Lead a Horse to Murder

A Reigning Cats & Dogs Mystery

Cynthia Baxter

BANTAM BOOKS

LEAD A HORSE TO MURDER
A Bantam Book / June 2005

Published by
Bantam Dell
A Division of Random House, Inc.
New York, New York

This is a work of fiction. Names, characters, places, and
incidents either are the product of the author's imagination or
are used fictitiously. Any resemblance to actual persons, living
or dead, events, or locales is entirely coincidental.

All rights reserved
Copyright © 2005 by Cynthia Baxter
Cover art by Bob Giusti

Bantam Books and the rooster colophon are registered
trademarks of Random House, Inc.

ISBN 0-553-58643-2

Printed in the United States of America
Published simultaneously in Canada

www.bantamdell.com

OPM 10 9 8 7 6 5 4 3 2 1

"In a similar vein to that of Susan Conant, Ms. Baxter does an excellent job of creating hysterical characters and providing plenty of descriptions of their four-legged companions. An extremely quick read, *Putting On the Dog* is a wonderful mystery that packs a lot of action and red herrings into a slim volume that avoids the pitfalls of pretentious punning. This is a great book to read while curled on the couch with your own four-legged friends." —The Best Reviews.com

DEAD CANARIES DON'T SING

"Dead canaries don't sing, but you will after reading this terrific mystery!" —Rita Mae Brown, *New York Times* bestselling author

"A little bird told me to read this mystery, which is awfully good. For the record, I would shred any canary who insulted me." —Sneaky Pie Brown, *New York Times* bestselling cat

"Should be on your summer reading list!" —*Newsday*

"An auspicious debut . . . Messages, murder and a menagerie of odd animals are along for the fun." —*Mystery Scene*

"Baxter's lighthearted, enjoyable mystery is an entertaining debut featuring a likable menagerie of characters, a few surprising plot twists and a touch of romance." —*Lansing State Journal*

"Clever, fast-paced and well-plotted, *Dead Canaries Don't Sing* stars an appealing heroine and furry sidekicks sure to enchant pet lovers. Five paws up for Cynthia Baxter's first in the *Reigning Cats & Dogs* series." —Carolyn Hart, Agatha, Anthony, and Macavity Awards winner

To Karen

Acknowledgments

In researching and writing *Lead a Horse to Murder,* I was overwhelmed by the warmth and enthusiasm of all the people I met who love horses and the sport of polo. I would like to thank the following individuals for their generosity in sharing both their time and their knowledge with me:

Carole Trottere and Nancy Albora, who started me off with Horse 101;

Greg Beroza, D.V.M., founder of the Long Island Equine Medical Center in Huntington, Long Island, and at Belmont Park Race Track in Elmont, who taught Jessie Popper everything she knows about treating horses;

Dick Fredericks, D.V.M., who taught me everything I know about polo, and the people he introduced me to in Wellington, Florida: Dave Blake and his sons Brad, Jeff, and Tom; Frank ("Butch") and Leigh Butterworth; and Dave Rizzo, who has run the Meadowbrook Polo Club for forty years;

Luis Rinaldini, who opened his home to me;

Fredric V. Vencl, Ph.D., of the Ecology and Evolution Department of Stony Brook University and the

Smithsonian Tropical Research Institute, who was instrumental in plotting the almost-perfect murder;

Officer Robert Boden of the Suffolk County Police Department's Information Office, who helped me find answers to my procedural questions;

Martha S. Gearhart, D.V.M., owner of the Pleasant Valley Animal Hospital in Pleasant Valley, New York, who, as always, serves a critical role as my dog and cat expert;

Eric Callendar, whose informative hands-on class in Animal First Aid at Suffolk County BOCES proved a valuable source of information about treating sick animals;

Trish, Rob, and Megan MacGregor, as well as Mike Bell, who, like me, found that uncomfortable bleachers were a small price to pay for the fun of watching polo on Long Island and in Florida;

Lisa Pulitzer, journalist, book author, and crime expert extraordinaire, who helps me make it all sound real;

And of course Faith Hamlin, my agent and my own personal cheerleader, and Caitlin Alexander, my editor, whose support, enthusiasm, and great ideas make it all happen.

A Note to Readers

Lead a Horse to Murder is a work of fiction, and all names and characters are the product of the author's imagination. Any resemblance to actual events, organizations, or persons, living or dead, is coincidental. Although some real Long Island places and some real people are mentioned, all are used fictitiously.

Lead a Horse
to Murder

Chapter 1

"A horse is dangerous at both ends and uncomfortable in the middle."

—Ian Fleming

My jeans and chukka boots were splattered with mud, my neck and armpits were coated in sticky sweat, I was practically choking from the pungent smell of manure trapped in the warm, humid air . . .

It doesn't get any better than this, I thought blissfully, closing my eyes and letting the early September sun bake a few more freckles onto my nose and cheeks. There's nothing like being around horses to make you feel grounded.

The ear-piercing sound of Max and Lou yapping their heads off snapped me out of my reverie. I turned to see what had sent my Westie and my Dalmatian, two whirling dervishes that masquerade as pets, into such a tizzy.

And then I spotted him. A few hundred yards away, a lone horseman had cantered onto one of the grassy fields that sprawled across Andrew MacKinnon's estate.

The steed was a magnificent Arabian, pure white with a massive chest and long, sturdy legs. From where I stood, he looked more like something Walt Disney had conjured up than a real animal.

But it was the rider who captivated my attention. He was clearly in control of both his horse and the mallet he gripped in his hand, exhibiting a combination of power and grace that mesmerized me. His shoulders, so broad they stretched the fabric of his loose-fitting dark blue polo shirt, hinted at his incredible strength. I watched, fascinated, as he leaned forward to hit the ball, sending it flying across the field.

Even from a distance, I could see he was extraordinarily handsome. His jaw, shadowed with a coarse stubble that gave him a roguish look, was set with determination. His dark eyes blazed as they focused on the ball. Yet a few locks of thick black hair curled beneath his helmet, making him seem charmingly boyish.

Though the sight of the accomplished horseman was enthralling, I reminded myself that it wasn't the joy of spectator sports that had brought me to Heatherfield this morning. The night before, I'd received a phone call from Skip Kelly, the manager of Atherton Farm, a horse farm a few miles from my home in Joshua's Hollow.

"A friend of mine's got a horse that needs seein' to," Skip had told me. "Guy name of Andrew MacKinnon. He's over in Old Brookbury, a mile or two from the Meadowlark Polo Club. Sounds like Braveheart's got a tendon problem. But Mac's usual veterinarian is in the hospital with a broken leg. Seems one of his patients wasn't too happy with the service he was getting."

"Occupational hazard," I commented.

"Mac said he wanted the best, so naturally I thought of you. I gave him your name and number, so I figured I'd let you know they might be givin' you a call."

"Thanks, Skip," I told him sincerely. That kind of

praise means a lot when it comes from someone you respect. I've known Skip for years. He's been working for Violet and Oliver Atherton since I first began making house calls with my clinic on wheels. But he's been involved with horses practically his entire life, growing up around them in Kentucky, then working on various horse farms and even a few racetracks.

"And Jessie?" Skip's voice had grown thick. "I've known Mac for years. Braveheart is his favorite horse. In fact, from what I can see, that gelding is the only animal he's ever really cared about. Take good care of him, will you?"

"Always," I assured him, not certain whether "him" meant the man or the horse.

I took special care to check my supplies and equipment before making the drive halfway across Norfolk County early that morning, wanting to be certain I arrived fully ready to treat a highly valued horse. I had a feeling Andrew MacKinnon's estate wouldn't exactly turn out to be typical of the suburban homes at which I usually made house calls. But I was completely unprepared for what I found.

I'd gotten some sense of the world I was about to enter as I maneuvered my twenty-six-foot van along Turkey Hollow Road. This entire section of Long Island's North Shore was like something out of an F. Scott Fitzgerald novel. In fact, Fitzgerald had written *The Great Gatsby* while living just a few miles from this very spot during the 1920's, immortalizing the flamboyant and often decadent lifestyle of the area's ridiculously well-to-do inhabitants.

In the early 1900's, some of the wealthiest individuals in the nation constructed palaces on Long Island, earning the North Shore the nickname "the Gold Coast." Frank W. Woolworth, the five-and-dime store magnate, had built a fantasy estate, Winfield, that shamelessly embraced his passion for the Egyptian occult. Teddy Roosevelt's rustic house in Oyster Bay, Sagamore Hill, became the summer White House during his two terms as president.

J.P. Morgan, William K. Vanderbilt II, and other wealthy industrialists—the Donald Trumps of their time, except with better hair—also built dream houses along the shores of Long Island Sound. Even the characters in the movie *Sabrina*—Audrey Hepburn and Humphrey Bogart in the original version, Julia Ormond and Harrison Ford in the remake—lived on Long Island's Gold Coast.

While the MacKinnon homestead, Heatherfield, wasn't on quite as grand a scale, it was definitely of the same ilk. Yet most people who passed along Turkey Hollow Road would never even have noticed its entrance, much less guessed that a sprawling estate lay beyond.

As I drove through the black wrought-iron gate flanked by two stone pillars, I wondered if I'd made a wrong turn. From the looks of things, I could easily have entered the grounds of a country club or even wandered into the Meadowlark Polo Club. But I'd noticed the name Heatherfield etched on a gold plaque set into one of the pillars.

"This must be the place," I muttered, glancing over at Max, my tailless Westie, and Lou, my one-eyed Dalmatian, who shared the seat beside me. Even they looked impressed. Or maybe it was just the endless stretches of green grass that had them spellbound. I could almost hear Lou thinking, *Somewhere out there, there's a tennis ball with my name on it.* Max, I suspected, was imagining all the squirrels and rabbits just waiting to be chased.

I had to keep my jaw from dropping to the ground as I drove along a paved road that curved through an amazing amount of land—especially given the outrageous property values on Long Island. Some of it was dense wooded areas: towering oaks and lush maples, their leaves already taking on a reddish tinge that warned that summer would soon be replaced by fall. But most of Andrew MacKinnon's estate had been divided into large, grassy paddocks. Many were empty, while a few housed a horse or two. In the distance, I noticed a brown-shingled building that looked like a stable. But on the phone, Heatherfield's barn manager had told me the stable was yellow, so I kept driving.

After nearly a quarter of a mile, I spotted an elegant stone house. Or mansion, depending on how much of a stickler for using the correct word you happen to be. Given the fact that it had enough rooms to pass for a small hotel, I suppose anyone who referred to it as a house would be guilty of understatement.

I finally caught sight of the stable. The one-story yellow building was U-shaped, a main section with two wings. I suspected it had originally been built as a carriage house.

And I was surprised that it wasn't still being used as one. So many vehicles were parked on the property that it looked like a used-car lot. A very *fancy* used-car lot. A Cadillac and a Mercedes sat on the paved semicircle in front of the house. Another half dozen vehicles lined the long driveway. Most were parked at haphazard angles, as if they'd been discarded by drivers who didn't consider them important enough to deal with properly. I spotted two SUV's, a Hummer, and a dilapidated station wagon. There were also two horse trailers, not hitched up to anything at the moment.

But the shining star of the makeshift parking lot was definitely the red Porsche, so low to the ground that the driver could probably feel pebbles on his butt. It bore an awfully close resemblance to a snazzy model I'd recently seen in a car magazine. Nick had shown it to me while we were browsing in a bookstore, marveling over its six-figure price tag. That was considerably more than the cost of the van that served as my clinic on wheels, and the Porsche didn't even come equipped with its own X-ray machine and autoclave.

I pulled my van up and opened the door. Predictably, Max and Lou shot out, acting as if they'd just been released from two years under house arrest. They spotted a tough-looking barn cat and immediately set off in his direction, hell-bent on checking out any living, breathing creature with the audacity to venture within a quarter of a mile of where they were.

I headed toward the stable, lugging a big black bag with most of the supplies and equipment I expected I'd need to treat Andrew MacKinnon's prized horse. As soon as I entered, I sensed someone else's presence. Actually, it wasn't as much an eerie, Stephen King kind of feeling as a distinctive smell. Cigarette smoke, stinging my nostrils and making my throat raw.

"Hello?" I called. "Anyone here?"

For a few seconds, nothing. And then a man stepped out of the shadows and planted himself a foot away from my face. His creepy entrance made me wonder if he'd orchestrated the whole scene for my benefit. Not a very promising beginning, I thought with annoyance.

He stood roughly six feet tall, lanky with knobby fingers that curled around his cigarette butt. His fashion statement was Aging Cowboy: jeans and a T-shirt, worn underneath a red plaid flannel shirt. His face looked as scorched as the Arizona desert. Despite the reptilian skin, I estimated his age in the mid-forties. And he positively reeked of cigarette smoke, as if part of his daily grooming routine involved dousing himself in Eau de Marlboro.

He studied me coldly, his eyes a pale shade of hazel

that contributed to his lizardlike appearance. "Who the hell are you?" he rasped.

"I'm Dr. Popper," I replied. "I got a call this morning about a horse that needs tending to."

"So you're the vet."

"That's right."

He continued to stare, as if he was waiting for me to say, "Naw, only kidding!" Instead, I stared right back.

"C'mon," he finally said, turning and heading in the opposite direction. "I'll take you to Braveheart."

"And you are . . . ?" I asked.

"Johnny Ray Cousins," he mumbled without looking back. "Mr. Mac's barn manager. I'm the one who called you."

I drew my breath in sharply when my charming host stopped in front of a stall labeled "Braveheart." Andrew MacKinnon's gelding truly was a beautiful animal. The sleek Arabian was a deep shade of chestnut with a flowing mane, intelligent brown eyes, and a proud demeanor.

"How're you doing, boy?" I asked him in a soft voice, stroking his nose gently. And then, even though I could feel Johnny Ray's eyes burning into me, I leaned forward and nuzzled Braveheart's nose with mine. It was something I'd seen horses do with each other, so I'd adopted it as my own greeting whenever I was getting acquainted with one I was about to treat. When in Rome, I figured.

I turned back to MacKinnon's barn manager. "What's going on?"

"Looks like his tendon pulled up a little bit sore, over there on his right back leg," Johnny Ray mumbled. "Happened yesterday. Braveheart probably took a bad step, maybe hit a divot. Course, he coulda been struck with a polo mallet, but I didn't see it happen. Anyway, he stumbled, but Scott, the guy who was riding him, picked up his reins and kept playing. He told me afterward he felt a funny step, but Braveheart here is a real trouper. He went on to score the winning goal.

"After the game, we took a look at it. It was a little bit filled with fluid and there was some heat. I iced it and gave him a couple of bute, but a few hours later, it was still sore to the touch. I talked to Mr. Mac about it this morning, and he insisted we give you a call."

Johnny Ray shot me a hostile look, no doubt making sure I understood that it had been his boss's idea to summon me—not his.

"Let me take a look." I set down my bag, ready to work.

Tendon damage is a frequent occurrence in polo ponies, ranging from a simple strain or sprain to a rupture that could put the animal out of commission completely. Injuries of this sort are especially common among horses that play the game at its most demanding level. Polo requires them to run fast, then make short stops and turns—moves horses simply aren't built for. Exhaustion is another factor, along with irregularities like stones or divots, clumps of earth pulled from the ground by galloping hooves or mallets. Still, polo fields are generally well maintained, and tendon injuries usually turn out to be mild.

"Okay, boy," I said. "I'm going to take a look at you. We just want to figure out what happened."

Braveheart stood still in his stall, patiently allowing me to examine his right back leg. From what I could see, Johnny Ray's analysis was correct. It looked like the gelding's injury was a simple soft-tissue injury—no open wound, no major bone fractures. Still, I wanted to be sure.

"I'm going to do an ultrasound," I said. I opened the carrying case that contained my portable unit. The nifty device consisted of two pieces, an extension probe and a processing computer with a monitor, yet it weighed barely two pounds.

As I ran the extension probe over Braveheart's bruised tendon, I studied the screen. Sure enough, the image clearly showed a pocket of excess fluid within the superficial digital flexor tendon at the back of the horse's right leg, an indication of minor structural damage.

"Okay, I see a weak spot in the tendon," I told Johnny Ray, pointing to the screen. "I'm going to put Braveheart on anti-inflammatories, phenylbutazone and Naquasone, for a few days. Give him half a Naquasone pill and one full bute in the morning and the same at night. I'd also like you to keep up with the icing or cold-hosing during the day, but put on a mud poultice overnight to draw out the heat and get the swelling down. During the day, keep the bandage on and keep him in the stall. I'll reevaluate his condition in a few days."

Johnny Ray barely acknowledged my instructions. "Now I suppose you want to get paid," he said gruffly. "I'll take you inside to meet Mr. Mac."

He tossed his cigarette butt onto the ground, half-heartedly snuffing it out with the sole of his boot—not the best idea around wooden stables and the horses confined in them. I opened my mouth to protest, then reconsidered. Andrew MacKinnon's barn manager and I hadn't exactly started out on the best terms, even though I suspected the reason was simply that I had the nerve to be female, a veterinarian, or a combination of both. Since he and I were going to be working together over the next week or two to ensure that Braveheart made a complete recovery, the last thing I wanted was to create any more bad feelings.

As we walked toward the house, I caught another glimpse of the elegant horseman I'd noticed earlier. "Who is that?" I asked.

Johnny Ray glanced at the field. "Oh, him. Eduardo Garcia. One of the Argies. He plays on Mr. Mac's team."

"Argies?" I repeated, confused.

"Argentines."

"Oh. I don't know much about polo, but it looks like he's really good."

"One of the best. Sometimes I come out here just to stand by the fence and watch him stick-and-balling. That means practicing. Y'know, hitting the ball around with the mallet."

Scowling, he turned so that his back was to the polo player. "Those Argies have a helluva life. I wonder if them spics even know how good they got it."

It was a good thing Lou and Max chose that moment to come bounding toward me, panting with glee as if thinking, *Isn't this place the greatest?* Their arrival provided just the distraction I needed to keep myself from giving Johnny Ray Cousins a piece of my mind.

Not that he hung around long enough to continue our fascinating conversation. He strode toward Andrew MacKinnon's mansion, walking fast enough to stay at least six feet ahead of me.

Fine with me, I thought, trailing after him. Even being treated like a second-class citizen by a man with a chip on his shoulder the size of that Hummer over there was better than attempting to converse with him.

I took a moment to appreciate the fact that, thanks to my career choice, I spent more time in the presence of animals than people. And to reflect on how ironic it was that animals, not people, were referred to as "dumb."

I followed Johnny Ray across a brick patio at the back of the house, but stopped short when we reached a pair of elegant French doors. I had a feeling that wet paws and damp noses wouldn't be particularly welcome inside, even though this was an estate on which animals were clearly a priority.

"Stay!" I instructed Max and Lou. They looked at me in disbelief, clearly indignant that they were being left behind. Reluctantly, Lou lowered his butt to the ground. Max, meanwhile, stared at me hard, as if thinking, "How *could* you?"

As Johnny Ray and I stepped onto the smooth marble floor of the hallway, a young woman appeared in one of the doorways and rushed over to us.

"Hey, Inez," he mumbled. "Mr. Mac around? Or has he gone into the city already?"

"Meester Mac is in his study," the pretty young woman answered, lowering her head shyly. "I will tell him you wish to speak with him."

"No need." The barn manager barged right past her—in the process, tracking dirt across what looked like a very expensive Oriental carpet.

"Meester Johnny!" she called. "*Por favor,* Meester Mac does not like—"

Johnny Ray ignored her, striding down the hallway. "Damn Port-o Rican," he muttered.

Horrified, I glanced at Inez, hoping she hadn't heard. If she had, she showed no sign of it. Instead, she kept her head down, not looking at either of us.

I trailed after Mr. Congeniality, hoping Andrew MacKinnon wouldn't hold his bad manners against me. Then again, I thought, Johnny Ray works for him, so chances are he already knows what a Neanderthal he's dealing with.

I decided to forget about Johnny Ray. Instead, I concentrated on my surroundings. My original assessment of Heatherfield, that it wasn't exactly in the same league as the thousands of ranch houses and split-levels that covered Long Island, hardly did the place justice. If the size alone weren't enough to knock your socks off, it was outfitted with tasteful, well-designed furniture, paintings, and other designer touches that made it clear that this part of Long Island still deserved to be labeled the Gold Coast.

Mr. MacKinnon's study drove that point home. As I stepped inside, I was enveloped by a room that had the restful feeling of a hideaway, created by the skillful integration of rich textures and intense colors. The walls were painted the same dark green as a billiard table, with dark mahogany wainscoting all around. The deep, masculine tones were echoed in the couches and chairs, which were upholstered in brown leather the color of creamy milk chocolate. I placed my hand on the back of a chair and found it was as thick as a saddle but as soft as a kitten's ear.

The walls were covered with pictures, hung at every possible height. Whether they were big or small, framed photographs or signed lithographs or huge oil paintings with gilt frames, they all featured horses. And most of those horses had polo players on their backs, their expressions grim and determined as they leaned forward to whack the ball.

I couldn't help being curious about the man who had amassed enough wealth to buy himself such an impressive playground. I had pictured Andrew MacKinnon as a suave James Bond type, wearing a burgundy-colored silk bathrobe and carrying a brandy snifter. Then I shifted to a slick Mississippi River boat gambler with a waxed mustache and a string tie and the distinctive gleam of greed in his dark, beady eyes. Next, I tried on a dignified Anthony Hopkins in a gray morning coat, smoking a cigar and reading the *Financial Times*.

None of the personas I'd invented for Andrew MacKinnon came even close to the paunchy man in his early sixties who stood up as we barged in, unannounced. Instead of the shiny, slicked-back hair of my riverboat gambler, he hardly had any hair left at all. What there was of it was almost completely gray, barely hinting at the fact that a decade or two earlier, he had been a red-head. He had a ruddy complexion to match, and pale blue eyes rimmed with nearly colorless lashes.

And forget the string tie. Ditto for the silk bathrobe. This particular captain of industry was dressed in wrinkled khaki pants that sagged in the back and a loose-fitting lemon yellow golf shirt marred by a small but distinct stain. His abundant stomach protruded like Santa Claus's, stretching the knit fabric more than I suspected its designer had ever intended.

It certainly wasn't easy picturing him riding the princely Braveheart, galloping across a polo field with a team of muscular young horsemen like the one I'd seen stick-and-balling earlier that morning. In fact, I had to remind myself that this undistinguished businessman actually owned the castlelike estate that surrounded us: the mansion, the cars and trucks and trailers, the stables, the polo fields, and of course the magnificent horses I knew were worth plenty.

"How's my horse?" he demanded, dropping the *Wall Street Journal* he'd been reading onto his chair.

"You'll have to ask Dr. Pepper," Johnny Ray replied sullenly.

I could feel my blood starting to boil. I've been called Dr. Pepper more times than I can count. But being mistaken for a rival to Coke and Pepsi was usually accidental. The sneer on Johnny Ray's face made it clear that his slip was completely intentional—and that he wanted me to know it.

I decided to ignore him. "Mr. MacKinnon, I'm Dr. Popper," I said, stepping forward and shaking his hand. "I checked out Braveheart, and it looks as if he's suffered some minor structural damage on the back of his right leg—"

A piercing scream, accompanied by the sound of quick footsteps across the marble floor, stopped me mid-sentence.

"What the hell...?" Andrew MacKinnon muttered, stepping out into the hallway.

"Meester Mac! Meester Mac!" Inez cried. "Come quickly! It's Eduardo! He fell off his horse—and he's not moving!"

Chapter 2

"It is not enough for a man to know how to ride; he must know how to fall."

—Mexican Proverb

The four of us—MacKinnon, Johnny Ray, Inez, and I—raced through the hallway and out of the house, sliding on the slippery marble and probably looking like the Keystone Cops. The fact that Max and Lou joined in, loping alongside us through the grass and barking, only added to the situation's feeling of unreality.

"I was looking out the window," Inez gasped, "and I see Eduardo fall off his horse. I thought he will get up, but he—"

"I have my cell phone," I volunteered. "I'll call nine-one-one."

"Not yet," MacKinnon insisted. "It could be nothing."

As soon as we reached Eduardo, I could tell it wasn't nothing. The polo player lay perfectly still on the ground, his muscular body twisted into an unnatural position. What was most horrifying was the strange angle of his head, which was frighteningly at odds with the rest of his body. His face was ghoulishly pale, made even whiter by its contrast with the thick black curls that framed it.

"Stay!" I instructed my dogs, my tone serious enough to prevent them from dashing over to Eduardo's body. Without even bothering to glance at MacKinnon, I pulled out my phone and dialed.

"Officer Spinelli, Tenth Precinct. Where's the emergency?"

"Heatherfield, an estate at twenty-five Turkey Hollow Road in Old Brookbury. A man's fallen off a horse. We need an ambulance—fast!"

I hastily gave him directions, then knelt on the grass, next to Eduardo. I pressed my fingers against his neck, trying to feel a pulse. Nothing.

I glanced up at the others to tell them the sickening news. But my throat had closed up, making it impossible for me to speak. It didn't matter. When I saw their stricken expressions, I knew the look on my own face told them everything.

"He may be in shock," I finally managed to say, even though I suspected I was being overly optimistic. "Someone should get a blanket."

"I go," Inez volunteered. As she turned and ran toward the house, Johnny Ray took off his flannel shirt and tucked it around Eduardo's torso.

"How could this have happened?" MacKinnon wondered aloud, sounding dazed. "The man's been around horses practically since he was born. He's the best rider I've ever come across in my life!"

The police arrived fifteen minutes later, trailing an ambulance that bumped across the field before stopping just a few feet away from where we stood. The driver and an EMT jumped out of the vehicle and sprinted toward Eduardo's inert body. Meanwhile, the two uniformed police officers who had emerged from a pair of white-and-blue Norfolk County police cars sauntered over to the three of us.

"I'm Officer Gruen." The burly man with dirty-blond hair hitched up his navy blue pants. "So what happened here?"

"Eduardo Garcia works for me," Andrew Mac-Kinnon said in a low, even voice. "This morning, he was stick-and...he was riding that mare over there." He pointed to the white horse, which was being led away by a dark-haired young man I assumed was a groom. "Next thing we knew, he'd fallen off his horse. My housekeeper, Inez, happened to look out the window, and she saw him lying on the ground."

"Ed-uar-do Gar-ci-a," Officer Gruen repeated slowly, writing down the name. "You say he works for you?"

"That's right."

"What is he, a groom or a stable boy or something?"

MacKinnon stiffened. "He's a polo player. One of the finest in the world."

"Okay, but you said he works for you. What exactly does he do?"

"He plays polo for me."

"Yeah, I got that. But what exactly does he—?"

I left the two of them to sort things out, heading over to Inez. Studying her for the first time, I saw how young she was—probably barely twenty. Long, straight black hair hung limply around a gaunt face that was pretty enough, although hardly striking. Her thin arms were wrapped around her slender waist, and a pair of spindly legs stuck out from beneath an ill-fitting skirt. Her only outstanding feature was her eyes, dark brown and slightly almond-shaped. Standing out here in the middle of the expansive field, hugging herself and wearing a distraught expression, she seemed extremely fragile.

"Are you all right?" I asked.

"Ees such a terrible thing! Eduardo, he is so young, so talented, with such a wonderful future ahead of him!" She looked as if she were on the verge of crying.

I patted her shoulder distractedly, shifting my focus back to the EMT worker. I was standing far enough away that I couldn't make out what he was telling the two police officers.

But the words didn't matter. The expression on his face told me my assessment had been correct.

Eduardo Garcia was dead.

I glanced at Andrew MacKinnon. All the color had drained from his face, and even though I guessed he easily weighed over two hundred pounds, he looked as if a mild breeze could have knocked him over. As for Johnny Ray, he was impossible to read. He simply wore the same ornery expression he'd had since I arrived.

Inez figured it out, too. She let out a cry, covering her face with her hands. Sobbing, she ran toward the house, her shoulders shaking and her thin legs zigzagging across the field.

I stood frozen to the spot, watching the ambulance crew take Eduardo's body away. MacKinnon and Johnny Ray followed them a few paces behind. With shaking hands, I pulled out my cell phone, stepped farther away, and dialed Nick Burby.

I knew perfectly well that he was consumed by his first weeks of law school. As a first-year student, he was taking four demanding courses plus an informal workshop in legal writing. Then there was the newness of his situation. Learning to think an entirely different way while digesting the details of hundreds of legal cases would be difficult enough at any stage of life. Given the fact that he hadn't been a student for a full decade made the experience even more daunting.

But this was an emergency.

If he's in class, I told myself as I listened to it ring, *he'll have turned his phone off. I'll probably get his voice mail, so I'll just leave him a—*

"Nick?" I cried as soon as he answered with a cheerful hello. "Can you talk?"

"Hey, Jess! Sure. For a minute, anyway," he replied. "I'm walking from one building to another." He hesitated. "Anything wrong?"

"I'm on a call at a horse farm." I had to struggle to keep my voice from shaking. "Actually, I'm on somebody's estate. The owner plays polo, so he has fifteen or twenty of his own horses... Anyway, about a half hour ago, one of his polo players fell off his horse. Nick, he's dead!"

"Oh, my God!" Nick breathed. "Jessie, are you okay?"

"I'm fine. But Nick, the whole thing is so bizarre! I mean, I was standing in a field, watching him practice, just a few minutes before it happened. I was completely mesmerized. He and the horse were practically one being, you know? They moved together with such assurance, such smoothness—"

"Look, we'll have dinner tonight and you can tell me all about it, okay? Sorry to cut you off, Jessie, but I've really got to go."

"How about you?" I asked quickly, wanting to talk to him just a little bit longer. "How are they treating you at law school?"

"You wouldn't believe how much I have to do," Nick grumbled. "I'm already overwhelmed by how much work Criminal Law is going to be. My Contracts class is going to be even worse. And everybody's telling me how important it is to be part of a study group. They say it's the only way to get through the first year. From now until the winter break, I'll be lucky if I have time to take a shower." He paused. "It's really cool!"

I couldn't help laughing, even though the sound that erupted from my throat was a cross between a chuckle and a sob. "Glad somebody's having fun," I told him. "See you later, Nick."

When I hung up, I became aware of an empty feeling that had settled deep in the pit of my stomach. Nick suddenly felt so far away—not physically, but as if he was so tied up in what he was doing that there wasn't much room for anything else.

Eduardo Garcia's death had hit me in way that surprised me. It was strange; I'd never even met him. In fact, I'd never heard his name until that morning.

But I'd seen him on a horse, in his element. His youth, his strength, his agility...He was like someone's fantasy, come to life.

Now, he was gone. Dead. Without warning, without reason, and way before his time.

I was glad I'd rescheduled my morning appointments, pushing them back later in the day since I hadn't known how long I'd be at Heatherfield. I desperately needed a cup of tea—and a long, comforting conversation with the person who was an expert at brewing it.

I could feel the tension in my neck and shoulders as Max, Lou, and I turned off Minnesauke Lane and drove up the long curving driveway that led to my cottage in Joshua's Hollow. Unlike much of Long Island, the quiet community on Norfolk County's North Shore still retains its rustic feel. The area has a rich history that dates back to the Revolutionary War, when it was the home base of a well-known spy ring that supplied General George Washington with crucial information about the movements of the British. Every once in a while, I can't resist squinting my eyes and peering into the dense woods, trying to picture a musket-bearing patriot in ragged clothes hiding behind a tree.

Housing on Long Island is insanely expensive, but I'd had the good fortune to hook up with a first-rate real estate agent named Mitzi, who had found me a charming stone cottage on an estate that had been built nearly two centuries earlier. The mansion on the property, which I affectionately call the Big House, was built by the grandson of one of the Culper Spy Ring's key members, Major Benjamin Tallmadge. While the older Tallmadge had dedicated his life to fighting for freedom, his descendent had spent *his* life benefiting from it, becoming a prosperous industrialist who owned several mills in the area. Every day, I thank my lucky stars for this place.

Usually, just pulling up in the circular driveway in front of the Big House fills me with a sense of peace. But today was an exception. I was haunted by the image of Eduardo Garcia lying on the ground, his handsome face ashen and his muscular body lifeless. As I put the van into park, I realized my hands were trembling.

The moment I opened the door, Max and Lou leaped out of the van, clearly as glad to be home as I was. I left them to sniff around happily as I made a beeline for Betty Vandervoort's front door.

While the Big House wasn't nearly as grand as Andrew MacKinnon's mansion, it was certainly an impressive residence. The angles of its stately white columns and brick façade were softened by the circular driveway. Well-tended flower beds and geometric bushes added to its solemn look.

Given the residence's formal appearance, anyone who didn't know its owner would probably have expected an equally dignified dowager to come to the door, draped in strings of pearls—or at least a pair of reading glasses on a chain. Not my Betty. In fact, just seeing her, dressed in purple linen pants, a boxy

turquoise blouse edged with beads, and chandelier earrings studded with brilliant stones that echoed both colors made me feel better immediately.

"Why, Jessica! What a lovely—" Within a split second, her expression changed. I'd long suspected that
Betty was a mind reader. Either that, or my distress was
clearly written all over my face.

"Goodness, are you all right?" she demanded.

"Not really." I cast her a pleading look. "But a cup of
tea might help."

"I'll put the kettle on."

As soon as I was settled inside Betty's kitchen, I began
to feel better. There was something comforting about
watching her bustle around. I watched in silence as she
filled her old-fashioned copper teakettle with water,
then retrieved delicate Limoges cups and saucers from
the china cabinet. Next, she grabbed a bottle off a
shelf, the secret ingredient that gave her tea its magical
powers.

"Tell me, Jessica," she said firmly, finally sitting down
at the table. "What happened?"

I took a deep breath. "I was making a house call on an
estate in Old Brookbury early this morning, and a man
who was riding there fell off a horse and was killed."

Her eyebrows leaped up to her hairline. "That's terrible! Was it someone you knew?"

"Not exactly. I'd only seen him once, practicing for a
polo match. Stick-and-balling, they call it. I watched
him—not for very long, just a few minutes. But seeing
him on that horse, so powerful and so much in control,
but at the same time so graceful and so...so *connected*
with his horse..." I shook my head slowly. "It's an image I'll never forget."

"And now he's dead." Betty's voice was practically a
whisper.

"It's hard to imagine, but yes."

We were both quiet for what seemed like a very long time. When Betty finally broke the silence, she spoke slowly, as if she were choosing her words carefully. "Jessica, I'm waiting for you to assure me that you have no intention of getting involved in whatever happened to this poor man. Especially since you'd never even met him."

"Don't worry. As tragic as his death is, it was an accident. Besides, it had nothing to do with me."

"Good. I just wanted to make sure this wouldn't turn into another one of those situations in which you'd take it upon yourself to ensure that truth and justice prevail." With a little smile, she added, "These days, we can leave that up to that Nick of yours. Speaking of Nick, how is he—and how is law school going?"

"Nick is fine. He's just busy. And stressed out."

"Nick?" Betty blinked in surprise. "But he's usually so calm! In fact, I didn't know he had it in him to get stressed out about anything!"

"Me, either. But classes just started last week, and I'm already seeing an entirely new side of him."

Actually, he'd been so busy that I'd hardly seen him at all—either his new sides or his old sides. And now he was talking about joining a study group, getting together once or twice a week with a bunch of other law students who would share their notes and pool their knowledge.

It's a good thing I keep a photograph of Nick next to my bed, I thought glumly, *or by now I'd have forgotten what he looks like.*

"I've been a little stressed out myself," Betty admitted, jumping up to silence the whistling kettle. "Opening night is only a week and a half away, and I'm getting jittery."

"But you love performing!"

Her face lit up in a smile. "That's certainly true," she

said, her sapphire blue eyes twinkling. "There's nothing like the sound of applause ringing in your ears—and knowing you've just put on a performance that deserves it." Her smile faded. "Still, I haven't been in showbiz for—well, for much too long for me to admit to. It's terribly exciting to be in a musical again, but between you and me, I'm finding that I'm a bit rusty. And of course getting on a stage always involves a few butterflies in the stomach, even for us seasoned veterans. I've loved the rehearsals, but with the opening around the corner, I'm finding the prospect of dancing in front of a real live audience after all this time a little frightening. I know I *used* to be good at it, but I keep wondering if I still am."

A few decades earlier, Betty had shown incredible gumption, saving a summer's worth of wages from her waitressing job at the Paper Plate Diner in Altoona, Pennsylvania, and buying a one-way bus ticket to New York City. Her pluck had paid off. She'd taken Broadway by storm, performing in musicals like *South Pacific* and *Oklahoma*.

In all the years that followed, her passion for musicals had never wavered. A few months earlier, back in June, I'd been thrilled to learn that Betty had decided to throw herself back into dancing. She'd auditioned for a community theater production of *Chicago*, winning the part of Katalin Helinszki in the electrifying "Cell Block Tango" dance number.

All summer, she'd bounded off to rehearsals with the Port Players four evenings a week, cradling her ballet shoes lovingly in her arms. Late at night, she'd knock at my door, her cheeks flushed and her eyes bright as she related the detail of every dance move, every comment the director made, every bit of intrigue among the cast members. It struck me that getting back into theater was precisely what she needed to stay young.

"Anyway," Betty continued, "let me worry about my

return to the stage. You can focus on that lovely boyfriend of yours. And be patient with him! I'm sure Nick could use a little moral support right now. Starting law school is no small thing—especially since he's been out in the world working for a few years since college. Hitting the books again is going to be quite a change from the freedom he enjoyed as a private investigator. It's going to take a lot of discipline. Plenty of back rubs, too."

"You're absolutely right," I assured her. I figured I could rise to the occasion, becoming a pillar of patience and strength for our hardworking law student.

Besides, those back rubs were sounding pretty darned good.

I still had a full day ahead of me, back-to-back appointments all over the island. I generally tried to group my calls to clients' homes, based on their location. But Long Island is well named—although an even better name would have been Long, Wide Island with Way Too Much Traffic.

Still, I never regret my decision to become a veterinarian-on-wheels. I love the feeling of having everything I need to ply my trade tucked neatly into a mobile unit. When it came to choosing a lifestyle, I really identified with that old cowboy song, "Don't Fence Me In." I've never stopped appreciating the feeling of freedom that comes from spending my days making house calls, tooling around in a van outfitted with heat and air-conditioning and running water, not to mention everything I need for performing diagnostic tests, surgery, and even dentistry.

Most of the time, I pretty much have total control over how I spend my time. Then again, sometimes my cell phone rings and my carefully constructed plans for the day go right out the window.

Which is why I eyed my phone warily when it began purring just as I was about to get onto the Long Island Expressway. Especially when I glanced at the name and number that appeared on the screen and recognized them immediately.

I eased off onto the shoulder, a firm believer in the New York State law that forbids talking on cell phones while driving. Max and Lou, wrestling for a primo spot on the seat beside me, looked surprised that we were stopping in such an unlikely spot.

"Dr. Popper," I answered crisply.

"Hi, Dr. Popper." I couldn't place the high-pitched voice. "I'm sorry to bother you. You don't know me. My name's Kathy Kelly. I baby-sit for the Weinsteins?"

I knew the Weinsteins well, at least Lindsay Weinstein and her twin toddlers, Justin and Jason. I also knew their German shorthair pointer, King. Almost a year earlier, he'd contracted two extremely serious illnesses that dogs get from ticks, Lyme disease and ehrlichiosis. Thanks to better living through chemistry—meaning wonderfully effective antibiotics like amoxicillin and doxycycline—the spirited pointer was soon playing Frisbee with the boys again.

"Anyway, Mrs. Weinstein's at the doctor with Jenny—that's the new baby—and I'm here alone with the twins," Kathy went on. "For the last hour or two, King's been acting really weird. I found a magnet on the refrigerator with your name and number on it. I hope you don't mind me bothering you like this."

"Not at all, Kathy," I assured her. "It's really good that you called. Now tell me what's going on with King."

"He keeps trying to throw up, but it's like nothing's coming out," she went on in the same frightened tone.

"He keeps looking at his side, and he's doing strange things like licking the air. He's also drooling."

"Okay, Kathy, you've done a great job of describing his symptoms. It sounds to me like King's got bloat." I made a point of sounding a lot calmer than I felt. "Stay there with him. I'm heading over to where you are right now. Just keep him quiet, and keep the kids away from him. I should be there in about fifteen minutes, okay?"

"Okay," Kathy replied in a reedy voice.

What I didn't tell her was that bloat—Gastric Dilatation-Volvulus, or GDV—is one of the most common causes of death in large dogs. Yet most dog owners have never even heard of it. Deep-chested dogs like German shepherds and retrievers are the most vulnerable. The dog's stomach can literally get twisted between the esophagus and the upper intenstine, trapping fluids, food, and gas inside.

GDV has to be dealt with fast. It doesn't take long before the animal's blood supply gets cut off and toxins build up inside the stomach. It's not unusual for the dog to go into shock, or even for his stomach to rupture.

I pulled back onto the road and headed toward the Long Island Expressway. Fortunately, I knew the way— and it was only a ten-minute drive.

Even before I'd pulled into the Weinsteins' driveway, their baby-sitter flung open the front door.

"He's in here," Kathy called as I climbed out of my van. "In the kitchen."

I left Max and Lou in the van, knowing I'd be coming right back with King. Kathy held the door open for me, ushering me inside. I'd assumed from her voice that she was sixteen or seventeen. But in person, she looked about fourteen. She was dressed in jeans and a faded Old Navy T-shirt, and she wore her long, chestnut brown hair straight down her back. I suspected she was one of those kids who was an A student and also found the time to belong to ten different clubs in addition to baby-sitting.

"It was really smart of you to call me," I told her again. "Do you think you could give me a hand?"

"No problem," she assured me. But I could see how frightened she was just by looking into her eyes.

The house seemed strangely quiet. Even the television was off. Usually, when I arrived at the Weinsteins', three-year-old Justin and Jason were acting like hellions—despite the thick blond curls, clear blue eyes, and sweet expressions that make them look like cherubs someone painted on a cathedral ceiling. Today, however, the two of them sat on the couch, holding hands and looking like they were on the verge of tears.

"King is sick," one of them informed me in a soft voice.

"I know," I replied. "Kathy asked me to take a look at him."

"Are you gonna make him better?" the other twin asked anxiously.

"I'm pretty sure he'll be fine," I assured him. I only hoped I'd turn out to be right.

I found the chocolate brown pointer lying in his dog bed in one corner of the spacious kitchen. His posture was hunched, and I could see mucus foaming around his lips. He recognized me immediately, and his tail thumped two or three times. I thought I could see a pleading look in his eyes as he fixed them on mine.

"It's okay, King," I told him softly. "We'll take care of this in no time." Turning to Kathy, I asked, "Do you think you could help me carry him into the van? The bed is stiff enough to serve as a stretcher."

Together, we managed to transport King across the lawn and into my van. As usual, Max and Lou seemed to sense that they were in the presence of a sick animal. They positioned themselves far enough away to keep from being underfoot but close enough to watch what was going on. I swear, if their IQ's were just a few points higher, I'd be able to train them to assist me. And they'd probably be great at it.

Once King was on my examining table, I had another thought. "Is it okay for you to leave the twins alone?" I asked Kathy.

"I have an idea," she replied. "I'll tell them to bring a few toys outside and sit on the front steps. That way, I can keep an eye on them while I help you."

I just nodded, figuring I'd tell Kathy just how terrific she was later on, after all this was over.

I knew the distension in King's stomach could be relieved with surgery. But I always consider cutting a last resort. With cases of bloat, I'd had good results with a procedure called gastric lavage. If that didn't work, then I'd have to think about a more invasive method of treatment.

The first step was getting King on an IV of fluids, along with an anesthesia that would knock him out. Kathy held him down, stroking him and talking to him softly, as I inserted the needle.

As soon as he'd lost consciousness, I intubated him with a trachial tube, then carefully inserted a hose into his esophagus. Once it was in place, I began pumping in water, pressing on King's stomach gently and watching to see if the tube would untwist his esophagus and the force of gravity would bring out the food trapped inside.

"Come on, boy," I muttered, even though I knew he couldn't hear me. "You can do this, King. Work with us."

Suddenly water and food began pouring out, a sign that the procedure was working. I let out a loud sigh of relief.

Kathy glanced at me hopefully. "Does this mean he's going to be okay?"

"He's going to be fine." This time, I made that statement with confidence.

After pumping out his stomach, I followed up with an X ray, just to be certain we were out of the woods. Sure enough, the positioning of King's stomach was back to normal.

"He's in great shape," I told Kathy.

"Thank goodness!" She clutched her hands to her heart like the heroine in an old-fashioned melodrama. "Dr. Popper, I've got to ask you. Did I do something wrong? Am I responsible for what happened to King?"

I assured her that she'd done nothing wrong—that by calling for help as promptly as she had, she'd done the best thing possible. Then I gave her a short lecture on ways of preventing bloat, simple things like feeding King two smaller meals a day instead of one large one and keeping him from exercising right after eating. I also assured her that I'd call the Weinsteins and pass along the same information to them.

"The only thing you *can* do," I told her, "is to restrict food and water until Lindsay—Mrs. Weinstein—gets home. I'll explain to her that she'll need to do the same for the next few days to prevent a recurrence."

"Can King play with us now?" either Jason or Justin asked as Kathy and I brought the pointer back into the house on our makeshift stretcher.

"Not yet, honey," I told him. "But soon. You know, you two guys were great. You really helped King by letting him rest. Now I'm going to ask you to do the same thing for the next couple of days, okay? And before you know it, King will be as good as new."

As I headed back to my van, I took a few deep breaths, needing to recover from the adrenaline rush that had carried me through the last half hour. I had to admit that I felt pretty good, knowing I'd made a real difference. Maybe the Weinsteins' dog wasn't as glamorous or impressive as some exhorbitantly priced polo pony. But he was probably even more important to Justin and Jason and their parents than Braveheart was to Andrew MacKinnon.

The same went for my own two canines. Before turning the key in the ignition, I gave Max and Lou a special hug, just to let them know how much I loved them and how glad I was they were healthy. And then I headed out to my next appointment.

By the time I pulled up in front of my cottage six hours later, I was looking forward to a relaxing evening—one that included my long-lost boyfriend, Nick. At the moment, however, I was just as pleased to see the other two members of my menagerie, the ones who didn't accompany me as I went traipsing around Norfolk County, making house calls.

"Hey, Cat!" I greeted Catherine the Great, my beautiful gray cat. She was curled up in her favorite spot, a tattered rag rug I keep in front of the refrigerator. Even though it still felt like summer, her arthritis invariably led her to the warmest spot in the house.

She stood up to greet me, walking over stiffly and meowing her hello. I scooped her up gently and petted her, taking care to avoid the nick in her left ear. A leftover from her previous life, it had remained sensitive even after it healed.

"How's my favorite pussycat, huh?" I murmured. She purred her response, which I suspected didn't mean "Fine" as much as it meant "Better, now that you're here."

Prometheus, my chatty Blue and Gold Macaw, wasn't

about to be forgotten. "*Awk!* Welcome home, Jessie! *Awk!*"

I returned Cat to her special spot, grabbed a slice of apple from the refrigerator, and went over to greet my bird. "Hey, Prometheus, how's the pretty birdy?"

"Prometheus is the pretty birdy," he told me proudly, as if I didn't already know.

"That's *how's* the pretty birdy, not *who's* the pretty birdy." I laughed.

I put out my hand and he hopped on, making ecstatic chortling sounds that indicated how thrilled he was to be reunited with the individual he believed was his mother. Frankly, I felt honored. I offered him a piece of the apple, which he tasted daintily. "Apple," he announced. "Prometheus loves apple. *Awk!*"

As for my canines, they weren't exactly grabbing the remote and hunkering down on the couch for an evening of spectator sports. Instead, Max and Lou assumed that coming home meant it was time for a few rounds of their favorite game: Slimytoy. This highly demanding game, which brings them both never-ending joy, consists of tossing and retrieving whichever saliva-coated rubber toy is the most favored at the moment. That happened to be a carefully coiffed hot-pink poodle that looked as if he'd practically lived at a doggy beauty parlor—at least before his head had been half ripped off, leaving a gaping hole that would have called for emergency surgery if he hadn't been made of rubber.

According to the rules of this sophisticated game, I threw Slimytoy and one of my dogs retrieved it. Of course, whenever the poodle landed behind a piece of furniture, it became *my* job to stretch and contort in an attempt at wresting it away from the hoards of dust bunnies that lurked beneath the couch and chairs. This particular job, which I considered the downside of being the only human being in the room, was made even more stressful by Max and Lou's insistence upon urging me on by making sharp barking sounds until the pink poodle finally resurfaced, sticky with saliva and covered in fuzzy gray material but nevertheless eager for another toss.

After my long day, I was too tired to send Slimytoy sailing across the room more than ten or twelve times. I left the dogs to their own devices, wondering why I'd never taken the time to teach them to read. Then I headed into the kitchen, where I spent another minute or two stroking Cat's soft fur and murmuring endearments before focusing on dinner.

I washed my hands well, not wanting to include any special ingredients in the meal I was about to throw together. Then I took a couple of chicken breasts out of the freezer, figuring I'd make the one passable dish I've mastered. Chances were they'd be just as frozen an hour from now, after I'd taken a shower and put on clothes that were not embroidered with the words "Jessica Popper, D.V.M." But thawing the chicken was less important than thawing Nick, who I hadn't seen since the weekend before.

"This schedule is absolutely insane," I mumbled, checking inside the refrigerator to make sure a bottle of white wine was chilling. I was relieved to spot a Ziploc bag of salad greens, the third critical ingredient required for assembling a collection of food items that could pass for dinner.

As for dessert, I knew for a fact there were two pints of ice cream in the freezer. Even so, I had a few ideas of my own that had nothing to do with anything that could be found in a supermarket.

I'd just come out of the shower with my wet head wrapped in a towel and was starting to feel like a member of the human species again when the phone rang. Nick, I hoped, telling me he was on his way.

Sure enough, caller ID informed me that I was at least right about the first part.

"Hey, Nick!" I towel-dried my head more enthusiastically. "What's up?"

"Torts," he replied gloomily. "That's what's up."

"I don't follow," I told him, even though the tone of his voice—and the sinking feeling in my stomach—told me exactly what he meant.

"I'm not going to make it over tonight," Nick said apologetically. "I'm really sorry, Jess, but I've just got too much to do. You wouldn't believe what my Torts professor dumped on us today." He sighed. "Everything they say about the first year of law school is true."

"Are you positive you can't come by—even for a little while?" I asked. Doing my best to sound seductive, I added, "You've got to eat, right? Besides, there's a back rub in it for you...and maybe something even more relaxing."

"Believe me, it sounds tempting," he said with a sigh. "But right now, I'm looking at a textbook that's about four inches thick. Can I take a rain check?"

So much for my feminine wiles, I thought. "Sure, Nick. Go study."

Great, I thought glumly as I hung up. I stuck the chicken back in the freezer and retrieved the unopened pint of New York Super Fudge Chunk stashed inside. Here I'd been looking forward to a hot night with Nick. Instead, it looked like I was in for a really *cold* night— with Ben and Jerry.

Chapter 3

"God forbid that I should go to any heaven where there are no horses."

—R.B. Cunningham-Graham

Three days later, on Friday morning, as my van bounced along the driveway leading into Heatherfield, I expected to find the same serene setting I'd encountered during my first visit to Andrew MacKinnon's estate. Instead, dozens of shiny, expensive cars were crammed onto the property, their chrome trim glinting in the early morning sun like drops of dew. Most of them were Mercedeses and BMW's—so many, in fact, that I wondered if the German Trade Board was holding a convention there. But the overpriced cars of all nations seemed to be represented, including enough Ferraris, Lamborghinis, Bentleys, and Rolls-Royces to reassure me that the entire European economy was doing just fine.

I spotted Johnny Ray hovering outside a shed that stood halfway between the house and the stable. As usual, he was engaging in his healthful habit of sucking in nicotine. I rolled my window all the way down and leaned out. Max leaped onto my lap from the passenger side, not about to miss out on an opportunity to stick his nose out an open car window. That seems to be an obsession with dogs, as verified by my leggy Dalmatian's look of envy.

"What's all this?" I asked Johnny Ray.

He paused to exhale, then peered at me with his pale, snakelike eyes. "It's for Eduardo." As usual, he uttered his words as if he found the act of speaking an extremely demanding task, something along the lines of hauling cinder blocks. "There was a funeral Mass this morning. Now everybody's over at the house for this big reception thing."

"I'd like to stop in later," I told him. "Pay my respects."

Johnny Ray gave a little shrug, making it clear that my plans were of absolutely no interest to him. "You better park over there," he said, pointing to a narrow dirt driveway that wound back around the barn. "Leave room for Mr. Mac's guests."

I waved, then placed Max back on his side of the van before veering off in the direction Mr. MacKinnon's ever-charming barn manager had indicated. The road was rougher than I'd anticipated, and my van rocked and rolled across the uneven terrain. I worried about how my equipment was faring. My dogs, too.

"Are you guys all right?" I asked, glancing over at Max and Lou, who were being jostled around the front seat.

I should have known they'd react with glee. For them, this was the canine version of bumper cars.

Chuckling at their unwavering joie de vivre, I turned my head back in the direction I was traveling—and immediately jammed on the brakes.

"What the—?"

Someone had darted right in front of my van. I'd come *this* close to hitting him.

My heart was pounding like the drummer in one of the classic rock bands Nick was so crazy about. I knew the near-miss was my fault, that I shouldn't have taken my eyes off the road. But it had never occurred to me that I'd encounter a jaywalker on Andrew MacKinnon's vast estate. Especially since my huge white van was pretty hard to miss.

Aside from looking surprised, the young man I'd come horribly close to hitting seemed fine. I put the van into park and opened the door. This time, both Max and Lou sprinted across my lap, pounding my poor thighs with eight muscular paws. As soon as they hit the ground, they both went into a sniffing tizzy, drunk with excitement over all the new smells.

I leaped out of the van after them, confronting the foolhardy pedestrian face-to-face.

"Don't you know better than to step in front of a moving car?" I demanded.

"Don't you know better than to take your eyes off the road?"

"Okay, I admit it was a bad idea, even though it was only for two seconds. But why on earth would you step right in front of me like that?"

"Because it never occurred to me that you'd come charging at me. I'm glad your reflexes are more highly developed than your common sense."

He looked as if he was in his mid-thirties, with gray-blue eyes and thick blond hair that softened into a mass of curls at the back of his neck. He wasn't exactly stocky; his frame was more along the lines of sturdy, with wide shoulders and muscular arms. Under his nubby brown sports jacket, he was wearing a pale blue cotton button-down shirt, so completely free of wrinkles it had to have been professionally cleaned and pressed. He looked so much like the classic preppy that I couldn't resist checking his feet to see if he was wearing Top-Siders without socks. Maybe because of the seriousness of the occasion, he was wearing black loafers—*with* socks. I also couldn't help noticing he stood amidst a cloud of cologne. Something musky and masculine, probably advertised as a surefire way of getting the babes into bed.

Before I had a chance to come up with a snappy reply to his last obnoxious comment, he glanced at the side of my van. "What is this thing, anyway? A traveling circus?"

"*No,*" I replied indignantly. At that moment, I happened to notice that both my wild beasts had gotten busy lifting their legs on as many tires as possible, leaving their mark on hundreds of thousands of dollars' worth of vehicles in an impressively short time. The fact that my operation was beginning to look very much like P.T. Barnum's road show only increased my frustration.

"I'm a veterinarian," I continued. "This is a mobile services unit. I make house calls, treating people's animals at their homes. I'm here today to check on one of Andrew MacKinnon's geldings."

He turned his eyes toward my van. I did the same, studying my twenty-six-foot-long white van and the blue letters stenciled on the door:

REIGNING CATS & DOGS

Mobile Veterinary Services

Large and Small Animal

631-555-PETS

"Interesting," he said. But his tone of voice made it clear that he found my operation more peculiar than interesting.

"What about you?" I countered. "Who are you—and what are you doing here?" Not that it was any of my business, of course—and not that I cared. I was just so put off by his attitude that I didn't want him thinking he was the only one who had a right to ask annoying questions.

Instead of responding to my question, he reached into his jacket pocket and whipped out a laminated ID card. In addition to a decent photograph and his name, Forrester Sloan, it was printed with the word, "Media."

"I write for *Newsday*," he informed me.

"Don't tell me," I said dryly. "You're doing an exposé on the hidden dangers of hitting balls with sticks while riding fast horses."

His mouth twisted into a deep frown. "I guess you haven't heard."

"Heard what?"

"The cops think Eduardo Garcia was murdered."

"But he fell off his horse!" I cried.

"True. But the medical examiner's office performed an autopsy, and apparently there were no signs of a trauma that would have led to his death. In other words, it wasn't the fall that killed him."

"Then what did?"

"The medical cause of death was determined to be an arrhythmia. That's an irregular heartbeat, either too fast or too slow—"

"I know what an arrhythmia is," I interrupted.

"Okay, but here's the thing: Eduardo was twenty-three, he was in perfect health, and he had no history of heart problems. So the forensic investigators have labeled his death suspicious. In other words, they're convinced there was more to it than the guy simply dropping dead for no good reason."

"Like . . . ?" I prompted.

He paused. "They think he was poisoned."

"Eduardo—*poisoned?*" I repeated, my voice reduced to a whisper.

"That's the focus of the investigation at this point," Forrester replied, sounding strangely matter-of-fact. "The medical examiner's office sent specimens to the State Crime Laboratory for testing."

My head was spinning. I felt as if I'd suddenly been transported from Andrew MacKinnon's luxurious estate to the pages of a mystery novel.

"But who—why—?" I sputtered.

"Precisely the questions I'm trying to answer," he said coolly. "That's what we folks in the newspaper biz do."

"Funny. I always thought that was what the folks in the homicide biz do."

"True, but they're not the only ones who are capable of asking questions and putting two and two together."

"In that case," I told him, my head still spinning but for some reason not wanting him to know it, "why don't you go play Magnum, P.I., and I'll get to work."

I pushed past him, my shoulder accidentally brushing against his. He snickered—which for some reason made me furious.

"Pretty tough, aren't you?" he commented.

I glared at him. "Does Mr. MacKinnon know you're here? Or Johnny Ray?"

"Johnny Ray and I made a deal." He mused, "Y'know, it's amazing how much you can still buy with a twenty-dollar bill."

"Look, none of this is even close to my concern," I shot back. "If you'll excuse me, there's a horse waiting for me." I gave my head a little toss to emphasize that I meant business.

I stalked off toward the stable, deeply inhaling the distinctive scent of hay, manure, and horse sweat.

Highly preferable to overpriced men's cologne, I thought angrily.

As I reached Braveheart's stall, I was pleased to hear footsteps outside—moving *away*. But the fact that Forrester Whatever-His-Name-Was was still chuckling raised the temperature of my blood by a few more degrees.

"Idiot," I muttered. "I hope Andrew MacKinnon employs a few security guards. Really nasty ones."

But my irritation over the cocky *Newsday* reporter was only part of the reason I was suddenly in a foul mood. I was truly distraught over what I'd just learned.

In fact, I had to lean against the wall of Braveheart's stall to steady myself. My knees had turned into Jell-O, and my heart was thumping so hard I was sure the horses around me could hear it.

Eduardo Garcia . . . *murdered?* No matter how hard I tried, I couldn't get the meaning of the words to sink in. The accidental death of such a vibrant young man had been difficult enough to comprehend. But the idea that someone had killed him was even harder to absorb.

I was glad that, for the moment at least, I had other responsibilities to engage my attention. Just by looking at Braveheart, I could see that his condition had improved. He seemed much more relaxed than the last time I'd seen him, and his dark eyes shone just a little bit brighter. Crouching down in his stall, I unwrapped the leg, washed off the poultice, and checked the gelding's tendon.

"So how's he doin'?"

I glanced up and saw that Johnny Ray had come into the barn, slinking in so silently that I hadn't even realized he was there. "He looks good," I replied. "The swelling is down. In fact, I think we can discontinue the poultice and the anti-inflammatories."

"Can I tell Mr. Mac he can start riding him again?"

I shook my head. "I still want to take things slow. Let's stick with hand-walking for about ten minutes twice a day. Cut his feed back, too. I'll check back again, but he's going to need another week to ten days."

I stroked Braveheart's nose and was rewarded with a grateful nicker. "Everybody deserves a few days off every now and then, huh, fella?"

I happened to glance over at Johnny Ray, who was scowling. *He probably disapproves of coddling the animals,* I thought bitterly. Still, the barn manager's chronic crankiness wasn't enough to make me change my ways.

Still stroking Braveheart's nose, I said, "I think we're set for today. Do you think I should check in with Mr. MacKinnon, or is he too busy?"

"I'm sure he'll want a full report." As was so often the case, Johnny Ray's mouth was pulled into a cross between a smile and a sneer. "Braveheart *is* his favorite horse, after all. And considering the fact that he just lost his favorite polo player, he could probably use some good news."

Am I imagining the insolence in his tone? I wondered, studying Johnny Ray's face and posture. Or am I just overly sensitive because the latest report on the cause of Eduardo's death is so devastating?

At any rate, I was looking forward to joining the group that had come together to mourn the young Argentine's demise. I hoped that being surrounded by others who had cared about him would help me put the terrible occurrence into perspective.

As I made my way toward the house after corraling Max and Lou into the van, I was surprised to see that Andrew MacKinnon really did employ security guards. A man in a gray uniform with a patch identifying him as an employee of a private security firm was stationed at the front door, checking names on a clipboard before letting anyone in. I wondered if that had been Mac-Kinnon's idea or the police's.

"I'm Jessica Popper," I told him when I reached the front door. "I don't think I'm on that list, since—"

"Here you are, Dr. Popper," he said, glancing at his clipboard. "Go right in."

I was about to do just that when I felt somebody brush up against me and grab hold of my elbow.

"I'm with her."

I glanced over at Forrester Sloan in surprise. "Hey! What do you think—?"

"Just go along with it," he whispered.

"Why on earth *should* I?"

"Because I need your help."

"*What?*"

"Besides," he went on matter-of-factly, "you owe me."

"For what?" I demanded.

"Don't tell me you've already forgotten. That you almost killed me, I mean."

"I think that's a bit of an—"

"Move ahead, please," the security guard urged, sounding a bit impatient. "You're holding up the line." He gestured toward two couples who had just arrived together. All four were dressed in stylish clothing that looked better suited to an art opening than a funeral. The women definitely fell into the trophy wives category, even if these particular trophies were starting to look just a little bit tarnished. I suspected that neither was a stranger to Botox, liposuction, and probably a dozen other procedures I'd never even heard of. Glancing at their husbands, a matching pair of classic balding businessmen with large stomachs, I hoped the luxurious lifestyle they'd bought with their smooth foreheads and perky breasts was worth it.

"Thanks, I needed that," Forrester said breezily as soon as we stopped inside the front room of the Mac-Kinnons' mansion. It was so crowded, and filled with so many different perfumes and colognes, I was surprised that gas masks weren't as de rigueur as tiny purses and very high heels.

"Exactly what do you think you're doing?" I demanded, wrenching my arm from his grasp.

"Like I told you, I'm trying to find out who killed Eduardo Garcia."

I cast him a cynical look. "I didn't think you were serious."

"Look," he went on, "scooping the story of who killed Garcia would make my career. And I really think I could do it. You've got to admit that I've got a couple of things going for me. One, I'm an experienced reporter. Two, the fact that I *am* a reporter gives me an excuse to nose around, asking questions. That's exactly what people expect reporters to do, even if they don't always like it. Third, I've got my preppy image working for me. I could probably do a pretty good job of fitting into this world. Don't you think I look like somebody who enjoyed a privileged childhood before going to prep school and graduating from Yale? With honors, of course. Double major in political science and philosophy. But then I rebelled against my parents to follow my dream of going to the Columbia University Graduate School of Journalism instead of going into the family business and becoming a successful corporate executive like my father. The whole story fits perfectly, don't you think?"

I had to admit that Forrester Sloan did, indeed, look like someone who'd be very much at home amidst the polo crowd. And he certainly had the self-confidence.

"I guess," I said begrudgingly. I couldn't resist adding, "Is all that true? About your background?"

He laughed, taking hold of my arm once again. "Come on. Let's mingle."

"Thanks," I said, slipping out of his grasp, "but I've already done my part by getting you in the door. As far as I'm concerned, you're on your own."

He just shrugged. "Catch you later."

"*Much* later," I muttered. "Like how about in my next life."

I glanced around, realizing I didn't know a soul in the room. Even though I'd wanted to pay my respects to Eduardo Garcia, I wondered if I'd be better off tracking down Andrew MacKinnon, giving him a report on his horse's status, and getting the heck out of there. But as I focused on the crowd, trying to find him, my eyes settled on the one familiar face I saw.

Inez, the MacKinnons' housekeeper, was making her way around the room, her eyes darting about uncertainly as she shyly proffered a tray of drinks. She needn't have worried about the possibility of social interaction. As far as these people were concerned, she was invisible, nothing more than a pair of hands floating in air for the sole purpose of supplying them with refreshments. The same held true for the other housekeeper circulating throughout the room with a tray, another Hispanic woman who was at least thirty years older and substantially wider than Inez. Both were dressed identically in plain black dresses and gleaming white aprons, with their hair pulled back into severe buns.

I moved over in the younger woman's direction. "Hello, Inez."

She looked surprised, probably shocked that someone had actually bothered to learn her name. "Dr. Popper!" Her tense face softened into a smile. "Would you like something to drink?"

"Thank you." I debated between iced tea and lemonade, deciding that when in doubt, go with caffeine. Peering into the tremendous dining room beyond a large doorway, its comically long table covered with heaping plates of food, I added, "It looks like the MacKinnons put out quite a spread."

"Yes, they use one of the best caterers on the North Shore," she replied.

"How about you?" I asked earnestly. "How are you bearing up?"

She sighed. "Such a sad thing. But of course, I hardly know Eduardo. He is—how can I explain, he is so busy with a different group of people."

The sadness in her eyes reinforced my initial impression of the bashful, soft-spoken young woman: that she'd harbored a serious crush on the handsome polo player. Looking around the room at all the beautiful young women who were part of the polo set, all of them with perfect makeup and expensive-looking clothes that showcased their well-toned bodies, I wondered if perhaps she hadn't been the only one.

"Still, it is *una tragedia* . . . how do you say, a tragedy? Someone so young, with such abilities with the horses."

"Yes," I agreed. I couldn't help asking, "Inez, was Eduardo friends with most of these people? Or are they friends of the MacKinnon family?"

"These people, I have seen them all here at the home of Meester MacKinnon before." She looked around before adding, in a whisper, "Some of them, the ladies, I know are special friends with Eduardo."

Doesn't surprise me, I thought, wondering just how hard to press her. But almost as soon as I had that thought, my curiosity about exactly how Eduardo fit in with the crowd of fashionably-dressed people around me hit a brick wall.

"Please excuse me, Dr. Popper," Inez said, looking

around nervously. "Meester Mac, he expects me to be working. Luisa, too. It would not be good for him to see that—"

"Of course, Inez. Don't let me keep you."

My interest in the emotional entanglements here at Heatherfield aside, I once again found myself with no one to talk to. I decided to find Mr. MacKinnon, report on Braveheart's improvement, and get on my way.

I studied the crowd in the spacious living room more carefully, then eased into the dining room to continue my search. I didn't see Andrew MacKinnon anywhere. After depositing my half-drunk iced tea on a tray of empties, I wandered down a short hallway that was lined with oil paintings of men and women with severe expressions and hardened eyes. At the end was the kitchen, an enormous room that was easily as large as most restaurant kitchens I'd seen. The walls were painted a pale yellow, while the curtains and cushions were covered in a deep rust-colored fabric printed with small sprigs of flowers, capturing the look of Provence—or at least an interior designer's interpretation of it. Huge cabinets, painted white, hung from the ceiling, the glass panels revealing so many bowls, plates, and glasses that I wondered if the catering service had bothered to bring its own. There were several sinks, interspersed among colossal refrigerators, industrial-looking stainless steel stoves, and more counter space than most diners.

I expected that the crowd would have spilled into this room, like most of the parties I go to. Instead, I saw only one person. Her back was to me, but I could see she was bent over a large tray of cookies, grabbing handfuls and stuffing them into her mouth so quickly that I suspected even my dogs would have been impressed.

I was about to sneak back out when I heard the loud

clicking of high heels against the ceramic tile floor right behind me.

"Callie, what is *wrong* with you?" the woman teetering on top of them demanded shrilly. She was tall and excruciatingly thin, dressed in a clingy black dress that anyone who'd ever eaten even a single French fry would find impossible to wear. Her smooth black hair, cut perfectly blunt, just skimmed her shoulders. Her features were delicate, complemented by a great deal of makeup that had been applied with an expert hand. I noticed that even with her life-endangering shoes, she was doing an excellent job of balancing a very large glass of something clear and brown. "Honestly, sometimes I think you *want* to be fat—that it's your selfish, malicious way of making me miserable!"

The cookie snatcher whirled around, still clutching some of her booty in her fists. She was a teenager, I saw, a chubby girl of fourteen or fifteen whose face was twisted into an angry snarl. The coarse, dark blond hair that streamed down her back looked as if it could use a good brushing, a strange contrast to the well-made but unflattering dark blue skirt and top she'd been stuffed into.

"It's always about you, Mother, isn't it?" the teenager returned angrily. "Everything in the entire universe is—"

She stopped, having just noticed that an interloper— me—had barged in on what was clearly meant to be a private mother-daughter moment.

"Don't you *knock* before you enter a room?" Callie barked, turning her fury on me.

"I'm sorry," I replied sincerely, my cheeks burning. "I—I was looking for Mr. MacKinnon."

"Figures Dad would just disappear, even on a day like this," Callie complained.

"Funny, him doing his usual disappearing act doesn't

bother me at all," the girl's mother mused. "But I suppose I have the magical powers of bourbon to thank for that." She held up her glass and peered into it admiringly. "But we haven't met, have we? I'm Jillian MacKinnon. The so-called lady of the house."

"I'm Jessica Popper," I told her, relieved that, at least for the moment, we were all back to addressing each other civilly. "I'm a veterinarian. I came to look at one of your horses."

"You mean one of *Andrew's* horses," she corrected me acidly. "And this is my lovely daughter Callie, who'll do anything in her power to break her mother's heart."

The withering look she cast her daughter was thrown right back at her.

"I can see you two are in the middle of something," I said, "so I'll just—"

"You're more than welcome to stay," Jillian countered. "In fact, I'd welcome your opinion, as an objective observer. If you were a fourteen-year-old girl who had grown up in total luxury, surrounded by every possible advantage and opportunity, yet you insisted on becoming your own worst enemy by stuffing every morsel of food you came across into your face—"

"Moth-er!" Callie screamed. "I hate you!" She flounced across the room, stopping only to grab a large dish of dainty, pastel-colored cakes the size of postage stamps and carry it out through the door with her.

Jillian turned to me and shrugged. "My advice to you? Have your tubes tied—*now,* before it's too late."

She turned away, picking up a bottle off the kitchen counter and refilling her glass. "If you really are interested in finding my husband—and frankly, I can't imagine why you would be—he's probably hiding in one of two places, his study or the stable. As I'm always telling my friends, if it's not related to either money or a horse,

don't expect Andrew to have the slightest interest in it."
She laughed, a raw, unpleasant sound, then gulped
down a large portion of her drink.

"Thanks. I'll check the study." I slunk out of there as
quickly as I could, my cheeks still burning. From what
I'd seen so far, Andrew MacKinnon's wife was drinking
herself silly and his daughter was eating herself into
oblivion. And to think that, at least from the outside,
the members of this family looked as if they had everything anyone could possibly want.

I headed down the hallway I remembered led to the
study. But as I neared the open door, I froze. Loud
voices, coming from inside, warned me that this might
not be the best time to poke my head in.

"Damn it, Winston!" I heard Andrew MacKinnon
shout. "Just stay out of this. None of it has anything to
do with you!"

"Nothing to do with me?" a voice I didn't recognize
shot back indignantly. The man it belonged to had a distinct British accent. "Andrew, my good man, we're talking about a *great* deal of money!"

Goodness, I thought, startled. *Can't* anybody *in this
household get along?*

"Keep your voice down!" MacKinnon hissed back.
"All we need is for the wrong person to overhear—"

"I certainly agree with you there," the stranger
replied. "Perhaps this is something that's best left to the
legal system to sort out."

"No!" MacKinnon barked. "That's the last thing we
want. But we can't have this discussion now, Winston.
Eduardo is *dead,* for God's sake. Please, let's talk about
this some other time."

I blinked, intrigued by their words but reluctant to
get caught eavesdropping. And it sounded as if their little argument was over, at least for the moment. I turned

and began to creep away, anxious to disappear into the crowd in the living room.

But before I could make it that far, the British-accented voice called after me, "Excuse me, miss. Is there something I can help you with?"

Chapter 4

"He who said he made a small fortune in the horse business probably started out with a large fortune!"
—Unknown

I turned, trying to look as if I hadn't overheard any of the unpleasantness that had just transpired between the two men. The one whose voice I hadn't recognized, a tall, slender gentleman—Winston, MacKinnon had called him—stood in the hallway, peering at me. His white hair and slightly stooped posture placed him somewhere in his seventies. Yet I got the feeling he had yet to let any of his standards slip, as indicated by his jaunty paisley-patterned burgundy bow tie and the matching silk handkerchief protruding from the breast pocket of his jacket.

"I was looking for Mr. MacKinnon," I said. "But if this is a bad time—"

"You might as well let him decide," Winston replied, glancing at the doorway wearily. He sighed, patting his jacket as if he was trying to smooth out more than just the wrinkles in the gabardine.

"Is that you, Dr. Popper?" MacKinnon called from inside the study. "Come in, come in. I'm anxious to talk to you."

Winston hurried past me, muttering to himself, as I strode into the study.

The dark mood lingering in the air stood in strange contrast to the room's peaceful décor.

Andrew MacKinnon was dressed better than the last time I'd seen him, sporting a coat and tie that he didn't look particularly comfortable in but which was certainly appropriate to the occasion. But his ruddy face had a flushed look. Probably the result of both the argument he'd just had and the large, nearly empty tumbler in his hand. I wondered if perhaps Jillian wasn't the only member of the MacKinnon clan who belonged to the Frequent Drinker Club.

"I'm sorry to disturb you, Mr. MacKinnon," I told him. "I know this is a bad time—"

"I'm anxious to hear how Braveheart is doing," he replied. Speaking more to himself than to me, he added, "Frankly, I could use some good news."

"Braveheart is doing wonderfully, but I'd like him to take it easy for another week or so. I'll check back then and see how he's feeling. In the meantime, Johnny Ray knows what to do."

"Excellent," he mumbled. "He's quite a horse."

"Yes, he is," I said sincerely. "I'll be on my way now. I'm sure you—"

"Don't go," he insisted. "Actually, it would be rather refreshing to spend some time with someone who's not part of the usual crowd. What can I get you to drink?" He headed toward a wooden armoire that was crowded with bottles and glasses.

I struggled to come up with an excuse, then realized that MacKinnon really did seem to want some company. "Thank you, but I'm fine."

"Nonsense. At least let me make you a G-and-T."

Silently I accepted the gin and tonic I didn't really want. I held it politely, hoping he wouldn't notice I wasn't actually drinking it.

Fortunately, he seemed to have forgotten I was in the room. "This is a terrible, terrible thing," he said, lowering himself into a chair and staring off into the distance. "Imagine, Eduardo *murdered*. I can't understand it. The man was one of a kind. A true prince."

I followed his gaze to a group of photographs artfully arranged on an end table. Most were shots of Andrew MacKinnon and the other three members of his polo team. With both hands he proudly held a large silver trophy. All four were dressed in the uniform of the game: white stretch pants, high black boots, and baggy polo shirts in the same shade of dark blue. A few of the other photographs captured the men on horseback, their expressions earnest as they leaned forward to take a whack at the ball.

But one of the pictures was larger than the rest. It was a framed photograph of an astonishingly handsome man I surmised was Eduardo. This was the first good look at his face I'd gotten. He had an irresistibly rugged look: the well-proportioned facial features of a movie star, set off by tanned skin and a roguish five o'clock shadow and framed by thick, wavy black hair. Intense dark brown eyes, lit up by a teasing glint, stared out at the camera. I also noticed a few tiny scars, no doubt souvenirs of all the time he spent on the polo field.

"He was also one hell of an athlete," MacKinnon went on. "I suppose you're aware he was a ten-goal player."

I shook my head. "Sorry. I know horses, but I don't know polo."

"Then let me give you a crash course." His face relaxed into a smile for the first time since I'd come into the room. "Being ranked a ten-goal player means you've been given the highest possible rating. At the beginning of every year, the United States Polo Association rates every polo player with a handicap from minus two to ten. The scores are supposedly based on a number of factors, like horsemanship and sportsmanship and even the quality of his horses. But when you come right down to it, the bottom line is how well someone actually plays.

"Often, especially in higher-goal games, a polo team is formed by someone like me who's enthralled with the game and has the means to hire three other players. They're usually Argies—Argentines—because they happen to be the best polo players in the world. There are exceptions, of course, a few Americans and the occasional South African who sneaks into the ranks of the ten-goal players. I have an American playing for me right now. Scott Mooney. Helluva guy—and a seven-goal player. To rank the team, you add up rankings of all four players.

"The patrons," he continued, "those men of means I mentioned, pay their teammates an annual salary, just like any employee. I suppose you've already heard the rumor that I paid Eduardo a million dollars a year."

I gasped, then immediately tried to hide my astonishment. "No, I hadn't heard that."

"It's one of the few rumors floating around that happens to be true. That wasn't always the case, of course. When I first brought him up here from Argentina, he was still pretty green."

"So you're the one who discovered him."

"Exactly right." MacKinnon paused to take a sip of whiskey. The sip turned into four or five. "I still remember the first time I laid eyes on him. In fact, it seems like yesterday." His voice had become soft, and his eyes had a faraway look. I couldn't tell if he was reacting to the memory—or the whiskey in his glass.

"It was a cool morning in April, so early that the sun was barely up. I was visiting a horse farm outside of Buenos Aires, trying to decide whether or not to buy a particular horse. The Argies are the best horse breeders in the world, as far as I'm concerned. The best horse trainers, too. Eduardo was still a kid—fifteen, sixteen. But I saw him out in a field, riding the horse I was interested in. He was just playing around, stick-and-balling with some of his buddies. But what a sight!" He chuckled. "To this day, the guy who ran the farm swears he didn't set the whole thing up. And to this day I don't believe him.

"I bought the horse, of course. I wasn't about to let Eduardo go, either. I could see he was a natural. His power in handling that animal, the graceful way he moved, that rare combination of strength and coordination that makes the whole thing look so easy..."

I remained silent, not mentioning that I'd had the same impression the first and only time I'd seen Eduardo Garcia on a horse, just a few days earlier. MacKinnon appeared to have gone into a sort of trance.

"At that moment," he went on, "it was as if I had the ability to look into the future. I could actually see the polo player Eduardo was going to be. And I was right on. Three years after I brought him up here, he was rated a ten-goal player.

"In the simplest terms," MacKinnon went on, "Eduardo was one of the best polo players in the world. And the man won a lot of games for me. But that was only part of it. The chance to play with someone of that caliber, to watch his mastery of the game so closely, out on the polo field amidst all the excitement, the speed, the *power*...well, I feel privileged that I was able to have an experience like that.

"As for Eduardo," he continued, "when he agreed to come to this country, he left behind everything and everyone he'd ever cared about. His village, his family, his childhood friends...Sure, he was dirt poor. Still, he abandoned the old Eduardo to become someone new. A new place, new friends, a new career...

"But he handled it all with amazing ease. The man was truly one of a kind. In fact," MacKinnon went on, his voice becoming strained with emotion, "he was like a son to me. Of course I love my daughters. Peyton and Callie are the center of the universe, as far as I'm concerned. But Eduardo...Eduardo was something special."

He shook his head slowly. "Losing him would have been a great loss to the game."

"Excuse me?" I asked, confused.

MacKinnon glanced up, looking surprised. I got the impression he'd been thinking out loud. For the moment, at least, he seemed to have forgotten there was someone else in the room.

"I said, 'Losing him is a great loss to the game.'" His gaze traveled back to the polo player's photograph. "Damn shame," he muttered. In a few hearty gulps, he emptied his glass, then rose to get himself a refill.

"Can I offer you another drink?" he asked politely, without looking up.

"I'm fine." I glanced at my glass, which was just as full as it had originally been. I put it down on one of the tables, hiding it between two framed photographs and hoping that someone would dispose of it later. "In fact, I should really be on my way."

I hesitated, wondering if our conversation had come to an end. But MacKinnon had picked up the photograph of Eduardo and was holding it in his hand, just staring at it. I slipped out of the room, not wanting to disturb him during what was obviously a private moment. Or maybe it was that, for the moment, at least, I'd had about all of the MacKinnons I could handle.

As I came out of the study, I nearly ran smack into the man who was striding down the hall.

"Excuse me!" I cried. "I didn't see—"

"Well, well, well. If it isn't Dr. Jessica Popper. You sure have a way of showing up in the most interesting places."

I blinked, caught off guard by the sight of the small, wiry man with the piercing dark eyes. But I immediately realized I shouldn't have been at all surprised that Lieutenant Anthony Falcone, Chief of Homicide, was among today's attendees. Still, seeing him here confirmed that the police believed that Eduardo Garcia's death hadn't been accidental, after all.

"Dare I ask what you're doin' here today?" he asked in his thick Long Island accent.

"If you're asking if I'm here because of Mr. Garcia's suspicious death, the answer is no. I happen to be treating one of Andrew MacKinnon's horses."

"You sure get around, don't you?" Lieutenant Falcone folded his arms across his chest. He reminded me of Napoleon—with a New York attitude. He was short, not even as tall as I was, and slight of build. His blue-black hair was slicked back, held in place by some substance so shiny I could have used the top of his head as a mirror.

"I hope you're not planning on gettin' involved in this investigation," he warned. "Murder is dangerous business."

"So I've learned," I replied coolly. "Although I seem to recall that the last time you and I met, even you had some complimentary things to say about how I handled myself."

I watched with no small sense of satisfaction as his mouth dropped open.

"Besides," I couldn't resist adding, "it seems to me that this investigation should be a cinch."

"Yeah?" Falcone's eyes narrowed suspiciously. "And why, may I ask, is that?"

"Apparently the medical examiner's office believes the man was poisoned. So all you have to do is find out who had access to his food right before he died and you've got your murderer."

"Sounds simple, doesn't it?"

"Like I said, a cinch."

"Except for one small problem," he growled. "The night before Eduardo Garcia died, he was one of three hundred guests at a party at the Old Brookbury Country Club, a celebration of the club's seventy-fifth anniversary. During the autopsy, the partially digested food that was found in his system indicated that the last time he'd eaten had been twelve to fourteen hours before his death—meaning that the last time he ate was at this fancy party and that it's therefore most likely where he was poisoned.

"In other words, Dr. Popper, at the moment we have two-hundred-ninety-nine individuals who could easily have slipped something in the guy's drink—including just about everybody you see here at Andrew Mac-Kinnon's estate today."

"I see," I said evenly, not willing to give him the satisfaction of admitting that maybe, just maybe, I wasn't quite the expert I'd pretended to be. Tossing my head, I said, "In that case, I'd better let you get to it. I guess it'll take you quite a lot of time to interview two-hundred-ninety-nine murder suspects."

I stalked off in the direction of the front door, determined to get out of there. In fact, by that point, there was nothing I wanted more. Which was why I was dismayed to find that the two women I'd seen come in right after me, the ones I'd immediately labeled trophy wives, were blocking the doorway.

"Excuse me," I muttered, expecting them to move out of the way.

Instead, one of them leaned forward and peered at me. "You're that... that animal doctor, aren't you?"

It sounded more like an accusation than a question. "Guilty as charged," I replied.

"Did I hear someone say that your name is Dr. Pepper?" the other one wondered aloud.

"It's Dr. Popper," I informed her through clenched teeth.

The second one, who was shorter, rounder, and louder, giggled. "That's a relief. Although I *was* wondering if you were a soft-drink heiress."

"Don't be silly, Viv," the taller woman chastised. "The Dr Pepper heiress lives in Texas. She's got a polo team of her own." Turning back to me, she added, "By the way, I'm Diana Chase. My friend here is Vivian Johannsen."

"Nice to meet you," I mumbled, hoping I sounded at least a little sincere. I had to admit that the two of them did make an interesting pair. Diana Chase was built like a model, so tall that her spiky high-heeled shoes seemed like overkill and so thin that the various bones that protruded almost looked like accessories. Sleek, dead-straight blond hair swooped down over her eyes. She had a breezy, confident air that advertised the fact that, thanks to her beauty, she was used to being admired and treated as someone special.

Even though this was supposed to be a somber occasion, she was dressed in a dangerously short white dress made from slippery fabric, with a complicated network of straps crisscrossing the tanned skin of her back. I wondered if she was unaware that we could all see the outline of her lacy white thong underwear—or if that was the whole point.

Her pal, meanwhile, was as curvy as Diana was angular. Vivian Johannsen had the classic hourglass shape, with hips as round as dinner plates, a tiny waist, and voluptuous breasts that threatened to pop out of the low-cut beige minidress she'd donned for the occasion. While Diana's jewelry was minimal, Vivian was decked out in large gold hoop earrings, an ostentatious necklace studded with glittering stones, and a diamond ring that was so big I was surprised she was able to lift her hand.

"How do you know the MacKinnons?" Diana asked casually. "Or were you friends with Eduardo?"

"I came here today to treat one of Mr. MacKinnon's horses."

Diana looked surprised. "Is that how it works? You mean people don't bring their animals to you?"

"Most horse vets make house calls," I explained patiently. "But I specialize in making house calls for all kinds of animals. Dogs, cats, even exotics like lizards. I have a van that's pretty much a clinic on wheels."

"How absolutely marvelous!" Diana cooed, suddenly interested. "You mean you actually go to your clients' homes—just like my personal trainer and my masseuse and my hairdresser?"

I forced a smile. "Same deal."

"Harlan would love that," Vivian interjected with a smirk. "Just think of all the pennies you'd save on gas!"

I blinked, wondering if they were joking. Diana hardly looked like a woman who had to worry about making ends meet.

As for Diana, she pointedly ignored her friend's comment. "In that case, when can you come by to take a look at Fleur? She's a Chartreux. I'm terrible at keeping track of schedules, but I don't think she's been to the vet in ages. She's probably due for some shots or something."

"Let me check my schedule," I told her, pulling my appointment book out of my bag.

"Me, too!" Vivian piped up. "I have a Himalayan named Liliana. Can you take her on as a patient?"

"I'd be happy to come by and check her out."

"See if you can fit me in, too!" she demanded, stepping in front of Diana and nearly crunching down on her foot.

Scheduling appointments wasn't easy, given all the tennis lessons, massages, and luncheons at Babbo, Bolo, and Nobu in New York City we had to work around. But both women managed to squeeze me in the following Monday—meaning I'd have to make the trip to this part of Norfolk County only once. After Diana Chase and Vivian Johannsen had punched me into their Palm Pilots, I was free to gather up my dogs and get on my way.

It wasn't until I was driving away from Heatherfield, with Max and Lou beside me, that I recognized what a bizarre morning I'd had. Here I'd expected to make a simple house call, examining Braveheart's tendon and then checking in with Mr. MacKinnon. Instead, I'd nearly run over one of the most obnoxious young men I'd ever encountered, learned that Eduardo Garcia had been murdered, attended his wake, and met some really peculiar people who'd actually made me glad I wasn't ridiculously wealthy.

I couldn't wait to tell Nick all about it.

Of course, that would have to wait. He was at school and I had a full day of appointments ahead of me.

As soon as I got home that evening, I took a few minutes to give every member of my menagerie a proper

greeting. Then I reached for my cell phone. As I dialed
the number of Nick's apartment, I replayed the events of
the day in my mind, trying to figure out how to tell him
all about it in a way that made sense.

"Hello..." I heard him say.

"Nick, it's me. Today was the craziest day—"

"...You've reached Nick, but I'm not able to take
your call right now. Please..."

I hung up, then immediately punched in his cell number. But the phone kept ringing, and I realized he wasn't
going to pick up.

"Damn!" I cried.

"Damn the torpedoes, *awk*!" Prometheus screeched.
"Full speed ahead!"

"Hardly," I mumbled. Unable to reach Nick, I was
suddenly hit with a tidal wave of loneliness. Wasn't
Friday night supposed to be a date night—at least for
someone who'd had the same boyfriend for four years,
more or less?

I was still feeling sorry for myself when I heard a
knock at the door. I flung it open—and was confronted
by the biggest mass of flowers I'd ever seen in my life.
The bouquet was so huge that it completely concealed
the head and torso of whoever was carrying it, making
it look like a creature from a science fiction movie who
was half floral and half corduroy-covered legs.

I couldn't be positive, but I thought I recognized
those legs.

"Nick?"

The face that poked itself out from behind the bouquet did, indeed, belong to Nick. It wore a big, apologetic grin.

"Are you still talking to me?" he asked sheepishly,
pushing back the lock of straight brown hair that was
always falling into his eyes.

"Why wouldn't I be?"

"Because I've been ignoring you."

A wave of guilt immediately rushed over me. "Oh, Nick, I know how busy you must be. After all, law school just started last week!"

I wasn't the only one who was happy to see Nick, though. Max and Lou shot over, yelping with joy and leaping up on him. He was suddenly surrounded by a flurry of white fur—some fluffy, some sleek and dotted with black—and eight paws sliding around on the floor.

"Hey, guys! I missed you, too!" Nick cried. "But you've got to let me put these down."

"Here, I'll take them," I offered. "Wow, these are really beautiful."

I relieved Nick of the shrub-sized bouquet, freeing him to crouch down and lavish attention on the dogs. His arrival had also prompted Cat to give up her warm, comfortable spot and amble over to say hello. Prometheus just shrieked, happy to be in the midst of any form of commotion.

The sweet fragrance of the yellow roses that were mixed in with half a dozen other varieties of colorful blossoms was already filling the cottage. "Thanks, Nick," I said. "That was really sweet of you."

He paused in his ear-scratching duties long enough to leer at me. "I have an ulterior motive. I expect to be thanked in a really big way."

I laughed. "One week of law school, and you're already depraved!"

"One week of sleeping alone, and you have no idea how depraved I can be!"

"No, but I'm looking forward to finding out. Let me just put these in a vase, and you can show me."

I went into the kitchen and stuck the bouquet into the biggest vase I could find. Then I grabbed two wineglasses, along with a bottle of red. On impulse, I picked up a couple of candles and a book of matches.

What the heck, I thought. *Might as well do this right.*

When I went back into the living room, Nick was nowhere in sight. Cat had sprawled out underneath the coffee table and Prometheus was attacking a slice of apple, but the dogs were gone, too.

Puzzled, I went over to the front door and opened it. "Nick?" I called, sticking my head out. So much for my theory that he'd taken Max and Lou out for a walk or a quick game of Frisbee.

Then I had a brainstorm. The bedroom. Of course. He'd said himself that he had big plans for the evening, our first together since the weekend before. And I noticed the door was closed.

Things were definitely starting to get interesting. Wearing a grin of my own, I stepped into the bathroom and checked my reflection in the mirror. I pulled the elastic band out of my hair, ran a comb through it, and smoothed it down around my shoulders. Then, just to get into the mood, I undid an extra button on my forest green polo shirt, embroidered with, "Jessica Popper, D.V.M."

I grabbed the candle and the matches. As I opened the bedroom door, my heart was pounding. I expected to see Nick lying on the bed, half-draped in a sheet, perhaps with a rose in his teeth. I could even picture a T-shirt thrown over the lampshade to help create the right mood.

Instead, the room was pitch black.

Even more intriguing, I told myself, my heart pounding even faster.

Moving cautiously in the dark, I set the candle down on what I knew was the top of the dresser. I was about to strike a match when I heard a deep, rasping sound that could only mean one thing.

Nick was snoring.

I lit the candle. Sure enough, he was sprawled across

the bed. Fully clothed and fast asleep. Lou was glommed onto one side, resting his chin on Nick's stomach and gazing at me woefully with his huge, brown eyes. Max was curled up between Nick's legs looking like a fur pillow—or maybe a fur hot-water bottle.

"Nick?" I said softly.

As I expected, I got no response.

I thought I hated lawyers, I reflected as I climbed into bed next to him with a loud sigh. But it turns out that I hate law schools even more.

Chapter 5

"When you're young and you fall off a horse, you may break something. When you're my age and you fall off, you splatter."

—Roy Rogers

I thought I'd seen the last of Heatherfield for a few days. But I found out I was wrong early the next morning. *Very* early.

When the shrill ring of my cell phone dragged me out of a deliciously deep sleep, I glanced at my alarm clock to see if it could possibly be as early as it felt. The red numbers glowed 7:01. *Somebody* had decided it was okay to call any time after seven, I thought crossly, even on a Saturday.

That somebody turned out to be Johnny Ray Cousins. I knew that as soon as I croaked "Hello?" and heard a gravelly, "Dr. Popper?"

"Yes," I mumbled, swirling my tongue around my mouth to clean out the cobwebs of sleep.

"We got a problem."

Those words were enough to snap anybody awake.

"Braveheart?" I demanded, my heartbeat instantly escalating.

"Nah, he's fine," Johnny Ray informed me. "But it looks like we got a mare with a bad impaction."

Serious, yes. An emergency that couldn't wait another hour or two, not really.

But by that point, I was fully awake. "I'll be there in about an hour," I told him. "In the meantime, hold back on feed."

"I'll be waitin'."

I glanced over at Nick, who was still fast asleep. Sighing softly, I climbed out of bed.

Of course, my animals were already in full gear. Promotheus was an early riser, since he was always— well, up with the birds. Cat was sleeping in more and more these days, lingering in a drowsy state as she lay on the rag rug in front of the refrigerator. Still, it wasn't much of a stretch for her to open her eyes, officially acknowledging the start of a new day.

Max and Lou, of course, were like two firefighters, on call twenty-four hours a day. Max, being a terrier, had a true type A personality, shifting into an energetic mode in the blink of an eye. As for Lou, as a Dalmatian he had an affinity for the fire-fighting life in his genes.

I couldn't say the same for my beau. I'd just gotten the coffee going when Nick stumbled into the kitchen, looking so dazed he could have been sleepwalking. A clump of his dark brown hair stuck up at a funny angle, and only one eye was open.

"Whazzup?" he mumbled, scratching his head and turning a bad hair day into a disastrous hair day.

"Go back to bed, Nick," I said soothingly. "I've got an early call. Another polo pony. I'll just let the dogs out and grab some coffee, and then I'll be out of here. But I should be home in a couple of hours."

"Leave the dogs." He paused to yawn loudly. "I'll

take them out for a run later. We could both use the exercise."

"Great. Now get some sleep. You need it."

Nick muttered something incomprehensible, then turned and shuffled back to the bedroom.

As the coffeepot burped and chugged, I threw open the front door and followed Max and Lou outside. There was a lot to be said for being up and at 'em this early in the day. The sun was low in the sky and the air was fresh, giving the world that pristine, Garden of Eden feeling. I felt like I was the only person in the world.

Until I heard a hearty, "Morning, Jessica!"

I turned and saw Betty emerging from the wooded area that surrounded the Big House. There would have been something romantic about the vision of a lone soul communing with nature except that the lone soul in question was dressed in orange sweatpants, a baggy pink New York City Ballet T-shirt, and shiny silver Nikes that looked as if they'd been issued by NASA.

"Good morning, Betty. You're certainly up bright and early!"

"Oh, I'm always up at this hour," she assured me, leaning over to pat Max and Lou, who'd immediately made a beeline for her. As she lavished affection on them and they shamelessly lapped it up, she said, "Best part of the day, as far as I'm concerned. Of course, used to be I was coming home around this time, my head buzzing from a long night of dreamy music and my feet barely able to keep still in my dancing shoes. Which reminds me: I've got some tickets for you."

"Tickets?"

"Five complimentary passes for opening night."

"Thanks, Betty. I'm really looking forward to it."

"I thought you might want to invite that nice friend of yours, Suzanne."

"That's a great idea," I told her—then immediately experienced second thoughts.

Suzanne Fox was one of my closest friends from our student days. While we were students at Bryn Mawr College, we had burned the midnight oil together in our efforts to get into vet school. And we'd both achieved our goal, with Suzanne going on to the Purdue University School of Veterinary Medicine in Indiana and me studying at the College of Veterinary Medicine at Cornell University. But over time, we lost touch. Demanding schedules have a way of making that happen. In fact, it wasn't until three months earlier, back at the beginning of the summer, that I'd learned that fate—and a now-defunct marriage—had brought her to Long Island.

But Suzanne would undoubtedly want to bring along her current beau, another vet named Marcus Scruggs. And *he* was another story entirely. The fact that I'd been the one to play matchmaker didn't make their blossoming love affair any easier to stomach—not when Marcus was about as appetizing as day-old sushi.

I was still ruminating over the pros and cons of spending an entire evening with Suzanne and a man who was very much like a congealing piece of raw eel when Betty interjected, "One of the tickets is for Nick, of course."

Which presented another potential problem. I hoped he'd manage to pencil Betty's opening night into his engagement book. I knew how hurt she would be if Nick wasn't there to witness her moment in the spotlight. Then again, he was extremely fond of her. He was also as excited as I was that she'd decided to jump back into musical theater, her lifelong passion.

Nick will find time for Betty, I told myself firmly. *Even if he can't necessarily find time for me.*

I hurried off, apologizing to Betty for not having

more time to chat. But I didn't want to keep Johnny Ray—or Andrew MacKinnon's poor horse—waiting. I shepherded Max and Lou back inside the house and headed off to Heatherfield.

As I chugged along the driveway of the MacKinnon estate, I spotted Johnny Ray, waiting for me outside the stable. He was leaning against the wall in a pose that I suspected had been inspired by James Dean. As if that weren't bad enough, he was playing out the part further by wearing scruffy jeans and a white T-shirt that looked as if they'd been supplied by the Costume Department. Of course, the deep grooves in his leathery face advertised the fact that he had two or even three decades on the actor.

Johnny Ray had adopted one more James Dean affectation: sucking on his usual cigarette. As I headed toward him, lugging a heavy bag, he took one last drag, then tossed the butt onto the ground and snuffed it out with the sole of his boot.

"You're late," he greeted me gruffly.

I raised my eyebrows in surprise. I was certain I hadn't committed to arriving at a specific time. I knew better than that, even at 7:01 A.M. Between traffic, roadwork, and a bunch of other unpredictable factors, driving times on Long Island are always tough to estimate.

"Anyways, you're here now," Johnny Ray mumbled. He turned his back on me and went inside the barn. I took that as an invitation to follow.

"This here's Molly," he continued, indicating the black mare in the corner stall. Gesturing toward the water bucket hanging from the side of her stall, he added, "It's been cool at night lately, so she hasn't been drinking much. You know how horses are. If it isn't hot, it doesn't always occur to them to drink. Anyways, yesterday I noticed she was looking kinda dull. She was unusually quiet and she kept her head down...she just didn't look right. In the late afternoon, maybe around four, she starts lyin' down in her stall—and Molly's one of them horses that never lies down. She kept looking at her flanks, and she started rolling around a bit." He shrugged. "The way I figure, since I know she ain't pregnant, it all probably adds up to an impaction."

"She hasn't passed any manure?" I asked.

"Nope."

"And she doesn't have any appetite?"

His mouth twisted into a sneer. "This morning, you told me to hold back on feed."

"I meant before that," I explained patiently.

He thought for a few seconds. "I guess I'd have to say she didn't have no appetite."

I just nodded, resisting the urge to cast him a look of total exasperation. Instead, I set down my bag. "I'll need some help stabilizing this horse."

I expected Johnny Ray to lend a hand. Instead, he yelled, "Hey, Hector! Get your ass over here."

Muttering to himself, he added, "Damn spics. Lazy as all get-out. Half the time, when he's supposed to bring the horses back in, I find him—"

Just then, a stocky young man with straight black hair who I assumed was Hector popped his head out of the tack room. As a newcomer, I decided to give him the benefit of the doubt—especially since I didn't consider Johnny Ray the most reliable character witness.

Smiling, I said, "Hello, Hector. I'm Dr. Popper. I could use some help subduing Molly while I examine her. Do you have a twitch we could use?"

He nodded and promptly retrieved one from the tack room. Fully cooperative, as far as I could tell. A twitch is basically a wooden stick with a loop of string at one end. Wrapping the loop around the horse's top lip has a tranquilizing effect, making it a really valuable way of maintaining control of the animal when you're doing something she might not be crazy about.

Once the young groom had applied the twitch, I went to work. I started by taking Molly's temperature with a rectal thermometer. It was slightly high, 101.5 degrees. When I listened to her heart, her pulse was 48, also somewhat elevated.

"Okay, Molly," I said to the mare in a gentle voice as I pulled on a plastic rectal sleeve. "I'm going to examine you now to see if we can figure out what's going on."

She just looked at me with woeful eyes.

I smeared on some lubrication jelly, pulled Molly's tail out of the way, and inserted my gloved hand. Sure enough, I felt a large mass of hard fecal matter.

"You're right, Johnny Ray," I reported. "That was a good call. Molly's got a significant impaction."

He grunted, which I supposed was his way of begrudgingly acknowledging that maybe I knew what I was doing, after all.

"I'm going to tube it with mineral oil and warm water," I told him. "First, I'll give her a little painkiller, just to keep her from experiencing any more discomfort." I injected the mare in the neck, then patted her and spoke to her soothingly while I waited for it to take effect.

She seemed to be fairly relaxed. Even so, I wasn't surprised that she jerked when I started to pass the stomach tube through her nose. Fortunately, Hector had anticipated her reaction and he tightened the twitch.

"It's okay, Molly," I reassured her. "Nobody's going to hurt you. Just take it easy, girl."

When I'd finished the procedure and removed the tube, Hector loosened the twitch and released her. The mare shuddered, shook her head, and let out a whinny—probably because she was relieved it was over. I turned to Johnny Ray.

"She's doing fine," I told him. "You'll get a setback of one or two days while we wait for this impaction to break up. Keep her muzzled for the next twelve hours, then limit her feed but give her free-choice water. She can go back to a small amount of wet hay after the impaction has passed. Call me if there's a problem. In fact, call me in the morning anyway, just to let me know how everything is going."

"Sure, Doc," Johnny Ray mumbled. "How about exercise?"

"It's okay to exercise her. And she should be up to playing again in about five days."

"You might mention that to Mr. Mac when you go up to the house to settle." He spoke without looking me in the eye. "He doesn't like bad news, and he won't be happy about Molly being out of commission."

I had a feeling that Andrew MacKinnon was depressed about a lot more than a polo pony or two being out of commission for a few days. But I wasn't looking forward to giving him something else to worry about.

As I headed toward the house, I happened to glance to the right. I noticed someone at the edge of the flat, grassy field that stretched far into the distance, sprawling across several acres dotted with colorful wildflowers and edged with a simple wooden post-and-rail fence. It was Callie, I realized, sitting with her back against a tall oak tree.

I was actually pleased to have a distraction that would delay going inside the house. As I drew near, I saw she was leaning over a large sketch pad, her dark blond tousled hair falling over her face and hiding it from view. I didn't want to startle her, so as I approached, I called, "Callie?"

She jerked her head up—and immediately looked guilty. As she peered up at me, she covered the white page of the pad with both arms.

"Oh, you, again. Dr. Popper, right?"

"You remembered," I said cheerfully. Gesturing toward the drawing pad she was working so hard to conceal, I commented, "That looks like a relaxing way to spend a Saturday morning."

"I'm not supposed to be—what did my mother call it? Oh, that's right, 'Sitting around on your butt all day, scribbling those pictures of yours.' I'm *supposed* to be getting some exercise."

"Can I see what you're working on?"

She hesitated, then said, "I'm just playing around. I mean, it's not finished or anything."

"I'm still curious. I'm not much of an artist myself, so I'm in awe of anybody who can draw."

"Whatever." She moved her arms away, but I noticed that her cheeks became flushed.

Glancing down, I saw that she was making a charcoal drawing, putting the finishing touches on a lovely rendering of the meadow that stretched out in front of her. She'd captured it all: the rolling fields covered with soft grass, the clusters of wildflowers, the backdrop of lush red maples.

"Why, Callie, that's beautiful!" I exclaimed.

"You sound surprised that I'm a decent artist," she replied curtly. "You know, no matter what the rest of my family thinks, I'm not a total loser. If you ask me, I'm the only one in my family who's got any talent at all. Except for my dad, of course. He's great at business. But my sister and my mother are good at being thin, and that's about it. Aside from that, they're a bunch of self-centered—"

"Callie, this is a difficult time for everybody," I reminded her gently, completely taken aback by her outburst. "With Eduardo's sudden death—"

"Hmph," she snorted, picking up her charcoal and

focusing on her drawing again. "Like anybody really cares about that egomaniac."

Her reaction startled me. "You sound as if you didn't like Eduardo very much."

"I hated him," she replied matter-of-factly.

"Really? Why?"

"Because he was just like the rest of them. Self-centered, totally clueless.... He was convinced the entire world revolved around him."

"It sounds as if a lot of people treated him like a celebrity," I observed, "and not without good reason." In part, I was thinking out loud. But I was also watching her, trying to understand her strange reaction. "From what I understand, Eduardo Garcia was one of the best polo players in the world. And while I never actually met him, I don't think I've heard anyone say a bad word about him. Instead, everyone's been talking about how charming he was. From the photographs I've seen, he was also incredibly good-looking."

She shrugged. "Everybody sure acts like he was this...this *star*, but I never thought so. He was simply one of those people who was so full of himself that everybody else assumed he deserved it. As far as I'm concerned, Eduardo just went around tricking people into thinking he was great even though there really wasn't much to him at all."

"I see." I decided not to pry anymore. "Are you taking drawing lessons?" I asked, changing the subject.

Callie shook her head. "I'd like to, but I haven't been able to find anybody I want to study with. At least, not around here."

"You might look into the Art Students League in Manhattan. I understand they have evening classes with some really great artists. You'd probably enjoy going into the city once or twice a week to study. You'd meet a lot of other people with the same interests as you, too."

"I've think I've heard of it," she said. "Maybe I'll check it out." Somewhat begrudgingly, she added, "Thanks for the tip."

Even though she was doing an excellent job of containing her enthusiasm, I got the feeling I'd made at least a ding in the barricade she'd built around herself. She reminded me of a dog or cat who'd been abused and as a result was slow to trust—kind of like Lou. "Who's your favorite painter?" I asked.

"Van Gogh. No contest. I love the way he swirls color. He was someone who was really troubled, you know? But somehow he managed to take all that inner turmoil and put it into his work, whether he was painting something beautiful like flowers or a landscape in the South of France or something as ordinary as a chair."

"Van Gogh is definitely at the top of my list," I agreed. "I also love Matisse."

"Me, too! He used such amazing colors!"

"Do you like his later work?" Calling upon what I'd learned in my Modern Art course in college, I added, "You know, he became arthritic later in life and couldn't paint anymore. That's when he started making those wonderful paper cuts. It was the only way he could express himself."

"I didn't know that," she said.

Something I hadn't known was also coming to light: Callie could be quite likable. Once she let down her guard, she was just a sweet fourteen-year-old girl who was extremely talented and who sincerely loved art—attributes that probably got lost among the oversized egos of the rest of her family.

"You know, I'd love to go to one of the museums in the city with you some time," I told her. "The Guggenheim or the Metropolitan...maybe even the Museum of

Modern Art. It would be really fun to look at paintings with you."

The wall instantly went back up. "You're just saying that," she said coldly. "You know as well as I do that it'll never happen." I was surprised at how quickly the other Callie had returned, the surly, childish one with a chip the size of the Louvre on her shoulder.

"My invitation stands," I insisted, handing her one of my business cards. "Call me when you've picked a date." Glancing toward the house, I told her, "Well, guess I'd better get going. I'll let you get back to your drawing."

"Whatever." With a shrug, she jammed my card in her pocket, grabbed her charcoal, and bent her head down over her drawing pad once again.

As I walked away, I felt unsettled by how quickly she changed. The girl had certainly mastered the art of defensiveness.

One thing was sure: Callie hadn't liked Eduardo Garcia very much. But as I left her behind, the question that continued to nag at me was Why not?

"Is Mr. MacKinnon home?" I asked Luisa when the MacKinnons' older housekeeper answered the door.

"Meester Mac is not here. But Meesus MacKinnon—"

"Is that you, Dr. Popper?" Jillian MacKinnon asked as she emerged from the front parlor. For a change, she didn't have a glass in her hand.

In fact, she looked much more relaxed than the last time I'd seen her. She also looked even more sophisticated. Her smooth black hair was pulled into a tight chignon, and she was dressed in crisp white capris and a pale pink linen blouse, an outfit that flattered her willowy frame. "He had an emergency meeting in the city—some *crisis* that had to be solved immediately, he claimed. But he told me to look out for you. His exact words were that I should 'be sure to take care of you.' To him, that means giving someone money." She stretched her mouth into a cynical smile, instantly obliterating all traces of prettiness.

"But please, come in and sit down. You must be dying from this heat. Would you like a cold drink? Luisa, could you—?"

"I'm fine," I assured her. "In fact, I should probably be on my way."

"We don't get much company," Jillian went on, ignoring my last comment and sweeping into the parlor. "Aside from the horse crowd, of course. But they don't really count. At least not in my book."

I followed, hoping we were moving toward the location in which she kept her checkbook. Chatting with Jillian MacKinnon wasn't exactly my idea of a good time, and I was anxious to get going.

As soon as we entered the parlor, however, Jillian sank onto a couch. "Please, sit down."

"Just for a moment." Dutifully I perched on a gold brocade chair that looked like it had once belonged to an emperor. An emperor who liked expensive fabrics and hard cushions. I glanced around self-consciously, hoping I hadn't tracked anything from the stable into this elegantly appointed space.

"Are you sure you don't want anything?"

"No, really. It's getting late, and—"

"You're right, it's after eleven," Jillian drawled, glancing at her watch. "Good. Time to start drinking." She jumped up, retrieving a bottle of red wine and a twelve-ounce tumbler from a table in the corner. Casting me a sly smile, she added, "Only alcoholics drink before eleven."

I watched her fill the glass almost to the top. She took

a few generous gulps, then closed her eyes as if savoring the effect.

When she opened her eyes, she fixed them on me in a way I found disquieting. "So you're a veterinarian," she said.

"That's right."

"How astonishing. Since you're a woman, I mean."

"Actually, veterinary medicine has become a predominantly female profession," I explained. "Since the 1980's, more than half the students in vet schools have been women."

"I meant it's astonishing that you have a job. I'm impressed that early on, you figured out it would be a good idea to have a life." She sat down and settled back in the cushions of the couch and helped herself to a few more healthy swallows of wine. From what I could see, it was already taking effect. Her shoulders were slumping downward, the corners of her mouth were headed in the same direction, and her eyes, the same startling blue as Callie's, were starting to look cloudy. "It took some of us decades to get to that point—and by then it was too late."

I glanced around at the opulent surroundings: the silk wallpaper, the thick velvet drapes, the end tables and cabinets hand-painted with lush flowers and succulent fruit. Choosing my words carefully, I observed, "If you don't mind me saying so, it doesn't look like you have too bad a life."

Jillian looked pensive for a few moments. "I don't mind you saying that at all. And you're absolutely right; that probably *is* how it looks on the outside. To someone who doesn't know any better, I mean."

"I suppose no one's life is perfect," I said, hoping my vague statement about the human condition would put an end to this "poor little me" discussion.

"I suppose it would help if I had a husband who

showed at least a little interest in me." Jillian's voice had become slurred, and she was staring off into space as if she were talking to herself, rather than to me. Hardly surprising, since she'd downed more than half her tumbler of wine in an impressively short amount of time. "It's funny, I know plenty of women who worry about their husbands falling for another woman. But I don't know a single one whose husband has fallen for another man."

I blinked, trying to comprehend what she was saying.

"Not that Andrew and Eduardo were lovers," she went on. "Nothing like that. At least that would be something I could understand. Instead, since the time Eduardo first came into our lives, it was like Andrew had this strange... *fascination* with the man. An obsession, almost." She paused to gulp down more wine. "Sometimes, I felt like I was invisible. I'm sure Callie felt the same way, even though she'd never admit that her father—or anybody else, for that matter—was capable of hurting her. Peyton, of course... well, that's another story. She and her father have been thick as thieves since the day she was born. Still, you'd think the man would have had *something* left over for the rest of us."

I was about to interject some well-meaning comment about how charismatic Eduardo Garcia seemed to have been when Jillian suddenly sprang from the couch with much more energy than I ever would have thought possible. "Time for a refill!" she cried.

And time for my departure.

"I really must get going," I said forcefully. "If we could just settle up..."

"Of course. You don't want to hear my life story. You want to get paid." Jillian grabbed the wine bottle and refilled her glass almost to the brim. She paused to take another few sips before staggering over to the ornately painted desk in the corner. Pulling a checkbook out of a drawer, she muttered, "How mush?"

Check in hand, I hightailed it out of there, thinking, *If this is Jillian MacKinnon at eleven-fifteen, what's Jillian MacKinnon like by the time cocktail hour rolls around?* The image I conjured up was chilling.

But even more chilling was my discovery that Jillian MacKinnon had actually been jealous of Eduardo Garcia. And given the fact that Eduardo had been murdered, maybe the possibility that jealousy had been his killer's motive wasn't that far-fetched.

A little voice inside my head warned that I was getting carried away. *Jillian is probably just a disgruntled polo widow,* I mused as I made a beeline for my van, *no worse off than a golf widow or a fishing widow.* Lots of women find it frustrating to put up with their husbands' passion for one sport or another. That doesn't mean they're driven to murder.

Then again, I thought, the more I saw of the MacKinnon household, the less I found surprising.

I was about to climb into my van when I heard someone calling, "Excuse me! If you have a moment—"

I turned, surprised. An older man dressed in a white suit and a straw hat was hurrying toward me, his face flushed from the effort.

"Dr. Popper, isn't it?" he said, a little out of breath as he drew near.

"That's right." I smiled as I struggled to place him. As soon as I did, I felt my smile droop. "Winston, right? I'm afraid I never got your last name." *That's the downside of eavesdropping on other people's arguments,* I thought. *You end up getting only some of the facts.*

"Winston Farnsworth. But Winston is fine."

"Then please call me Jessica. Or Jessie." I eyed him

warily, still not sure what I thought of the dignified English gentleman. He was wearing a bow tie again—yellow, this time, his attempt at looking more casual, I supposed. Still, the touch of whimsy the bright shade brought to his look was canceled out by the matching handkerchief carefully folded in the breast pocket of his white jacket.

But while he looked like an upstanding citizen, the fact that I'd caught him arguing with Andrew Mac-Kinnon on the day of Eduardo's funeral had left me unable to choose a side—if there was even a side to choose. I decided to wait until I had more information before forming an opinion of Winston Farnsworth.

"Dr. Popper—Jessica—I wondered if I might trouble you...and please, if this is an inappropriate request, don't hesitate to tell me."

I leaned forward, my curiosity piqued.

"Would it be possible for you to stop over at my house to take a look at my dachshund, Frederick?"

I glanced at my watch. According to my calculations, Nick would probably be at the park with the dogs at least until lunchtime. At least, the *old* Nick, the pre–law school version. Who knew how much time he penciled in for leisure these days? Still, today *was* Saturday, after all, and I was itching for a day off—or at least part of a day—with or without Nick.

"Perhaps I'm being overly cautious," Winston continued, "but for the last couple of days, Frederick's been scratching one of his ears incessantly. It's a little red inside, and I'm seeing some kind of discharge. I'm worried that it's gotten infected."

From Winston's description, it certainly sounded like an ear infection. Bacterial, or perhaps yeast. Nothing serious, but undoubtedly annoying, if not actually painful, for the poor little guy. Even though the strange concept of a day off sounded pretty enticing, the idea that Winston's dog might be uncomfortable or even worse made it impossible for me to say no.

"Of course," I told him. "I'd be happy to come by."

"Excellent!" Winston beamed. "Perhaps you'll even allow me to make you a cup of tea. I'm afraid I don't get many visitors these days. Being a bachelor is rather a lonely life."

"Tea sounds perfect," I told him. After my friendly little chat with Jillian MacKinnon, a little caffeine was definitely in order.

"Then why don't you follow me? My house is just a mile or two up the road, but locating my driveway has been known to give some people pause."

I climbed into my van, curious to see which of the vehicles parked along the MacKinnons' driveway would turn out to be Winston's. When the gleaming cream-colored Rolls-Royce Corniche pulled out in front of me, I thought, *Of course.*

A little over two miles north on Turkey Hollow Road, the Rolls's right-turn signal blinked. I followed the car onto a long driveway and through a wrought-iron gate decorated with an elaborate letter "F."

"Not too shabby," I muttered.

The driveway, lined with magnificent oak trees, cut straight through an immense, perfectly manicured front lawn the size of a small airport. It led to a huge brick house with elegant white columns. White shutters framed three stories of windows, and a neatly trimmed row of bushes, all exactly the same height, lined the front. At first glance, the estate was as dignified as its owner.

As we walked toward the house, I expected a house-keeper to greet us. Instead, Winston pulled a ring of keys from his pants pocket and unlocked the front door himself.

"I have live-in help during the week," he volunteered,

as if he'd anticipated my surprise. "But my housekeeper goes home to her family on weekends. Actually, I prefer having the house to myself. I've never been completely comfortable having people wait on me."

He must have noticed that my eyebrows shot up.

"My dear girl, I haven't always been this wealthy," he said, his hazel eyes sparkling with amusement. "I happen to be one of those chaps who pulled myself up by his own bootstraps. A rags-to-riches tale, as they say. I grew up in London's East End, raised by a loving mother who worked her fingers to the bone as a maid in a house very much like this one."

"But the way you speak sounds so..." I searched for the right word. "...refined."

Winston chuckled. "These are skills that can be easily acquired," he replied. "All it takes is determination."

As I followed him through the door, I concentrated on the house. Even though my knowledge of decorating consists solely of what I've learned from watching the Home and Garden Channel, I easily identified Winston's décor as Early Horse. Nearly every element of the room reflected his passion for anything and everything equine.

The library was no exception. Like Andrew Mac-Kinnon's study, the fawn-colored walls of the cozy room Winston led me to were covered with photographs, drawings, and paintings of horses. Most of them carried humans who were intensely absorbed in either jumping, fox hunting, racing, or, most frequently, polo.

But that was just the beginning. The hooked rug in front of the fireplace had a horse design, and a big overstuffed chair was upholstered in dark blue fabric covered with gold horses. No fewer than three different lamps had horse-themed bases and shades. I spotted a horse ashtray, horse candlestick holders, and horse bookends, propping up books about—you guessed it— horses.

"Horses have always played a large role in my life," Winston said, sounding almost apologetic. "But I suppose you already figured that out."

"I can see it's your passion," I observed diplomatically, sitting on a love seat that was covered in dark blue velvet, one of the few items in the room without any horses on it.

"In fact, my first job, when I was a boy of nine, was mucking out stalls at an equestrian club just outside of London. Throughout my life, I've been fortunate enough to enjoy all sorts of pastimes," he went on. "Stock-car racing, jumping from airplanes, even hang-gliding. Sailing, too. Many years ago, I competed for the America's Cup. But polo has always given me a thrill that nothing else comes close to.

"They say it's the most dangerous sport—that it's basically ice hockey on horseback." Winston lowered himself into the overstuffed armchair. "But it's more than that. There's a sense of power that comes from playing the game that I've never experienced anywhere else. Then there's the unity you feel with the horse. It's as if the two of you are connected, somehow. As if you share the same soul. You become one tremendous beast with four mighty legs and two strong arms, thundering up and down the field with one singular purpose. It's hardly surprising polo is considered the game of kings. In fact, at an ancient polo ground in northern Pakistan, tucked away in the mountains near Gilget, there's a famous stone with a poem in both English and Arabic. It's attributed to a man named J.K. Stephen, and it reads, 'Let other people play at other things: The King of games is still the game of Kings.' In fact, polo actually originated as a game for royalty. Do you know much about its history?"

"I'm afraid not," I admitted.

"The game is believed to date back some twenty-five

hundred years, when it was played in Persia—present-day Iran. A Persian poet and historian who called himself Firdausi first wrote about it at the beginning of the last millennium. Even so, the game could well date back even further, at least to the sixth or seventh centuries B.C.

"But even then, it was the 'game of kings,'" Winston continued. "Queens, too, and emperors. The game spread to China, then Japan, where both Samurai and common people enjoyed the sport. In those days, the balls were made of all kinds of materials. Leather, ivory, even the roots of certain plants and trees. Willow was used quite commonly. In fact, the word 'polo' comes from 'pulu,' which is the Tibetan name for the willow root.

"The British heard about the game—and witnessed it, as well—long before they began playing it in India in the 1850's. They founded their first polo club in India, in a town called Silchar. That was in 1859. It's gone now, but the Calcutta Polo Club, which was founded three years later, is still around. It's considered the world's oldest.

"Before long, just about every regiment in the British cavalry had its own team. Many of the maharajahs—the princes who ruled various states throughout India—formed teams, as well. They created the India Polo Association in 1891, the organization that was the first to standardize the rules of the game. The game came to England around then, getting its first permanent home in the 1890's when the seventh Earl of Bathurst founded a polo club near Cirencester, on his own estate. It also became popular in Argentina around then—but heavens, I'm boring you."

"Not at all," I told him sincerely. "It's fascinating."

"I appreciate how polite you are, Jessica, patiently listening to an old man going on and on. But I haven't forgotten that I promised you a cup of tea. If you'll just excuse me."

I took advantage of his absence to examine his books. They ranged from dusty first editions that looked as if they might be valuable to brand-new volumes with slick covers. They covered every aspect of horses, from breeding them to training them. The shelves were even stocked with novels in which horses played a prominent role.

I was perusing a dog-eared copy of *Black Beauty* I'd pulled off the shelf when I heard a voice behind me say, "Quite a collection, isn't it? I'm afraid I'm a bit of a fanatic when it comes to both books and horses. A combination of the two is simply irresistible."

Winston set down a tray with two porcelain cups and a china teapot on a low table. "I'm sorry, but I don't have anything to go with the tea. Cookies or little sandwiches, I mean." Smiling apologetically, he added, "I'm afraid a doddering old bachelor like me isn't very good when it comes to entertaining guests."

"This will be fine," I assured him, returning to the settee.

"By the way, you're welcome to borrow any of the books that pique your interest. I think of books as my friends, and I truly enjoy introducing them to other friends. Especially *new* friends."

"Thanks, at the moment I'm up to my ears in veterinary journals," I told him. "But I would like to hear more about polo. When did it come to the United States?"

"We have an American publisher named James Gordon Bennett to thank for that. I understand he was quite an adventurer. He happened to catch a polo match while traveling in London in 1876. He was so intrigued by the game that he brought polo balls and mallets back to New York with him. Soon afterward, he held an indoor exhibition match in New York City, and a short time later, the first public match took place in Prospect Park in Brooklyn. Ten thousand spectators turned out for the event.

"Within a decade, polo clubs had sprung up all over the east. But Long Island became the real center, hosting international matches that drew more than thirty thousand spectators at a time. Even Teddy Roosevelt played. He belonged to a club in Oyster Bay that unfortunately no longer exists.

"Today, polo is played all over Europe, Hong Kong, Malaysia, Russia, in just about every country you can think of. And the international center is in Wellington, Florida. But during the summer months, Long Island's polo tradition is still alive and well, I'm pleased to report."

Winston paused to sip his tea. "Not bad. Especially for someone who's about as comfortable in a kitchen as a bull in the proverbial china shop." He raised his cup to his lips again, then stopped midway. "You know, Jessica, I'm glad we're having this chance to get to know each other a little. I'm afraid you caught me at rather a bad time the other day."

"It was a bad time for everyone," I replied. "I'm sure everybody who knew Eduardo was shocked by his death."

"You mean shocked by the fact that he was murdered." He shook his head in disbelief. "I can't remember anything in my life that's been more tragic. It's so senseless! Such a promising young man. Eduardo was so full of potential!"

His characterization of Eduardo as "full of potential" surprised me. I was tempted to ask him what he meant. It seemed to me that if anyone had ever fulfilled his potential, it was the charismatic polo player. He was one of the few ten-goal players in the world; he was handsome and charming; he was worshipped by just about everyone who knew him... Was it possible that Winston expected even more of him?

Leave it alone, I told myself. *You're reading too much into Winston's comments.* "Full of potential" is a phrase people use all the time, especially when they're talking about young people.

Besides, I could see how distressed this topic of conversation was making him.

"Perhaps I could take a look at Frederick now," I suggested, figuring this was a good time to dispense with the socializing and get down to business.

"Of course. I've already taken up too much of your time. As I mentioned, bachelors like me have a tendency to get lonely, and as a result we may be guilty of talking too much. He's penned out back. I'll just bring him in...."

As Frederick bounded inside, I saw that he was an energetic wire-haired dachshund with fawn and tan fur. He headed right over to me and jumped up to say hello, wagging his tail so hard I was afraid he'd fall over. Like most dachshunds, Frederick was an affectionate, sweet-tempered house pet. It was difficult to believe they were originally bred to hunt badgers, slipping into their narrow burrows and dragging them out. In fact, the name, *Dachs Hund,* was German for "badger dog."

"Let's bring him into my van," I told Winston. "I'll check him out there."

"Lead the way," he said gallantly, reaching down to scoop up Frederick.

Not surprisingly, the dachshund tensed up when he found himself in an unfamiliar environment. "I'm not going to hurt you, Frederick," I assured him as I held him in my arms and scratched him behind the ears to help him relax. Glancing over at Winston, I saw that he looked a bit nervous, too.

"Okay, Frederick, we'll start with something easy," I said, placing him on the scale. I was pleased with the results: just under ten pounds.

"It's good that he's lean," I observed as I moved him to the examining table. "Dachshunds have a tendency to become overweight, which can result in intervertebral disc disease."

Winston patted his own lean torso self-consciously. "It's something Frederick and I work on together. We take long walks to stay in shape."

"Sounds like a great idea." I stroked the nervous dachshund's back, then ran my hands over his spine more carefully, checking his vertebrae.

"So his activity level is good," I observed. "Have you noticed any change in how much he's been eating or drinking? Any coughing or sneezing? Vomiting or diarrhea?"

"None of the above, thank goodness," Winston replied. "As far as I know, the only trouble he's been having is that ear I mentioned. It's the left one."

I looked into Frederick's ear with an otoscope. Sure enough, it was raw, with a thick brown discharge.

"Looks like Frederick's got an inflamed external ear canal," I said. "It could be bacterial or yeast or a combination. From the smell, I'd say there's definitely yeast present. It's not uncommon in dogs with long ears. They cover the ear canal, keeping air out." I checked his other ear, which looked fine. "Chronic yeast infections can also be caused by allergies. But in that case, both ears would be affected."

"Goodness, I hope it's not serious," Winston exclaimed.

"No, but it's no wonder Frederick's been acting bothered. I'm going to clean out his ear, but I don't want to go in too deep. I'll give you a cream that's a steroid, an antibacterial, and an antifungal. You'll need to squirt it into his ear twice a day. I'll also give you some fifty-milligram hydroxyzine pamoate capsules. It's an antihistamine that will help stop the itching. Give him one capsule twice a day. And I'll give him a shot of cortisone, too, which will also reduce the itching."

I finished up by checking his eyes and his teeth, then announced, "All done, Frederick. You were such a good boy!"

He looked up at me gratefully with his dark, almond-shaped eyes and wagged his tail.

"We're both so thankful, Dr. Popper," Winston said. "I can see that old Frederick already looks like he's on the mend. I must say, I'm extremely impressed. Is there any chance I could begin using your services regularly?"

"I'll give you my card." I opened my purse—and the tickets to Betty's opening night immediately popped up. Two of them actually flew out, landing on the floor of my van.

"Let me get those for you," Winston insisted gallantly. He swooped down before I could protest. "*Chicago,* eh? Don't tell me you're as big a fan of musical comedy as I am!"

"I'm an occasional fan," I replied. "Actually, someone I know is performing in a local production. The Port Players are putting it on in Port Townsend. My friend Betty has a featured role in one of the big song-and-dance numbers."

"How marvelous! Perhaps you could tell me how I might obtain a ticket."

Before I'd even had a chance to consider what I was about to say, I blurted out, "I have an extra ticket for opening night, if you'd like one."

"Really? Why, that would be lovely." An expression of such genuine gratitude lit up his face that I was glad I'd offered it to him.

Even if I still hadn't made up my mind about him.

Maybe spending a little time with Winston Farnsworth—away from Old Brookbury—will give me more insight into what makes him tick, I told myself, glad I'd found a way of rationalizing my impulsiveness.

At the very least, there would be one more person sitting in the audience on opening night, cheering Betty on.

I climbed into my van, my stomach suddenly grumbling angrily. Lunchtime had passed, and it wanted some attention beyond Winston's cup of Earl Grey. I decided to head into Laurel Valley in search of a sandwich. Besides, I figured a break would give me the chance to digest what I'd spent the morning learning.

As I drove along Turkey Hollow Road, gripping the wheel of my van tightly while I maneuvered the neverending series of turns, I noticed with annoyance that a dark green vehicle was following very closely on my tail. It was one of those SUV's that looks capable of driving up the side of Grand Canyon. Personally, I believe that there should be a special punishment for tailgaters—maybe being tied to a chair and forced to watch infomercials all day. In fact, every time some idiot is following me so closely that I can see the whites of his eyes, I fantasize about plastering on a bumper sticker that reads, "I Brake for Tailgaters."

I tried speeding up. Didn't work. Next, I tried slowing down. He didn't take the hint. Finally, I put on my right-turn signal, stepped on the brake, and turned onto a narrow side road.

"Damn!" I muttered, peering into my rearview mirror. "This nut is *following* me!"

I pulled over to the side of the road, figuring he'd either give up and pass me or stop. He stopped.

When the door on the driver's side opened, I ascertained the identity of the nut in question.

Great, I thought sullenly. I'd already spent my precious Saturday morning dealing with a macho man who suffers from a cowboy complex, a surly teenager who identifies with a tormented genius who cut his own ear off, a fading beauty who thinks Jack Daniels is the Breakfast of Champions, and a kindly older gentleman whose hobbies may include polo and poison.

After all that, I told myself, *fending off a man whose ego is as big as Heatherfield should be no more challenging than a rousing game of Slimytoy.*

Chapter 6

"Take most people, they're crazy about cars. I'd rather have a goddam horse. A horse is at least human, for godsake."

—J. D. Salinger, Catcher in the Rye

I flung open the door of my van, slamming it shut—*loudly*—before marching over to the driver of the SUV that was pretending it was a tank.

"Where did *you* learn to drive?" I demanded. "The bumper cars at Six Flags?"

"Hey, you're not exactly Shirley Muldowney," Forrester Sloan replied loftily.

"*Who?*"

"Famous woman race-car driver? Three-time winner of the National Hot Rod Association World Championship? Subject of the movie *Heart Like a Wheel*?"

"Sorry," I returned acidly. "I guess I'm just not lucky enough to have your vast stores of general knowledge at my fingertips. But at least I'm smart enough to know how dangerous tailgating is."

"Sorry if I scared you."

I cast him the most scathing glare I could manage. "I don't scare that easily."

"Good. Then you're just the woman I'm looking for."

"Somehow, I doubt that. Besides, I'm already spoken for."

He waved his hand in the air, as if that wasn't the point. "I was following you for a reason, you know. I'd like to buy you lunch."

"Thanks, I can buy my own lunch."

"I don't doubt it. But there's something I want to talk to you about." He cocked his head to one side. "Come on, Popper. I know a great little restaurant about a mile from here. They've got the best clam chowder on the North Shore. And it really is on me. I insist."

"Thanks, but—"

"I've got some information I think you'll find pretty interesting. Information about Eduardo Garcia."

I hesitated. That, I realized immediately, was a mistake.

"Good." Satisfaction was written all over his annoying face. "This time, *you* can follow *me*."

I opened my mouth to protest, then snapped it shut. What the heck, I figured. It couldn't hurt to find out more about the polo player who'd been murdered. As obnoxious as Forrester Sloan was, he *was* a reporter, which meant he was in a position to find out more than your average Joe. Besides, I really was hungry, and the best clam chowder on the North Shore was pretty hard to turn down.

I followed him to a ramshackle eatery in Baytown called Barnacle Billie's, a beachside restaurant I'd never been to before. I had to admit it had a certain charm, mainly because it was housed in a dilapidated building covered in gray, weather-worn shingles that made you want to call out "Ahoy!"

In back, a rustic deck stretched out over the water. If you looked down between the cedar slats, you could see the waves of Long Island Sound swirling below. Definitely not for anyone with a tendency toward seasickness.

"This isn't bad," I admitted as we sat down opposite each other in a pair of matching plastic molded chairs. "I guess you have taste after all."

"Actually, I have excellent taste," Forrester countered, waving his napkin in the air flamboyantly and draping it across his lap. "Excellent manners, too."

Fortunately, a waitress appeared before I had a chance to stick a pin in his overinflated ego. After we each ordered clam chowder and shrimp cocktail, I eyed him warily. Maybe the food here was good, but I was pretty sure the company was going to give me indigestion.

"You know, Popper," Forrester said breezily, "I was thinking about you last night while I was in bed."

"Why do I have the feeling I don't really want to hear this."

He ignored my comment. "I was lying there, thinking, 'I have a sense that Jessica Popper is the ideal person to work with.' "

I raised my eyebrows. "Don't tell me. You're secretly Dr. Dolittle, in disguise."

"Nope. But I'm actually Clark Kent."

Wryly, I observed, "Which implies that some of the time, you're Superman."

"Or at least implies that I need a Lois Lane."

I sat back in my seat and folded my arms across my chest. "Okay, Sloan. What are you after?"

His steely gray-blue eyes bored into mine. "I need somebody to help me find out who murdered Eduardo Garcia. And that somebody is you."

I just stared back at him.

"Interesting," he mused. "You don't seem totally astonished."

"Actually, I'm more curious than astonished," I told him. "What on earth makes you think I'd be the least bit interested in helping you?"

The way he smiled made me realize he'd been waiting for that question all along. "I've been asking around about you."

"Really? I'm not particularly well-known."

"Actually, it turns out a lot of people know who you are."

"Like...?" I prompted.

"Like Lieutenant Anthony Falcone, Chief of Norfolk County Homicide."

"Oh," I mumbled. I could feel my cheeks burning, a sure sign they were turning as red as the cocktail sauce that had just arrived at our table with the shrimp. *"Him."*

"Yes, him. Apparently you've made quite an impression on him. Seems there was this little matter that came up back in June—"

"Okay, so I've...dabbled. But why would you think I'd want to get involved in another murder investigation? And why this one?"

"Same reason you've gotten involved in the past." He leaned across the table, so close that our noses were almost touching. "The challenge of the mind games, your sense that justice must be served...Then, of course, there's the fact that you happen to be damned good at it."

I had to admit that he certainly knew the right things to say. Even though I could hear Betty warning me somewhere in the back of my brain, even though I could see Nick's disapproving frown looming in the distance—

and even though I hadn't forgotten the dangerous, even life-threatening situations I'd gotten myself into in the past—I could feel myself being drawn in.

"Okay," I said, settling back in my plastic chair, wanting to keep my distance, "let's just say—and this is purely speculative—that I *did* decide to help you. What would be my role?"

"You're already an insider," he replied as our waitress delivered two bowls to our table. "The people who were closest to Eduardo already know you. They trust you, too. Even Johnny Ray admitted that you're good at what you do."

"Probably at gunpoint," I observed dryly.

"Even more important," Forrester continued, "you have a reason to be around the people who were part of Eduardo's circle, and to keep going back again and again. You're the perfect person to ask questions without anybody suspecting that you're doing anything more than making pleasant chitchat."

I picked up my spoon and began shoveling in clam chowder. I acted like I was half starved, but I was actually trying to come up with some good, solid reasons to tell Forrester Sloan to find himself another undercover agent.

Before I had a chance, he said, "I've already found out some pretty intriguing stuff. It's amazing what you can learn by doing a little research."

"You mean book research?"

"I mean talking to Richard Stokes research."

"The Norfolk County medical examiner," I said. "I'm impressed." Curious, too, but I tried to look indifferent.

"Impressed, but not that interested, right?" Even though he'd barely made a dent in his food, he scrunched up his paper napkin and threw it on the table.

"In that case, I'm sorry I wasted your time. I guess you're just too busy to—"

"Will you stop the theatrics and tell me what Stokes said?" I insisted. So much for my poker face.

"So you *are* interested." Forrester smiled triumphantly.

"Of course I'm interested."

"Good." He folded his hands in front of him. "Then you'll love this. The forensic investigators are becoming increasingly certain that Eduardo Garcia was poisoned. It certainly explains why a guy in his prime of life suddenly died of an arrhythmia. Toxicology is doing tests to determine what was in his system at the time he died. However, I learned something interesting: They only test for the most common poisons."

I didn't let on that my heart was beating wildly. In fact, I was glad the seagulls shrieking in the sky above made it difficult to hear. "And?"

"The key word here is 'common,'" he went on. "Meaning that the tests only screen for the most likely candidates. See, the simple fact is that most people aren't very creative when it comes to murder. If they decide to poison someone, they generally use something obvious. Something that's found around the house, or at least pretty easy to get hold of. And that's usually a substance that the M.E.'s office can easily identify. However, this was not the case with Eduardo Garcia's murder."

"Go on," I prompted, keeping my voice even.

"The toxicologists ran a routine procedure called paper chromatography," Forrester continued. "Basically, you use a special machine to run a sample of the victim's blood through paper. Different chemicals have different 'partition coefficients,' which means they migrate at different rates. Then you compare the migration rates of the substances you found in the blood sample with the migration rates of 'known' chemicals. If nothing matches, you can conclude that none of the usual substances—the most commonly used poisons, in this case—are present."

He paused—for effect, no doubt. "In other words, they're convinced Eduardo Garcia was poisoned, but they don't know with what."

"So his murderer was fairly crafty," I mused, thinking out loud. "At least, crafty enough to poison him with something that would be difficult to detect once he was dead."

"And given Eduardo's activities the night before, it looks like the murderer was also clever enough to pull it off at a function that was attended by hundreds of people," Forrester added, "making it really difficult to reconstruct exactly what happened."

The wheels were turning in my head. "Wait a second. How do the police know the poisoning wasn't accidental?"

"It's not impossible. But no one else who attended the same party experienced any symptoms, so they've ruled out tainted food. And the cops did a thorough search of his house, a little place in Morgan's Cove about a ten-minute drive from the Meadowlark Polo Club. They didn't find anything to indicate that he'd inadvertently poisoned himself. No bottles of prescription drugs, no strange chemicals, nothing questionable in the refrigerator."

I nodded. *So the cops covered that base,* I thought.

But something else nagged at me, a question I wanted to ask even though it hadn't quite formed in my mind.

Before I had a chance to figure out what it was, Forrester added, "I've learned a few other interesting tidbits, too."

He looked at me expectantly.

"Okay, out with it," I finally said. "You know I'm dying to hear whatever you've got."

I hated the look of satisfaction that crossed his face. But I figured that was the price I had to pay.

"I've also been doing some research on polo," Forrester announced. "And I've dug up some pretty incredible stuff."

"I know a little about the game's history," I volunteered. "A friend of Andrew MacKinnon's, Winston Farnsworth, gave me a quick lesson on 'the game of kings.'"

"Hah!" Forrester returned. "How about 'the game of barbarians'? Did you know one of the first fans of the sport was Genghis Khan? His Mongolian troops played polo using the heads of their enemies—which they'd personally chopped off. I think they were more interested in sending a message than having fun out on the field. And from what I've been learning, the equipment may have changed, but the spirit can be just as brutal."

"Sounds a little harsh," I observed. "I thought polo was nothing more than a few guys on horseback hitting a ball."

"It is. Except that these particular guys usually happen to be some very rich and very powerful individuals. You should see how they live, Popper," Forrester said. "Some of them have estates that stretch on forever, with five polo fields on each—and the regulation size is one hundred fifty by three hundred yards, even bigger than a football field. They can own as many as one hundred fifty polo ponies. Horses start at twelve or thirteen thousand dollars, but the good ones go for thirty to fifty thousand.

"The mansions on their estates look like castles. But

in addition, there's always a swimming pool, tennis courts, the whole works. Then there are the stables and the grooms' quarters. Most of the time, they're just as luxurious as the main house. White stucco walls, red terra-cotta roofs, palm trees and flowers planted everywhere... You or I would probably be perfectly happy living in one of the stalls—and I'm not exaggerating."

"How many people actually live on this scale?" I asked.

"Only about thirty. They're mostly American, but they come from all over the world. A few are well-known movie actors, but the majority are industrialists. One owns the Down Under restaurant chain. Another is a member of the family that owns the biggest soft-drink company in the world. Then there are two brothers who are part of a famous beer family.

"Then you've got the internationals. One Frenchman is from a famous family of art collectors. Another guy, a South African, has his own polo fields and horses, but never competes. He just plays for fun on his own estate—like playing croquet in your backyard. Know where his money comes from?"

"I can't begin to guess."

"He owns an army, Popper. His own private army, complete with mercenary soldiers, fighter jets, tanks, the whole kit and caboodle. If you're the president—or dictator—of a country and you need an army, his is for hire."

I didn't even try to hide my astonishment. "I had no idea that kind of thing even existed!"

"Yeah, no kidding. Anyway, a lot of the patrons are from Argentina. Their families have been playing polo for generations. One patron from South America owns a bank, an oil company, a car manufacturer, and a couple of other little side businesses. He has an estate in Wellington, Florida, a ski chalet in Utah, a mansion in the city of Buenos Aires, and a thirty-million-dollar polo complex somewhere else in Argentina. It's right on the ocean, but it also has a three-and-a-half-acre swimming pool. Three and a half acres, Popper. He's also got a couple of yachts with their own helicopters and helicopter pads and two full-size jets that go for about thirsche million apiece. He happens to like cars, and he's got a red Enzo—a Ferrari—that cost one and a half million dollars. They're special-edition supercars, and the company only built three hundred ninety-nine of them. Compared to that, the hundred-thousand-dollar Porsche he owns looks like a weekend station wagon."

"In other words," I interjected, "when we're talking about polo, we're talking about major money."

"You got it. And the stuff I'm telling you about is just the tip of the iceberg," Forrester went on. "Even these guys who have multimillion-dollar estates in Wellington mostly just play on the weekends. They fly down to Florida in their private jets on Sunday morning, play a couple of hours of polo, have a drink or two, and fly back home.

"Of course, not everybody is involved with polo on the same scale. There are people who have a couple of polo ponies and play occasionally. For them, it's more like a hobby. You'd recognize a lot of the names. Some rock stars, a whole bunch of actors, a television producer who used to have his own talk show, a Broadway producer who was behind one of the biggest musicals of the late 1960's.

"But then there's a whole subculture of people whose entire lives revolve around polo. The polo players, of course. They're on salary, working for the patrons. It's not uncommon for them to get paid a million dollars a year. Some of the better players get paid five thousand dollars a game—which comes to about thirty thousand a month. But some of them only get five hundred bucks for each game. And of course they all have their own horses and grooms."

"Sounds expensive," I commented.

"Sure. A lot of them end up having to do something else on the side, anything from training horses to modeling. Whatever they can do to make a buck. Not all of them get paid on the scale that MacKinnon paid Eduardo. I heard his salary was a million a year."

"I heard that, too—from MacKinnon himself." I added, "Speaking of Andrew MacKinnon, what's his story?"

"Nothing suspicious there—at least, not that I've been able to uncover so far," Forrester replied. "He grew up wealthy, right here on Long Island. He's the son of a successful entrepreneur who started a company that manufactures machine parts. Fasteners, fittings, those boring little pieces of metal that make the world go round—or at least the world's machines. Andrew joined the company at a young age, learned the business, and took over when Daddy retired. All he had to do was keep the family business running smoothly. It's a feat he's managed nicely, from what I can tell."

"What about his relationship with Eduardo?" I asked. "Was he really as enamored of him as he claims?"

Forrester shook his head. "That sounds like a subject you know more about than I do."

"He seems sincere," I mused. "He did make kind of a strange comment, though. Yesterday, right after the funeral, he said that losing Eduardo would have been a great loss to the game. Then he corrected himself and said that losing Eduardo *is* a great loss to the game. It just struck me as odd."

Forrester shrugged. "Probably just the grief talking. People get confused."

"Could be." I frowned. "But there was something else. I heard MacKinnon arguing about Eduardo with that man I mentioned—Winston Farnsworth. Do you know anything about him?"

"No. But I'll see what I can find out." He jotted down the name on his pad of paper. "What kind of argument?"

"I only caught the tail end. But I heard Farnsworth say something like, 'We're talking about a tremendous amount of money!'"

"Money, murder..." Forrester muttered. "The two often go hand in hand."

"As seems to be the case in Eduardo Garcia's murder," I added. I sighed, suddenly overwhelmed by what we were trying to wrap our heads around.

"Could be. Especially since we're dealing with a bunch of people who aren't exactly the nicest guys around."

"Lifestyles of the Rich and Felonious," I muttered.

"Some people might say 'rich' and 'felonious' are synonymous," Forrester commented. But he said the words so softly I wasn't sure I was supposed to have heard him.

"If you're from such a privileged background," I couldn't resist asking, "how come you weren't already an expert on polo?"

"Actually, my sister's the equestrian in the family. And she was into dressage." He shook his head, as if he was still having trouble taking it all in. "This polo thing is really over the top."

"I agree. Which doesn't make investigating Eduardo Garcia's murder any easier. Where do you suggest we start?"

He grinned. "Welcome aboard, Popper. Glad you

decided to join the team. It just so happens there's a polo game at the Meadowlark Polo Club tomorrow at three. I think you and I should both be there."

"Sounds like fun." I made a point of adding, "I'll bring a date."

Forrester looked startled. "If you must. But don't forget that we're there to work."

"You're making it sound like so much fun."

"Don't worry, Popper. It'll be fun."

Even though Forrester had turned out to be a much more engaging companion than I'd expected, I suddenly found myself glancing around the restaurant's outdoor dining area. It wasn't that I noticed anything extraordinary. In fact, the thing that struck me happened to be extremely *ordinary*.

Looking around, I spotted a young couple sitting at one table, sharing a plate of fried calamari. At the table beside them sat two female friends, laughing together over a pitcher of margaritas. Behind them was an older couple, barely speaking but looking surprisingly comfortable in their shared silence. In the back corner, three men gathered at a round table, talking loudly. The question that had been nagging at me had finally come into focus.

"Forrester," I said, "what about *before* the party?"

He frowned. "I'm not following."

"Falcone seems pretty convinced that Eduardo was poisoned at the party. And that certainly strikes me as a strong possibility. After all, the occasion provided the perfect opportunity. Crowds of people, loud music, a lot of different things going on at the same time... Given all the noise and activity, slipping something into his food or a drink probably wouldn't have been that difficult."

I leaned forward. "But what if he wasn't murdered at the party? What if he actually ingested the substance that killed him *before* the party? Over lunch or dinner...or even coffee with a friend?"

"It's possible." Narrowing his eyes, Forrester demanded, "Okay, Popper. Where are you going with this?"

With a shrug, I explained, "I'm simply thinking that it wouldn't be a bad idea to reconstruct exactly what Eduardo did—where he went, who he saw—the entire day before he died."

"I'm sure the police are doing that."

"Maybe." Then again, I thought, Lieutenant Anthony Falcone has been known to miss seeing the obvious. Maybe that came from having such a swelled head.

"Look, Popper," Forrester continued, "I encourage you to follow your gut. If you think you've got some lead that the cops are likely to miss—"

"Could you please stop calling me Popper?" I interrupted, not even trying to keep the irritation out of my voice.

"I *like* calling you Popper. You *seem* like a Popper."

"And exactly what does a Popper seem like?" I couldn't believe we were having this conversation.

"Tough. Tenacious. Smart as a whip."

"Sounds like you're describing an Airedale."

He laughed. "They are pretty tough, aren't they? Speaking of which," he went on, "I'm hoping that one of these days, you'll tell me about the other murder investigations you've been involved in."

"Maybe," I said loftily.

He leaned forward and gently brushed a strand of hair away from my face. "How about over dinner? I could swing by and pick you up in a few hours. I know this terrifically romantic little place that most people have never even heard of—"

I peered at him through narrowed eyes. "Are you flirting with me?"

He looked surprised. "Isn't it obvious?"

"Look, Sloan, if you and I are going to work on this murder thing together, we have to have an understanding. No flirting."

"Sure, Popper. Whatever you say. But I've got to warn you, I can be pretty charming."

"I've noticed," I said dryly.

"Good," he returned, a smile playing at his lips. "Then I'm doing better than I thought."

On my way home, I cruised through Port Townsend, passing by Theater One. Not only was the elegant freestanding building a hundred-year-old piece of the village's history; it was also the home of the Port Players. As luck would have it, a truck parked right in front was pulling out. I couldn't resist taking advantage of the unexpected appearance of a parking space to poke my head in to watch a few minutes of Betty's rehearsal.

The lobby was empty—not surprising for the middle of the day. I quietly pushed open the heavy door just beyond, finding myself inside an eerily dark theater. But the stage was aglow. I sank into one of the dark red velvet seats, taking care not to let the hinge squeak too loudly.

Six women stood onstage, forming a loose half-circle around a tall, gangly man with a goatee who was clutching a clipboard. The director, I surmised. The women were all of different ages, and all were dressed differently. One wore a leotard and brightly colored leg warmers, one wore sweatpants and a pale pink T-shirt, one wore bicycle shorts and a halter top.

Betty looked the most fetching, dressed in a black

tank top and a red satin tap skirt I'd seen before. Gold hoop earrings the size of coasters glittered in the glaring spotlight.

"You're looking good, ladies," the director exclaimed, his voice resonating through the empty auditorium. "This number, 'Cell Block Tango,' is going to be one of the highlights of the production. Layla, let's get those kicks a little higher. Jasmine, watch those arms. We're putting on a musical here, not sending semaphore signals. Betty, you're dancing like a dream. Don't hold back. The audience is going to love you, so show them what you've got.

"Now take five," he continued. "Then we'll take it from the top."

As the dancers eased offstage alone or in pairs, I stood up and waved my arms. Betty spotted me and waved back.

"How are those pre–opening night jitters?" I teased as we met halfway up the aisle.

"Under control," she replied. Sighing, she added, "At least that's what I keep telling myself."

"If the director's happy, seems to me you've got nothing to worry about," I pointed out. "By the way, I found someone to use that fifth ticket."

"Anyone I know?"

I shook my head. "Someone new. I've just met him myself. But he seems to be a fan of musical comedy."

"The more, the merrier, I always say."

"I should probably get going," I said, suddenly aware that I didn't exactly fit in with my glamorous surroundings. Especially since the odor I was emitting was an unpleasant contrast to Betty's flowery perfume. "I desperately need a shower. That's what happens when you spend the morning at a horse farm."

Betty's expression clouded. "Have you learned anything new about the death of that poor polo player?"

I hesitated. My Friend the Mind Reader frowned. "Jessica?"

"I wasn't going to mention it, but since you brought it up..." I took a deep breath. "The medical examiner determined that the cause of death was poison."

"Poison!"

I nodded. "Apparently they haven't identified the substance, but they're pretty sure that poor Eduardo Garcia was murdered."

"Good heavens!" She shuddered. "What a terrible thing. That poor young man! I feel so sorry for his family. At any rate, I'm glad that at least *you* have no intention of getting involved in his murder."

Without quite looking her in the eye, I mumbled, "I didn't exactly say that."

Betty drew her lips into a straight line. "Now, Jessica..."

"There's this reporter," I began. "He asked me to help him." Quickly, I added, "I'm not really going to get *involved*. It's more like I've agreed to keep an eye out for anything that might be related to the case. Maybe— maybe—ask a few questions. Until Andrew MacKinnon's regular vet is back in business, I'm going to be spending a fair amount of time at Heatherfield. That puts me in an ideal position to serve as an extra pair of eyes and ears. But honestly, that's *all* I'm going to be doing."

I wasn't about to mention that I was already finding the incident as fascinating as it was disturbing. Of course, how Forrester Sloan fit into all this was another matter entirely.

"I suppose if that's *all* you intend to do, that's not too dangerous. That is, as long as you don't get carried away." The look of doubt on Betty's face told me she had every suspicion that getting carried away was exactly what I was likely to do. "But this reporter... he's not someone you..."

"No!" I assured her, not even having to hear the rest of her question. "As far as I'm concerned, Forrester Sloan is two steps higher than Marcus Scruggs on the evolutionary scale. That *still* puts him about six notches below a slug."

"Good. I'd hate to think that anything could get in the way of your relationship with Nick. It's still fragile, Jessica. Besides, with all the pressure he's under right now—"

"Okay, dancing inmates!" the director called, leaping onto the stage and clapping his hands. "Where are my dancing inmates? I want to run through 'Cell Block Tango' one more time...."

"The show must go on," I said cheerfully, standing up and gathering my things. Deciding you couldn't go wrong with overused theatrical expressions, I added, "Break a leg, Betty."

"Certainly, Jessica," she said, heading toward the stage. Glancing back at me over her shoulder, she added, "Just promise me *you* won't break any hearts."

As soon as I opened the door of my cottage, my animals threw their usual welcome home party. The only thing missing was the confetti and the paper hats. Unfortunately, there were no other human beings in attendance.

At least Nick had left a note, I thought dejectedly, picking up the sheet I found in the middle of the piece of furniture that served as dining room table, desk, and message center.

Hey, Jess,

I tried to wait, but I had to get home to hit the books. By the way, the dogs and I had a great workout at the beach. Those guys sure can run!

Dinner tonight?

N.

Absence makes the heart grow fonder, I told myself, gritting my teeth.

Still, I recognized that my resentment over seeing so little of Nick simply proved that I really loved him. I decided to bury my frustration and enjoy the anticipation of a romantic Saturday night tryst with my elusive paramour.

It must have worked, because my heart actually fluttered a little when Nick showed up on my doorstep that evening, wearing jeans and his favorite Led Zeppelin T-shirt and smelling faintly of Safeguard soap. This time, he'd brought something even better than a bouquet of flowers: enough Chinese food to feed General Tsao's army.

Max and Lou were as happy to see him as I was. They scampered around, yapping and frolicking like animals in a cartoon. Prometheus began shrieking, making sure that no one would forget that an affection-starved bird was in the room. I knew it was only a question of time before Cat emerged from the kitchen, demanding equal time.

But for the moment, I was top dog. "Hey, Jess," he greeted me, leaning forward to plant a light kiss on my lips. "I got all your favorites. Garlic Triple Crown, steamed dumplings with chili sauce, sesame noodles, spring rolls, the whole kit and caboodle."

"You thought of everything," I returned. "All that's missing is a real kiss."

"Oh, yeah?" His voice softened. He put down the plastic bags, took me in his arms, and gave me the same kind of kiss Rhett Butler gave Scarlett O'Hara during the siege of Atlanta. And just like Rhett, Nick had the ability to leave his ladylove breathless.

"I've missed you," I told him once I was able to speak again.

"I've missed you, too," he murmured. "But tonight, I'm not even going to think about law...hey, what are you guys doing?"

I looked down, suddenly as distracted by the sound of rustling plastic as he was. Max and Lou had abandoned their shameless adoration of Nick and were instead nuzzling the white cardboard cartons of Chinese food, trying to figure out how to stick their noses inside.

"Get out of there!" I shrieked, my voice almost as high-pitched as Prometheus's.

Nick laughed. "I'm as starved as they are. Let's eat."

So much for romance. Still, sesame noodles and dumplings weren't a bad alternative. We sat side by side on the couch, the cartons laid out on the coffee table and our plates balanced in our laps.

"So how's that horse?" Nick asked, deftly wielding a pair of chopsticks. "The one who dragged us out of bed at dawn this morning."

It took me a few seconds to remember what he was talking about. Treating Andrew MacKinnon's mare seemed like something that had transpired days ago, instead of less than twelve hours earlier. So much had happened since then. Dealing with Johnny Ray's grouchiness, Callie's defensiveness, and Jillian's chronic unhappiness would have been demanding enough. But I'd also endured an entire lunch with Forrester Sloan— and agreed to help him investigate Eduardo Garcia's murder.

It was that last part that stood out as the real highlight of the day. Still, I knew from past experience that bringing it up was practically guaranteed to ruin my evening with Nick.

So I simply answered, "She'll be fine. It was just a simple impaction, which is very common. Horses' anatomy makes them prone to intestinal obstructions. In other words, grass and food stop up their pipes, and they—"

"That's okay," Nick interrupted quickly. "As long as she's going to be okay."

I suddenly remembered that not everyone finds the workings of animals' digestive systems quite as fascinating as I do. Especially during mealtime.

"Speaking of horses," I continued, "how would you like to go to a polo match at the Meadowlark Club tomorrow afternoon? It should be really fun." *Not to mention a chance for us to spend some time together,* I thought.

I expected his response to be something along the lines of, "Oh, boy! Can't wait!" Instead, my suggestion was greeted with silence.

"Jess," he finally said, "I can't go to a polo game tomorrow."

"Why not?"

"I have to study."

My blood instantly turned as hot as the chili sauce. "Nick, this is insane! You only started at Brookside last week, and you already qualify for Missing Persons status! Do you mean to tell me that law school is going to take up every single moment of your life?"

"Yes, as a matter of fact." I could tell he was trying to keep the defensiveness out of his voice. Or maybe it was something else that was making him sound funny, like irritation. "Isn't that what happened when you went to vet school? Didn't it monopolize your entire life from the very start?"

"Sure, but that was—" I stopped myself. To be perfectly honest, I didn't know how I'd intended to finish that sentence. But I realized there was no way I *could* finish it without sounding condescending. Nick already knew that I wasn't exactly crazy about his decision to become a lawyer. There was no point in bringing it up again.

"Okay," I said, doing my best to calm down. "I guess I'm just going to have to get used to this. But you don't mind if I go to the polo match without you, do you?"

"Of course not. I don't expect you to put your life on hold just because I'm changing careers. I'll tell you what: Let's have dinner together tomorrow night, and you can tell me all about the game. In fact, you can give me a play-by-play. And I *promise* that this time I won't cancel at the last minute."

"Or fall asleep?"

Grinning, he said, "I'll drink six cups of espresso, if that's what it takes." He reached over and put his arm around my shoulders. Always the gentleman, he shifted his body to avoid dumping sesame noodles all over me. "And I've got something to tell you that I've kind of been putting off. I figured it was bad news, but I'm beginning to think that maybe it's good news."

Not a very encouraging introduction. "What?" I asked warily.

"My apartment's being painted next week. I'm pretty much going to have to move out while they get the job done. I figured I'd stay here—which means we'd be seeing a lot more of each other."

I was already starting to feel as if the walls were closing in on me. "For how long?" I was glad that the sudden dryness in my throat hadn't made it impossible for me to talk.

"Just a few days. Don't worry; I won't crowd you. Besides, it'll be kind of fun, don't you think? Kind of like a long sleepover."

"Okay," I croaked, taking deep breaths.

I grabbed my chopsticks and began shoveling in food without even tasting it.

He's just going to be staying here for a few days, I thought. It's only temporary.

After all, it's not as if he's moving in.

Chapter 7

"Horse sense is the thing a horse has which keeps it from betting on people."

—W.C. Fields

As I drove my red Volkswagen past the small, tasteful sign reading "Meadowlark Polo Club," I actually experienced a wave of disappointment. This was my first polo game, and I'd been expecting something grand. I'd imagined a dignified clubhouse surrounded by manicured gardens—the type of place F. Scott Fitzgerald would have devoted at least a couple of paragraphs to describing. Instead, the club, whose history included serving as the world's center for polo during the 1920's and '30's, consisted of nothing but a few well-worn buildings with faded gray shingles and polo fields lined with uncomfortable metal bleachers.

Still, the hordes of people who were flocking onto the grounds for the three o'clock polo match scarcely seemed to notice. They were too busy sizing each other up—or, more accurately, peeking at everyone else in the crowd to make sure *they* were being sized up, and that they were eliciting a favorable reaction.

The men wore the typical casual costume of khaki pants and polo shirts, and most accessorized with large, round stomachs. As for the women, they were dressed to the hilt in skimpy sundresses and strappy sandals. Most of them looked as if the primary component of their fashion statement was being extremely thin.

I spotted Diana Chase, wearing white again. But this time, she wore tight capris and a loose-fitting white jacket over a tailored mint green shirt. Very tasteful. Her sidekick, following a few paces behind, was also wearing an expensive-looking outfit, made of a pale pink knit fabric that emphasized her curves. But Vivian Johannsen's skirt spiked high enough and her halter top dipped low enough to capture lustful glances from most of the males in attendance, along with an equal number of envious looks from the females. I couldn't help wondering how much of her voluptuousness was real and how much had been purchased on Park Avenue—from a plastic surgeon.

I also spotted Jillian MacKinnon, clutching her usual fashion accessory: a glass. This time, it was only a plastic tumbler, but her unsteady gait told me its contents were having the desired effect. Callie trailed a few feet behind, her arms folded across her chest and her mouth pulled into a frown. Even she was decked out for the occasion, stuffed into a tight, bright yellow sundress I was certain would send her mother back to the bartender again and again.

What an interesting segment of society, I thought, and one that few outsiders even realize exists, much less ever view firsthand: men and women who look at owning a stable full of horses the way most people see owning a cat, whose vehicles easily cost more than most people's homes, who think nothing of flying to Florida for an afternoon's polo match—or to England for just the weekend.

But for today, at least, I was as much a part of the event as anyone else. I headed for the bleachers, noticing that they were close enough to the field to provide an excellent view of the action—*on* the field, as well as *off*.

Unfortunately, the degree of comfort they offered wasn't nearly as impressive. I'd just gotten settled and was wondering how my back would ever manage to make it through the afternoon when Forrester Sloan plopped down beside me.

"Hey, Popper, glad you could make it," he greeted me.

"Are you kidding? I wouldn't have missed this for the world," I returned. "I'm flabbergasted by all the competitiveness, the obvious displays of killer instinct... and the polo match hasn't even started yet."

"Now you're getting it," he said, chuckling. Glancing around, he added, "Where's that date you threatened to bring?"

"Otherwise engaged."

"Gee, that's a real shame," he returned sarcastically. "I'm really gonna miss having him here."

"I've never been to a polo match before," I said, changing the subject. "I'm actually pretty excited."

"A novice, huh? In that case, let me give you a quick lesson in Polo 101." Forrester, too, was back to business. "A match consists of six segments called chukkers. Each one lasts seven minutes. The point of the game is to get the ball across the line between the goalposts. It doesn't matter if it's hit with a mallet or the horse kicks it across. There are four players on a team, and each one plays a different position, although they all pretty much do whatever needs to be done. Number One is the most forward offensive player, Number Two is also offensive but plays a little deeper, and Number Three switches between offense and defense. Number Four is the defensive player. He protects the goal."

"I see you've done your homework," I observed, only half teasing.

"Good reporters always do their homework," Forrester returned, sounding a trifle defensive. "It's part of the job."

A booming amplification system interrupted our conversation. *"Good afternoon, and welcome to the Meadowlark Polo Club,"* the commentator began crisply. *"Before today's match gets under way, we'd like to take a moment to say good-bye to one of our most beloved players, Eduardo Garcia. Eduardo was one of those rare individuals who was well-known for his sportsmanship off the polo field as well as on it. He was generous, warm, and loved by all who knew him. He will be sorely missed. And now, a moment of silence."*

I noticed that most of the people in the stands bowed their heads respectfully. But not all of them. Diana Chase took advantage of the silence to fumble through her purse. She could have been looking for a tissue to dab at her moist eyes, I reasoned. Or maybe she was simply making a point by refusing to pay her respects. Someone else in the bleachers also made a point of showing how uninterested she was in paying tribute to the fallen polo star. Callie kept looking around, rolling her eyes and sighing and just generally making it clear she'd rather be someplace else. *Anyplace* else.

The commentator's voice took on a more upbeat tone. *"We'll commence play with the umpire bowling the ball between the players...Scott Mooney hits the ball...that's Pancho Escobar on the ball for the Blue Heather team, keeping the ball in play, towards the goal..."*

I watched, fascinated, as the eight players on horseback raced after the ball.

"*Vamos!*" one of the players called.

"Easy, easy, easy!" cried another.

"*Now it's taken by Johnny Ray Cousins, who's playing for Blue Heather,*" the commentator continued. "*Wait—we have a whistle on the play.... We appear to have a penalty, Number Three, from forty yards to an undefended goal.... The ball will be thrown in...the ball is cut, sliced across the field by Escobar, who steadies his pony...*"

The sight of the spirited horseman, galloping across the field on his mighty horse, brought the crowd to its feet.

"Pancho's pretty amazing," I commented to Forrester. "But what's Johnny Ray doing out on the field?"

"Apparently he used to be quite the polo player back in his younger days. Believe it or not, he was rated an eight-goal player. But a bad accident messed him up for a couple of years. He seemed to think part of the recovery process was liquid therapy. Even when his back healed, his addiction didn't. Word got around that he was unreliable, and that was the end of his career."

"Sad story," I commented.

"Sad guy."

"But it looks like he's trying to make a comeback."

Forrester cast me a meaningful glance. "Hey, with Eduardo out of the picture, MacKinnon needed somebody to fill in—fast. Enter Johnny Ray."

"Interesting," I returned, my eyebrows shooting up to my hairline. "A little factoid that's worth filing away."

"*He knocks the ball down toward the goal...and it's a score!*" the commentator announced excitedly. "*Pancho Escobar for Blue Heather puts the ball through!*"

"Wow, Pancho is really something!" I cried, exhilarated by the superb skill the lean, muscular Argentine who played on Andrew MacKinnon's team had exhibited.

"Yeah, these guys are all pretty incredible," Forrester admitted.

"And here I thought it was impossible to impress a seasoned newspaper reporter like you," I returned teasingly.

"Hey, these horses are moving at thirty or forty miles an hour. And the ball is going a hundred. This game is *fast*."

"Ice hockey on horseback," I said, repeating the catchy little phrase Winston had taught me. "I heard that from a true devotee of the sport. And speaking of devotees, I noticed that Andrew MacKinnon's riding around out there with the rest of the Blue Heather team, but he hasn't been mentioned once so far. He's not exactly in the thick of things, is he?"

"He's probably one of those guys who plays the game in order to watch the action up close and pretend he's part of it, without ever actually hitting the ball." Scornfully, he added, "Expensive way to get a front-row seat, don't you think? But the guys who finance the game, the patrons, play just for fun. There's no prize money to compete for, and there's no chance of ending up on a Wheaties box or making a killing on TV commercials. Yet that doesn't keep them from spending megabucks on their little hobby. These guys play polo the way you and I might play badminton in somebody's backyard at a barbecue."

I figured it was just as well we watched the rest of the chukker in silence. I really was enjoying the game and while Forrester's commentary did give me additional insight, I was happy to have the chance to concentrate on the accomplished players and their remarkable horses.

The game proceeded so quickly that I was surprised when the commentator announced, "*We're at halftime, and we invite you to come onto the field and replace the divots...."*

This, it seemed, was part of the festivities. Forrester and I dutifully followed the throngs of spectators who abandoned the bleachers and headed onto the polo field. Some people halfheartedly pressed the clumps of grass that had come loose back into place. But most of them put much more energy into meeting and greeting. The younger women teetered across the grass in their high-heeled sandals in order to flirt with the young men. The older men slapped one another on their backs, no doubt recognizing this as valuable networking time. Their wives gathered in small groups, meanwhile keeping watchful eyes on their men.

I spotted Callie halfway across the field, standing a few feet away from her mother and wearing a bored expression.

"Look, there's Callie MacKinnon," I told Forrester, pointing. "Andrew's younger daughter. Let's go over and say hello."

Callie actually looked mildly pleased when she noticed us making a beeline in their direction. Or maybe her expression was simply one of surprise.

"Hey, Dr. Popper," she said with an unenthusiastic wave. "What are you doing here?"

"Enjoying the polo game," I replied. "It's really fun, don't you think?"

She shrugged. "Like I haven't already been to a million of these. Hey, you want to come over to my house afterward? My parents are having this cocktail party thing."

I glanced at Forrester, wondering if he was thinking the same thing I was: that it was just a tad surprising that the MacKinnons were having a party two days after Eduardo had been buried.

Callie noticed my reaction. "It's not a party, really.

It's just this little gathering that takes place on Sundays. Everybody takes turns having people over right after the polo game. It was my mom and dad's turn, so they figured they'd just go ahead and do it. It's nothing fancy. Just standing around on the patio, getting drunk."

Forrester leaned over, placing his mouth next to my ear. "Take notes," he whispered.

I ignored him. "Thanks for the invitation, Callie, but I'd planned to have dinner with my boyfriend. He's in law school, and we don't get to spend much time together."

"Bring him."

"That's really sweet, but your parents might not want me to—"

"Mom, I just invited Dr. Popper over to the house after the game," Callie called, interrupting Jillian's conversation with the small group of women. "It's okay, isn't it?"

Jillian turned. For a moment, she looked stricken. Then her facial muscles relaxed. Maybe it was because she didn't want to look inhospitable, or maybe she was actually trying to be nice to her daughter, but she replied, "Sure, why the hell not? I shuppose there's always room for one more."

"Good," Callie said. "She's bringing her boyfriend, too."

Jillian cast a panicked glance at Forrester.

"Not him," Callie informed her. "Some other guy. He's a law student."

"In that case, he's welcome, too." Jillian glared at Forrester, as if wanting to make sure he understood that even though Nick and I were invited, *he* hadn't made the A-list.

"Sorry about that," I told him after we'd moved on and Callie and Jillian were out of earshot.

"About what?" Forrester looked surprised.

"Jillian's rudeness. Inviting Nick and me, but being so obvious about not inviting you."

"Don't worry, I won't take it personally. Besides," he added, "her unwillingness to open her home to a member of the press just makes her look more suspicious."

My eyes widened. "Do you think it's possible *Jillian* murdered Eduardo?"

"Popper, it's possible that anybody you see here today murdered Eduardo. They're all suspects, as far as I'm concerned." He glanced around the polo field. Then, with a bitterness in his voice that surprised me, he added, "Believe me, Popper, the rich really *are* different. Don't ever doubt for a second that any one of these people could be a cold-blooded killer."

His tone warned me not to press him any further. But he clearly had strong feelings about the wealthy. I was more curious than ever about where they'd come from—and whether he'd developed them from the outside, looking in, or whether they came from having grown up in their midst.

It seemed like a good time to call Nick to tell him about our cocktail party invitation and give him directions to Heatherfield. Even though I had to admit that I was getting used to Forrester Sloan—and that maybe I even liked him, at least a little—there was something about him that made me uneasy. And that something, whatever it was, made me appreciate Nick even more.

Like the citizens of Old Brookbury, Heatherfield had also gotten spruced up in honor of the post–polo match cocktail party. I got the feeling an entire team of landscapers had spent days getting ready, trimming grass, pruning trees, and planting flowers that provided a colorful and fragrant backdrop for the event.

The patio was festooned with colorful paper lanterns,

and even though the sun was still shining brightly, tiki torches burned around the perimeter. The landscapers' efforts were also apparent here. Not a single weed, or even a limp-looking blossom, dared to mar the profusion of shrubs and flowers that enclosed the area.

Luisa and Inez were working hard, passing platters of hors d'oeuvres so rich and elaborate that they could easily have constituted dinner. I noticed that as Luisa headed back inside, probably to the kitchen to refill her tray, Inez stood alone at the edge of the patio, watching the crowd of people. She looked tired, as if all she wanted was a chance to sit down. I was struck by the dramatic contrast of the thin, dark-haired young woman in a plain black dress framed by a cluster of graceful white flowers atop slender stalks. I realized it would have made a pretty picture—and wondered if Callie's interest in art was starting to rub off on me.

With Nick not yet there, I had no one to talk to. I wandered over to the Polynesian-style bar, an intentionally crude-looking hut with a thatched roof set up in one corner of the patio. A bartender in a straw hat was dispensing frozen tropical drinks that were as colorful as the bright flowers splashed across the fabric of his loud Hawaiian shirt.

I grabbed a frozen strawberry drink and surveyed the faces of the people gathered on the patio. There weren't many I recognized.

Fortunately, there was one face I knew, even though I'd only seen it from across the polo field. Scott Mooney, one of the players on Andrew MacKinnon's team, was standing alone, gobbling cheese and gulping down ginger ale. He'd changed out of his polo garb into jeans and an olive green T-shirt that was tight enough to show off his lean, muscular torso and sculpted arms. His straight, sandy blond hair, which he wore long, kept falling into his eyes, and he kept pushing it away. I couldn't tell if it was a nervous gesture or a calculated effort to bring attention to his handsome features. He had the look of a California surfer—or maybe a midwestern farm boy.

I sidled over to him, eager to grab a few minutes of what would hopefully look like casual conversation. Not only had Scott known Eduardo Garcia; he'd galloped across polo fields just inches away from him.

"Great game," I told him, glancing up from the cheese tray I was pretending had been the main attraction. "You played really well. Of course, since it was the first polo match I've ever seen, I'm not really in the best position to judge."

He flashed me a wide smile, showing off two rows of perfectly straight teeth so white they almost twinkled. Up until that point, I hadn't been close enough to realize that in addition to being strikingly handsome, he exuded an easy self-confidence that told me his good looks had made life easier for him than it was for most people. I also saw that, like Eduardo, he had a few scars—a nick on his cheek, a tiny line near one of his unusually green eyes.

"How did you like it?" he asked. "Your first polo match, I mean."

"It was incredible," I told him. "What an exciting game! And the skill that's required to play is just unimaginable." I paused to sip my drink before adding, "I wish I could have seen Eduardo Garcia play. I understand he was really something out on the polo field."

"Yeah, it's really a shame." Scott shook his head. "Eduardo was such a cool guy. And like you said, a hell of a polo player. But polo wasn't his whole life, if you know what I mean. The guy really knew how to have fun."

"Fun . . . as in other sports?" I probed.

Scott grinned. "That's not exactly the kind of fun I was talking about. Actually, Eduardo was quite the ladies' man." Lowering his voice, he continued, "He used to brag to me that women told him things they wouldn't even tell their husbands." He paused, sipping his ginger ale. "Or, to be more accurate, things they *especially* wouldn't tell their husbands."

"Sounds like he was pretty popular," I observed.

"Yeah, Eduardo pretty much had it all. Good looks, charm, athletic ability... You know, he came from nothing. The guy started out dirt poor—and I'm talking the kind of poverty we just don't have in this country. But he adapted just great, once he got to the U.S. of A. He never stopped being grateful for the chance to come up here and play on Mac's team. He fit right in. In fact, Eduardo became part of this set in a way most Argies never manage."

Most intriguing. "You're talking about the women he...*befriended*, right?"

"He hung out with their husbands, too. Hell, entire families around here welcomed him with open arms. The guy was the toast of Old Brookbury! Everybody liked Eduardo. Trusted him, too. In fact, we used to tease the poor guy because he was always going to parties that the rest of us weren't invited to. It was like he was on the inside track with these folks. He broke through the invisible barriers that separate the players—especially the Argies—from the patrons."

He took another sip of ginger ale and frowned. "And you know, I never bought any of those rumors. Not for a minute."

"They *are* kind of hard to believe, aren't they?" I commented, not letting on that I didn't have the slightest idea what he was talking about.

Or that I was absolutely dying to know.

"Anybody could get into financial trouble, the way he did," Scott continued. "I mean, living the high life, hanging out with people with the kind of money Mac and his friends have ... It wasn't his fault. In fact, you could almost say it was inevitable." He shook his head. "Still, I don't buy what they say about him taking money from his lady friends. It just doesn't fit, you know?"

I just nodded, trying to look knowledgeable and wise without letting my astonishment show through.

"Hey, there's Pancho," Scott said suddenly. "I gotta ask him something. Nice talking to you!"

I watched him disappear into the crowd. Eduardo taking money ... as in gifts? I wondered. Or maybe cash payments for his services?

Or were the rumors Scott was referring to even more ominous—perhaps even something along the lines of blackmail?

I made a mental note to tell Forrester about my intriguing conversation with Scott. In the meantime, I set my sights on Callie, who was tucked away in a corner of the patio, sipping a foamy lime green drink through a straw. I eased over in her direction.

"Hey, Callie," I greeted her cheerfully. "This isn't too shabby a way to spend a Sunday evening, is it?"

She shrugged without lowering her drink from her mouth. Was it my imagination, I wondered, or was she even more surly than usual?

I tried again. "Thanks again for inviting me. Heatherfield looks pretty spiffy. It must be terrific, living in such a beautiful place."

"Seems kind of dumb, since it's just the four of us," Callie mumbled. "And Peyton's hardly ever here any more. She's been in Europe all summer, taking some ridiculous course in Italian architecture. As if she ever opened a book or showed up for a class. I have a feeling she learned a lot more about the club scene than the cathedrals."

"When you get older, I'm sure your parents will let

you study abroad, too. And you're right: You'll probably get much more out of it, since it's something you really care about."

"I can hardly wait," Callie agreed. "Frankly, I'm looking forward to the day I can move out and live on my own. Someplace exciting, like London or Rome."

"Still," I said, glancing around, "this is such a peaceful spot."

Callie snorted. "That's what you think. Wait 'til my sister comes home."

"Really?" I asked, genuinely surprised. "Why?"

Her eyes met mine, but only for a moment. "You'll see," she said smugly, then turned back to her drinking straw.

It didn't take long for me to find out exactly what Callie meant.

A few minutes later, as I was about to emerge from the guest bathroom off the front hallway, I heard the front door open. While I watched in the mirror above the sink, a tall, thin young woman breezed in. Behind her, a man struggled with no fewer than five suitcases. I could see that a taxi was parked out front, and I assumed he was the driver. He wasn't exactly a small guy, yet he looked as if he'd met his match in this woman's luggage collection.

"Just put those over there—be *careful*!" she shrieked. "Those are Louis Vuitton!"

It was difficult to imagine why her bags were so heavy, given the fact that her preference in clothing appeared to run along the lines of the skimpiest garments available, made from the thinnest fabrics that could possibly be manufactured. The amount of space between her clingy, pink-flowered skirt and her stretchy white low-cut halter top could have qualified her as a belly dancer. Still, I had to admit that she was strikingly pretty. At least, I assumed she was, under all the makeup she'd plastered on. Her straight blond hair completed her look as the quintessential rich-girl-cum-party-girl.

"Gee, a whole dollar," I heard the taxi driver say sarcastically.

"You're lucky you got a tip at all. I'm positive you scratched the accessories pouch!"

"Have a nice day," he returned. The door slammed behind him.

"Moth-er!" she cried, her voice echoing through the entire first floor. "Dad-deee!"

I chose that moment to poke my head out the door.

"Moth...oh, hello." Peering at me, she demanded, "Who are you?"

"Jessie Popper. I'm a veterinarian, and I've been—"

"Where is everybody?" She clearly wasn't the least bit interested in me or the reason I happened to be standing in her house. In fact, her accusing tone implied that I was responsible for hiding the other members of her family from her deliberately.

"On the patio. Your parents are having a cocktail party." I managed to smile graciously. "You must be Peyton."

"Of course I am," she replied irritably. "Who else would I be?"

"You're early."

Peyton and I both turned at the sound of another voice. Her mother had come into the house, one hand on her hip and the other wrapped around a glass.

"Actually, I'm late," Peyton returned crossly. "That stupid taxi driver insisted on taking the Long Island Expressway, even though I told him the Northern State would be better. Honestly, you'd think he—"

"Why didn't you just call Ramon?" Jillian demanded. "What do you think we employ a chauffeur for?"

"Oh, Mother, you know what a mob scene it is at the airport. It just seemed simpler to jump into a cab."

"Whatever. How was your trip?" Jillian asked distractedly. I had to admit that I was surprised by how underwhelmed she seemed by her daughter's return after an entire summer in Europe.

"Fabulous, of course."

"Come outside for a few minutes," Jillian ordered. "I'm sure there are people here who'd like to see you." She turned and walked back outside.

However, her other parent chose that moment to appear, wandering in from the patio. "Peyton!" he cried, his face lighting up.

"Daddy!" Peyton dropped her designer purse and flew across the immense foyer, throwing her arms around her father.

"There you are, sweetie! I was getting worried! I tried your cell phone, but—"

"Oh, Daddy! I've missed you so much!" From what I could recall, it was the first time I'd seen any member of this household show even the slightest bit of affection.

"I missed you, too, angel."

"Why didn't you come visit me?" Peyton pouted, sticking out her lower lip like a four-year-old who'd had her lollipop taken away. "You could have jumped onto that Lear jet of yours and come over any time. And don't tell me you've been too busy. That's the excuse you always use!"

"That's because it's always true, cupcake."

"Then you're working too hard," she insisted. "You have to start finding time for the things that really matter—like me!"

He chuckled indulgently. "Don't tell me you didn't get the checks I sent."

"Of course I did! Otherwise, how would I ever have been able to buy this fabulous outfit?" She jumped back, modeling the handkerchiefs that doubled as clothing.

"You look beautiful," Andrew MacKinnon said admiringly. "But you always do."

"Oh, Daddy, you're *so* good to me," Peyton cooed, throwing her arms around him once again. "I'm the luckiest girl in the world!"

"Let's go outside," Andrew suggested. "The McPhersons are here, and so are the Batchelders. I'm sure they'd like to say hello."

"Whatever you say, Daddy," Peyton cooed, wrapping her arm around his and leading him away. "And I can tell you all about my trip."

Andrew beamed. "I wouldn't have it any other way."

I was relieved to see Nick standing on the front steps, glancing inside the house uncertainly.

"You're in the right place," I told him, striding over. "Just in time, too." Leaning closer, I whispered, "Thank you for saving me! These people are like characters in a David Lynch movie."

"Come on, how bad could they be?" Nick returned.

I decided to let him find out for himself.

I led him out onto the patio, which by that point was fairly crowded. Andrew and his adoring daughter were making the rounds, with Peyton giving air kisses to everyone she encountered. Jillian, standing at the other end of the patio, was commanding Luisa to bring out more wine. To me, it looked as if she was already having enough trouble standing up. Callie, meanwhile, stood in the corner with her shoulders slumped, still clutching her hideous lime green drink. I suspected she was wearing her usual scowl, but her stringy dirty-blond hair was obscuring her face.

Suddenly, the atmosphere shifted. Peyton's eyes had drifted away from her father long enough to zero in on Nick. Within a fraction of a second, her expression changed. Daddy's Little Girl was gone. In her place was a Big Girl—one who, from the looks of things, knew exactly what she wanted.

She strode across the patio so quickly I was afraid she'd knock over a few of the guests.

"Well, well, well," she gurgled, sidling up to Nick and batting her eyelashes as if she were a cartoon character. "What have we here? Or should I say, *who* have we here?"

"This is Nick Burby," I answered stiffly. "He's, uh, my boyfriend."

"Another veterinarian?" Peyton asked, flicking her silky blond hair over her shoulder. I noticed that a glint had appeared in her emerald green eyes—a glint that set off alarms in my head.

"Actually, I just started law school," Nick replied. He didn't seem to have noticed that he'd been identified as possible prey. "Last week, in fact. I was a private investigator, but that was something I kind of fell into after college. Now, I feel I'm finally on a path that makes sense for me."

"How admirable," Peyton returned. "I was saying just the other day that the one thing this world needs more of is lawyers."

"That's not exactly how everybody feels," Nick replied, his cheeks reddening just a bit. "Like Jessie here, for example. But I feel there's a lot I can do with a law degree. A lot of good—"

"*Definitely!*" Peyton gushed. "My goodness, just think of all the instances of social injustice we read about in the newspapers every single day!" Her lower lip protruded in a dramatic pout—her signature facial expression, I concluded. "All those poor, underprivileged individuals who get beaten down by the system..." Her features softened into a seductive smile, and she wrapped both arms around one of Nick's as if she were one of those African vines capable of strangling people to death. "Now, Nick, I won't let you get away until you tell me all about law school. It must be *fascinating*."

"It is pretty cool, actually," he replied, taking a baby step in the opposite direction. I didn't even know if he did it consciously. At any rate, his instinctive movement *away* from Peyton made me smile. "Of course, I'm just getting started, but I'm already finding—"

"Not that I know anything about this, but my advice is to major in Business Law," Peyton purred. "My father is always complaining that there's a surprising shortage. Of really good attorneys, I mean. Oh, I'm sure there are plenty of hacks, but I'm talking about the really skilled ones. The real players. The people who can make a difference."

"Right," I found myself muttering. "The ones who know how to twist the meaning of a supposedly ironclad contract to their own advantage."

I was greatly relieved that at that moment, Luisa came over, bearing a tray piled high with some kind of hors d'oeuvre made with layers of pastry. I couldn't identify the ingredients, but that didn't keep it from looking delicious.

"Check these out, Nick," I said. "Too bad we didn't line our pockets with Ziploc bags."

My hunch about the power of food was correct: Chowing down, especially on goodies of this caliber, was even more of a draw than flirting with a gorgeous young woman.

Nick wasn't the only one who was a slave to his stomach. Callie suddenly appeared, reaching toward the tray so energetically that she nearly knocked her sister over.

"Hey!" Peyton snapped. "Do you think for once in

your life you could act less like a wild animal and more like a human being?"

"Do you mind?" Callie countered. "I happen to be famished."

"When are you *not* famished?"

"Do you think it'd be better if I were anorexic or bulemic or whatever you are that keeps you looking like a stick figure some five-year-old drew?"

"Just because I happen to be capable of maintaining a little self-control—"

"Being around you is enough to give anybody self-control," Callie shot back. "Just being in the same hemisphere as you makes me want to throw up!" She stomped off—but not before scooping a large percentage of the hors d'oeurves off the tray and carrying them away.

"There's no place like home," Peyton muttered. Then she glanced up at Nick, this time sliding her hand down his arm and clasping his hand. "So, Nick, I insist that you tell me all about the classes a first-year law student takes!"

"That was fun," Nick commented as we walked away from the MacKinnons' front door, me toward my VW and him toward his Maxima. *"Not!"*

"You mean you didn't enjoy making such a nice new friend?" Sliding my arm around his waist, I teased, "For a minute there, I thought I was going to have to pour a bucket of cold water on that girl."

"Yeah, she's really something, isn't she?"

"Still, isn't it nice to know younger women find you irresistible?" I couldn't help adding.

"Thanks, but baby-sitting doesn't appeal to me," Nick grumbled.

The right answer, I thought, relieved that my spurt of

jealousy turned out to have had more to do with me than with Nick.

"Still, it's kind of sad," I went on. "All that wealth, yet the MacKinnons seem so miserable. Andrew has an angry alcoholic for a wife, Callie's horribly jealous of her sister, Peyton's completely wrapped up in herself...I guess what they say about money not being able to buy happiness is true," I replied. "At least, where that family's concerned."

"You're right," Nick agreed. "An evening with those folks is enough to make you give up all your worldly goods."

I was about to make a comment about Nick's new-found values and how they might not fit in all that well with law school, but fortunately we'd reached our vehicles.

"Coming over?" I asked.

"Sorry, Jess. I've got an early morning. And before I crash, I want to go over the cases we're covering in Contracts tomorrow. But I'll call you tomorrow, okay?"

"Sure," I said, keeping what I genuinely felt like saying to myself. "You know the way out, right?"

"Yup." Nick gave me a peck on the cheek, then climbed into his car. I figured his thoughts were already wrapped up in Jones versus the Toonerville Trolley Transportation Company or some other obscure case.

I went over to my car, noticing for the first time that the warm, sunny day had turned into a cool, dark evening. Even though September was just getting under way, I could already detect a hint of autumn in the air. Breezes sent the thick foliage on the maple trees swaying to and fro, making eerie shushing sounds. I shivered, wishing I'd thought to bring a jacket along.

As I unlocked my car, I noticed something white sticking out from under the windshield wiper.

"That's odd," I said aloud. It wasn't as if I were in a

public parking lot, where someone might have stuck an advertising flyer on my window. And I couldn't imagine the Old Brookbury police department issuing parking tickets on their well-connected residents' private property. I grabbed it and quickly unfolded it.

Even in the dim light from the lamp above the Mac-Kinnons' distant front door, I could see that the note was composed of letters from a magazine, cut out and pasted together to form words. It was the kind of thing I'd seen in movies, but could never imagine anyone actually doing.

Seeing one in real life was unexpectedly chilling.

Especially when I pieced together the uneven letters to read the words:

TO O ma NY q UE s T ions. MIN d yo U r o Wn b US ness.

Chapter 8

"I prefer a bike to a horse. The brakes are more easily checked."

—Lambert Jeffries

I stood frozen to the spot for a long time, just staring at the bizarre note. But I was more puzzled than frightened.

Whoever had sent this note had clearly noticed that I'd suddenly become very much a presence in the world that Eduardo Garcia had once inhabited. My conversations with all four of the MacKinnons, my visit to Winston Farnsworth's house after running into him here at the estate, my interrogation of Scott Mooney... *someone* was paying attention to my comings and goings.

Of course, I thought, this could just be somebody's idea of a joke—or a way of telling me I'm acting like a busybody.

Or that I don't really belong in this world.

I tucked the note into my purse, figuring I wouldn't mention it to anyone. At this point, I had no way of knowing *what* it meant. If I told Forrester, he'd undoubtedly tell Falcone—and the last thing I wanted was him getting on my case about me getting *off* the case.

By the next day, I'd all but forgotten about the note. Monday morning meant a return to my usual routine of back-to-back appointments all over Long Island. I'd barely dragged myself out of bed and into the kitchen before Max and Lou were practically doing handsprings. Well, paw springs. They knew the routine. The smell of coffee early in the morning, combined with me getting dressed in the dark, meant only one thing: another exciting adventure for Wonder Westie and the Dynamic Dalmatian, Super Vet's enthusiastic sidekicks.

Unfortunately for them, I had other plans. Call it a hunch, but I had a feeling that neither of my first two clients of the day, Diana Chase or her sidekick Vivian Johannsen, would find the antics of my two spirited beasts amusing. Maybe it was because Diana actually owned white clothing.

"Sorry, guys. You're staying home today," I told them. To make it up to them, I squeezed in a quick game of Slimytoy before hitting the road.

As I drove my van up to Diana Chase's humble little home, I was certain I'd made the right choice leaving Max and Lou back at the cottage. I shuddered to think of the damage they might have done to the pale pink house, which looked like a country retreat in the South of France. The house itself was a complicated arrangement of walls and roofs, half hidden behind lush shrubs and trees. The grounds surrounding it stretched on for acres, but were broken up by walls of hedges, complicated rose gardens, and intimate sitting areas that looked as if no one had ever sat in them. Not only did it make for an impressive display of wealth; the Chase estate was also breathtakingly serene. Aside from the sweet chirping of birds, the only sound interrupting the silence on this peaceful morning was the soft *pop-pop* of tennis balls being lobbed across a clay court.

I knocked on a side door, since that was where I'd parked my van. Through the glass panels, I could see a pretty young woman—the housekeeper, no doubt—frowning as she passed through the kitchen. She was dressed in jeans and a beige polo shirt, her hair pulled back with a white scrungi.

"Can I help you?" she snarled in a thick Long Island accent.

She's certainly rude enough to be French, I thought. *But she doesn't come close to having their sense of style.*

I had a much higher opinion of the elegant animal that stood alongside her, rubbing against her leg and peering at me curiously. She was a real beauty, with dark gray fur and large glowing eyes the color of copper.

I forced myself to smile. "I'm Dr. Popper," I informed her. "Diana Chase asked me to come by today to take a look at Fleur. I have my mobile services unit right here—basically, a clinic on wheels. Is she here?"

"Yeah." The housekeeper bent down and scooped up the cat. Then she handed the animal to me as impersonally as if she was delivering a broken toaster to a small-appliance repairperson.

"Actually, I was talking about Ms. Chase."

"Ms. Chase is having her nails done," she told me haughtily. "She can't be disturbed."

"I see," I said, even though I didn't. If my cat was being examined, I thought, I'd want to be there to hear firsthand how she was doing. Through gritted teeth, I added, "I was hoping to get some information about Fleur's medical history."

"Ms. Chase said to tell you that you're authorized to do whatever needs to be done. She'll sign whatever's necessary once her nails are dry."

"But it would still be helpful for me to know—never

mind." Chances were good that Fleur received excellent medical care. That was usually the case with a specialty breed like this one. Whoever had chosen a Chartreux was probably a serious cat lover, since this was a breed you didn't see every day of the week.

It also happened to have a particularly fascinating history. According to legend, the Chartreux dated back to thirteenth-century France, when knights began returning home from the Crusades, bringing the unusual booty they'd picked up on their travels. That included blue cats that the monks at Le Grand Chartreux monastery had begun breeding whenever they weren't too busy making Chartreuse liqueur.

The result was a gentle, devoted animal that made an excellent house pet. Chartreux were also extremely quiet. In fact, many were completely mute, able to purr but not able to meow. From what I'd seen of Fleur so far, she fell into that category.

As I carried Fleur to my van, I noted that she seemed extremely comfortable with strangers—another characteristic of the breed. Or maybe she was simply attention starved, I thought. I couldn't help wondering what life was like with Diana Chase, her unfriendly housekeeper, and whoever else lived in that house.

"Poor little rich girl, huh, Fleur?" I murmured, nuzzling her soft fur with my cheek. "I have a feeling that instead of tennis courts and a Jacuzzi, you'd much rather have a nice warm lap to curl up into."

She purred in agreement.

"At least you have a pretty name," I pointed out. "Fleur, French for 'flower.'"

She just blinked.

"Okay, my little flower, let's have a look at you," I said. I ran my hands along her spine and palpated her internal organs, then checked her eyes and her ears.

As I'd expected, Fleur seemed to be in fine shape. The

only thing she needed was a booster shot for rabies, since according to the tag on her collar, she was due. I also gave her a distemper and upper-respiratory booster. Usually, I warn the cat's owner that a small lump might develop from the rabies vaccine, but that it was nothing to worry about unless it didn't go away within a month. But Fleur and I were on our own.

"You're in good shape," I told her, lifting her off the examining table. "And you seem like a lovely pussycat. I only hope your owners appreciate how lucky they are to have you."

She blinked again, acting as if she didn't have the slightest idea what I was talking about.

Carrying her in my arms and petting her velvety fur, I returned to the side door and knocked. The same housekeeper answered, looking surprised to see me.

"Back already?"

"Fortunately, Fleur's in good shape," I informed her. "Now if I could just speak to Ms. Chase—"

"Is that you, Dr. Popper?" I heard a familiar voice call from somewhere in the house. "Angeline, bring her in here, will you?"

Angeline grunted. I took that to mean "okay."

I followed the Happy Housekeeper down a long hallway to a large room in the back of the house. One entire wall was covered with floor-to-ceiling windows. They provided a spectacular view of a seemingly endless expanse of thick green lawn. The furniture was ornate: a dramatic lounge-chair-style "fainting couch," end tables with elaborate scrolled legs, and uncomfortable-looking chairs covered in brocade fabrics interlaced with shiny gold thread. Even the wallpaper fell into the decorating category of "overdone froufrou," at least according to my taste. It looked as if it were silk, a soft shade of rose with a floral design.

One more feature of the room caught my eye: the

collection of fashion magazines that was spread haphazardly across a coffee table. I spotted *Vogue, Elle,* and *Harper's Bazaar,* not only the U.S. editions but French, Italian, and British editions, as well. I longed to flip through them to see if any of the letters had been cut out.

But I wasn't exactly alone. Diana was draped across a couch, her hands hanging in midair as if she were a bird that had damaged both wings. The talons at the end of each finger were painted a gleaming shade of fire-engine red. Her feet were bare, showing off ten toenails that were the same brilliant shade.

"Excuse me for not getting up," she purred, sounding very much like Fleur. "My nails aren't quite dry. Tell me: how is my little pussycat?"

"She's in very good health," I reported. "I did a general exam, and I gave her a distemper and upper-respiratory booster. I noticed she was also due for a rabies booster, so I—"

A glazed look had come over Diana's eyes, a sure indication that she hadn't heard a word I'd said.

"You know," she interrupted, "I didn't want to say anything at the MacKinnons' the other day—and I hope you won't take this the wrong way—but you could really benefit from a makeover."

My mouth dropped open so far I could practically feel the silken threads of the Oriental carpet on my chin.

"Excuse me?" It wasn't much of a snappy comeback, but given how astonished I was, I felt I deserved credit for managing to say anything at all.

"It's nothing personal," she went on coolly. "Oh, I know you're a busy lady, one of those successful career-woman types. But that's no excuse for not looking your best."

"Thanks, but I don't think—"

"Sometimes, it's the little things that make the biggest

difference. Your hands, for instance." Before I had a chance to hide them away in the pockets of my khaki shorts, Diana reached over and grabbed hold of them. The calm expression on her face immediately turned to horror. "Just *look* at your fingernails. There's absolutely *no* reason for this. None at all."

"Given the type of work I do," I protested, "it doesn't make sense for—"

"Lee-Lee!" she yelled. "Could you please come in here? There's something you need to see."

"Ms. Chase, if you don't mind, I have a lot to do today. Now that I've finished with Fleur, I have to go over to—"

A small Asian woman wearing jeans and a plain white T-shirt hurried into the room. She appeared to be in her late twenties, with perfectly smooth white skin and shiny, dead-straight black hair. Barely five feet tall, she was so thin I suspected I could have lifted her with one arm.

"Lee-Lee, take a look at these." Diana was determined to ignore my protests. Easing out of this situation appeared to be impossible. She was gripping my hands so firmly that to release myself would have required a struggle. "But prepare yourself. We have what I'd consider a real nail emergency on our hands."

I was about to point out that she'd just made an awful pun when Lee-Lee gasped. I blinked in astonishment, never having dreamed that my fingernails could be capable of eliciting such horrified reactions.

"Oh, no-o-o," she cried. "No, no, *no-o-o!*"

"I told you," Diana said with satisfaction. "An emergency. Do you think you can help?"

"I try," she said, still looking so aghast that I suspected she'd just met up with the challenge of a lifetime.

"We *definitely* have to choose a polish that really makes a statement," Diana insisted.

"I have good color," Lee-Lee said, obviously trying to be helpful.

"Something kicky. Something *fun*." Diana peered at me for a few seconds before adding, "You impress me as someone who needs to have a little more fun."

Lee-Lee began rifling through her bag of magic potions, finally pulling out a pale pink I was pretty sure I could live with. "How about Chase Me Pink?" she asked, presenting it to Diana.

"No, no, *no*!" she replied, shaking her head violently. "How about that pale shade of melon we used for the tennis tournament? That had such a nice summery feel."

"Serene Tangerine?" Lee-Lee pulled out a bottle of something so garishly orange it could have been used to paint detour lines around construction sites.

"No, no, that other one. What was it called? That's right: Never Tango With a Mango. Jessie—may I call you Jessie?—this will look absolutely fabulous on you."

The mere name Never Tango With a Mango was enough to make me shudder. As for the color of the polish in the little glass bottle, it wasn't much of an improvement over Serene Tangerine. The idea of having certain parts of my body covered in it practically made me break out in hives.

But Lee-Lee had already sat me down at a cunning little wooden desk that looked like something Empress Josephine would have used to jot down her grocery lists. She had brushed some mystical clear liquid on my fingertips and was attacking my cuticles with the vengeance of a samurai.

"Angeline?" Diana shouted. "Bring us some lemonade, will you?"

By the time the sour-faced housekeeper had appeared with a tray of what I suspected was an equally sour beverage, it was too late for me to drink it. Lee-Lee had grabbed hold of my hands and was energetically kneading them, having already smothered them in a thick white citrus-scented lotion that smelled good enough to eat. Still, Angeline deposited a tall, icy glass next to me, not even bothering with a coaster.

"Don't worry; it's not made with sugar," Diana assured me from the couch. "Equal."

I glanced at it longingly, wondering if Angeline could be coerced into bringing me a straw.

"You must enjoy being a veterinarian," Diana said. "Working around animals all the time. Personally, I adore animals."

"It's pretty rewarding," I replied as Lee-Lee meticulously began painting my nails with a color that, unfortunately, did resemble the bright orange of a mango. An overly ripe mango, one that was just about ready for the mulch pile. "Of course, any career has its negative aspects. But overall, I'm glad I—"

"You work with horses, too, right?"

"That's right. In fact, that's how I met the MacKinnons. One of Andrew MacKinnon's horses, Braveheart, contracted tendonitis, and I was called in to treat him."

"So you're a polo fan?"

I thought we'd made a little leap in logic, but I was willing to go with the flow. "Not really. I mean, I'd never been to a polo match before yesterday."

"I noticed you were sitting with that reporter," Diana commented. "Are you two...friends?" She sounded as cool as the lemonade that was sitting next to me.

All of a sudden, I got it. I'd been set up. This little tête-à-tête that she'd orchestrated had nothing to do with the sorry state of my fingernails.

It was all about Eduardo—and providing Diana with an opportunity to give me the third degree about the investigation of his murder.

"If you ask me, that reporter doesn't really belong around here," she continued. Her tone had escalated to icy. "He's already written his story about Eduardo's murder. It made front-page news, so he got what he wanted out of it. I can't imagine why he's still hanging around here." Turning her entire body so that she faced me, she pointedly asked, "Do *you* know why?"

"I think he discovered what a fascinating game polo is." I was glad that at least some of the time, I was capable of thinking on my feet. "I suppose that once he got a taste of it, he was hooked."

"I see." Diana didn't look convinced. "And what about you?" Her questions were being thrown at me like darts.

"I love watching the horses as they play," I told her. At least that part was true. "And you know, Diana, you were absolutely right when you so astutely observed that I'm somebody who needs to have more fun. I think becoming a polo fan is a great place to start. You know, it's considered the game of kings."

Diana smiled blandly. "So I've heard. I wonder how the police are doing with their investigation. That Lieutenant Falcone person . . . is he any good?"

"I wouldn't know," I said, all innocence. Without pausing to take a breath, I added, "How close were you and Eduardo?"

She looked startled. "I barely knew him!" She gave me her answer a little too quickly—and a little too vehemently.

I remarked, "A man that handsome—and from what I hear, charming—seems like he'd be of interest to every woman who ever met him."

"Except those of us who happen to be happily married," she replied indignantly.

A loud clattering sound made everyone jump. Lee-Lee scrambled to retrieve the bottle of nail polish she'd just knocked over.

"So sorry!" she cried. I noticed that her cheeks had turned bright red, and that she kept her eyes down.

"But you came to his funeral," I persisted, unwilling to let Diana off the hook. Especially given Lee-Lee's reaction.

"That was business," she returned.

"How so?"

Panic flickered in her eyes. At least, if I was reading her correctly. "My husband. Harlan. He and Andrew... but none of this could possibly be of interest to you." Her voice had become slippery smooth, and the tension that had been building in her face vanished in an instant. "Lee-Lee, aren't you done yet? We don't want to keep poor Dr. Popper here forever."

Glancing down, I noticed that Lee-Lee had finished applying a thick coat of shiny orange to my fingertips. I held them up for Diana to see.

"What do you think?" I asked her. "The new me?"

"Definitely," she replied. "Lee-Lee, you're a genius."

Even though she'd eased back into her other persona, the one that was dripping with sweetness, I sensed that Diana was disappointed she hadn't been able to extract more information. Yet while I was pleased that I'd managed to dodge her probing questions, I was also disappointed that I hadn't learned much, either.

Then there was the fact that I was stuck with the ten ridiculous protrusions at the ends of my hands, as bright and shiny as orange M&M's.

Forrester Sloan, you owe me, I thought, seething. *Big-time.*

Still, chatting with Diana Chase did reinforce my suspicion that—in the words of the MacKinnons' housekeeper, Inez—Diana Chase was one of the ladies who had been "special friends" with Eduardo.

The question was, had things between them gone

wrong—perhaps even wrong enough for her to want him dead?

If Diana Chase's palatial home had been a petite piece of Provence, Vivian Johanssen's homestead was a tribute to Tuscany. The white stucco villa was only two stories high, but it sprawled across enough square feet to make the Medicis feel at home. The red terra-cotta roof was complemented by colorful hand-painted tiles that framed the front door, and elaborate wrought-iron gratings decorated the windows while increasing security. On a warm September day like this one, when the sun was shining brightly, I could almost hear the *paesani* crooning "O Sole Mio!"

While Diana and Vivian were neck and neck in the race for the most luxurious estate, Vivian definitely outshone her buddy in the animal-lover department. In addition to a large stable and several paddocks holding at least a dozen horses, I spotted three Shetland ponies, two angora goats, a llama, and a large yellow Lab sleeping on the driveway in a small patch of sunshine.

I braced myself for an encounter with another rude housekeeper. Instead, Vivian answered the door herself, dressed in crisp khaki capris and a white linen blouse. Despite her casual outfit, she was decked out in enough flashy jewelry for the Academy Awards.

"Dr. Popper! You're right on time!" she greeted me. "Come on in. Can I get you a cold drink?"

If nothing else, these women of leisure were certainly polite when it came to offering visitors refreshments. I figured social skills had been drummed into them at an early age.

"I'm fine, thank you. Actually, I'm running a little behind schedule, so I'd like to check out Liliana—" I stopped mid-sentence. I realized as I stood in the hallway that I was talking over a loud din. It sounded mechanical, like a microphone that had been left on. "What's that sound?" I couldn't resist asking.

Vivian cocked her head to one side, looking puzzled. Then, relieved, she said, "Oh, you must mean the doves."

The expression on my face must have been completely blank because Vivian gestured for me to follow her. We stepped through a short hallway, into the kitchen. Two of its windows opened onto a large sunroom that was easily twice the size of my cottage. Two of the sunroom's walls were made completely of glass, providing a calming view of the lush plantings that ran along the side of the house. But what was most interesting was that it was filled with doves.

There were dozens of them. Perhaps even hundreds. They gathered on the stone floor and perched in the trees stuck in large terra-cotta pots and positioned throughout the room. The cooing sound such a large number of birds made was as much a presence as the classical music that was piped through what I imagined was a state-of-the-art sound system.

"Goodness! You really are fond of animals," I commented.

Vivian beamed. "They're beautiful, aren't they? Of course, they can't stay here forever. Bill and I will have to have a separate building constructed. But for now, I enjoy having them here. I find them so calming."

"I noticed you have a few Shetland ponies, too," I commented. "Do you have children?"

She nodded. "They're away at school. Chandler is starting her sophomore year at Exeter, and Porter's a senior at Choate Rosemary Hall." Anxiously, she added, "You've heard of those two schools, haven't you?"

"Sure," I replied, struck by how much it appeared to matter to her.

"Diana has two sons." Vivian sniffed before adding, "They're both at *Andover*." She pronounced the word as if she were saying "Leavenworth" instead of naming one of the most prestigious prep schools in the country.

"Speaking of Diana," she continued, "did you stop at her house this morning?" From the strange tone of her voice, I had a feeling she was trying to sound casual, but that there was actually a lot more to her question than met the eye—or ear.

"Yes, I checked out Fleur. She was in fine shape."

"Diana?"

"Fleur." Even though I barely knew either of them, I had a nagging feeling that the two women's relationship was much more complicated than it appeared. "How long have you and Diana been friends?"

"Oh, forever. Like five years."

Very close to forever, I thought.

"She has a lovely home, doesn't she?" Viv asked. "It's almost as many square feet as mine. If you count the sunroom, of course. Which I do."

An awkward silence descended over us. I felt like a houseguest who wasn't holding up her end of the social pleasantries.

"Let me take a look at your cat," I said. "I'll need to bring her out to my van."

Once we were inside my clinic-on-wheels, I placed Liliana on the examining table. She was a gorgeous Himalayan, a lilac-cream lynx with luxurious white fur and dramatic lilac-toned points, meaning her face, ears, legs, and tail. She also had blue eyes that could melt an iceberg.

"Hey, Liliana. Aren't you a beauty?" I exclaimed, stroking her ears.

"She is, isn't she?" Vivian agreed, standing up a little straighter. "And rare, right?"

Her comment surprised me. "Actually, a lot of people

have come to appreciate how beautiful and intelligent Himmies are." Liliana, it turned out, had something she wanted to say. She meowed loudly, as if she were carrying on an intense conversation with me.

"They're also vocal," I added, laughing.

Vivian frowned. "You make it sound as if they're really ... you know, common."

"They've gotten to be increasingly popular," I commented, palpating Liliana and looking for irregularities with her internal organs. So far, so good. "The breed wasn't developed until the 1920's and '30's, when a Swedish geneticist and some people at Harvard both tried crossing a Siamese female and a black Persian male, which turned out to be critical in creating the unusual coloring. But you probably know all this already."

"Actually, I don't." For some reason Vivian actually seemed distressed. From what I could tell, her sulky mood began when I'd failed to exclaim over Liliana's uniqueness.

"Well, you've got yourself a beautiful cat," I assured her. "Himmies have some of the best qualities of both breeds: the dramatic markings of the Siamese and the big eyes, silky coat, and incredibly cute face of Persians. They're also incredibly playful and very connected to humans. It's no wonder so many people enjoy having them."

"But I don't know anyone else who has a Himalayan," Vivian persisted. "Don't you think they're more rare than—oh, let's say, a Chartreux, for example?"

Suddenly, I got it. Vivian's main concern wasn't having the sweetest or most playful cat on the block. Not even the most beautiful. Her goal was having a cat that would outshine Diana Chase's.

"You don't see a Chartreux every day of the week," I admitted. Maybe Vivian was interested in playing a game of one-upmanship that was based on animal ownership, but I had no desire to go there. "Now, has Liliana been experiencing any unusual symptoms? Vomiting, diarrhea?"

"No, nothing like that." Vivian hesitated. "So how did it go at Diana's this morning?"

"Fine." Chuckling self-consciously, I held out my hands. "I even got a manicure."

Vivian sniffed. "You know, she's *obsessed* with cosmetics."

"Really? I hadn't noticed."

"I'm not talking about wearing them. I'm talking about making money from them. She's got a real thing about nail polish."

I suddenly felt shallow for having allowed the vile stuff to be applied to my fingernails, however reluctantly. I was glad Liliana's fur was long enough to help conceal the garish orange dots that were now part of my body.

"For as long as I've known her," Vivian continued, "she's been saying she wanted to be the Gloria Vanderbilt of nails."

I blinked. "Sorry?"

"I guess you're too young to remember Gloria Vanderbilt. She was already one of the wealthiest women in the world, but in the late 1970's, she started designing jeans—or at least putting her name on them. At first, everyone thought she was nuts. At least *we* did. I mean, who'd ever heard of a socialite—a ridiculously rich one, no less—putting her name on women's behinds?

"But she proved all of us wrong. Instead of being ridiculed, she won tremendous respect. Those stupid jeans made her somebody really special, not because of who she was and what her last name was, but because of what she proved she was capable of doing.

"Gloria Vanderbilt is Diana's idol. Only she always talks about building a nail polish empire, as bizarre as *that* sounds." She paused. "At least, she used to. For the past few months—a year, maybe—Diana hasn't said a word about her dream."

"Do you think she gave up the idea of ever fulfilling it? Or is it possible she actually went ahead with her plan, but didn't want anyone to know?"

Vivian sat up a little straighter. "I can assure you that if Diana was going to jump feet first into something like that, I'd be the first to know. I mean, we *are* best friends."

"Of course," I said. Just like Caesar and Brutus.

"Besides, as much as I adore Diana, even I have to admit that she'd probably never have the guts. Her husband, Harlan, is one of the wealthiest men around, but he's also one of the biggest skinflints. He keeps her on a pretty short leash, money-wise. He's one of those guys who'll take six people out to one of the most expensive restaurants in the world, then spend ten minutes arguing with the waiter because the check is a dollar more than it's supposed to be. I mean, my Bill's not perfect, but at least he's not a cheapskate!"

"I see," I replied noncommittally.

What I saw most clearly, in fact, was that life in Old Brookbury wasn't exactly the way it appeared to be on the surface. Penny-pinching multimillionaire husbands, philandering polo players, wandering wives, daughters that ranged from ornery to oversexed...Even though I was very much an outsider, getting just a glimpse of what went on inside, I could see that day-to-day life here had as many layers as a well-written soap opera.

As I made my way out of Vivian's house, I turned a corner and suddenly found myself face-to-face with a man I didn't recognize. At least, not at first—maybe because practically bumping into him caught me completely off guard. After a few seconds, I realized that I'd seen him before, and that he was Vivian's husband, Bill. I also noticed for the first time that he bore an uncanny resemblance to a large hog, except for the fact that hogs are generally better looking. In fact, I've always kind of liked hogs. Unfortunately, Bill Johannsen had a body that was just as sturdy as one of his porcine counterparts, and it happened to be blocking the door.

"Excuse me," I said, smiling. "I'm just letting myself out."

"Not so fast." He stepped closer, putting his face right up against mine. "Exactly what are you up to?" he hissed.

I blinked. "What do you mean?"

"I overheard you talking to my wife. You were asking an awful lot of questions."

"In the veterinary profession, our patients can't tell us what's bothering them or anything about their medical history. So whenever I treat an animal, especially one that's a new patient, I find that the best way to—"

"Don't play innocent with me. You know damned well that's not what I'm talking about." Eyeing me warily, he added, "I've noticed that you've become quite a presence around Old Brookbury all of a sudden. You— and that nosy reporter. Everybody saw the two of you, sitting with your heads together at the polo game. You think we don't know what you're up to?"

"He happens to be covering the story of Eduardo Garcia's murder." I could hardly believe I was defending Forrester Sloan.

"Fair enough. Then he has an excuse. Which brings us back to you."

I stood up straighter, narrowing my eyes and staring right back at him. "Not that it's any of your business, but I find it extremely disturbing that someone's been murdered. Especially someone as well-loved as Eduardo. If there's anything I can do to help bring his killer to justice, I'm not about to let anyone or anything get in my way." Just for the hell of it, I added, "And that includes anonymous notes."

A look of confusion crossed his face. Either he was an excellent actor or he had absolutely no idea what I was talking about.

"Look," he said impatiently, "I suggest you stick to veterinary medicine and keep your nose out of matters than don't concern you."

"Is that a threat?"

"It's a piece of good, solid advice. People who go snooping around places they don't belong may find out things they'd be better off not knowing."

He turned and strode off.

That certainly sounded like a threat, I thought, rage surging in my chest. But instead of scaring me away, it further convinced me that Eduardo Garcia had been embroiled in something unsavory. Perhaps even something unsavory enough to get him killed.

Figuring out what that was was going to be the hard part. Especially since the more time I spent with the people of privilege who made up his circle, the more impenetrable that circle seemed.

Chapter 9

"Show me your horse and I will tell you who you are."

—Old English Saying

A s I tromped toward Andrew MacKinnon's stable to do follow-ups on Braveheart and Molly Wednesday morning, I kept glancing from side to side. While I'd truly enjoyed working with the animals who lived in Old Brookbury, I'd found the people they lived with to be some of the most complicated humans I'd ever encountered in my veterinary career. I hoped I'd come early enough to avoid any social interaction.

I should have known better. As soon as I stepped inside the cool, dark stable, I was hit with the unmistakable smell of stale cigarette smoke.

"Hello, Johnny Ray," I said, even before I'd spotted him.

He rounded the corner, wearing a smirk that by now was as familiar to me as his white T-shirt and jeans.

"Well, well. If it isn't Dr. Popper," he returned.

I decided to ignore his ability to make even a short

statement like that one sound contemptuous. "So how's Molly making out?" I asked.

"She finally passed some manure," he informed me, warming up a little. "It's kinda hard. But I can see some of the oil coming through."

"Great. So we're out of the woods. How about Braveheart?"

"He's doin' good, too."

"I'll take a look."

He stood in the entrances to the horses' stalls as I checked them, first Molly and then Braveheart, studying every move I made. It was a bit unnerving. In fact, I felt like I was back in veterinary school. Still, my first concern was the horses. Even greater than my annoyance over Johnny Ray's obnoxious behavior was my relief that his assessment had been correct. Both the gelding and the mare were doing fine.

"Let's give Braveheart a few more days just to be safe. I want to be sure that tendon has completely healed. I'll check him again this weekend to see if he's well enough to play in Sunday's game."

"You should probably stop in at the house on your way out and tell Mr. Mac," Johnny Ray grumbled. "But I got to get goin'. Can't stand around here all day."

"Nice to see you again," I couldn't resist saying to his back as he swaggered off.

A minute or two later, I was about to head out of the stable when I heard a rustling sound in the tack room. I stepped inside the cool, dark space, inhaling the rich scent of leather. "Johnny Ray? Is that you?"

Out in the stalls, a horse neighed. The tack room was empty. But I got the distinct feeling that someone had come in behind me. I whirled and found Pancho Escobar blocking the doorway.

"Hello," I said. "I didn't realize you were here."

Pancho just stared at me, his dark eyes burning with a strange intensity.

"Uh, that was a great game Sunday," I went on, anxious to break the uncomfortable silence. "How long have you been playing on Andrew MacKinnon's team?"

He hesitated. "Four years," he finally replied.

"I see." My heart began to pound as I debated whether to push things a little further. Even before I'd decided, the words burst out of my mouth: "So you must have known Eduardo Garcia for quite a long time."

His eyes narrowed. "Yes."

"In that case, maybe you could help me out with something." Speaking a little too quickly, I continued, "Everyone keeps talking about what a great guy Eduardo was. He's practically taken on mythical proportions. But I find it hard to believe he was as flawless as people are making him out to be."

" 'Flawless?' " Pancho repeated, looking confused.

"Perfect. Without any faults."

"Hah!" Pancho had finally let his guard down. In fact, his comment reeked with insincerity.

"You make it sound as if there was another side to him," I observed, trying to sound casual.

His mouth stretched into a sneer. "Oh, yes. Two years ago, thees 'other side' of Eduardo caused me to lose an entire season." He stopped himself. "But ees not good to speak ill of the dead."

"It sounds to me as if you're simply telling me what happened," I said. "Facts are facts. Especially if he broke the rules. Is that what Eduardo did?"

Pancho hesitated. "He cheated," he finally replied with a shrug. "Ees as simple as that."

"Really!" My astonishment was sincere. "But he didn't get caught?"

"Not the gr-r-reat Eduar-r-rdo Garcia!" he sneered.

He glanced around before continuing, as if wanting to make sure we were alone. "You see, he and I were not on the same team at that time. Like any sport—baseball, basketball, whatever sports in which the stakes are high—there is much trading of players, much buying and selling of talent. Eduardo was playing for Andrew MacKinnon, as he always has. But I was playing on another team, Rosewood. During one game early in the season, I was right behind Eduardo on the field, trying to get the ball away from him. And then, with no warning, he violated one of the most basic rules of polo."

"Which rule?" I prompted.

"If you miss the ball, never stop short. If you do, the horses behind you will run right into you." His expression darkened. "And that is exactly what he did. He missed the ball and lost control of it. And then he stopped. My horse collided with his, and I fell off. I broke my leg and was unable to play for the rest of the season.

"I have always known he did it on purpose," Pancho went on. "There was a special competitiveness between us from the start, one that went far beyond a normal desire to be the best. He didn't like me, and there ees no doubt in my mind that he was prepared to do whatever it took to get me out of the game. And that is exactly what he did.

"Of course, it was impossible to prove that what he did was intentional. Eduardo claimed his horse had stumbled. But I knew the truth. I was close enough to see him pull on the reins. And if there had been any doubt in my mind, I could see from the look in his eyes as they carried me off the field on a stretcher—a look of triumph—that he knew exactly what he had done."

"Did you tell anyone?" I asked.

He laughed coldly. "I tried, but of course no one would listen. No one could believe that Eduardo Garcia was capable of such behavior. But the cost to me, both financially and in terms of my ability to play, was tremendous. So my heart was not broken when soon afterward, I heard rumors about Eduardo being in serious financial difficulty."

"I haven't heard any of those rumors," I lied, hoping he'd fill me in on the details.

"Ah. Then you are one of the few. Eduardo Garcia, the patron saint of polo, at least in Old Brookbury, was badly in debt. You see, he had this nasty habit of spending much more than he made. Even though he was paid handsomely, he could not resist indulging in baubles for his lady friends and toys for himself. He also insisted upon having the finest polo ponies in the world. Nothing but the best would do for our friend Eduardo!"

"I see."

And I *did* see. Pancho was right; with the exception of Andrew MacKinnon's immediate family, just about everyone who had known the dashing young polo player *did* talk about him as if he was in the running for sainthood. Yet no one could possibly be that pure, especially someone who was plucked out of a poverty-stricken village and thrown in with some of the wealthiest people in the world—including some of the most beautiful and desirable women imaginable.

But Eduardo wasn't the only person surrounded by questions. Pancho raised a few of his own. His appearance in the barn—unannounced and unexpected—troubled me. Did he make a habit of hanging around in the shadows, waiting for the opportunity to spread the word about the *real* Eduardo Garcia?

Or had he been watching me? Was it possible that he'd noticed I'd been asking a lot of questions—and that he wanted to make sure I got the right answers?

• • •

I was still ruminating over our odd conversation as I made my way toward the main house. When Luisa answered the door, it took me a second or two to remember what I'd come for. Fortunately, the MacKinnons' motherly housekeeper helped me out.

"I am so sorry, Dr. Popper," she said. "Meester Mac ees not here. The car took him to the city—"

"Luisa, who is it?" Peyton sashayed down the dramatic circular staircase that dominated the front hallway, the skinny straps of her sheer sundress slipping down her shoulders. "Oh, it's you. The animal doctor."

Somehow, she managed to make my chosen career sound extremely unflattering.

"Hello, Peyton," I said evenly. "Nice to see you again."

"Eef you will excuse me," Luisa said, bowing her head and dropping her shoulders. "I have work in the kitchen."

"Of course, Luisa." Somehow, I got the feeling Luisa didn't like her employer's older daughter very much. I also got the feeling she was completely justified.

With the housekeeper gone, Peyton focused her attention on me. "Your timing is excellent. The rest of my luggage just arrived from Europe. Would you be a dear and help me carry these suitcases into my bedroom? You must be as strong as a bull, working around horses and all that. The stupid FedEx people just left them at the front door. You'd think they'd have the decency to deliver them to the room they're headed for, wouldn't you?"

If not wash and press everything inside, I thought, decrying the low standards we'd all settled for.

However, the chance to do a little snooping was irresistible.

"Sure," I told her. "I'd be happy to help."

Without so much as a thank-you, Peyton picked up the smallest piece of luggage—pretty much a cell phone carrier with a handle—and headed back upstairs, leaving the two humongous valises for me. I gritted my teeth, telling myself that the possibility of learning something interesting about Eduardo was worth a few pulled muscles.

I followed her up the stairs and down a long hallway, lugging the two suitcases. Finally, we reached a large bedroom that was decorated in soft shades of peach and mint green. French doors that led out onto a balcony had been left open, sending the sheer white curtains that covered them billowing in the breeze.

"Put them down anywhere," Peyton instructed me.

I was about to ask her if I should expect a bigger tip than the one she'd given the taxi driver when she let out a long, loud sigh.

"I absolutely *despise* unpacking," she grumbled, flicking a strand of hair over her shoulder. "I'd have Inez do it, but she always puts things in the wrong place. I swear, I don't know *why* Daddy keeps her around."

"She seemed really upset when she learned Eduardo was dead," I interjected. I held my breath, hoping Peyton wouldn't notice how quickly I'd changed the subject from the cruel hand fate had dealt her—that is, having to unpack all by herself after her difficult summer of clubbing and sunbathing all over Europe—to the dead polo player.

"You know, I'm not stupid," Peyton said calmly. "I know exactly what you're doing." In response to my blank look, she added, "You're trying to figure out who killed Eduardo."

"Well, no, I was just—"

"I'm not judging you," she insisted. "It's a natural thing to wonder. Except you don't have to work at it this hard. All you have to do is ask me."

"Ask . . . *you*?"

"Right. Ask me who killed Eduardo." She shrugged. "I'm not going to lie."

"Okay, then. Who killed him?"

She frowned, then placed her hands on her nearly nonexistent hips and glanced around the room. "Where are my cigarettes? I can't imagine..." She spotted her pocketbook lying on the bed, grabbed it, and spilled the contents out. In addition to the Chanel wallet, Tiffany keychain, Gucci credit card holder, MAC lipstick, Mont Blanc pen, and all the other items that came pouring out, was a packet of Silk Cuts. British, I thought, pleased that I'd learned something useful from reading *Bridget Jones's Diary*. She wasted no time lighting up with—what else?—a gold Cartier lighter, then turned her attention back to me.

"My father."

I didn't even try to hide my astonishment.

"It was almost inevitable," she went on, pausing to take a puff. "You see, he's very possessive."

"Possessive of what?" I asked.

"Of me." Her matter-of-fact tone was chilling. "He knew Eduardo and I were lovers. Even more importantly, that we were madly, passionately in love. And Daddy had no intention of ever letting us do anything as extreme as get married."

I studied her, thinking that I had yet to see any indication that Peyton had had even fond feelings for Eduardo, much less that she'd been "madly, passionately in love" with him. In fact, it was difficult to imagine someone so wrapped up in herself feeling that way about anyone besides the reflection she saw in the mirror.

"My impression is that your father adored Eduardo," I told her.

"Oh, he did. At least, on the polo field. Eduardo was a great player, but he was still an Argie. Believe me, my father wasn't about to let his precious daughter marry one of *them*.

"You see, my father isn't quite what he seems," Peyton went on. "The Argies are good enough to ride his horses and share his table and make him look good on the polo field. But letting one of them marry his daughter—and gain serious access to his money—well, that's something else entirely."

She paused, smoking her cigarette and thinking. "Of course," she finally said, "it could have been me who murdered Eduardo, too."

"*You?*" Her remark caught me entirely off guard. "Why would you have done something like that?"

She shrugged. "Jealousy, most likely. I know perfectly well that Eduardo had other lovers. That vile Chase woman, for example, who's had so much fat pumped out and so much collagen and Botox and Lord knows what else pumped *in* that it's amazing she doesn't float into the air like a badly dressed helium balloon." She took a few more puffs, then mused, "I have to change. What should I put on?"

She strolled over to her closet and studied a row of white blouses. From where I stood, they all looked pretty much the same. Finally, she pulled out one that was hanging neatly on a padded satin hanger. "There *is* one small problem with that theory, of course. I have an airtight alibi. I was out of the country until Sunday, five days after he died. Even *I'm* not clever enough to murder someone from three thousand miles away. Which, of course, brings us back to Daddy." She focused on the blouse, sticking out her lower lip in her usual childish pout. "For heaven's sake, will you *look* at what Inez did to this blouse? You'd think someone who claims to be such a skilled housekeeper could manage to get a simple caviar stain out of linen, wouldn't you? Honestly, if this happens one more time...Inez? Inez, where are you?"

She stalked off, her high heels clicking angrily against the wooden floor in the hallway as she went to chastise her servant. It was a very Marie Antoinette moment. *Maybe there really* is *something to this reincarnation business,* I thought.

I was about to leave her bedroom when I noticed that all the items from her pocketbook were still lying in a heap on the bed. One in particular caught my eye. An oversized envelope, the kind the airlines give out with a boarding pass. I glanced at the doorway. There was no one in sight. I could hear Peyton downstairs, berating poor Inez, shrilly lecturing her on the importance of maintaining high standards in the workplace—a topic on which she obviously considered herself an expert.

I stepped over to the bed, trying to get a better look at the boarding pass. The printing was facedown. Glancing around one more time to make sure I was alone, I picked it up. Paris to New York on Air France, just as I'd expected. This was the ticket Peyton had used to come back to the United States.

But my stomach lurched when I focused on the date: September 2, five days *before* Eduardo's death.

She *lied,* I thought, my head spinning as I maneuvered the curves of Turkey Hollow Road and headed back to what I'd come to think of as my real life. Not that it was the least bit difficult to believe that someone who was that spoiled—and that full of herself—was capable of dishonesty. But she'd gone out of her way to tell me her alibi, then either carelessly or craftily laid out the evidence that it was completely invalid.

Is Peyton MacKinnon so out of touch with reality that she thinks she's above suspicion—and perhaps even above the law? I wondered. Or is she playing some other game—a game that for some reason has something to do with me?

Thanks to the full day of appointments I had scheduled, I quickly forgot all about Peyton and Eduardo. In fact, it wasn't until I got home that evening that I remembered that I had something much more personal than the polo player's murder to deal with.

The sight of Nick's black Maxima, parked in what I considered the van's unofficial parking space, reminded me.

Of course. Today was the day Nick had moved in.

Temporarily, I reminded myself, taking a few deep breaths before opening the front door.

The dogs were instantly all over me, ecstatic that the leader of their pack was home. Prometheus also squawked his hello. And there was a new addition to the household: Leilani, the Jackson's chameleon Nick and I had brought home from Hawaii, blinking at me from her glass tank on the coffee table.

But Nick was nowhere in sight. And here I'd expected to find him relaxing in the comfortable upholstered chair in a velvet smoking jacket, reading the paper and sipping brandy from a snifter.

"Nick?" I called. "I'm, uh, home."

He poked his head out of the kitchen, looking unusually frazzled. "I'm so glad you're here! The leader of my study group called an emergency meeting. And it's my turn to host. Don't we own an ice bucket?"

I let his use of the word "we" breeze by me. "They're meeting *here*?" I demanded. "But this place is so tiny! Can't they meet at your place?"

"It's too chaotic, Jess. I stopped in before to pick up some stuff I forgot to bring over this morning. There are drop cloths all over the furniture, the entire place smells so strongly of paint that I practically gagged..."

"Exactly how many people are in this study group?" I asked.

"Just four, besides me."

"All right," I agreed. The last thing I wanted was to be a bad sport. Even if I suspected that having that many people inside my tiny cottage at one time violated the fire code.

"Great," Nick said, sounding relieved. "Jess, you're the best. No wonder I'm so crazy about you." He hesitated. "Would it be pushing my luck to ask you to hold down the fort while I take a quick shower? The members of the group should be here in a couple of minutes. If you'd just let everybody in—"

"Of course. In fact, I'd be happy to."

"And I stopped at the supermarket and picked up some stuff for everybody to eat. But I didn't have time to do the Martha Stewart thing and make it look all nice and presentable...."

"I'll take care of that, too," I assured him. I just hoped he didn't have any illusions about me coming even *close* to Martha's standards.

As I pulled bottles of soda and wine out of the refrigerator, I actually found myself looking forward to the evening ahead. Meeting some of Nick's fellow law school students will be fun, I thought. I pictured all of us relaxing together after the group's intense night of debating the fascinating intricacies of the law, sipping wine and intelligently discussing world events. In fact, this whole law school thing was starting to sound better and better. Nick's involvement in a brand-new sphere was bound to open up an entire world of clever people with a burning commitment to maintaining justice in an increasingly chaotic and confusing world.

I was even inspired enough to hunt down six matching glasses. Then I dumped a box of crackers into a crystal bowl that had somehow found itself in my possession, first wiping it out to remove the dust. Next I set out some cheese—a slab of Jarlsberg and a wheel of Brie—on a wooden cutting board. All right, so I wasn't exactly ready for my own televison show. But it would do.

When the doorbell rang, I almost wished I owned a long velvet skirt or some other garment that was the female equivalent of a smoking jacket. I scooped up Max before answering, figuring a cute, fluffy white dog was a nice touch. After all, I wanted to convey the image of a sophisticated woman who felt at home among both intelligent humans and our animal friends.

By that point, I was expecting to find Cary Grant and Diane Sawyer standing on my doorstep. My enthusiasm was dampened by a quick dose of reality.

"Am I in the right place?" A tall, scrawny guy—at least six foot four and maybe one hundred fifty pounds—leaned forward and peered at me through the thick lenses in his tortoiseshell eyeglasses. The heavy frames were completely out of proportion, given his gaunt face and small, beady eyes. He was dressed in jeans that looked as if they'd been dry-cleaned. His light blue shirt was obviously brand-new, since the creases that demonstrated precisely how it had been folded in the package created a grid across his sunken chest. I just hoped he'd remembered to take the pins out.

But it was the bow tie that really got me. He didn't come close to carrying it off the way Winston Farnsworth did.

"Are you looking for the study group?" I asked politely. "Nick Burby?"

"That's right. We're looking for Nick." A short woman who bordered on rotund stepped out from behind him. She was dressed in a batiked skirt that reached almost to her Chinese canvas shoes. A shawl made of coarse, undyed fabric was wrapped tightly around her shoulders. Even so, I could see she'd draped half a dozen strands of colorful beads around her neck. Her long red hair, shooting out from her head like an aura, was just as coarse. My first impression of her face was that she reminded me of a pug. But while a flat, squishy nose and small dark eyes looked unbelievably cute on a canine, on her those features didn't have quite the same effect. "Is Nick here?"

I forced myself to smile. "You've come to the right place."

"Good," the geeky guy said, pouting. "I was sure we were lost."

The woman looked me up and down critically. Narrowing her eyes suspiciously, she demanded, "Who are you?"

"Jessica Popper. Nick's girlfriend."

"Nick didn't say anything about a girlfriend."

"He told us we were meeting at his friend's house," the man insisted.

"Yes, but he didn't say it was a girlfriend's house," the woman hissed back.

"I'm sorry, I didn't get your names," I said as politely as I could through gritted teeth.

"I'm Wendy Harnik. And this is Jerome Sidlanski."

And here I'd been so sure they were going to introduce themselves as Cary and Diane.

As I was ushering them inside, I saw that another member of Nick's study group had arrived. A remarkably thin woman who'd pulled her shiny black BMW up onto the grass, taking out a few of Betty's flower beds in the process, slammed the car door. Then she headed toward the cottage, teetering on a pair of high heels that didn't quite mesh with the badly paved piece of road that served as my driveway. She wore a black pantsuit and several pieces of large jewelry and was clasping a cell phone tightly against her ear.

"I don't give a *damn* what they told you," she shrieked into the phone. "A deal is a deal. You tell those bastards—look, I can't talk now. I'll have to get back to you on this." Her thickly lipsticked mouth was frowning as she slammed her cell phone closed, then stuck it into the tremendous leather purse that dangled from her shoulder. She strode toward me, arranging her mouth into a smile when she realized someone was watching.

"Nick Burby's place?" she asked.

I nodded.

"And you are—?"

"Nick's girlfriend. Jessica Popper."

"Oh, that's right. The vet. He told us all about you." She sighed tiredly, as if she'd already heard quite enough. "So can we call you Jessica? Or are we supposed to call you Dr. Pepper?"

I ignored the reference to soft drinks, accidental or otherwise. "Jessie is fine. And what should I call you?" I'd already come up with a few ideas of my own.

"Stephanie Walcott. God, is there someplace I can get a glass of wine around here? Oh, damn!" The last comment was in response to her cell phone, which had begun to bleat out an annoying melody. Rolling her eyes, she jammed her hand deep into the mailbag in search of it, muttering to herself when it failed to materialize.

I was actually glad when the fourth and final member of Nick's study group came up behind her and I had an excuse to turn my focus elsewhere.

"I got so *lost!*" whined the pudgy young man with a remarkably pasty complexion. "Nobody told me you couldn't see the house from the road! Why didn't anybody say anything? I'm not familiar with this area at all. How were we supposed to *find* this place?"

"Well, you're here now!" I told him brightly. "I'm Jessie, Nick's girlfriend."

"Ollie Sturges. Actually, Oliver J. Sturges the third.

Oh, my God. That's not a *cat*, is it? Nick didn't say anything about any cats. I'm *so* allergic. You've got to put that animal outside. Oh, my God, did I bring my *inhaler*?"

By this point, Nick had emerged from the bedroom, his skin still flushed from his shower. Buttoning the cuff of his shirt, he said, "Hey, everybody. Glad you found us."

I picked up Cat and shut her inside the bedroom, then grabbed the dogs' leashes.

"You're not leaving, are you?" He frowned, pushing the damp strand of dark brown hair out of his eyes. "I don't want you to feel you have to leave your own house."

"I don't mind." In fact, I was tempted to tell him I could hardly wait to get out of there. "Come on, Max. Let's go, Lou."

As I hurried out the door with my two canine pals, I could hear Ollie Sturges III whining, "This Brie is *cold*! It's *supposed* to be served at room temperature!"

But before anyone could respond, he was cut off by the singsong chirping of Stephanie's cell phone.

I sat in my VW for a few minutes, thinking. My dogs couldn't understand what we were waiting for. Max kept jumping up on the window, and Lou wouldn't take his nose away from the glass—their way of saying, "Are we there yet?" Even their extraordinary cuteness wasn't enough to pull me out of my dark mood. I was too busy feeling rejected by Nick—or at least left out in the cold by his decision to reinvent his life and himself.

I whipped out my own cell phone and dialed.

"Hey, Forrester. How's it going?"

"Hey, Popper," he replied breezily. "What's up?"

"I have a new theory," I told him. "What do you think about Peyton being the murderer?"

"MacKinnon's older daughter, right?"

"Yup. She told me she and Eduardo were lovers. And she claimed she had an alibi, but—"

"Sounds like you've come up with some great stuff," he interrupted. "But I'm about to head into a town board meeting I'm covering. Some big blowup over a proposed zoning change. Can I catch up with you later?"

I've got bigger plans for "later," I thought—*and they revolve around Nick, not playing "Clue."* "How about tomorrow evening?"

"Perfect. Dinner, okay? We'll talk." And he was gone.

It seemed like the ideal occasion to take Max and Lou to the beach for a run on the sand. Or maybe I was the one who needed to get away from it all. Long Island may be congested, but it has what I suspect are the most spectacular beaches in the world. There are rolling blue-green waves on the South Shore and calm waters guaranteed to soothe the soul on the North Shore. Both are lined with velvety white sand as far as the eye can see. Add a few seagulls to keep things interesting by driving my canines wild and you've got yourself a relaxing interlude with Mother Nature.

Of course, I couldn't help bringing at least some of my baggage with me. Even as Lou played tag with the gulls and Max cavorted in the surf, I kept thinking about Eduardo. I pulled off my shoes and trudged through the waves, watching the water swirl around my ankles. I had to agree with Forrester. Any one of the people who'd known him could have killed him. Peyton MacKinnon, the jealous lover who had lied about having an alibi. Diana Chase, the *other* jealous lover—at least, the only other one I knew about for sure. There was also Vivian Johannsen, who could have been a jealous lover—or not. And Callie, who claimed to hate him but had yet to explain why.

And those were just the women in his life. Then there was Pancho Escobar, who'd admitted to me that having Eduardo dead wasn't necessarily a bad thing. Scott Mooney, who seemed too good to be true. Andrew MacKinnon, who said himself he'd thought of Eduardo as a son but whose daughter claimed he couldn't accept adding an Argentine to the MacKinnon family tree.

Winston Farnsworth? Possibly, although I had yet to determine a motive. There was just something about him I didn't trust. The same went for Jillian. For all I knew, she'd poisoned him in a drunken rage and didn't even remember it. Johnny Ray was someone else who made me uncomfortable—and he certainly didn't have much good to say about the dashing young polo star.

My head was spinning so hard from running down the list of murder suspects that I didn't notice that the sun was about to go down. When I finally did, I let out a sigh. The sky was streaked with pink and purple, creating one of those truly breathtaking moments that gets stored away in your memory forever.

I decided to think about something more comforting than Eduardo Garcia's murder. Something like...Nick.

I waited for a feeling of peace to come over me. Instead, thinking about Nick didn't turn out to be much better than thinking about Eduardo.

Why did things suddenly seem so unsettled with him? I wondered, kicking at the surf and noticing for the first time how cold my feet were getting. Here we were supposed to be working on our relationship, and here *he* was pursuing an exciting new course in his life...yet it seemed as if we kept getting our wires crossed. Now, we were under the same roof—if only for a few days. And even now our schedules didn't mesh. How were we supposed to walk hand in hand into the sunset when I seemed to be the only one who managed to pencil in any beach time?

I gathered up my companions and headed home. As I pulled into the driveway, I saw that Nick's Maxima was still parked in the same spot. Fortunately, by this point, it was the only vehicle that remained, aside from my van. From inside the cottage, I could hear Robert Plant of Led Zeppelin howling about his plans to give me his love.

I found Nick in the kitchen. Not surprisingly, he hadn't heard me come in. He was too busy dancing to the song's throbbing beat while drying my wine glasses. If there was any food left over from his study group's little get-together, it was packed away. In fact, both the kitchen and the living room looked neater than I could remember them looking in months.

"Hey, you're back!" He stopped dancing long enough to give me a welcome-home kiss. "Everybody told me to thank you for letting us use your place."

I had my doubts about that. "How did it go?" I asked.

"Great. I learned a lot."

"Good." I wandered back into the living room and dropped into the overstuffed chair that, for once, was free of four-legged creatures. "Well, I'm bushed. I think I'll turn in."

Nick came out of the kitchen, looking astonished. "But it's so early!"

I raised my eyebrows. "Isn't this what's commonly known as a school night?"

"I guess. But this is a special night."

I thought for a few seconds, wondering what I was missing. "And why is that?"

He looked surprised that I didn't know. "It's our first night as roommates."

Temporary roommates, I thought. But I kept the correction to myself.

"Right. Uh, exactly how long did you say it's going to take the painters to finish your apartment?"

"Just a couple of days. I can probably go back this weekend." He dropped onto the arm of the chair and put his arm around me. "That is, if you can bear to let me go."

Before I had a chance to respond, he exclaimed, "Oh, man, 'Stairway to Heaven'!" He turned up the volume on the CD player so loud that even Prometheus protested.

"How about 'Stairway to Sleep'?" I said, leaping off the chair. "I've had a long day, and I'm going to bed. Hopefully, *without* Robert Plant."

I flounced off, not exactly slamming the bedroom door after me but not quite closing it quietly, either. I figured that I was entitled. After all, this was *my* house.

Chapter 10

"No ride is ever the last one. No horse is ever the last one you will have. Somehow there will always be other horses, other places to ride them."
—Monica Dickens

As I drove to Niamogue to meet Forrester for dinner the following evening, I was annoyed to discover that a couple of butterflies were doing the Virginia reel in my stomach.

Cut it out, I scolded myself. *It's not as if this is a date. It's a business meeting, for heaven's sake!*

Still, there was something about sneaking out to meet the reporter for dinner without bothering to mention my plans to Nick that made me feel guilty. Even though Forrester Sloan *was* one of the most arrogant, self-centered people I'd ever met.

The fact that we'd decided to meet at Gianelli's, a small neighborhood restaurant tucked away on a quiet street, didn't help. I knew perfectly well that my motive in choosing it had been to avoid being spotted by anyone who was associated with Eduardo Garcia's murder—especially the person whose hobby was playing cutouts with magazine letters. Still, setting up clandestine meetings like this made me feel like the polo shirts I wore as part of my work outfit should be embroidered with a scarlet "A" instead of "Jessica Popper, D.V.M."

"You made it," Forrester greeted me as I sat down opposite him. It had taken me a minute or two to spot him, hidden away in a back corner of the dark restaurant. Between the compact room's wood paneling, its tiny windows, and its high-backed booths, it was easy to lose someone in the shadows.

"You sound surprised," I replied.

He shrugged. "I didn't know how tight a leash that boyfriend of yours keeps you on."

My blood began to boil as if I'd just sat down on a stove, rather than a red leatherette banquette. "Do you go out of your way to sound objectionable, or is it something that just comes to you naturally?"

He laughed. "It's fun to tease you, that's all. It's so easy to get a rise out of you."

"I'm glad you find me entertaining," I shot back.

" 'Entertaining?' " The look in his eyes softened. "That's the least of it."

"I think we'd better order," I said pointedly, grabbing one of the menus the waitress had just set down on our table. "I'm starving."

He drew in his breath, then hesitated. I got the impression he'd stopped himself from saying something he wasn't sure he should say. Much to my relief, he commented, "I understand the pesto here is terrific."

After we'd ordered, I sat back in my seat with my arms folded primly across my chest. "I've been learning some interesting things about the life and times of Eduardo Garcia," I told him.

"Do tell." He leaned forward.

"Even though Andrew MacKinnon thought of him as a son, not to mention someone who could do no wrong, it turns out that not everybody saw Eduardo that way. Even MacKinnon's other polo player, Scott Mooney, alluded to the 'rumors' that surrounded him. And Scott's one of those blond surfer types who sees life as one long day at the beach, someone you'd expect to be reluctant to breathe a bad word about anybody. According to Scott, Eduardo was a real ladies' man. And he wasn't only popular in bed; he was also the confidante of both his lovers *and* their husbands."

"Sounds like quite an accomplishment," Forrester mused, "managing to win the trust of the men whose wives he was sleeping with."

"Old Eduardo seems to have been a pretty accomplished player—and I'm not just talking about polo." I paused, thinking back. "Scott also mentioned that he'd gotten into some financial trouble—and that he had to do some 'things' to get himself out of it."

Forrester looked as interested as Max does whenever I open the refrigerator. "What kind of 'things'?"

"He didn't specify—and I couldn't find a way to make him. But he did say he didn't believe all the rumors that had sprung up around Eduardo." I sighed. "Unfortunately, no one's bothered to whisper any of them to me."

"Too bad. Still, it sounds pretty likely that our murder victim was involved in some games that had nothing to do with polo," Forrester observed.

"So it seems. And according to some other sources, Eduardo may have had a bit of an unethical streak."

"Meaning...?"

"Meaning Pancho Escobar, who plays for MacKinnon's team now but played for someone else a couple of years ago, claims Eduardo cheated during one of the games. But Eduardo was never blamed—largely because of his reputation as a golden boy. But it cost

Pancho a season of playing, and all the money that goes with it."

"It also gave Pancho a reason to be pretty damned angry with Eduardo," Forrester noted. "Maybe even angry enough to kill him."

"Let's get back to the women in Eduardo's life," I suggested. "I believe he was having an affair with Diana Chase."

"The tall, willowy blonde? The gorgeous one?"

I experienced something that felt an awful lot like a twinge of jealousy. I chalked it up to low blood sugar.

"I guess you could describe her that way." I grabbed a roll, thinking that tall and willowy simply weren't in the cards for me. "Anyway, I spoke to the woman who claims to be her best friend but who reminds me of the evil cheerleader in one of those teen flicks. She's a tad—shall we say, competitive. She gave me the impression that Diana tried to start her own business, but lost a ton of money. If that actually happened, Diana might have been afraid that her husband would find out."

Forrester shook his head. "You lost me. In terms of the connection to Eduardo, I mean."

"Eduardo might have been one of the few people who knew about her business failure. Maybe even the only one. It's possible he threatened to tell her husband. Maybe he was even blackmailing her."

"And therefore giving her a very strong motive for bumping him off."

"Exactly."

"Of course," Forrester went on, "we're ignoring half the motive-plus-opportunity equation. You seem to be finding plenty of motives. But adding slow-acting poison to somebody's hors d'oeuvres isn't necessarily easy."

"If only we could reconstruct how Eduardo Garcia spent his final hours," I said, thinking aloud. "Specifically, who he saw during the day, who he talked to at that party..." I sighed. "Speaking of food, I'm afraid I can't entirely rule out Callie."

Forrester's eyebrows shot up. "MacKinnon's younger daughter? She's just a kid."

"A very *angry* kid. But sweet, at the same time. Vulnerable. Hurting. I'd hate to believe she could be guilty of anything worse than stealing chocolate éclairs. But for some reason, she seems to bear a real grudge against Eduardo."

"Could be sibling rivalry," he offered. "You said yourself that MacKinnon treated him like a son."

"It's possible. Or maybe Callie simply developed a schoolgirl crush on him and then resented him because he was someone she could never have." I paused to butter another roll. These carbs were definitely habit forming. "Speaking of Andrew MacKinnon's offspring, what's your impression of Peyton?"

Forrester shrugged. "Don't have one. I haven't actually met her, so I haven't had the chance to form one."

I eyed him critically, thinking that he probably wouldn't have too much trouble catching her interest. In fact, given that he was a male between the ages of fifteen and eighty-five, I suspected he'd have a better chance of finding out what made that girl tick than I ever would.

"Well, not only have I met her," I told him, "I've decided she definitely deserves a place on our list of suspects."

"Sounds intriguing. What have you found out?"

"First of all, Peyton made a point of telling me that she and Eduardo were lovers. *More* than lovers. Then she came right out and said that her father could well have murdered Eduardo because he didn't want his daughter marrying an Argie."

"Interesting theory. But why does that make her a suspect?"

"She also went out of her way to convince me that as a jealous lover with a rival—Diana Chase—she could also have murdered him. Then she delivered the punch line. She told me she had an airtight alibi: she was out of the country until after Eduardo died. But it didn't take me long to discover that her alibi was about as airtight as a torn Hefty bag. She left the contents of her purse lying around, and I took the liberty of checking her airline ticket. Peyton MacKinnon arrived back in the U.S. the second of September, five days *before* Eduardo was murdered—and ten days before the date she's pretending she came home."

"*Really.*" I could practically hear Forrester's mind clicking away, processing what I'd just told him. "Good detective work, Popper. You've got a wonderfully devious mind."

"I've never trusted that girl." I didn't bother to mention that her fascination with my boyfriend might have had something to do with it. "Besides, she made it ridiculously easy. I don't know if she was just being careless or if she's much more calculating than she lets on."

"She definitely sounds like someone I've got to learn more about."

Just be careful she doesn't ensnare you in her web, I thought. Aloud, I said, "Bring a machete. A really sharp one."

"Huh?"

I waved my hand in the air. "Forget it. Anyway, at this point, I'm suspicious of just about everyone who had anything at all to do with Eduardo. Or Andrew MacKinnon, for that matter."

"I don't blame you. There's something about captains of industry and their entourages that makes them all seem suspect."

Narrowing my eyes, I said, "You know, I think I'm

going to take a detour and investigate somebody who's not on our list of suspects."

"Who are you talking about?"

"I'm talking about Forrester Sloan, the enigmatic reporter."

"Me? I'm as transparent as glass." But from the way he was grinning, I could tell he was flattered.

"I wonder. I know you try to portray yourself as this preppy who grew up amidst tremendous wealth—and consequently developed a deep dislike for it. Not to mention an even deeper distrust. But how do I know you're not really somebody like...like Winston Farnsworth? Somebody who comes out of humble circumstances but who manages to convince the world that he's right at home in the world of privilege."

"For that matter, how do you know Winston Farnsworth is telling the truth?"

"I don't. But Winston's not nearly as intriguing as you are."

"Intriguing, huh? Now there's something I don't get called very often. Especially by an attractive woman who I'd love to—"

"Who ordered the linguini?" Our waitress chose that moment to arrive at our table, bearing plates. At first I was sorry. I was genuinely curious about how Forrester intended to finish that sentence.

But then I realized what I'd been doing. *Flirting.* I'd been shameless, in fact. Playing with my hair as if I'd graduated summa cum laude from the Peyton MacKinnon School of Charm, cocking my head to one side, making leading statements...

Saved by a bowl of pasta, I thought, plunging into my dinner and resolving to calm down.

Just because Nick is too busy for you these days doesn't give you license to flirt, I reminded myself. Or anything else along those lines.

"Let's get back to Peyton," I suggested. "I think we need to take a close look at her."

"Makes sense," Forrester agreed. "It's possible that in the days before the murder, she and Eduardo had a lovers' quarrel. Maybe he was getting ready to dump her." He paused to wrestle with his crab cake. "From what you've said, Peyton MacKinnon sounds like somebody who wouldn't like the idea of being dumped."

"Frankly, from what I've seen of Peyton, I wouldn't put the ability to commit murder past her. Especially if there was a rival for Eduardo's affections."

"You mean Diana Chase."

"Exactly."

"Well, Eduardo sure picked the wrong married woman to have a fling with."

My ears pricked up like Max's when he hears the crinkling of plastic wrap—a sign that food might be on the way. Now it was *my* turn to lean forward.

"What do you know about Diana Chase?" I demanded.

"I don't know anything," Forrester replied. "But I do know plenty about her husband, Harlan. Mainly that he's a ruthless son of a bitch. He's very big in the New York City media scene. He owns a few magazines, and has been putting out his feelers for some cable stations. But he's widely known as an incredible cheapskate."

"So Vivian wasn't exaggerating."

"Vivian?"

"Vivian Johannsen. Diana's best friend? Or at least the woman who pretends to be her best friend..."

"Johannsen." He frowned. "As in Bill Johannsen?"

I blinked. "What do you know about that charmer?"

"He's another member of Andrew MacKinnon's clique. They have a few things in common, mainly that they both love horses and money. Johannsen owns a chain of supermarkets. Mostly in New Jersey and

Pennsylvania, with a few upstate. He's another one who's been known to use a few tactics that were considered questionable. Finding ways of getting around the unions, driving out his competitors by initiating lawsuits that couldn't hold water but which still cost the little guys enough that they were ruined, charming little ploys like that."

"Then I guess I shouldn't be surprised by our interaction," I mused.

"What do you mean?"

"He cornered me while I was at their house, treating their Himalayan. That's a cat, by the way. Anyway, he basically threatened me. He told me that people who go snooping around places they don't belong sometimes find out things they'd be better off not knowing."

"Interesting," Forrester observed, frowning.

"And while we're on the subject of interesting threats," I continued, "I suppose I should mention that somebody left me an anonymous note."

"*What?*" This time, Forrester froze.

"It's kind of hard to take it seriously. I mean, the thing is made from letters cut out of magazines. How Mickey Mouse is that?"

"Popper, given the fact that you're involved in a murder investigation, I wouldn't take anything lightly—especially a threatening note. What did it say, exactly?"

"I think I still have it in my purse." Sure enough; it was right where I'd left it. I pulled it out and handed it to him.

" '*Too many questions. Mind your own business,*' " Forrester read aloud.

"Not much of a speller, huh?"

"Have you gone to the police?"

"*No.*" I grabbed the note out of Forrester's hands. "Anthony Falcone and I are not exactly on the best of terms. The last thing I need is a lecture on how I should leave police work to the police."

"Or to a clever and determined reporter," Forrester added teasingly. But his expression remained serious.

"It sounds like you're not going to turn me in," I observed as I tucked it away. "That you'll keep my little love letter here a secret."

"For now. But Popper, you should think about talking to Falcone. He's not really such a bad guy, you know. And as amateurish as that thing looks, whoever sent it to you was probably dead serious."

"I'll consider it," I told him. "Now, if you don't mind, I'd like to concentrate on eating. Thinking about the cast of characters we've just put under our microscopes has depleted my blood sugar."

For the rest of the meal, we managed to keep the conversation considerably lighter. But I noticed that Forrester Sloan wasn't big on revealing very much about himself—unless he was telling stories about the creative ploys he'd used to rise to the position of top reporter.

Finally, after we both said no to coffee, he snatched up the check, glanced at it, and tossed some bills on the table.

"How much is my share?" I asked, reaching for my wallet.

"I've got it."

"You don't have to—"

"It's fine."

"Then I'll get the next one."

He didn't acknowledge my comment. In fact, he was silent as we walked out to the parking lot together. When we reached my car, he turned to me. "Hey, Popper? There's something I'd like you to think about. Besides Eduardo Garcia's murder, I mean."

"What?"

Without looking me in the eye, he said, "Dumping that boyfriend of yours. I know for a fact that you could do better."

He finally glanced over, giving me a wink. Much to my surprise, a flush came over his face. Then he turned away and disappeared behind his SUV.

Even though I avoided checking my reflection in the rearview mirror, I had a feeling my own cheeks were as red as my Volkswagen as I drove home from the restaurant. I didn't like feeling confused like this. Here I'd believed that Forrester and I were getting together solely to discuss what we'd learned about Eduardo Garcia's murder. Yet he'd taken the occasion to make it clear that the polo player's killer wasn't the only person he was pursuing.

And what about my role in this? I wondered. What kind of signals was I sending out to Forrester that made him feel it was okay to be so...so blatant?

By the time I got home to my empty cottage, I'd decided that at least some of this was Nick's fault. While the rational part of me understood that going back to school was bound to make anyone busy, I also resented the fact that I seemed to have practically fallen off his list of priorities.

In fact, I was slumped on the couch with Max dozing in my lap and Lou leaning his head against me, wondering if calling him would be more productive than channel surfing, when I heard a knock at the door. Max raced over, with Lou a foot or two behind. From their reaction, I suspected it was Nick.

When I opened the door, I saw that I was right. At least I *thought* I was right. All I could see was a huge bouquet of balloons, every color of the rainbow. Yet the pair of legs that stretched below them, covered in brown corduroy, backed up my original suspicion.

"Nick?" I asked. "Or am I being kidnapped and forced to join the circus?"

"It's me," I heard Nick's voice reply. "I'm back here, behind this purple one."

The sight of all those balloons immediately sent Max into overdrive. I'm sure he thought he was being confronted by a dozen tennis balls gone berzerk. In fact, he went a little berzerk himself, leaping up and down again and again like a fuzzy white wind-up toy. Lou, a considerably more timid soul, decided that whatever they were, they were dangerous. He began barking at them furiously, meanwhile doing a sort of tap dance. He sounded really tough, although the fact that he was half-hidden behind the oversized, overstuffed upholstered chair did a lot to detract from his threatening look.

I, however, was neither frightened nor overjoyed.

"You know, I can't be bought off with a bunch of balloons," I told Nick tartly. "Besides, don't you know how dangerous these are to animals?"

Nick paraded inside, still clutching the balloons. I noticed that each one was tied with a long ribbon in the same color—a very nice touch.

"How can balloons be dangerous?" he asked. He finally let go, sending the colorful cluster up to the ceiling and sending the dogs into a tizzy. Even Prometheus looked unsettled. He started squawking uncontrollably. At least he wasn't swearing.

Only Leilani was taking the chaos in stride. As usual, she was emotionless, although I did notice her gaze travel upward a few times.

"Not only are they making my animals crazy; if one breaks and Max or Lou gets hold of it before I do, they could choke on the rubber!" I cried.

"I didn't think of that. Sorry." Nick looked so guilty that I couldn't stay angry. And keeping track of a dozen balloons wouldn't be *that* difficult. "Besides, you can't be mad at me tonight. Not when I came here looking for sympathy." He paused before adding, "I found out today that I'm being evicted from my apartment."

"*You*? The best tenant anyone could ever hope for?"

"Thanks for the compliment, but that's not the issue. You know the apartment I live in is illegal. That area of Port Townsend isn't zoned for apartments in houses, unless family members live in them. And that's exactly what's about to happen. The landlord's daughter is getting divorced, and she came back home. That's why the place is being repainted. Putting her in that second-floor apartment is perfect for the family's situation. Unfortunately, it's not so perfect for mine. In fact, it leaves me without a place to live—on very short notice."

"How short?"

"The end of the month."

"But that's only two weeks away!"

"When you're living in an illegal apartment, your landlord doesn't have to play by the rules—mainly because there aren't any rules," Nick replied grimly. "Actually, he told me he's doing me a favor by giving me that much time. His daughter's staying in her old bedroom right now. She can't wait to get her own space. In fact, every time I pass her in the driveway, she glares at me."

"Oh, Nick, that's awful."

"So now, besides keeping up with my classes, I'm going to have to start looking for a new apartment. A *cheap* apartment."

"I'll help," I offered, wondering how I'd ever find the time to go apartment hunting. My schedule was already packed. Of course, abandoning my unofficial investigation into the murder of Eduardo Garcia would free me

up. But by doing that, I'd be letting Forrester down...
wouldn't I?

I kicked myself—metaphorically—for putting Forrester's needs ahead of Nick's. If Nick needed help finding a place to live, of *course* I'd help him.

"First thing tomorrow, I'll call the woman who found
me this place," I told him, putting on my optimistic
voice. "Mitzi something. I'm sure I have her card somewhere. She's terrific. She'll find you something."

"I hope so," Nick said tiredly. "Otherwise, I might be
pitching a tent on your lawn."

That was one possibility, I mused. There were others,
of course. But at the moment, even the idea of contemplating them was simply too overwhelming.

Mitzi was apparently taking Friday off for a long weekend. There was nothing to be done about Nick's living
situation, so instead, I tried to focus on the two of us
having a good time as we hauled off to Betty's opening
night at Theater One in Port Townsend.

The century-old building looked as if it had been
spiffed up for the occasion. The dark red velvet seats
and the thick curtain made from a similar fabric looked
luxurious in the dimly lit theater. The gold-toned walls
glowed, showing off the hand-painted murals that had
originated in the 1930's and had recently been refur-
bished. The air felt electrified—or maybe it was just my
excitement over my friend's long-overdue return to the
stage that made me feel that this evening was magical.

The fact that all the members of the Betty Vandervoort Fan Club had dressed for a night at the opera
added to that feeling. I'd put on a flowered sundress,
confident that its colorful fabric was an appropriate accompaniment to the flecks of orange that still clung to
my fingernails. Nick looked particularly lawyerly in

khaki pants and a pale blue shirt with a button-down collar.

Even Marcus Scruggs looked presentable. Thanks to his tall, lanky frame, his loud Hawaiian shirt and baggy olive green cargo pants actually looked stylish. His dark blond hair was smoothed back with some kind of hair gel. If he could only have done something about his facial expression—a perpetual leer—I might have actually been able to keep myself from cringing every time he opened his mouth to speak.

But it was my college pal and fellow veterinarian Suzanne Fox who turned heads as the happy couple headed down the aisle toward Nick and me a few minutes after we arrived. She had abandoned the long braid she'd worn since college, instead getting her thick orange-red hair cut into a frenzy of different lengths, each section going its own separate way. She'd also defied nature by somehow managing to make it dead straight, banishing the waves that had always given her a romantic, pre-Raphaelite look.

She appeared to have broken a few laws of physics, as well, with the skin-tight, celery green dress that enveloped her curves. Suzanne doesn't exactly fall into the slender category, yet she displayed absolutely no self-consciousness about showing a little thigh and a lot of cleavage. Her beau Marcus seemed powerless to stop himself from touching any and every bit of her exposed flesh, even in public. For all his faults, I admitted to myself begrudgingly, at least he was someone who appreciated the non-anorexic female form.

But I wasn't able to give the incomprehensible chemistry that bonded Suzanne and Marcus together more than a passing thought. I had no idea how bad Betty's opening-night butterflies were, but mine were throwing a wild party. As I sat in the fifth row with Nick on one side and Suzanne on the other, I hoped she was coping better than I was.

But it was also exciting. I just knew her star quality would shine through—and that she'd be an absolute hit.

"Here's her name, in the program!" I exclaimed. "This is absolutely thrilling! I'm so glad Betty's gotten back into show business."

"Sounds like she's not the only one who's cultivating her hobbies," Suzanne said meaningfully.

"What hobbies are those, Popper?" Marcus asked.

"I called Betty a few hours ago to wish her luck," Suzanne said, her cornflower blue eyes shining. "She told me all about what Jessie's been up to."

I hoped Nick hadn't overheard. And from the way he was thumbing through the program, it seemed that he hadn't.

At least until Marcus bellowed, "Sounds intriguing, Popper! What *have* you been up to?" Leering, he added, "Or is it something you can't talk about in polite company?"

Nick glanced up, looking puzzled. "What's he talking about, Jess? Your work at Heatherfield?"

"That's what it's called: Heatherfield," Suzanne chirped. "That's the estate where he died, right? The guy whose murder you're investigating?"

"You're investigating a murder?" Nick asked. I could tell he was trying to keep his tone light. I also knew him well enough to hear the heaviness that was *really* there.

"I'm not exactly *investigating*," I told my rapt audience of three. "I simply agreed to help out a reporter. Forrester Sloan. It's no big deal, really. He just asked me to keep an eye out for anything that might seem...*unusual* while I was around the estate, treating Andrew MacKinnon's horses."

"Just a low-key, casual kind of thing, huh?" Nick asked in the same strained tone. "Asking the occasional murder suspect a question or two as you're examining one of this guy's horses?"

"Something like that."

"Just like when you were in the Bromptons back in June," Suzanne commented, eagerly adding, "What have you found out so far?"

Fortunately, at that moment I saw Winston Farnsworth trudging up the aisle, looking baffled. I raised my hand and waved.

"Time to change the subject," I said pointedly. "Here comes one of our suspects now."

"Sorry I'm late," Winston said, huffing and puffing a bit as he slid into the empty seat next to Nick. "Took me a bit longer to drive here than I'd expected."

"At least you made it," I told him. "Thanks for coming."

"Thank you for inviting me," Winston returned heartily. "It's a real pleasure to be going to the theater again."

I'd just finished a quick round of introductions when the lights began to dim. The five of us settled back in our seats.

Almost instantly, I forgot all about Eduardo and Nick and everyone else who played a role in my life. I was too busy concentrating on the action onstage. I was immediately pulled into the story of two women, Roxy Hart and Thelma Kelly, whose love lives landed them in jail.

True, it wasn't the most polished stage production I'd ever seen. Some of the dancing was a little ragged, and more than one actor flubbed a line or two. Still, it was obvious that every person involved in the production was excited to be part of it—and that every one of them was giving it their all.

As much as I was enjoying myself, I couldn't get rid of the kernel of anxiety lodged in my stomach. Betty had yet to come onstage. Until she'd finished her dance number, I wouldn't be able to breathe normally.

Finally, the orchestra played the beginning bars of "Cell Block Tango." In my head, I sang along: "He had it coming . . ."

I leaned over to Nick, whispering, "This is it."

"She'll be great," he whispered back. But he reached over and squeezed my hand.

The six women who had taken the stage each struck a pose as a voice offstage identified them as "the six merry murderesses of the Crookem County Jail." I fixed my eyes on Betty, my heart pounding wildly in my chest.

One by one, each of the women gave a short monologue about the murder she'd committed, alternating with singing and dancing by the entire group. Finally, it was Betty's turn. I held my breath.

I watched, enthralled, as she delivered her lines with ease—even though the character she was playing, Katalin Helinszki, spoke only Hungarian. She carried it off like a real pro, winning over the audience with her polished performance. Her dancing, meanwhile, was positively mesmerizing. I wasn't exactly an expert on ballet, but it seemed to me that Betty did a fabulous job.

The rest of the audience thought so, too. When she finished her dance number, the crowd applauded wildly, even though the scene hadn't yet come to an end.

"They love her!" I whispered to Nick. Even though my vision was clouded by tears, I could see by the glow in Betty's eyes that their enthusiasm meant everything to her.

When intermission rolled around, I was still on cloud nine.

"What a glorious night!" I exclaimed. "Betty was spectacular!"

"I think the audience responded to her even more than the two leads," Suzanne added.

"Your friend is certainly talented," Winston commented.

"You kidding? The lady's dynamite!" Marcus exclaimed.

"We'll go backstage later, and you can meet her," I told Winston. "I'm sure she'd appreciate hearing how much you enjoyed her performance."

For the moment, however, I had much more concrete concerns. So did Suzanne. The two of us took advantage of the break to head to the ladies room.

"There you go, heading to the ladies room in pairs," Marcus jeered, grinning as if he'd just said something terribly clever instead of repeating what I'd considered a tired old joke practically since college. "You know, we guys can't help wondering what you do in there that requires two of you. Of course, some of us have a really good imagination...."

"Oh, Marcus," Suzanne cried, giggling. "You are just too funny!"

I didn't know who I felt like swatting more, him or her. I had to admit, my friend's attraction to a man I found barely tolerable baffled me. Then again, matters of the heart always hold an element of mystery. Which I suppose is why most people find them endlessly fascinating—including me.

"So how are things going with Marcus?" I asked Suzanne as we stood in line with all the other theatergoers who'd been foolhardy enough to consume liquids within the previous twelve hours. I tried to sound casual, even though I was braced for anything, from a tirade about Marcus's belief that he was second only to Elvis in desirability to complaints about various exotic sexual habits.

"Oh, Jessie, at the risk of sounding like a character in a romance novel, Marcus is the man of my dreams! He's everything any woman could hope for. He calls me three times a day to make sure I know he's thinking about me, he's constantly showering me with presents, he treats me like a goddess in bed...And I have you to thank."

Or to blame, I thought woefully, dreading the conversation I could imagine us having six months from now.

"Suzanne, I'm glad things are working out so well. But at the risk of sounding like a spoilsport, I do feel compelled to—"

In the mirror, I saw Suzanne's expression go from enraptured to troubled in about three seconds flat.

"There is *one* complication in my love life," she said haltingly.

Here it comes, I thought, my stomach tensing as I braced myself for the punch line.

"It has nothing to do with Marcus, though. Not directly, anyway." She hesitated. "It's Robert."

"Robert?" I repeated, confused. It took me a moment to remember that Robert was the name of Suzanne's ex. "What's going on with him?"

"He's got a new woman in his life. Jessie, he's getting married!" Suzanne's blue eyes suddenly looked wet, as if they'd been painted on with watercolors, and her creamy skin was covered with red blotches. "I ran into somebody who used to be friends with both of us. I haven't talked to him in ages. But we'd barely said hello before he started telling me all about Robert's wedding plans. He and this...this *woman* are getting married at the exact same place we did, and having the same best man. Robert is taking all the things that were special to us and throwing them in my face by repeating them with her. He's making a mockery of our entire marriage! He's even taking her to Puerto Rico for their honeymoon!"

"Maybe he's trying to recapture what he sees as really fond memories," I offered. "Or maybe he really *liked* Puerto Rico."

"Are you kidding? He hated it! We had a terrible time! Robert insisted on renting a car, and we got horribly lost in San Juan late one night. We ended up in the city's worst slum, La Perla. It's the one place they warn tourists about. And they weren't exaggerating. A bunch of guys who I swear were drug dealers surrounded the car—"

"Maybe he just doesn't have enough imagination to come up with another idea," I suggested.

Suzanne sniffled. "I guess I'm just jealous. After all, Robert's the one who decided to end our marriage, not me. I know, in my head, that it really is over and that it's time for me to move on. And I truly believed that I had. At least, until I found out about all this. Since then, I've been feeling like the floor dropped out from under me." She looked at me mournfully. "I don't want the past to get in the way of the present, Jess. Most of all, I don't want to screw things up with Marcus."

I struggled to come up with the right thing to say. Suzanne was certainly correct about her relationship with Robert being old news. He'd clearly moved on. And she'd made great strides in doing the same—even if it was with a man I happened to consider in the same league as the mold that grows on shower curtains.

But when it came to relationships—at least the human variety, as opposed to the human-and-animal type—I wasn't exactly in my element. I'd spent most of my life running away from commitment, so I was hardly in the best position to play Dr. Phil.

I was relieved that a bell suddenly rang, signaling the

end of intermission and putting an abrupt end to our conversation.

As I took my seat and the lights dimmed, my head was throbbing. *This love stuff sure is complicated*, I thought, settling into my seat to watch the rest of the play. *Just* look *where it landed Roxy and Thelma.*

I wasn't surprised when the conclusion of Act Two elicited a standing ovation. And when Betty took a bow, the building practically shook from the applause.

It took seven curtain calls, but the show finally ended and the five of us headed backstage. We found Betty in the dressing room with most of the other cast members, her face lit up as if it was her birthday, New Year's Eve, and the Fourth of July, all rolled up into one.

"Betty, you were great!" I exclaimed, throwing my arms around her.

"Ah, Jess, you're just saying that." She hugged me back, then pulled away and smiled. "I was pretty darned good, wasn't I?"

"You stole the show," Nick assured her, giving her a squeeze. "You've still got the same star quality that wowed 'em on Broadway."

Suzanne and Marcus hovered a few feet away, waiting for their turn to shower Betty with praise. But she focused on Winston, her expression turning into one of pleasant surprise.

"And you are...?"

"This is Winston Farnsworth," I told her. "He's a new client. But even more, he's also a fan of musical comedy. When he learned I had tickets to *Chicago*, he..."

I got the feeling Betty wasn't listening to a word I was saying. Instead, she was batting her eyelashes so hard I was nearly knocked over by the breeze.

"Mr. Farnsworth." Betty held out her hand. Her left hand, I noticed, the one that clearly had no wedding ring on it. "What a pleasure."

"The pleasure is all mine." Winston took her hand, but instead of shaking it, raised it to his lips. "And thank you for such an enjoyable evening. Having the opportunity to watch you dance was a magnificent gift."

Betty giggled. "With such impeccable manners, you must be European."

"Guilty as charged," he returned, his eyes twinkling. "I'm actually a Londoner."

"Ah, London." Betty sighed. "One of my favorite cities in the world."

"Then we must compare notes."

By that point, the two of them looked ready to book a flight. I hadn't seen such chemistry since I finished my lab requirements for veterinary school.

It's cute, I told myself firmly. I tried not to think too hard about the fact that the sight of Betty and Winston making goo-goo eyes at each other was tying my stomach up in knots.

I understood the reason, too: When you came right down to it, I didn't really know anything about Winston Farnsworth. Oh, sure, he was charming and all that. With his English accent and his continental manners, he was as suave as Sean Connery.

But it was possible that he was also a murderer. I hadn't yet ruled him out as a suspect. Even though I didn't know what his motive might have been, he was involved closely enough with Andrew MacKinnon that I had to wonder about his relationship with the man's fellow polo player and surrogate son, Eduardo.

The memory of his argument with Andrew—on the day of Eduardo's funeral, no less—echoed through my head. *Something* was going on, something I unfortunately knew nothing about. And the last thing I wanted was for Betty to start throwing herself at him before I'd had a chance to find out what it was.

I made a mental note to talk to her about him the very first chance I got. But for now, the evening was hers to enjoy, and I, for one, had no intention of doing anything that might diminish it.

Chapter 11

"I ride horses because it's the only sport where I can exercise while sitting down."

—Joan Hansen

I was caught up in a bizarre, complicated dream—something about prison inmates in ballet shoes singing about murdering a handsome polo player—when a harsh ringing dragged me awake. Forcing my eyes open and glancing at the clock, I saw it was just past eight. I stuck my arm out of the covers and flailed around for the phone, wondering when Saturdays had lost their special status that made it impolite to call before, say, ten in the morning.

"Hello?" I croaked.

"Dr. Popper? Andrew MacKinnon here."

"Mr. MacKinnon!" I sat up abruptly, automatically assuming he was calling me about a horse-related problem.

"It's not too early, I hope."

"No, not at all," I assured him, meanwhile wondering, *Why do people always say that?* "Is something wrong? With one of the horses, I mean?"

"Everything is fine. Actually, I'm calling with an invitation. My way of thanking you for all you've done since my regular vet landed himself in the hospital. I'm wondering if you'd like to come to an *asado* tonight."

"Uh..." One thing life had taught me was never to accept an invitation unless you know enough about what the event *is* to have a pretty good idea what to wear.

MacKinnon picked up on my confusion. "An *asado* is an Argentine-style barbecue. Jillian and I are throwing a birthday party for one of my players, Pancho Escobar, here at Heatherfield tonight. I thought you might like to come. And of course you're welcome to bring a guest."

I glanced over at the most likely candidate, who was snoring softly beside me with the pillow pulled over his head. This *asado* sounded like fun, as well as a chance for Nick and me to enjoy a night out together.

The fact that it was being held at the Scene of the Crime didn't hurt, either.

"I'd love to come," I said sincerely. "And I'll plan on bringing my boyfriend, Nick."

"Then I look forward to seeing you both. Six o'clock?"

"We'll be there."

By that point, Max and Lou were already in high gear. Telephones tend to have that effect on them. They associate them with adventure, since they've lived through so many occasions on which the ringing sound has been followed by a mad dash out of the cottage and into the van. Lou was standing with his nose a couple of millimeters away from mine, tickling me with his moist breath. Max, meanwhile, was wagging his stub of a tail, gnashing his teeth against his hot-pink poodle. He just assumed that I found its desperate squeaks as enticing as he did. From the other room, I could hear Prometheus, muttering to himself like someone who was hearing voices. Occasionally, he squawked something of interest, like "Shake your booty! *Awk!* That's the way I like it!" When Cat wandered in, meowing a considerably more dignified greeting than her feathered roommate, I knew it was time to get up.

I whispered, "Good morning!" to Leilani, then let Max and Lou out, noting that it was another perfect September day. The sky was clear and the sun was casting the world in a golden glow. I stood in the doorway, watching the dogs chase a squirrel and stretching my arms high in the air.

I jumped when someone grabbed me from behind.

Fortunately, it turned out to be the one person I *like* having grab me.

"I didn't mean to wake you," I told Nick, clasping my arms over his and leaning back so my head rested against his shoulder.

"Are you kidding? By this point, I've already forgotten what a good night's sleep is."

I hesitated, wondering if I dared to say what I was thinking. But the words started pouring out even before I'd decided. "It's turned out to be a big change, hasn't it? You going back to school, I mean. Bigger than we anticipated."

"Yeah. It's one of those things you think you're ready for, but until it actually happens, you can't really comprehend how it's going to play out." He sighed deeply. "I know it's Saturday, but I have to head over to the library first thing. I expect to be there all day."

"I figured. By the way, we have a dinner invitation for tonight, at Heatherfield."

I felt his body tense. "Not another trip into a parallel universe, I hope?"

"This should be better than last time. Andrew MacKinnon's having a birthday party for one of his polo players, Pancho Escobar, so I assume there'll be a lot of people there. The food should be good, too. They're barbecuing, Argentine-style."

"Sounds like fun."

"Speaking of fun..." I wriggled around so I was facing him. Our bodies still pressed together, I said, "You don't have to go the library *immediately*, do you? We have to at *least* wait for the coffee to drip."

"Mmm. It would be a shame to waste those five minutes, wouldn't it?"

"Five minutes!" I slid my hands up under his T-shirt. "Give me fifteen, and I'll really make it worth your while."

"Deal."

By the time we sat down to coffee—a full thirty-five minutes later, I noted with satisfaction—we were both feeling considerably better about our situation. But as Nick passed me one of the English muffins he'd just toasted, I noticed that his expression had grown tense.

"What is it, Nick?" I asked, trying to keep my tone light. Something about the sudden coolness in the air told me I wasn't going to like whatever had caused it. The first thought that popped into my head was our unfinished conversation from the night before. I braced myself for a lecture on my unhealthy obsession with murder investigations.

Nick cleared his throat. "I've been thinking that, well, maybe it wouldn't be a bad idea if—"

"Don't tell me," I interrupted tartly. "You've been thinking that maybe it wouldn't be a bad idea if I kept away from murder investigations, if I simply kept my nose to the grindstone and concentrated on my veterinary practice...."

He blinked. "Actually, I was going to say I've been thinking that maybe it wouldn't be a bad idea if you and I moved in together."

My mouth dropped open—literally. I quickly ordered

myself to snap it shut. "You mean...but...wait, you're saying that—"

He stood up, walked over to my side of the table and wrapped his arms around me. Lou immediately wandered over, wagging his tail and sticking his nose between us. "You know, Jess, you're awfully cute when you're flabbergasted." He chuckled softly. "Have I ever told you that?"

"No. I mean, yes. I mean...let's stop and think about this, Nick. I mean, living together is a big decision."

"You know what?" he asked, gently rubbing my back. "Sometimes you think too much. In certain situations, it's better to just go with what you feel."

I wasn't about to tell him that I was feeling pretty darn close to panic. While I've never thought of myself as claustrophobic, for some strange reason the walls of the room suddenly seemed to be growing closer and closer.

"I love you, you know," Nick said. Somehow, he made the whole thing sound so simple.

"I know," I said, trying to hide the fact that I was practically choking. Why hadn't I left the front door open, to let some air in? "I love you, too."

"And things between us have been going pretty well lately."

"*Very* well," I agreed.

"If you think it's hard for us to find time together now, wait until my classes really get rolling. If you and I were living together, at least we'd see each other at breakfast every morning, and pass each other on the way in and out of the bathroom...." He slid his hands under my shirt. The skin of his palms felt warm and smooth against my back. "And just think how nice it would be to snuggle up in bed together every night."

The memory of the spectacular half hour that had led up to this moment was making it hard for me to think straight. "I know you said I think too much, but can I think about this?"

He looked startled. It clearly wasn't the answer he expected. At least, it wasn't the one he wanted.

He dropped his hands. "Sure."

I could tell he was disappointed. And I couldn't really blame him. Not when I'd let him down by not throwing my arms around him and exclaiming, "Yes! Yes!"

Then again, this wasn't the first time Nick had asked a question I hadn't answered correctly. A really *important* question.

His eyes didn't meet mine as he sat back down in his seat, way over on the other side of the table. You've never seen anybody gulp down an English muffin and a cup of coffee quite so fast.

With equally impressive speed, he headed out of the cottage, stopping only to peck me on the cheek and mumble, "See you later." And even though he left me standing in the doorway with a panting Dalmatian, a rawhide-chewing Westie, a cat who was rubbing against my leg and meowing for attention, a chameleon blinking lazily in her tank, and, just a few feet away, a macaw who was singing the pirate song Nick had once taught him, the cottage suddenly felt remarkably empty.

As soon as Nick's car disappeared up the driveway, I sprinted across the yard to Betty's house. There was something to be said for having your own personal therapist, fortune-teller, and surrogate mother right there on the premises.

Even though it was still fairly early, Betty greeted me at the door in full makeup, complete with lavender eyeshadow and crimson lipstick. Somehow, on her it looked good. So did the long, gold earrings which, upon close examination, turned out to be shaped like flamingos. For her casual morning at home, she was dressed in a mustard-colored caftan whose folds draped dramatically over her tiny frame. It was laced with shiny gold threads, making her look as if she'd just stepped out of the Casbah.

"Jessica, are you all right?" she greeted me.

"Yes. I mean, no. I mean—Betty, I could really use a cup of tea." Actually, given the adrenaline rush I had on top of the caffeine buzz from my morning hit of coffee, tea was the last thing I needed. The same went for Betty's secret ingredient. But it would give us a chance to talk.

"Coming right up." Betty cast me a worried look. "I think I'd better make it a double."

As I plopped down at the kitchen table and laid my palms flat on its surface, I saw that my hands were trembling. "I'm shaking," I observed, surprised.

Betty glanced over from the sink, where she was filling the kettle. "Why am I sure that whatever you're about to tell me has something to do with Nick?"

I didn't blurt out the thought that popped into my head at that moment, that I'd long suspected she was capable of reading minds. At least, *my* mind.

But my news couldn't wait for the water to boil. "Nick suggested that we move in together."

Her eyebrows shot up so forcefully that her long gold earrings swayed from side to side. "Well, it's about time. And I wouldn't raise the rent, if that's what you're worried about."

"That's the least of my concerns."

"Why don't you tell me exactly what your concerns *are*?"

"Giving up my independence, of course! Sharing my space with someone else...with a man." I swallowed hard. "Even if that man is someone as wonderful as Nick. I mean, the closets in that place are tiny, and...

and the kitchen's so small there's barely room for one person to move around, much less two. And the dogs are used to running around as much as they want, jumping on the furniture and leaving their saliva-covered toys all over the place..."

"I think what we're really talking about here is making a commitment," Betty said gently.

"Well...yes." I paused, thinking. "Of course, there are some practical reasons to go for it. For one thing, Nick is about to be evicted from his apartment. His landlord's daughter is getting divorced, and she's moving back home to that second-floor apartment. Then there are financial considerations. With Nick in law school full-time, he's living off his savings. Saving money by sharing a place makes perfect sense."

"That all sounds very practical," Betty said, nodding. Her mouth drooped down just a little as she muttered, "*Too* practical."

"Then there's the fact that with Nick becoming a student again, we hardly get to spend any time together," I went on. "He's always in class or at the library or...or with that obnoxious study group of his. If we lived together, at least we'd pass each other going in and out of the bathroom every morning."

"Not to mention snuggling up together in bed," she interjected.

"That, too."

Betty stood up and focused on retrieving the sugar bowl from the shelf above the stove. Without looking at me, she demanded, "Jessica, do you love Nick?"

"I—what?"

"You heard me. Do you love Nick?"

"Well, I...yes. Yes, I love Nick."

"Do you love him enough that you believe, deep down, that there's a good chance you'd be happy spending the rest of your life with him?"

I squirmed in my seat. "That's the tricky part! Whenever I hear that phrase 'for the rest of your life,' I start to feel as if the entire room is—"

"Jessica, answer my question," Betty insisted.

I took a large gulp of tea, largely to counteract the dryness of my mouth. "Yes," I finally croaked. "I love him that much."

"Then I believe we've answered the question."

"You're just like Nick! You both make it sound so simple!" I protested.

"It's not very complicated," she countered. "At least, it doesn't have to be."

She reached across the table and took my hand. "Jessica, you know what a romantic I am. I think you and Nick living together is an excellent idea. You're both crazy about each other, and the two of you should be together. Sharing that cottage, where you already feel at home, would be a good way for you to get used to the idea of letting somebody into your life without feeling trapped.

"In my day, of course, the natural next step in a relationship like the one you and Nick have would have been marriage. It's much better these days, when two people in love can take a less drastic step without raising too many eyebrows. Living together isn't as big a commitment—but you're right to give it serious thought. It's definitely not something to take lightly."

She paused to sip her tea. "Jessica, you know I absolutely adore Nick. And since I think of you as a daughter, I'd be tickled pink to see the two of you make a real commitment to each other. If you want my opinion—and even if you don't—I think you should give it a try."

Her answer didn't surprise me.

Unfortunately, neither did my reaction to the idea of letting Nick get a little closer. Okay, a *lot* closer. Even scarier than the idea of sharing my closets was the idea of sharing my entire life.

Of course, there would be advantages. Logistical ones, but even more important, emotional ones. Nick and I would be getting even closer, moving our relationship to an entirely new level.

The problem was that I couldn't simply focus on what I'd be gaining. What loomed even larger in my mind was what I'd be giving up.

My inability to embrace Nick's latest idea about modifying our living arrangements resulted in a sort of—shall we say, *tension* between him and me. In fact, it quickly took on a life of its own. It sat between us like a cranky child as we drove along the Long Island Expressway that evening, heading toward Old Brookbury for Pancho Escobar's birthday celebration.

"This should be fun," I said with forced cheerfulness as I veered my red VW into Heatherfield.

"Yeah," he said noncommittally, glancing up from the law book he'd been reading as I drove.

"It's really nice that Andrew MacKinnon invited me," I went on. "I mean, *us*."

"Look, why don't you get out here and let me park?" he suggested. "It's a mob scene. Besides, you're the one who's friends with this crowd. I'll catch up with you in a few minutes."

"Sure." I hopped out and followed the sound of laughter and clinking glasses, noting that tonight's celebration was taking place right outside the stable. Much better than being inside, I thought, especially on such a warm evening. For the occasion, the courtyard that the three sides of the U-shaped building created had been turned into a party room. A "ceiling" had been created with strings of tiny white lights that crisscrossed overhead, while brightly colored paper lanterns added a festive look. A small group of musicians played tunes that were unfamiliar to me but which seemed to have a Latin flair.

I glanced around, noting some familiar faces. Andrew and Jillian MacKinnon. Diana Chase and Vivian Johannsen, standing together and looking as if neither had the slightest intention of ingesting any food this evening.

I turned my attention to the huge platters of food that were laid out on a long table. Guests were already crowding around the cheese plates and salad bowl. The bread, I noticed, was virtually untouched—no doubt the legacy of Dr. Atkins.

There was one exception. I wasn't surprised to see that Callie had already staked out the food table and was busily loading poppy seed rolls onto her plate.

I was about to head over to say hello, in fact, when someone grabbed my arm a little more roughly than I would have considered neighborly. Glancing over my shoulder, I found myself face-to-face with Bill Johannsen.

"I see you're still hovering around," he hissed.

"I don't hover," I returned indignantly, wrenching my arm away. "I happen to be an invited guest. And I don't appreciate being manhandled."

"I'm watching you," he countered, narrowing his beady little eyes so that he looked even more like one of Miss Piggy's relatives than usual. "That reporter, too."

"I don't doubt it," I returned. "The question in my mind is, why?"

I impressed myself with how cool I'd remained during our brief but unsavory interaction. But as soon as he moved away and disappeared into the crowd, I realized I was shaking. Whether it was from anger or fear, I couldn't be sure. One thing I *was* sure of, however, was that this entire day was turning out to be more trying than I cared for.

I was relieved when I turned and spotted Andrew MacKinnon heading toward me.

"Dr. Popper!" he greeted me warmly. "I'm so glad you could make it."

"Thank you for inviting me. This probably doesn't surprise you, but I've never been to an *asado* before."

"In that case, let me give you a short lecture on the traditional Argentine roast. It even includes the fifty-cent tour."

He took my arm—much more gently than the last person who'd felt I was up for grabs—and led me out of the courtyard. A hundred feet way, at the edge of a field, an elaborate metal grill had been set up over an open fire. Just beyond, I saw rows of wooden picnic tables and chairs, covered by a huge white tent.

"As you can see, it's very much like an American barbecue," Andrew said, clearly proud of the setup. "Different cuts of beef and *chorizos*—sausages—are cooked on an open fire."

"It smells great," I commented. "What exactly is all this?"

"The barbecue grill is called the *parrilla*. In Argentina, you'll find a *parrilla* at almost every *estancia*—every ranch. There, the cooking is done inside a little house that's usually made from mud bricks with a dirt floor— Hector, would you mind serving our special guest?"

As soon as Andrew and I sat down at one of the tables, Hector approached carrying a small grill, the charcoal still glowing red. It was laden with meat.

"This is called a *parrillada*," Andrew informed me. "It's basically an assortment of different meats and *chorizos*."

"Thank you, Hector." I eyed the food nervously, suddenly remembering my real agenda in coming to Heatherfield this evening. Less than two weeks earlier, someone had died right here on the property—and the victim had been poisoned.

Still, I couldn't suddenly claim to be a vegetarian or dream up some other excuse to avoid eating the food in front of me, even though this festive event was crawling with murder suspects.

"Dig in," Andrew insisted. "I want to know what you think."

I glanced up and saw that he was watching me expectantly. Cautiously I tasted one of the sausages. I had an immediate reaction, all right: sheer ecstasy over the heavenly mixture of distinctive spices and subtle flavors that electrified my taste buds. "This is delicious!" I told him sincerely.

He looked pleased by my reaction. "This is how people eat in the Pampa region in Argentina. Argentina beef is the best in the world. The cattle eat only pampas grass. No hormones, no chemicals. The result is a taste that's completely unique, no matter how it's cooked. And there are several different methods: burying the meat in a hole with a fire, roasting it on a spit, or grilling it, like we did today. And I've learned from the Argies that there's a trick: making sure the fire is just right. The secret is to let the coal burn until a thick layer of white ash forms before putting the meat on the grill. Then you need to give it time, letting it cook slowly."

He filled me in on some more of the fine points of the art of the *asado*, then stopped abruptly. "I hope I haven't been boring you."

"Not at all!" I assured him sincerely.

He smiled, looking a little sheepish. "You're very kind to indulge me. My daughters are always complaining that I get carried away. But in fact, I really should leave you to eat in peace while I get back to some of my other guests. Enjoy!"

"Hey, smells great!" Nick came up behind me, just missing Andrew MacKinnon's impromptu lecture on Argentine cooking.

"Help yourself," I replied. "There's enough meat here for a pride of lions." I was relieved that our ability to make normal conversation had finally returned—and that the cranky child had disappeared, at least for now.

However, just as I'd begun looking forward to a fun evening with Nick, I noticed another cranky child. Unfortunately, this one was heading in our direction.

Even though this event was the South American equivalent of a barn dance and everyone else was dressed casually, Peyton was decked out in a party dress that looked much more suited to bars than barns. It was very pretty, made of a flowing fabric with swirling flowers in soft shades of lavender and pale green. However, the material happened to be sheer enough to reveal the fact that she wasn't wearing a stitch underneath.

She zeroed in on my boyfriend like a heat-seeking missile. "Hel-*lo*, Nick," she purred, sweeping back her veil of pale blond hair and threading her arm through his. "How lovely to see you again! I'm *so* glad you came—even though this barbecue thing is so hokey. My father makes such a big deal about it. I guess he figures it makes the Argies feel at home. But if you're as bored as I am, we could probably find something more interesting to do...."

"Hi, Peyton," I said brightly.

She glanced in my direction for all of two seconds. "Oh, hi, Jessica," she said dully. Immediately she turned her attention back to Nick. "You haven't seen the swimming pool yet, have you, Nick?" She ran her hand up and down his forearm. "We'll have to take care of that right away. It's *definitely* one of the highlights of the tour."

"Jess?" Nick's voice was practically a whimper. "Want to come see the pool?"

"She's already seen it," Peyton said sharply.

"Actually, I haven't," I informed her.

Glowering at me, she said, "This is the *private* tour."

Nick cast me a desperate glance. At least, I thought he looked desperate. Maybe something else was turning his cheeks the same shade of red as the pieces of raw meat that were just starting to sizzle on the grill.

"Nick?" I croaked. "Are you sure about this?"

"I don't want to be rude," he countered. "I mean, this is her house, after all. We're invited guests."

Stay out of the cabanas! I was tempted to call after them as I watched them saunter across the field, Peyton's arm slung loosely around Nick's shoulders.

"She is pretty, no?"

I turned and saw Inez standing next to me, holding a plate of food. For once, she wasn't dressed in a stern black uniform. Instead, she was wearing a pale blue sundress that struck me as much more befitting of a slender twenty-year-old woman.

"I suppose so," I replied begrudgingly. Given the fact that Peyton had nearly dragged my boyfriend away bodily—and he hadn't put up much of a fight—I wasn't feeling particularly charitable toward her. I decided to change the subject to something that wouldn't give me heartburn. "How nice that you're helping Pancho celebrate his birthday," I said, thinking, *And that you're here today as a guest, rather than a servant.*

"Pancho, he invited me. We have known each other for a long time. And we both knew Eduardo..." Her expression darkened.

"I can imagine how terrible you must feel, losing a friend."

"Oh, Eduardo and I, we were not really friends," she

said, looking shyly to the side. "He did not really notice me."

But you noticed him, I thought. "Still, he was so young and so full of life."

"You are interested in what happened to Eduardo?" she asked, focusing her dark almond-shaped eyes on me once again. "I heard Meester and Meesus MacKinnon saying you have become friends with a newspaper reporter...?"

"Forrester Sloan," I said. "We were both at the polo game last Sunday. I suppose a lot of people saw us sitting together."

"They say they think the two of you, together, are trying to figure out who killed Eduardo. Ees correct?"

"I think we all want to know what really happened to Eduardo," I replied. "And you're right: That includes me. Inez, I'm doing everything I can to find out who killed him."

"Meester and Meesus MacKinnon, they also say the police think he was poisoned at the big party at the club...?"

"That's the theory the cops seem to think makes the most sense. But I think it's a mistake to focus on that one event."

"Excuse me?" she asked, looking confused.

"I've got a theory of my own: that it's just as likely he was poisoned before the event. Sometime during the day, or even earlier that evening. What I intend to do is learn more about who he might have been with during the hours before the country club party. Don't worry, Inez," I assured her. "I know Eduardo meant a great deal to a lot of people, and I promise you I'm going to do whatever I can to find out who killed him. You've got my word on that."

She nodded slowly. "Then thees ees good. You sound like you are trying very hard to find out who did thees terrible thing to Eduardo..." She stopped, choking on her words. Her eyes were wet as she said, "Now eef you will excuse me, I must go find Luisa. She, too, ees here as Pancho's guest today."

As I watched her wander off, I was reminded once again of what a tragedy it was that someone as young and vibrant as Eduardo Garcia had been murdered. The injustice of it made my blood boil.

I took a few deep breaths, then turned back to the plate of meat that was still waiting for me. I was about to resume my sausage-eating frenzy when I noticed the guest of honor standing nearby, next to the barbecue. Figuring that questioning a suspect was bound to be healthier than O.D.'ing on protein, I edged my way over to him.

"Happy birthday, Pancho," I said boldly.

As he glanced up, a look of shock crossed his face. I guess he hadn't realized this was a surprise party.

"Dr. Popper! What are you—?"

"Andrew MacKinnon invited me," I explained. "It was so kind of him. I've never been to an *asado* before."

He stared at me for a few seconds, his eyes filled with distrust. I could almost hear the wheels turning in his brain.

"The other day," he said, lowering his voice, "I say too much. I am afraid I was not in such a good mood when you and I talked."

"Actually, I appreciated your honesty," I told him.

He shrugged. "We all have a good side and a bad side. In that way, maybe Eduardo and I are not so different."

"I think that's true for all of us."

"But I do not want you to think I am such a bad person."

"Not at all," I assured him. *In fact,* I was tempted to

add, *you may be one of the most truthful people I've met here at Heatherfield.*

"Good." The smoldering look in his eyes faded. "Then I will see you tomorrow, at the polo game?"

Actually, that hadn't been on my schedule. But it wasn't a bad idea. I'd been planning another trip to Heatherfield on Sunday to give Braveheart the final okay before the game, anyway, and I liked the idea of combining business and pleasure. Besides, spending the afternoon in the area would give me another chance to do some snooping. "I'll be there," I told him.

"Good," he said, nodding.

Why was he suddenly concerned about me thinking he's not such a bad guy? I wondered as I drifted away, back to my table.

There were two obvious possibilities. One was that good old Pancho was hoping our budding friendship might have the potential to head into a different direction. My ego wasn't inflated enough to buy that one. But the other was just as unsettling. And that was that he was keeping an eye on me while trying to ingratiate himself—all because he knew I was involved in the investigation of Eduardo Garcia's murder.

It was an interesting thought. Yet I suddenly remembered that at the moment, I had something more immediate to worry about than Pancho's agenda: my wayward boyfriend and his predatory tour guide. As I sank back onto the wooden bench, contemplating the slabs of meat still waiting for me, I glanced around. I hoped I'd spot him somewhere in the crowd, mingling with someone other than Peyton. No such luck.

What on earth is keeping him? I wondered. *Surely it doesn't take this long to look at a stupid swimming pool.*

"This seat taken?" I looked up and saw Callie hovering near the table, carrying a plate piled high with food.

She didn't wait for an answer before plopping down opposite me.

"Be my guest," I said anyway.

"Where's your boyfriend?" she asked. "I thought I saw him earlier."

"He's taking a tour of the house."

"Ah," Callie said knowingly, sticking a wad of bread into her mouth. "Peyton's got her claws in him."

"She's just being hospitable," I returned, fully aware that it was me I was trying to convince, not Callie.

"Right. My sister is Miss Manners. If I were you, Dr. Popper, I'd keep an eye on her. Nick is pretty cute. If he were my boyfriend, I'd do everything I could to hang on to him."

"Nick's not going anywhere," I insisted.

"Whatever," Callie said, making a face. "By the way, I'm thinking of following up on your suggestion about taking art lessons. I checked the Art Students League's Web site, and it looks like a pretty cool place. My school offers classes, but the teachers aren't very good. I mean, it's not like they're real artists or anything. I go to Porter Hills Academy. Do you know it? It's a private school, full of snobby kids from the North Shore."

"Maybe the other kids are a little stuck-up," I told her, "but I bet you're getting a great education."

"I guess. This year, we're doing Shakespeare. We're starting with *Romeo and Juliet*. In fact, we're having a quiz tomorrow. Yuck."

"That sounds like fun," I commented. "I took a class in Shakespeare my sophomore year of college."

"Then maybe I should ask you to help me cram for this stupid quiz," Callie grumbled. "There's all this stuff on imagery we're supposed to be learning—" She wrenched her head around, suddenly distracted. "Hey, look! They're bringing out dessert! Check out that birthday cake. It's huge!"

Funny, I thought. The fact that Nick still hadn't materialized had completely taken away my appetite.

He still hadn't turned up by the time we'd all sung "Happy Birthday," applauded one of the world's top polo player's astounding ability to blow out twenty-three candles in one breath, and eaten a large portion of the cake. I kept glancing around, feeling like one of those poor, pathetic dogs that's left tied to a parking meter while his owner goes inside. I could only hope that the reason for his disappearance was that Peyton was treating him to the grand tour—and that it was strictly architectural.

By that point, most of the guests had left. After saying good-bye to Callie, I headed toward the parking area in search of my red VW, hoping that sooner or later, Nick would do the same.

As I neared my car, my heart suddenly felt as if it had gained twenty pounds. Another white square stuck out from beneath the windshield wiper.

Maybe it was just a note from one of the Mac-Kinnons, I told myself. Something like, "Please don't park here with our invited guests—use the servants' parking lot." But as I slowly unfolded the single piece of paper, I saw it was another note comprised of glossy letters cut from magazines.

One anonymous note could be chalked up to a practical joke. But two? Somebody was trying awfully hard to get my attention.

I drew my breath in sharply as I read the message.

MeEt mE in SIDe Hether FILd StaBle
SEve n oclOC k Sun Day NITE

I stared at the note for a long time, only vaguely aware of the churning inside my stomach and the sickening pounding of my heart. Who besides Pancho

Escobar knew I'd be coming to Old Brookbury for the polo game the following day? Or did whoever sent the note know that no matter what I'd planned, I'd be curious enough to show up for a secret rendezvous that could very well yield information about Eduardo Garcia's murder?

"Jessie! *There* you are!"

I jerked my head up, relieved to see Nick rushing over in my direction. I quickly folded the note and tucked it away, deep inside my pocket.

As he got closer, I saw that his cheeks were as flushed as I suspected mine were. At first, I assumed it was from jogging in the warm late-September air. Then I remembered where he'd been all evening.

"Did you have fun with Peyton?" I had intended to sound teasing. Instead, my voice sounded accusing.

"Yeah," he answered noncommittally. "Quite a place the MacKinnons have got here. I guess she showed me most of it."

I'll bet. "Did she behave herself?" I couldn't resist asking as we got into the car.

"Y'know, she's not such a bad kid," Nick replied. I noticed that his eyes didn't quite meet mine. "You should really try to get to know her a little."

"Right. I'll do that." An uncomfortable silence fell over us. I pretended the reason was that I was focused on easing my VW out of its parking space. Finally, as we rode along the MacKinnons' long driveway, I said, "By the way, there's another polo match tomorrow, and I was wondering if you'd like to—"

"Sorry, Jess. I can't. Sundays are the best day for me to study."

"Right," I mumbled. "I should have anticipated that."

It wasn't until we'd pulled onto Turkey Hollow Road that I realized how tired I was. Between anonymous notes inviting me to clandestine meetings and spoiled socialites who'd never learned what the word "no" meant, the day had turned out to be more eventful than I'd expected.

I also realized how glad I was to be leaving Heatherfield, even though I knew I'd be back the very next day. And what *that* visit held in store for me, I couldn't begin to imagine.

Chapter 12

"I can always tell which is the front end of a horse, but beyond that, my art is not above the ordinary."
—Mark Twain

As I headed toward Heatherfield early Sunday afternoon—*alone*—I opted to take a different route. I figured I might as well take advantage of being footloose and fancy-free—*again*—to enjoy the sights.

I rolled down the windows as I wound along the tree-lined back roads of the North Shore, enjoying the warm, sunny September day with its pale blue, cloudless sky. This part of Long Island was idyllic, probably much the way it had been during the days the area had been the world's polo center. I drove past country clubs and golf clubs and mansions tucked behind large elms and high stone walls, noting how perfectly manicured every inch of the countryside was.

My route took me into the charming village of Laurel Valley. There wasn't much to the exclusive downtown area, just two crisscrossing streets lined with small businesses. I drove past gift shops that appeared to specialize in highly breakable items and chic clothing boutiques that mainly sold cashmere sweater sets and little black dresses. I also spotted a cigar bar and a French restaurant. Wedged between them were the headquarters of a posh interior designer. The store windows were draped in elegant fabrics suitable for decorating châteaux, with signs advertising Scalamandré and Schumacher and several other top-of-the-line brands I recognized from the Home and Garden Channel.

As I cruised along the main street, I noticed another shop, one I'd driven by dozens of times: the Laurel Valley Tack Shop. On impulse, I pulled my VW into the first parking space I spotted. I didn't have any grand plan in mind, just a vague notion that I might stumble upon something that could be of use.

As I wandered inside, I saw that the tack shop was basically a supermarket for horse lovers. Separate departments sold everything related to horses in any way, shape, or form. The merchandise ranged from saddles and bridles to grooming equipment to specially made cookies for horses.

But the shop's wares went far beyond items designed for the actual care of horses. Its inventory seemed to include any and every product with a horse theme that had ever been manufactured. There was a rack of greeting cards with pictures of horses, a jewelry counter displaying earrings, bracelets, necklaces, and toe rings with horsey images, and leather purses with horseshoe-shaped clasps. I saw drinking glasses and carafes etched with a polo motif, linen dish towels silk-screened with horse heads, a doormat with a picture of a polo player, and a license plate frame that said, "I'd Rather Be Playing Polo." Still, I could have done without the bumper sticker that read, "It Takes Wooden Balls to Play Polo." Given all the variations on the same basic image—

polo ponies carrying mallet-bearing riders—I was surprised the place wasn't crawling with lawyers from Ralph Lauren's staff, looking for lawsuits. Other than being impressed by how many different ways there were to use horse designs, I didn't learn anything new.

In fact, I was on my way out when I noticed a bulletin board near the exit. I stepped closer and scanned the ads that had been thumbtacked up haphazardly: the business cards of various professionals whose skills might be of use to horse enthusiasts, handwritten ads for used trailers and saddles, photographs of horses that were for sale.

But one particular piece of paper caught my attention. Staring back at me was an eye-catching color photograph of an estate that looked oddly familiar. I leaned forward to read the fine print.

OLD BROOKBURY TREASURE

Tucked away on seven landscaped acres, this gracious Country Manor offers Old World elegance amidst a bucolic setting with lush Gardens and specimen trees. Elegant Living Room with fireplace, formal Dining Room, charming Study, state-of-the-art gourmet Kitchen with Butler's area, sun-filled Solarium. Master Suite with skylight, 4 additional BR's, each with own Bath. Guest/Service Wing includes Living Room, Eat-in Kitchen, 2 BR's, Bath. Pool with Pavilion, Sauna, Jacuzzi, Tennis Court, 8-stall stable w/ Tack Room, 4-car Garage. Price Upon Request.

Winston's estate. And it was for sale.

I blinked hard, trying to digest what I was seeing. My head was already buzzing. But I forced myself to calm down enough to scan the rest of the ad. The real estate agent was listed as Dagny Phipps of Stevens Ellison Properties, located on Turkey Hollow Road in Laurel Valley.

Just a few steps away.

I left the tack shop and strode purposefully toward the storefront that housed Stevens Ellison Properties. Out front sat a wrought-iron park bench surrounded by colorful flowers bursting from huge terra-cotta pots. The store window was covered with photographs of homes that were for sale, each one more luxurious than the last. Glancing at the listings, I saw that tennis courts, servants' quarters, and stables were as standard in Old Brookbury as refrigerators and bathrooms were for us common folk. I also noted that nothing seemed to be selling for under seven figures. *Mid*-seven figures.

I smoothed my hair, took a few deep breaths, and put on my snootiest demeanor before waltzing inside, trying to look like someone who *needed* servants' quarters. I had a feeling I wasn't doing a very convincing job, but I wasn't about to let that stop me.

The interior was quiet and dignified, with thick carpeting, upholstered couches, and four large, important-looking desks. The perfect atmosphere for writing large checks.

"Good afternoon," I said brightly, addressing the sole person in the office.

"Good afternoon," the woman replied in a soft, breathy voice. She appeared to be in her late forties or early fifties. Her neat blond pageboy was held back with a black velvet headband and she was extremely thin, dressed in a crisp white blouse and a dark pleated skirt that peeked around the edge of her desk. She reminded me of the headmistress of a prep school for girls. Or at least my fantasy of what such a person would look like.

"Is Dagny Phipps available?" I asked.

"Oh, I'm sorry." She cocked her head to one side

sympathetically. "Ms. Phipps isn't here. She's out, showing a house. I'm just the receptionist, but perhaps I can be of assistance."

"Maybe. I'm interested in an estate that I just learned is up for sale. I believe it belongs to a gentleman named Winston Farnsworth."

Her eyes moved up and down like a yo-yo as she checked me out more carefully. "Is this for ... *you?*"

"My parents," I said quickly. So much for my attempt at appearing suitably snooty.

"Of course." She looked relieved. "Yes, the Farnsworth property is for sale."

"So it's true. Winston really *is* selling his house," I said, still not quite believing what I'd just verified.

"You sound surprised," she observed.

"Well, sure," I replied, taking advantage of the opening she'd inadvertently provided. "I mean, I know Winston Farnsworth. I'm a veterinarian, and his dog, Frederick, is my patient. But I had no idea—"

"We're really not supposed to gossip about our clients," she sniffed, primly folding her hands on top of the desk.

"Of course not!" I agreed. "That would be just awful! Especially in Winston Farnsworth's case!"

She narrowed her eyes. "What do you mean?"

"Surely you've heard the rumors! I mean, someone in *your* position, right in the center of things—why, you must know the true story behind just about everything that goes on in the area. After all, you're one of the key players!"

She looked startled. "Actually," she replied, sounding annoyed, "nobody tells me anything. They don't think it's important to include me, because I'm 'just the receptionist.'" Lowering her voice, she added, "But believe me, I know *plenty*. I keep my ears open, and I hear all kinds of things."

I decided it was time to lay all my cards on the table. "Then you must know if the rumors are true."

A look of uncertainty crossed her face. "You're talking about his financial difficulties, right?"

"Naturally," I said. "And given the fact that he's put his estate on the market, they obviously *are* true."

"That's what happens when you make bad investments," she returned, sounding smug. "I heard he even had to let his housekeeper go. After eleven years! Poor Dora. Such a lovely person. And such a hard worker!"

"Yes, poor Dora," I echoed. "Imagine!"

"If you ask me," she continued, "it was only a question of time before the chickens came home to roost."

I blinked. "Exactly what chickens are you talking about?"

Arching her eyebrows so dramatically that they looked like an advertisement for McDonald's, she said, "Well, from what *I've* heard, the man simply isn't who he pretends to be. Everybody around here seems convinced that he's an absolute charlatan. A fake. Last week, I heard Dagny—uh, Ms. Phipps—talking on the phone, telling somebody that his people were 'nobodies.' She was saying that he never really fit in here, and that it was hardly surprising that his little charade had finally come to an end!"

She suddenly looked stricken, as if she'd realized that maybe, just maybe, she'd said a bit more than her employers would have liked.

"But that doesn't mean he's willing to come down in price." Her tone had become crisp and businesslike. "The Farnsworth property is still a real gem, and we expect it to bring in top dollar."

"Maybe I'd better come back when Ms. Phipps is here," I said. Quickly, I added, "So I can take a look at the estate, I mean. And see if it's right for my parents. The, uh, Vanderbilt-Guggenheims."

The woman smiled at me brightly. "I'm sure they'll love it. Here, I'll give you her card. Thanks for coming in!"

But as I headed back to my car, I found myself wishing I'd stayed a bit longer. I wanted to know more. Like exactly what the rumors about Winston Farnsworth were—and what people were saying was the cause of his sudden financial loss. I was also curious about just how much of a "charlatan" he was considered to be.

Especially since the argument I'd overheard Andrew MacKinnon and Winston having the day of Eduardo's funeral kept playing through my head.

"Andrew, my good man," I could distinctly remember him saying, "we're talking about a *great* deal of money!"

And from what I could tell, that financial loss had had something to do with Eduardo.

When I reached Heatherfield, I was still shaky from what I'd learned about Winston's recent reversal of fortune. I headed straight for the stable, glad that, for once, Johnny Ray was nowhere in sight. In fact, the only sign of life, aside from the few horses that remained in the barn, was Hector.

We exchanged a few words, partly in English, partly with sign language, and partly using the few Spanish phrases I'd picked up from dealing with Spanish-speaking clients. Then I examined Braveheart. He not only seemed fine; he seemed to be telling me, through the burning intensity of his dark brown eyes, that he was itching to get out on the polo field again.

"*Braveheart es bueno*," I told Hector. "*Y Molly es buena.*"

Glad that at least one thing in my life was going smoothly—my medical practice—I stopped at the house, figuring I'd give Andrew MacKinnon the good news that both his horses were doing just fine.

I rang the doorbell, then waited. There was no response. I walked around to the back door, the one that opened onto the patio. As I peered through the screen door, I didn't see any signs of life. But I could hear music playing softly—a radio, maybe, or a CD player.

"Hello?" I called a few times. When no one answered, I wondered if the music was drowning out my voice. I opened the screen door and tried again. "Hello? Anyone here?"

I stepped inside, wondering if I'd find Andrew MacKinnon in his study. Still calling "hello" so my unexpected appearance wouldn't startle anyone, I took a few steps down the hall and stuck my head inside. The room was empty.

I decided to leave him a note, since Braveheart needed to warm up if he was going to play polo at three o'clock. I also wanted to recommend that the gelding be allowed to take it easy. I glanced around, wondering where I might find a pen and a piece of paper. I didn't see any in the study. As I stepped back into the hallway, I realized the music was coming from upstairs.

"Hello?" I called again, standing at the bottom of the stairway and hoping whoever was on the second floor would hear me. I walked up the stairs slowly, finally reaching the landing.

I still hadn't gotten any response. But the music was clearly coming from one of the bedrooms. Callie's room, from the looks of it.

"Callie? Are you up here?" I called, going over to the doorway. Sure enough, a radio was blasting, but no one was there.

I stepped inside. *You shouldn't be in here,* a little voice told me. I decided to ignore it.

The bright, sunny bedroom was the realization of

what was undoubtedly most little girls' fantasy. Unfortunately, from what I knew of Callie, there was no way it was hers. The furniture was white, hand-painted with delicate flowers in pale shades of pink and lavender. If that wasn't sweet enough to provide a sugar rush, the effect was augmented with white ruffled curtains, a white satin bedspread edged with throw pillows in the same pastel colors, and fluffy pink carpeting.

Even if Callie *had* been the kind of little girl who'd appreciated living in Barbie's Dream House, at this point she was much too grown-up to be comfortable in such surroundings. The CD's, DVD's, and copies of *Teen People* and *Us* were proof. As I surveyed the clutter, I spotted a large sketchbook. Glancing around to make sure no one had snuck up on me, I carefully slid it out, taking care not to let Christina Aguilera or Ricky Martin fall.

I began flipping through the pages, marveling over the girl's drawings. Callie really had talent, I thought. She seemed to enjoy drawing the things that mattered to her most. She'd done several landscapes that captured the rustic beauty of Heatherfield, charcoal drawings of grassy fields edged with lush red maples and lofty oaks. A few of her sketches were of horses. I recognized Braveheart, standing proud and alone. I wished I could suggest that she frame it and give it to her father to hang in his study, but since I wasn't supposed to be snooping around in the first place, I couldn't let on that I'd seen it. Another drawing was the cat I'd seen hanging around the stable, the target of Max and Lou's wrath. She'd done a lovely drawing of him sleeping in the sun, capturing shadow and light with amazing deftness.

I flipped over to the next page—and froze. The pencil sketch was a well-executed portrait of Eduardo that expertly captured every detail of his face: his dark liquid eyes fringed with thick lashes, his strong jawline, his sensual mouth. Callie had even included the scars I'd noticed in his photograph. Even more startling was the way she'd managed to capture the distinctive liveliness that was reflected in his eyes and the almost jeering twist of his lips.

My mind was spinning. Was it possible Callie made this rendering just by looking at a photograph? I wondered. Maybe—but my hunch was that she'd gotten up close and personal. It was simply too good a likeness. Yet she claimed to despise Eduardo Garcia. Was she using that as her cover story, reinforcing my theory that she was determined to conceal a secret crush?

I turned the page, still feeling a little unsettled. The next drawing was also of Eduardo. He sat astride Braveheart, his handsome face tense with concentration as he prepared to swing the mallet in his hand. Once again, Callie had done an amazing job of capturing both his strength and his grace.

There were several more. I leafed through the sketchbook, admiring a drawing of the handsome polo player in the barn, adjusting Molly's bridle, then another that showed him standing at the edge of a field, staring off in the distance.

My heart skipped when I turned the next page. Eduardo again.

But this time, he was completely naked.

He lay stretched across Callie's bed, his head framed by the same hand-painted headboard that was right in front of me. Like the others, this drawing was expertly executed, detailing Eduardo's well-developed muscles, his tanned skin, even the dark curly hair on his chest. And the taunting expression I'd seen hinted at before was in full force here.

I stared at the sketch, wondering, Did this really happen? Did Eduardo actually pose for her—*naked*? Or was all this simply the fantasy of a little girl who had a crush on a roguish polo player who offered her little attention besides the occasional pat on the head?

I jumped when I heard a noise. Footsteps, hurrying along the hallway. Someone was coming.

I flipped the sketchbook shut, trying my best not to look like someone who'd almost been caught doing something she wasn't supposed to be doing. I also tried desperately to think of an excuse for being in Callie's room.

I glanced around, then noticed that the bedroom had its own private bathroom. Not surprisingly, the tile and fixtures were pink. I darted inside and turned on the sink faucet, then began humming, as if choosing the bathroom adjoining Callie's bedroom to wash my hands were the most natural thing in the world.

When I heard someone come in, I turned off the faucet and took my time drying my hands, still humming. As I stepped out of the bathroom and saw Peyton standing just inside the bedroom doorway, I made a point of looking startled. Then I smiled.

"Oh, hello, Peyton," I said casually. "I didn't hear you come in."

"What are *you* doing here?" she demanded.

"I just popped into the bathroom to wash my hands." I held my breath, wondering if she'd buy my story, which was about as flimsy as the peach-colored piece of gauze currently masquerading as her skirt. I needn't have worried.

"Well, if you see that obnoxious sister of mine, tell her I'm looking for her," she returned with a pout. "Somebody stole the September issue of *Vogue* out of my room, and I can guess who it was!"

"I'll tell her," I returned.

She turned on the heel of what I suspected was a very expensive leather sandal and stalked out of the room.

I waited until she was out of sight, then slunk out.

But the anxiety created by nearly being caught red-handed, or at least *wet*-handed, was already behind me. Instead, I was busy pondering what Callie's relationship with Eduardo Garcia had been—and why she'd been so insistent about hating him when her drawings clearly indicated otherwise.

Of course, there was one obvious answer. But the possibility that Callie had killed Eduardo was simply too devastating to contemplate.

I was so lost in thought that I didn't notice I'd taken a wrong turn as I wandered along the path that led away from the MacKinnons' mansion. At least, not until I suddenly found myself facing a small Tudor-style cottage I hadn't seen before. It was so tiny, in fact, that I wondered if it was a playhouse, built years ago for Andrew's two daughters to enjoy.

Unable to contain my curiosity, I strolled around the side, wondering if I dared peek into a window. But as I reached the back, I saw that a door that led into a kitchen was ajar, and that Inez was standing inside.

"Oh, I'm sorry!" I exclaimed. "I had no idea someone lived here!"

"Ees all right," she assured me with a shy smile. "Ees nice to have some company."

"This is certainly a cute little building," I observed. "Do you live here alone?"

She nodded. "A few of us who work for Meester Mac live here on the property. Luisa, she live in the house. Johnny Ray has a small apartment above the stable. Hector, too, has a small room there. But I am the most lucky because I have the nicest place to live. Ees very comfortable. Would you like to see?"

"Sure," I told her, partly because I didn't want to

seem rude and partly because I really was eager to see if the interior was as charming as the exterior.

As I stepped inside, however, I saw that the guest cottage hadn't been maintained with quite the same care as the rest of the estate. The kitchen looked as if it hadn't been redone since the 1970's, as indicated by the cracked linoleum and the avocado green refrigerator. Still, it was very clean, and Inez had added some homey touches. A large bouquet of wildflowers was centered on the small kitchen table, and a row of flowerpots lined the windowsill. They included an herb garden as well as two or three ornamental plants that appeared to be basking in the sunlight. A collection of photographs was haphazardly stuck onto the refrigerator with magnets shaped like fruit.

"Is this your family?" I asked, stepping over to the refrigerator.

"*Sí,*" she replied. "All of them are still at home, in Puerto Rico. Luisa, she has family here, so on the weekend, like today, she goes to visit with them. But me," she added with a little shrug, "I am the only one in my family brave enough to come to thees country."

I scanned the photographs of her cousins and uncles and aunts, posed together in various combinations. There were so many different faces, people of all ages and body types. Inez had clearly come from a very large family, yet here she was alone.

"Would you like to see the rest of the house?" she offered proudly.

"I'd love to," I told her. "Especially since you've added so many nice touches."

I followed her into the small living room, outfitted with bland beige curtains, a sagging couch, and a low coffee table made of dark wood. Through an open door, I could see the third room of the cottage, a bedroom that was barely big enough for the double bed. On it was a well-worn chenille bedspread that looked more Sears than Scalamandré.

Still, Inez had made her mark in these rooms, as well. She had tacked travel posters of Puerto Rico up on the walls, glamorous shots of magnificent beaches dotted with palm trees. I suspected that she hadn't actually spent much time sunning herself on the beaches of Porta del Sol while growing up there, but the posters did add color. She had lined the windowsills with healthy-looking houseplants, and a ragged-looking stuffed tiger sat on the bed. The one small table in the living room, as well as the night table next to the bed, were covered with framed photographs that I surmised were more family members.

"You've decorated it very nicely," I observed, glancing around. "The photographs make it so homey. Do you get back to Puerto Rico to visit very often?"

"No, not so often," she said. "I mees them all very much." She paused to shrug. "But I am very busy, working for Meester Mac and his family. They have all been so kind to me."

"Except Peyton," I couldn't help interjecting.

"She is young," Inez said softly, as if youth and rudeness were interchangeable.

I didn't bother to point out that Inez and Peyton were probably only a few years apart—yet life had dealt them both very different hands.

"Well, I'll let you get back to whatever you were doing," I said. "Thank you for the tour."

I glanced at my watch and saw that it was getting late. The afternoon's polo match would be starting soon. And after that, I had an important appointment that I was determined to keep—even though I didn't know who it was with or what it was designed to accomplish.

• • •

While I'd found my first polo game a fascinating experience, I suspected that I'd have trouble concentrating on my second one. The mysterious meeting scheduled for later on that day was simply too much of a distraction.

At least this will keep me busy, I told myself as I walked through the Meadowlark Polo Club's parking area, toward the playing field.

I was about to take a seat in back, someplace discreet that offered a good view of the action, when I spotted Forrester. He was sitting smack in the middle of the bleachers. I climbed up to his row and plopped down next to him.

"My, my, fancy meeting you here," I remarked. "Goodness, these days even polo seems to attract riffraff!"

Forrester grinned. "I see you're in top form today, Popper. Ready for your advanced class in polo?"

"Thanks, but I've already learned plenty. All I need is a mallet and a good pair of boots and I'll be ready to play."

"Hey, polo's not just a male sport, you know."

"I never said it was."

"In fact, I'm sure someone as well versed as you are in the sport of polo is familiar with Louise Hitchcock."

"Don't tell me. Shirley Muldowney's long lost twin, right?"

"Not even close," Forrester returned, "unless speed counts. Lulie—Louise—Hitchock is considered the mother of women's polo, not to mention a significant figure in Long Island's history. In the early 1900's, she founded a polo school less than a mile from here. A co-ed polo school, with boys and girls competing against each other. Pretty revolutionary, in those days. A few years later, Lulie put together a team that included her and her two daughters and played against one of the men's teams. It attracted quite a large crowd."

"Goodness, you're just a font of knowledge, aren't you?"

"Don't tell me you don't find this stuff as fascinating as I do, Popper."

Before I could come up with a snappy reply, the commentator's voice came over the amplification system, loud and clear. "*Good afternoon, ladies and gentlemen...*"

"Showtime," I muttered.

"Really?" Forrester commented, putting on a pair of dark sunglasses and glancing around. "And here I thought the real show was in the stands."

"*The ball is hit by Pancho Escobar...*" the commentator's voice boomed. "*That's Johnny Ray Cousins on the ball for Blue Heather....*"

"He's really good," I said, leaning forward as Johnny Ray deftly smacked the ball and sent it flying down the field.

"There's something to be said for clear eyes and steady hands," Forrester returned. "And now, with Eduardo out of the way..."

"*Scott Mooney taps the ball into play... He accelerates his pony, keeping the ball in front... The ball is hit by Pancho Escobar... and that's Johnny Ray Cousins at Number Two for Blue Heather... and a score!*"

"Go, Johnny, go!" Forrester exclaimed. Turning, he peered at me over the top of his frames. "What do you think, Popper? Is the missing piece of the puzzle Johnny Ray wanting to make a comeback? Is that what Eduardo's murder is all about?"

"There's got to be an easier way to get out on the polo field," I replied. "Unless there's some past history between them..."

"Frankly, our pal Johnny Ray doesn't strike me as the most stable guy in the world. All that smoldering anger. He's kind of creepy, don't you think?"

"If I had to describe him in twenty-five words or less," I told him, " 'creepy' would definitely be one of them."

I wondered how good a speller he was.

I considered telling Forrester about the anonymous invitation. But I was afraid that his sense of chivalry would kick in and he'd insist on coming with me—or worse yet, that he'd notify Falcone.

And that would completely ruin my chances of learning whatever my secret pen pal was so anxious to tell me.

However, Johnny Ray wasn't the only murder suspect at the game that day, either on the field or off it. I glanced around the stands, studying the spectators and wondering if I'd find one of them waiting for me inside the MacKinnons' stable. I knew my mysterious pen pal could easily be any one of them. The idea that whoever it was might also be watching *me*, trying to gauge my reaction to our face-to-face meeting, made it nearly impossible for me to pay attention.

Yet as I drove up the driveway at Heatherfield a few minutes before seven, a strange feeling of tranquillity settled over me. Finally, there was going to be some resolution. Even being threatened in person was better than all this secretiveness.

At least I'd find out who was warning me off the case.

I parked in the driveway, glancing around and noticing how unusually quiet Heatherfield seemed. It was hardly surprising, on a Sunday evening. Most of the people who'd attended the polo game had gone directly to the Old Brookbury Country Club for some social event. I was sure that included at least some members of the MacKinnon clan.

In fact, the estate felt like a ghost town.

Somebody did a good job of planning this, I thought

wryly as I trekked toward the stable. *There's no one around to hear me scream for help.*

Only kidding, I told myself as I neared the main door. Still, I took a few deep breaths and tried to slow the pounding of my heart.

"Here goes," I muttered. I reached up and pulled on the door's handle, surprised when I met with resistance.

That's funny, I thought, yanking on the handle a few more times. Why would the stable be locked?

Peering between the door and the jamb, I could see a metal bolt. Still puzzled, I went around to the side of the building, where there was a second door. That one turned out to be locked, too.

I frowned. At that point, there was only one other door to try, located behind the building. That one led inside the tack room. I went around to the back, wondering if the person who'd sent me that anonymous invitation had planned on making things so difficult—or if our "secret meeting" was simply becoming unexpectedly complicated because of bad luck.

As I rounded the corner, I saw that the tack room door was ajar. *Finally,* I thought grimly. *So I haven't come here on a fool's errand after all.*

I was heading toward it when something on the ground caught my attention. The sudden movement startled me, making me jump.

I glanced down—and instantly my heartbeat quickened. Even in the darkening shadows of dusk, I could see a long, narrow shape slithering across the stubble of grass. The shape was covered in gray leathery skin with dark blotches. From where I stood, it looked as if it was about three feet long—and it was heading in my direction.

"Oh, my God!" I gasped, reeling backward. "A rattlesnake!"

Instinctively, I began running in the opposite direction.

It wasn't until I'd gone nearly twenty feet that I remembered that we don't *have* rattlesnakes on Long Island. Actually, we don't have much in the way of snakes at all.

The only variety I knew of, in fact, was the Eastern hognose snake.

Standing half hidden by a tree, I peered at the slithering reptile, trying to remember the last time I'd forced myself to look at a picture of a hognose. That was a tough call, since even photographs of Serpentes practically make me break out in hives. Though I've dedicated my life to helping animals, I can't help having a visceral reaction to snakes. It's not something I'm particularly proud of, but it's something I've never been able to overcome.

Even from my vantage point, I could see that this snake had the distinctive snout that had earned it its name. This beast was undoubtedly a hognose—which meant it wasn't dangerous. True, they have a hood that makes them resemble a cobra, and they exaggerate that look whenever they're threatened as a means of discouraging predators. But they're nonvenomous, and the worst thing they're capable of doing is rolling around in their own feces and emitting a horrible-smelling secretion to repulse any birds of prey that might be considering them as a possible luncheon entrée.

But my reaction to snakes has never been based on logic. And this encounter was no exception. No matter what my brain told me, the shuddering throughout the rest of my body made it clear there was no way I was going to tangle with this character.

Keeping my distance, I continued eyeing the loathsome reptile. I figured that sooner or later he'd move away from the doorway. Then, I'd be able to go into the stable and confront my mysterious pen pal. But instead of cooperating, the snake slithered back toward the building. Then he curled up like a Christmas wreath right in front of the door, blocking my only means of access.

Great, I thought. *Now what?*

But I knew the answer. I was going to have to find a way to get past the one living, breathing creature on the planet that I had a difficult time dealing with.

Think, I instructed myself, aware that the seconds were ticking away. I glanced at my watch and saw it was already five minutes after seven. The person who was expecting to meet me was probably already inside the stable, wondering where the heck I was.

And then a lightbulb went on in my head. *An umbrella,* I thought. There was one in my car. If I could gently remove the obstacle from my path, without having to get too close to him...

I immediately retraced my steps, going around to the front of the stable and continuing on to my car. I moved quickly, afraid that I'd miss my rendezvous, thanks to the uninvited serpentine interloper.

I'd just reached my car when I became aware of a familiar smell. It was an unpleasant smell...and a dangerous smell, one that immediately sent adrenaline surging through my veins.

Something was burning.

In my confusion, I frantically examined my Volkswagen. There was no sign that anything was out of order. I turned, scanning the grounds that surrounded me, anxiously searching for signs of fire.

And then I saw it. A cloud of dark smoke, wafting upward from the stable.

"The stable's on fire!" I screeched, racing toward the building. "Fire! Fire! Somebody call nine-one-one!"

As I said those last words, I realized I had my cell phone with me. I pulled it out and dialed the three numbers. Still jogging across the field, I cried, "There's a fire at Heatherfield, in the stable! The address is twenty-five

Turkey Hollow Road in Old Brookbury. Please send help—and hurry!"

By then, I'd reached the MacKinnons' house. I flung open the front door, yelling, "The stable's on fire! Come quick!"

Then I ran back toward the stable, my heart racing so hard I felt nauseous.

The horses! I thought as I drew near and saw the cloud of black smoke that encircled the yellow building. Bright flames licked the edge of one window. *There are horses inside!*

That idea sickened me even more than the jackhammer pounding of my heart or the thickening smoke that was beginning to burn my nostrils.

As I approached the stable, I could hear shouts. I was relieved to see that Johnny Ray, Hector, and Andrew were already on the scene. Callie was charging across the lawn, pulling on a bathrobe and looking dazed. Inez, meanwhile, came running from the direction of her cottage. But even the realization that help was on the way couldn't keep my stomach from wrenching at the sight of the orange flames shooting out of one of the side windows and the huge cloud of smoke hovering above the building.

"Damn it, get the hose!" MacKinnon shouted. "Callie, Inez . . . anybody!"

"I've got it, Daddy!" Callie yelled back. "Inez, help me!"

As he raced toward the building, he demanded, "Hector, which horses are inside?"

"Five horses, in the east wing!" Hector yelled back. "Braveheart, Molly, Stryder, Austin, and Dani."

"Johnny, Hector, help me with this," MacKinnon cried. "We're going in!"

I started to follow, but Johnny Ray called over his shoulder. "Stay out, Dr. Popper! We've got this covered!"

"The horses!" I cried.

"Damn it, we don't want to be responsible if anything happens to you!"

Andrew MacKinnon reached the main door first. He yanked on the handle, then cried, "Damn it, it's locked! Who the hell locked this thing?"

Hector and Johnny Ray were already heading around the side of the building.

"This one's locked, too!" Hector called, trying the side door.

"This one, too!" I heard Johnny Ray yell. "What the hell—?"

But MacKinnon hadn't waited. He'd pulled out a ring of keys and was already wrestling with the lock. It only took him a second or two to wrench it open.

I stood by helplessly, watching the three men race inside. Glancing back, I saw Inez and Callie struggling with a garden hose, dragging it toward the stable. From inside the burning building, I could hear the terrified whinnying of the horses. The smoke was getting thicker, and the flames were now licking the edge of a second window.

Without waiting another second, I dashed into the stable. The clouds of thick black smoke that were quickly spreading through the interior burned the inside of my nose, but I could still see well enough. At the end of hall, Hector was leading two of the horses out. Their eyes were wild with fear, but they allowed him to drag them toward the door. Johnny Ray was nowhere to be seen.

My head snapped around at the sound of a frightened whinny. I saw that Braveheart was still in his stall. MacKinnon was trying to get him out, but the gelding had panicked. He reared up, whacking MacKinnon in the chest with his front right leg. MacKinnon cried out in pain and stumbled backward, instinctively covering his face with his arm.

The gesture seemed to frighten Braveheart even more. The horse reared up again, this time flailing against the wooden wall of his stall.

"It's okay, Braveheart!" I cried, stepping into the fray. I tore off the light cotton sweater I was wearing and dunked it into the water pail. After wringing it out quickly, I draped it over the terrified horse's head, blindfolding him.

He immediately calmed down. I grabbed his halter and snapped on a lead rope, then guided him out of the stable.

"I've got Braveheart," I yelled to Andrew MacKinnon. "Make sure all the others are out!"

As I led the horse out into the yard, I saw that Johnny Ray had the last two. He took hold of Braveheart's lead rope, and he and Hector led all five frightened horses toward the safety of a distant paddock.

"Dr. Popper, get out of there!" Callie yelled. She ran over and grabbed my arm, pulling me away. I was so dazed that it took me a few seconds to realize that the high-pitched noise reverberating in my ears was the sound of sirens.

"Thank God!" I muttered as two fire engines came bumping across the driveway, their sirens shrieking and their lights flashing. They'd barely stopped before half a dozen firefighters sprang from the trucks and began readying the hoses.

"The horses are safe!" MacKinnon called to them. "There's no one inside!"

I was suddenly exhausted. I realized I was trembling as Callie led me to a grassy spot a safe distance away.

"Are you okay?" she demanded anxiously. "Did you breathe in any smoke? We learned in school that—"

"I'm fine," I assured her, my breaths sounding like

gasps. "All the horses got out, right? We're absolutely sure of it?"

"They're all out," she replied. "My dad would never let anything bad happen to them."

I just nodded, too depleted to speak.

I watched the firefighters douse the burning building with water, subduing the flames but sending clouds of ugly smoke upward to darken the sky. The five horses were out of danger. Hector, Johnny Ray, and Mac-Kinnon were standing with Inez, a safe distance away.

It was only then that I fully comprehended what had happened.

Someone deliberately set the stable on fire, I realized. Someone who thought I was locked inside ...

Someone who wanted me dead.

Chapter 13

"A canter is the cure for all evil."

—Benjamin Disraeli

We all watched in dazed silence as the firefighters finished the job. But my head was buzzing so loudly I was surprised everyone else couldn't hear it.

It can't have been a coincidence, I thought. I *was supposed to be in the stable.* Two of the doors were already locked, meaning I'd have had to enter through the back door. Once I was inside—or at least *believed* to be inside by whoever planned this whole thing—it was a simple matter of locking the third and last door, setting the building on fire, and sneaking away.

Which is exactly what would have happened if it hadn't been for that snake.

The scenario was almost too horrifying to imagine. Yet it kept playing through my head as I stood with Callie still clutching my arm, watching the fire trucks pull out of Heatherfield.

Seconds after they left, another vehicle came barreling onto the property, sending up a spray of pebbles and dirt.

A dark blue Crown Victoria that I recognized as Lieutenant Anthony Falcone's car.

My heart sank even further. *How could today get any worse?* I wondered.

I shouldn't have asked. The sight of a dark green SUV trundling up the driveway, a few yards behind Falcone's car, gave me my answer. It jerked to a stop less than ten feet in front of me.

"What the hell is going on around here?" Forrester demanded, springing out of his monster-sized vehicle and planting himself in front of me.

"You tell me," I replied wearily. "You're the ace reporter."

He shook his head in disbelief. "First murder, now arson..."

"How do you know it was arson?" I shot back.

"I *don't* know—at least not yet. But you want to bet there's an arson inspector here within an hour?"

I glanced at Lieutenant Falcone, who was standing a hundred feet away. He looked like he was finishing up the earnest conversation he was having with Andrew MacKinnon. I cringed when he headed in my direction.

"Dr. Popper. We meet again." His beady black eyes traveled up and down, as if he were evaluating the subject standing before me: me. "Ever notice that the only time you and I run into each other is when something terrible has just happened?"

"Maybe we should schedule a lunch date," I suggested. I tossed my head, trying to appear a lot more confident than I happened to be feeling at the moment.

He didn't look the least bit amused. "Wanna tell me what happened here?" he asked. As usual, his tone had a taunting quality that made my blood boil. It was almost as if he expected that the MacKinnons' stable being set on fire was somehow *my* fault.

A debate was raging inside my head. I had seconds to decide whether I should come clean and tell him about the anonymous note that had been designed to put me inside the stable at the exact time it was being set on fire—or keep that piece of information to myself.

The decision was made for me.

"This might be a good time to tell him about the note," Forrester prompted.

Lieutenant Falcone focused his eyes on mine. They burned with the intensity of lasers. "Dr. Popper?" he demanded. "What's he talkin' about?"

I was about to cast Forrester the nastiest glare I could manage. But I realized that he was probably right. It no longer made sense to keep silent about the anonymous communications I'd received.

I cleared my throat nervously, bracing myself for Falcone's response. "Two notes, actually."

Forrester looked surprised, but he remained silent. As for Falcone, he drew his lips into a straight line.

"Go on," he said in a cold voice.

"I found the first one last Sunday. Somebody left an anonymous note on my van while I was here at Heatherfield. I'd gone to the polo match at the Meadowlark Polo Club, and afterward the MacKinnons invited Nick and me to a cocktail party."

" 'Nick?' " he repeated.

"Nick Burby. My boyfriend. I believe you two met briefly. In the Bromptons? Back in June?"

"Sure, sure. I remember. Go on."

"Anyway, after dinner, when I went out to my van, I found a note on the windshield. It was composed of letters that had been cut out of a magazine."

"And exactly what did this note say?" Falcone was beginning to sound irritated.

"Here, I can show it to you." I retrieved it from my purse, unfolded it, and handed it to him.

" 'Too many questions. Mind your own business.' " Falcone's eyes narrowed as he read it aloud. There was something else in his expression I couldn't quite read. Something hard.

"Do you happen to have any idea why somebody might have left you a note like this?"

"Obviously someone thought I was getting a little too close to figuring out who murdered Eduardo Garcia."

"And do you know *why* somebody might have thought that?" Lieutenant Falcone demanded.

I stood up a little straighter. "I've been doing a lot of work for Andrew MacKinnon over the past two weeks. His regular veterinarian broke his leg, so I've been filling in. I've also picked up a few new clients in the area and I've been treating their dogs and cats."

"So you're saying it's just bad timing."

"Something like that."

He remained silent. But while he didn't say anything, he kept watching me. I just watched back.

"What about the second one?" he finally asked.

"I have it here," I said, pulling it out. "This one was left on my windshield yesterday. I came to Heatherfield for Pancho Escobar's birthday celebration."

His facial muscles tensed as he ran his eyes over it. "So you were supposed to be in the stable at seven, the same time the fire broke out."

"My God, Jess!" Forrester blurted out.

"So it seems," I replied.

"These notes should have been entered as evidence!" Lieutenant Falcone barked, finally letting loose. "Don't you know obstructing a police investigation is a serious offense?"

"I didn't consider those notes evidence," I replied archly. "In fact, I didn't take the first one at all seriously. It wasn't until I saw the stable go up in flames that I understood that I was being set up."

Pointedly, Falcone turned around to glance at the charred building. A cloud of smoke hovered ominously over the wreckage. "I'd say this is pretty serious, Dr. Popper."

"Well, I know that *now*."

"I'm taking them with me for fingerprinting," Falcone insisted.

I handed the second note over, countering, "Don't you think whoever went to the trouble of making them was clever enough to wear gloves? After all, he figured out he should use cutout letters so we wouldn't identify him through his handwriting."

He ignored my question. Instead, he fixed his piercing eyes on me again. "What exactly do you think you're doing?" he asked accusingly.

I blinked. "Excuse me?"

"You seem to think you're some self-appointed private investigator at large or somethin'. Every time I turn around, you're smack in the middle of one of my murder investigations. It's like you're tryin' to do my job. In the meantime, you got no credentials, no training, no experience—"

"Excuse me," I interrupted, this time using quite a different tone. "I don't know where you get off telling me I'm 'trying to do your job.' As a matter of fact, I'm trying to do *my* job. Aside from a cocktail party and celebrating Pancho Escobar's birthday, the only reason I have ever come to Heatherfield—or anywhere else in Old Brookbury, for that matter—has been to treat sick animals. Andrew MacKinnon's barn manager asked me to come here on several occasions to treat their horses.

I've also treated dogs and cats belonging to people who live in the area. Winston Farnsworth, Diana Chase, Vivian Johannsen..."

I paused to take a deep breath, trying to calm down. It didn't work. "And you're right about me having no credentials or training in the area of homicide investigation. Which is why I've been spending my time practicing veterinary medicine, a field in which I *do* have credentials—a Bachelor of Arts degree in Biology from Bryn Mawr College and a Doctor of Veterinary Medicine degree from Cornell University. If you'd like to see my diplomas, you're welcome to step into my van any time.

"As for recent events," I continued hotly, "if someone around here has decided to make me the target of a twisted letter-writing campaign—and if that same someone or some *other* someone gets off on setting barns on fire and endangering the lives of people and animals, not to mention destroying valuable property—and that person manages to get away with these things without getting caught, then I'd say that someone who *does* have credentials and training and experience in the field of homicide investigation isn't exactly doing *his* job!"

Falcone just stared at me. I stared right back, not even blinking.

"I don't want to see you anywhere near here again," he finally said, speaking in a low, angry tone.

I stood up a little straighter. "Unless you've got some legal ground to stand on, I'd suggest that you refrain from telling me where and how to conduct my professional life," I returned. "I am licensed to practice veterinary medicine throughout New York State, and that's precisely what I intend to continue doing."

Falcone's lip curled into a sneer, and his black eyes blazed. I sensed he was trying to come up with a retort.

But I didn't wait. Instead, my hands clenched into fists, I turned away and stalked off toward the MacKinnons' house.

Unfortunately for Forrester, he caught up with me as I neared the front door.

"Way to go, Popper!" he breathed. "You sure held your own with Falcone!"

Maybe under other circumstances, I would have been amused, or even flattered, by what Forrester clearly meant as a compliment. However, given the fact that I'd nearly come up close and personal with a fire that was raging inside a locked wooden building, I wasn't exactly in the mood for clever repartee.

"Forrester, do me a favor," I said crossly.

"Sure, Popper. You da *man*!"

"Good. Then listen to 'da man' and just go away."

I barely had time to notice that his expression had changed from admiring to astonished before I turned away and headed inside the house. Frankly, I hoped it was the last time I'd ever see Forrester Sloan's face again.

However, I immediately confronted another face I recognized. As I stepped into the foyer of the MacKinnons' mansion, not even bothering to knock, Callie came down the stairs with a large sketchbook in hand. Her tousled blond hair was pulled back into a loose ponytail, and she was dressed in jeans and an oversized T-shirt.

"Are you okay?" she asked anxiously.

"I'm fine," I assured her. *At least physically,* I thought. As for coming *this* close to being trapped inside a burning building...that was something I was going to have to find a way to deal with. And it was going to take some time.

As if she knew what I was thinking, Callie commented, "At least nobody got hurt."

I nodded. "Yes, thank goodness no one was in the barn." Suddenly, a horrifying thought popped into my head. "Where's Peyton?" I demanded. "I haven't seen her all day."

"Don't worry," Callie assured me. "She never goes into the stable. Besides, she's not even home. She stormed out of here hours ago."

I frowned. "Is something wrong?"

"She had a huge fight with my parents."

"About what?"

"Apparently my mother opened a piece of her mail and found out she'd been thrown out of her summer program." Callie laughed disdainfully. "Like anybody should be surprised that Peyton spent, like, no time in class because she was so busy hanging out at clubs and taking off for the beach.

"Anyway, she's not getting any credit, and they made her move out of the dorm early. And of course they're not giving any of the money back, even though it cost a fortune. So my mother went nuts, screaming about how she and my father have always given her whatever she wants, but she still keeps screwing up. Even my dad was furious with Peyton, and that *never* happens. So she started crying and moaning about how they don't appreciate how hard she tries...like anybody believes *that*. Anyway, I don't know where she is right now, and frankly, I couldn't care less."

I didn't say anything. I was too busy digesting what I'd just learned. At least I now knew why Peyton had come home from Europe early. I also understood that she'd had good reason to lie about it, since she hadn't wanted her parents to find out. Of course, that still didn't account for how she'd spent those extra days back in the New York area....

And then something else became clear: If Peyton had

left Heatherfield hours ago, she couldn't have set the fire. Unless, of course, she'd snuck back....

"Frankly, I'm *glad* she got in trouble, for a change," Callie went on. "She always gets away with murder. And instead of appreciating the fact that she's got my parents wrapped around her finger—well, my dad, anyway—she thinks she's entitled to, like, the whole world. She thinks it's fun to play with people, you know? To her, everything's a game. It's like she's convinced she can do or say whatever she wants, and there's never any consequences."

I couldn't agree with you more, I thought. *Especially since I'm one of the people she seems to enjoy playing with.*

"Anyway," Callie asked, already losing interest in the topic of her sister, "what's that homicide guy doing here? Falcone, or whatever his name is."

"Lieutenant Falcone. He's here because somebody most likely started that fire on purpose."

"Arson?" Callie's blue eyes widened. "But then why wouldn't the police send an arson guy?"

I hesitated, wondering how much to tell her. "They will. But Lieutenant Falcone thinks the fire was related to Eduardo Garcia's murder." In response to her puzzled look, I added, "It's possible that whoever set the fire was trying to scare me away from investigating the case."

She frowned, looking more confused than ever. "Wait a sec. I thought you were a veterinarian. You mean you're not?"

"I am a vet, Callie. But I also have this habit of sticking my nose where it doesn't belong. Mainly, into murder investigations. It's kind of like a hobby."

"You mean you've done this before?"

"Once or twice," I replied wearily.

"I get it. So *you're* the reason somebody set the stable

on fire—and it was probably done by the same person who killed Eduardo."

"Exactly."

"Wow." Callie blinked. "In that case, you must be freaking out!"

"I am," I admitted. "In fact, if you don't mind, I think I'd just like to use your bathroom for five minutes so I can clean up and go home."

"Sure. I don't blame you."

I was about to leave when I heard her call, "Dr. Popper?"

I glanced back over my shoulder.

"Just tell me one thing," she said. "Did it work?"

I shook my head to show I didn't understand her question.

"Did nearly getting trapped in a burning building make you decide to butt out?"

I thought for a few seconds, caught off guard by her question—and the blunt way she asked it.

"I guess it did," I told her, then turned away.

As I headed toward the door, I was already agonizing over how I would ever manage to tell Nick about this. Given the fact that he wasn't exactly crazy about my penchant for nosing around murder investigations, I expected a long string of *I told you so*'s. Or worse, he wouldn't say anything. He'd just look at me so mournfully that I'd know exactly what he was thinking: *What if something had happened to you? What would I do then?*

As much as I was dreading the conversation I was inevitably going to have with Nick, I couldn't wait to get away from Heatherfield. But when I heard someone call my name softly, I turned.

"Dr. Popper? Can I speak weeth you? I am so sorry to bother you, but eet ees important."

"Of course, Inez." I could see from the earnest look on her face that something was troubling her. Even though I was exhausted and upset, I figured I could spare another couple of minutes.

"Please, come into the kitchen," she said, glancing around nervously. "There, no one will hear."

I followed her, my curiosity piqued. She closed the door before speaking.

"I hope I was not wrong to keep silent for so long," she began, leaning against the counter. Her hands fluttered in front of her like hummingbirds. "I thought I should say something, but I was afraid of—how do you say, getting involved."

"It's all right, Inez," I assured her. "I'm sure you didn't purposely withhold any information." I tried to sound calm and matter-of-fact. But I held my breath as I waited to hear what she had to say.

"I am only trying to help. I can see that someone— maybe the person who killed Eduardo—is very dangerous. To start a fire like that, to try to hurt you and all those horses . . . ees such a terrible thing. And Dr. Popper, you have always been so nice to me. If there is even one small way I could help . . .

"Maybe thees means nothing," she continued, "but a few days before Eduardo was killed, I heard him talking with Meesus Chase."

"Eduardo was speaking to Diana?" I asked.

She nodded. "Eet was more like arguing. Meesus Chase, she was so angry."

"What was she so angry about?" I asked gently. I didn't want to let on that my heart was pounding.

"Something about a secret she had told him. Something to do with money. A *lot* of money." She hesitated, biting her lip. "Money she invested badly—and lost.

Eduardo, he just laughed. He said she was a bad businesswoman. Then he said something else, something that made her even more angry."

"Do you remember what that was?"

Once again, Inez glanced around, as if wanting to be absolutely certain no one else could hear. "He said he thought Meesus Chase's husband would be very interested to learn about all the money she lost."

I drew in my breath sharply. "Inez, do you remember exactly when you heard all this?"

She nodded. "It was Sunday evening. Two days before Eduardo was killed."

By that point, my head was spinning. Based on what Inez was telling me, Diana Chase had just leaped into the number-one spot on my list of the polo player's probable murderers. She certainly had a motive. If she *had* gone ahead with her plan to try to launch her own nail products company, then failed miserably and lost a substantial amount of money, she would have been in a very bad position with her husband. In fact, she would have undoubtedly been desperate to keep that information from Harlan. If Eduardo was the only person who knew about her failure, if he was threatening to expose her and perhaps even blackmailing her, who knew what she was capable of?

I certainly didn't know, at least not for sure. But I had my suspicions.

"Thank you for being so honest, Inez," I told her. "You did the right thing in telling me."

I turned and headed for the door, wishing I could find some satisfaction in the possibility that Inez had just helped me identify the person who had murdered Eduardo—and almost murdered me. But at that point, I just wanted to go home.

• • •

As I closed the front door of my cottage behind me, I was instantly smothered with dog love and inundated with welcoming screeches from a very excited macaw. I was also surrounded with the sounds of Jimi Hendrix, a sign that someone of the human variety had also been awaiting my return home. Sure enough, Nick glanced up from the couch, where he was sitting with a ridiculously large book balanced in his lap. He slammed it shut, his face lighting up.

"Perfect timing!" he greeted me, leaping off the couch. "Believe it or not, I just finished my work. I thought that maybe tonight we'd—" His expression quickly turned from cheerful to deep concern. "What's wrong, Jess? You look like you've just seen a ghost."

"Not quite," I returned, trying to keep my voice light. "But I almost became one."

"Somehow, that doesn't strike me as particularly funny."

"It's not." I sank onto the couch, suddenly exhausted. Even worse, my entire body had started to shake. Now that I was home, whatever defense mechanisms had kept me relatively calm and collected in the face of such grave danger had fallen away. Finally, I was reacting to the horror of what had just happened.

"Hey, Jess?" Nick said softly. "Why don't you tell me what's going on?"

I eyed him warily, taking deep breaths. "I think you'd better sit down for this."

Once we were sitting side by side, he turned and fixed his eyes on me. "Let's hear it."

Speaking in a low, even voice that was oddly devoid of emotion, I told Nick about the fire at Heatherfield. As I watched all the color drain from his face, I was glad I'd made sure he was sitting. Still, he did his best to remain expressionless, listening silently until the very end.

"Did you contact Falcone?" he finally said, his voice strained.

I nodded. "He showed up at Heatherfield right afterward."

"What did he say?"

"What do you *think* he said? That I was swimming in dangerous waters and that I should get back on dry land."

He reached over and gently pushed back a strand of hair that had fallen against my cheek. "He's right, you know," he said gently.

"I know," I mumbled.

"It sounds as if whoever murdered Eduardo Garcia knows you've been poking around, asking questions," Nick went on. "What's even more important is that he's extremely serious about stopping you."

I nodded, my gaze wandering over to Leilani's tank. From the small branch on which she stood, she gave me a knowing look, as if she, too, thought I should reconsider.

"Do you know what I think?" He draped his arm around me and pulled me closer. I leaned my head on his shoulder, nestling into that special place in men's chests that seems to have been created specifically for that purpose. "There's no reason for you to have anything more to do with Eduardo Garcia. Or Heatherfield, for that matter."

Maybe I'm just contrary by nature, but what should have been comforting words prompted a disconcerting idea to pop into my head. *What about promising Forrester I'd help him with his investigation?*

I hated letting anyone down. Still, I could hardly ignore the fact that my involvement in the investigation of Eduardo's murder had escalated into a game with high stakes. *Extremely* high stakes. At this point, even Forrester couldn't fault me for reneging on my promise to help him. After all, whoever had set that fire had made it clear that not only was I in danger, so were Andrew MacKinnon's poor, innocent horses.

Besides, at the moment, Forrester Sloan, Heatherfield, and Eduardo Garcia seemed far, far away. The idea of leaving all of it behind—and forgetting all about the bizarre cast of characters who comprised the MacKinnon clan and their entourage—sounded very attractive indeed.

"You're absolutely right," I told Nick.

A great sense of relief immediately washed over me. It was as if a dark cloud that I hadn't even realized was hovering overhead had suddenly disappeared, leaving behind a clear blue sky.

The weather forecast changed less than thirty-six hours later. Tuesday morning, as Nick and I bustled about the cottage, getting ready for a new day, my cell phone rang. Not a particularly unusual occurrence. But when I glanced at the caller ID and saw a number I recognized, I could practically feel a cool breeze in the cottage as the sun ducked out of sight.

"Dr. Popper," I answered crisply. "Uh-huh. Uh-huh...I'll be there later this morning."

"An emergency?" Nick asked, glancing up from his bowl of cereal.

"I'm not sure." I grabbed my coffee mug, chagrined to see that it was almost empty. "Actually, Stryder's symptoms sound a little puzzling."

"Stryder?" Nick repeated. "Is that a dog or a cat?"

I made a point of staring into my mug.

"Jess," he said, sounding exasperated, "don't tell me Stryder is a horse."

"Okay," I replied halfheartedly.

He sighed. "I thought we agreed that Heatherfield was history." I could tell he was trying to sound calm. I hated it when he did that—mainly because he was so much better at it than I was.

"We did agree. At least, in terms of investigating Eduardo's murder. But this is different. This is about a horse that's in trouble."

"And I suppose you're the only veterinarian on Long Island who's capable of treating an ailing horse," he said sarcastically.

"I'm the only veterinarian who has a relationship with the people over there, aside from the poor guy who's laid up in the hospital," I replied, sounding a little more defensive than I'd planned. "I'm also the only veterinarian who can get over to Heatherfield in under an hour."

"Jessie . . ."

"I'll be fine. I promise. Horses only. No dead bodies." I looked at him searchingly.

"I'm not trying to tell you what to do," Nick said. "I'm just trying to keep you from becoming one. A dead body, I mean."

He chose that moment to glance at his watch—and to realize that if he didn't hit the road immediately, he'd never make it to his first class by nine. Despite the fact that the atmosphere inside the cottage had grown considerably more strained, I couldn't help thinking how strange it was to be having breakfast with a grown man who was worried about being late for school.

Still, as I watched him dash off, a wave of despondency swept over me. I felt the same way I imagined Max and Lou feeling as they sat by the front door, whimpering and watching me leave. Even Cat had left the room, creeping back to the kitchen to settle onto the rug in front of the refrigerator now that Nick was gone. Only Prometheus seemed unaffected, cheerfully singing

"Happy Birthday" even though not one of us had a birthday coming up in the near future. Leilani, as usual, simply stared, blinking every once in a while in a way that made her look terribly wise.

I sat with my hands wrapped around my coffee mug, even though it was empty. I hated having Nick leave while there was still tension between us. Somehow, it seemed one of us was always hurrying out, worried about being late for something important. It was part of modern life, I supposed. At least, *our* modern life.

Still, one of the worst things about both of us having such busy schedules was that there was hardly ever enough time to kiss and make up.

I was relieved to find that Heatherfield had the same ghost-town atmosphere it had had Sunday night. Still, the sight of the partially burned stable, with its charred shingles and boarded-up windows, made my stomach wrench.

Fortunately, one of the few signs of life was a team of workmen tearing down the wreckage and preparing to rebuild. And the horses looked as if they were enjoying the crisp, sunny fall day in their paddocks. Only one dapple gray mare, Stryder, remained in her stall.

"You're back," Johnny Ray greeted me. He'd adopted a new affectation: chewing on a toothpick. Better than a cigarette, I thought grimly. At least I don't have to worry about the dangers of secondhand sawdust. "Didn't know if you'd actually show up."

"I told you on the phone that I'd be here," I returned irritably.

"Sure. But tellin' and doin' are two different things. I figured you might get spooked about coming back here, after the fire and all."

I just looked at him coldly. "Tell me more about this horse's symptoms."

"She ain't eatin' and she ain't drinkin'," Johnny Ray informed me. "Her eyes look kinda yellow, too."

I examined the animal and discovered other problems. All in all, she was exhibiting a somewhat baffling combination of symptoms. I decided to check in with another vet. I never hesitate to seek advice from someone who's more knowledgeable than I am—even if that someone happens to be Marcus Scruggs.

"He-e-ey, Jess," he greeted me, answering his cell phone on the second ring. "What can the Marc Man do you for?"

Ever since I'd introduced him to Suzanne, he'd treated me like his best friend. I, of course, was still holding my breath, waiting for what I was convinced was inevitable disaster.

"I'm looking at a mare who's exhibiting depression, anorexia, and dehydration," I told him. "She's also jaundiced, with an accelerated heartbeat and respiration rate."

"Hmm... probably not EIA," Marcus mused.

I had already considered EIA—Equine Infectious Anemia or swamp fever—an untreatable viral disease that's spread by flies and other insects. But it's virtually unheard of in the northeastern United States.

"Sounds to me like acute hemolytic anemia with methemoglobinemia," Marcus finally said. "Any chance the horse has been eating the leaves from a red maple tree?"

Of course. As soon as Marcus said the words, everything clicked.

Stryder had been poisoned.

Several of the paddocks were surrounded by red maple trees—*Acer rubrum*. And red maple leaves are extremely poisonous to horses. It's a problem year-round, but it's much more common in the fall, when the leaves start to turn. Horses can get at them more easily when they start drying up and falling on the ground.

Eating the leaves causes a condition called hemolytic anemia in which red blood cells are destroyed, making it impossible for the blood to carry oxygen. It often goes hand in hand with methemoglobinemia, another condition that makes red blood cells unable to carry oxygen.

"Bingo," I breathed. The irony of the fact that one of the horses at Heatherfield had ingested poison—even though it had been accidental—wasn't wasted on me.

"In that case, the mare might need a blood transfusion," Marcus continued. "But if ingestion is recent, activated charcoal should do the trick. She'll also need intravenous fluids to counteract the dehydration. Because of the likelihood of methemoglobinemia, I'd give her vitamin C, too, to oxidize her blood."

"Thanks, Marcus," I told him sincerely.

"Hey, no problem. In fact, I was going to call you anyway." Lowering his voice, he added, "This doesn't happen very much—like *never*—but I could use a little advice in the love-life department."

Oh, no, I thought. *Please, can't you just send an e-mail to the "Playboy Advisor"?*

"It's Suzanne," he went on. "She's been acting funny lately."

"What do you mean by funny?" Even as I said the words, I hoped I wasn't getting into something I couldn't handle.

"It's almost like she's pulling away." He snorted. "Imagine, a chick pulling away from the Marc Man."

"Imagine that," I said dryly. Not surprisingly, my sarcasm was completely wasted on him.

"I can't decide if I should lay low or race full speed ahead with my usual irresistible charm," he went on.

"Maybe you should try talking to her about it," I suggested.

"Hey, that's a really good idea! Thanks, Jess. You're the best."

That was a first, I thought as I hung up. Me—giving advice to the lovelorn. Even if this particular individual was about as psychologically complicated as an amoeba.

Still, he'd given me some good insights into the probable cause of the mare's symptoms. Maybe Marcus is a slimeball, I thought, but he's a slimeball who knows his stuff.

I decided to hold off on the transfusion. From the information I was able to drag out of Johnny Ray, it sounded likely that Stryder had eaten the leaves that were making her sick only recently. I administered activated charcoal and vitamin C and put her on an IV to address the dehydration.

"Keep an eye on her," I told Johnny Ray. "I think we're out of the woods, but the next few hours are important. You've got my cell phone number, right?"

"Yeah." I was heading out of the barn when I was pretty sure I heard him mumble, "Thanks."

As I neared my van, I noticed a white square on the windshield. *No,* I thought, my stomach clenching. *Not again.* Even though I'd decided that I'd had enough of murder investigations, it looked as if the person who enjoyed playing with paper as much as matches had no idea that I'd come to that conclusion.

My mouth was dry and I had a dazed, sick feeling as I approached my vehicle. When I reached the windshield, I hesitated, wondering if I dared ignore the message that had clearly been left for me. But I figured there was nothing to be gained by hiding my head in the sand. Gingerly, I reached for the square of paper and unfolded it.

YOur Play ing WTH fiRE.
STop or thEr Will b AnotheR viCTum.

Even though my recent discussion with Lieutenant Falcone about my role in the investigation of Eduardo Garcia's murder had been less than rewarding, I did what any other mature person would have done in a similar situation: I immediately dialed his number on my cell phone. Of course, I was actually immature enough to experience a great wave of relief when I got his voice mail.

I left him a message about having received a third anonymous note, then put the incident out of my mind.

Instead, I concentrated on something I was sure I'd find much more fulfilling: a full day of calls that sent me zigzagging all over Long Island. With the horses at Heatherfield occupying so much of my time and energy lately, getting back to my usual routine felt as comfortable as slipping into a well-worn pair of sneakers.

The day's appointments included a follow-up with King, the Weinsteins' German shorthair pointer. I was heartened to see that he had made a full recovery. In fact, he was wrestling with both Justin and Jason at the same time, doing a fine job of holding his own.

Another long day, I thought as I pulled into the driveway that led to my cottage a few minutes past seven. I was looking forward to a relaxing evening, one that hopefully included a hot bath. I was glad that Nick was back in his apartment, enjoying the new paint job even though the days he and Leilani would be spending there were numbered. A little quiet time was exactly what I needed.

But as I neared the end of the driveway, the sight of

something incongruous made me blink. In the wooded area just past Betty's house, at the far end of the property, I spotted a wide expanse of cream-colored metal, surrounded by tree trunks and leaves.

I gasped when I realized what it was: a cream-colored Rolls-Royce, half hidden by the thick growth of trees.

Chapter 14

"A horse's eye disquiets me: it has an expression of alarm that may at any moment be translated into action."

—E.V. Lucas

Winston! I thought, my stomach immediately tensing up. *What on earth is* he *doing here?*

My mind raced as I imagined the worst scenario possible: that Winston was the one who had noticed from the start that I was asking too many questions, that he had been sending me threatening notes, and that he was guilty of trying to impress his message upon me even further by setting the MacKinnons' stable on fire while he believed I was locked inside. And that his latest maneuver was striking at me through one of my most vulnerable spots, my dear friend Betty.

I opened the back of my Volkswagen and rifled around for the heaviest tool I could find. The tire iron looked pretty imposing, so I grabbed it. I took care to close the door of the trunk gently, not wanting to make any noise that would call attention to the fact that I'd arrived on the scene to rescue my poor neighbor.

Easing across the lawn as stealthily as a cat burglar, I crept around to the side of the house. Once I reached the back door, I placed my hand on the knob and slowly gave it a twist. As usual, Betty had left it unlocked.

Oh, Betty, you're so trusting! I thought mournfully. *Leaving yourself vulnerable like this...*

Moving in slow motion, I opened the door, hoping it wouldn't squeak or bang against anything. It cooperated fully. So far, so good.

My hands were sweating as I clutched the tire iron, furtively treading across the tiled kitchen floor. I continued down the long hallway, grateful for the thick carpeting that helped keep my presence a secret. I hoped it was also muffling the sound of my pounding heart.

There were still no signs of life. There were, however, *sounds* of life—coming from upstairs. The creaking of a floor, a hard bang, a voice I was certain was Betty's....

I'm coming! I wanted to scream. *I won't let him hurt you!*

The dramatic staircase I confronted next presented a bit of a challenge. I knew for a fact that it squeaked. Still, given all the activity I could hear upstairs, I didn't think anyone would notice the sound of my footsteps. Besides, even if they did, I had no choice but to strike—and fast.

I hurried up the steps, hoping my weapon wouldn't slip out of my sticky wet palms. When I reached the top, I saw that the door to the master bedroom—Betty's bedroom—was closed. From inside, I heard grunts and moans.

Oh, my God! I thought. *He's hurting her!*

Adrenaline surged through every vein, giving me such a powerful burst of energy I felt as if I'd just gulped down a triple espresso. I sprinted toward the bedroom door, pausing for just a second to take a deep breath and make sure I had a firm grip on the tire iron. Then, I flung open the door, holding my weapon high above my head.

I stood poised to attack, waiting for my eyes to adjust to the darkened room. I finally spotted Betty, lying limply across the bed dressed in nothing but her favorite bathrobe, a pale pink silk kimono. I let out a shriek. Then I realized Betty was also shrieking.

"Jessica, stop!" she cried, leaping off the bed. "Have you completely lost your mind?"

I blinked, needing a few seconds to digest the fact that Betty actually seemed *distressed* by my arrival on the scene, rather than grateful.

"Betty! Are you all right?" I demanded breathlessly.

"For heaven's sake, put that thing *down*!" she insisted. "And I'm fine—aside from nearly having a heart attack because of someone bursting into my bedroom, brandishing a monkey wrench!"

"It's a tire iron," I shot back, whipping the metal bar around in the air a few times for good measure. "Where is he?"

"Where is *who*?"

"That fiend! That monster! That...that..." My voice trailed off as the bathroom door opened and Winston emerged. His mouth instantly fell open in astonishment.

I wasn't surprised by his shocked expression. However, I *was* surprised that he was dressed in only a towel. It was wrapped modestly around his middle, revealing a chest that was thickly covered with silver hair and a surprisingly trim torso. The only other thing he was wearing, in fact, was a look of complete embarrassment.

"Jessica!" he exclaimed, desperately grabbing at his towel to make sure it wouldn't slip. "Isn't this, er, a lovely surprise!"

"Jessica, *please* put that horrible thing down!" Betty cried. "You're frightening me!"

I looked at Betty, then Winston, then lowered my arms. Suddenly, *I* was the one who was embarrassed.

"I thought..." I sputtered. "When I saw Winston's car hiding in the trees..."

"We were trying to be discreet," Betty said evenly. "We wanted some privacy. But I see that we were asking too much."

I glanced around the bedroom. The blinds had been drawn, and the only light came from candles that had been placed on the dresser and the night table. The dresser also sported a tremendous bouquet of long-stemmed yellow roses, carefully arranged in a large crystal vase. Next to it was a long, thin box, the distinctive shade of robin's-egg blue that meant it had come from Tiffany. I also noticed two fluted glasses, half-filled with champagne. From the looks of things, it had pretty much lost its fizz.

I'd also lost my fizz.

"I guess I owe you both an apology," I said meekly.

"I believe you do," Betty returned, wrapping the belt of her robe around her waist more snugly.

"Not at all!" Winston boomed. "I understand completely. You were simply looking out for your friend's safety. That's quite noble of you!"

"I'm sorry," I told Betty. I only hoped she could tell *how* sorry. "I guess I'll be going. You two can, uh, get back to what you were doing."

I turned and raced out of there. My brain was buzzing. For the first few seconds, it was complete and utter mortification that had me running on overdrive. But even before I'd reached the bottom of the stairway, a different type of emotion was riling me up.

What on earth is that man doing in Betty's house—and in her life? I wondered. *For heaven's sake, he's a fraud. A phony! And from the looks of things, he could even be a murderer!*

My original suspicion, that Winston was using Betty to get me to back off from the murder investigation, loomed large. I could easily imagine him stooping that low: wangling his way into her affections, then using her as a shield, his protection from me trying to find out the truth.

As I headed down the stairway, much more quickly than I'd gone up it, my entire body shook. The incident had literally left me trembling with rage. It had also left me more determined than ever to prove the guilt of Eduardo Garcia's murderer.

An hour or so later I was still agonizing over the shocking scene I'd witnessed at Betty's house. Even the hot bath I'd taken to calm myself down hadn't helped. I'd sat amidst the bubbles as tense as if I was sitting in a dentist's chair, mystifying poor Cat, who lay curled up on the bathmat, with my constant muttering. As I sat on the couch, towel-drying my hair, I still couldn't stop ruminating about Winston Farnsworth's ruthlessness.

I froze at the sound of a knock. The dogs launched into their usual barking routine, sounding fierce but wagging their tails, thrilled over the prospect of company. I just stared at the front door, hoping it wasn't Betty, coming over in her bathrobe to explain.

And *really* hoping it wasn't Winston.

I was incredibly relieved when Nick opened the door and poked his head in.

"Anybody home?"

"Come on in," I said, wondering why he was getting so formal.

"I'm not alone. I brought a friend." He hesitated. "I hope you don't mind."

Just as long as my surprise guest for the evening doesn't turn out to be one of the obnoxious members of your study group, I thought.

"The more, the merrier," I told him. "Bring him in."

"It's a she, actually," he said as he came inside.

I stared at Nick, confused. From what I could see, he was alone.

Don't tell me he's developing a split personality, I thought. *Given everything that's happened over the last couple of weeks, I really don't think I could handle—*

And then he reached into the pocket of his jacket and brought out what looked like a teeny-weeny, ridiculously fluffy orange ball. Fake fur, I figured. A pair of earmuffs, or maybe a big key chain.

Then the ball meowed.

"Oh, my," I cried, reaching for the tiny kitten. "You sweet little thing! Where did you come from?"

She was tiny enough to fit in the palm of my hand—yet she had the coloring and markings of a ferocious tiger. Her fearful mewing turned to a contented purr as I stroked the amazingly soft, silky fur on her head with one finger.

"Who's lucky enough to be owned by you?" I asked her, holding her face up to mine and gazing into her huge, golden eyes.

"See, that's the thing," Nick returned. "She's homeless."

I glanced up at him. "You found her?"

"She was abandoned, right on campus. I was cutting across the grass to the parking lot, and next to the curb, I found a cardboard box. She was in it."

"Oh, you poor baby!" Anger rose inside me as I tried to comprehend the horror of leaving a poor, defenseless animal all alone like that. Didn't whoever was heartless enough to just leave her like that understand that her chances of survival were horrendously low?

"What's the matter with these people?" I cried. "Don't they have any sense? To do something that cruel and that heartless is unforgivable! If they're not responsible enough to have their pets neutered—which is reprehensible enough—then the *least* they can do is find a home for the puppies and kittens! People like that shouldn't be allowed to have pets! In fact, anybody who abandons a poor, helpless animal should face criminal prosecution!"

Nick blinked. "Wow. I knew you felt strongly about this, but this is even more than I expected!"

"I'm sorry." I suddenly felt like one of the balloons Nick had brought over—right after all its air had been let out. "Of course I feel strongly about people's senseless treatment of animals. But you also happen to have caught me at a very bad time. I'm not exactly in the best of moods right now."

"What's wrong?" he asked, settling onto the couch beside me.

I took a deep breath, looking down at the darling kitten in my lap and hoping her cuteness would help improve my mood. But even the miniature tiger gazing up at me with golden eyes the size of planets couldn't manage that. "I just found Betty in bed with Winston Farnsworth."

Nick's eyebrows shot up in surprise. "Whoa! The distinguished guy in the bow tie who came to opening night? With the English accent?"

"That's the one."

"Way to go, Betty!" he crowed.

"*Wrong!*" I countered crossly. "This is not a good thing, Nick. In fact, it's terrible!"

"Explain," he said, shaking his head in confusion.

"You should see the way he's treating her!" I cried. "Sneaking over to her house in the middle of the day for a clandestine rendezvous, bringing her big, showy bouquets of flowers, buying her expensive presents..."

"I can see why you're so freaked out," Nick observed dryly. "Such horrible mistreatment would upset anyone."

"You're missing the point!"

"Which is?"

"I don't trust him, Nick! I know for a fact that he's not who he says he is—"

" 'For a fact?' " he repeated. "I don't remember you saying anything about doing a background check on the guy. Or did I miss that while I was up to my ears in torts?"

"I have a sixth sense about these things," I replied archly.

"No offense, but your track record isn't exactly all that impressive," Nick replied. "I could name a few people you were convinced were good guys who turned out to be bad guys. I could also name a few you thought were *bad* guys who were actually *good* guys."

"Winston Farnsworth is just plain shady," I insisted. "That's all there is to it."

"Do you know what I think?" Nick asked.

I was glad he was finally going to make a comment of the constructive variety. "No. What?"

"That you're guilty of ageism."

"Me?" I sputtered. "I don't know what you're talking about, Nick! I'm simply looking after Betty's best interests. She's one of my dearest friends—"

"And she happens to have gone a bit beyond the sweet blush of youth," Nick finished calmly. "Look, Jess, the fact is you can't imagine a man—any man— being interested in Betty for who she is, can you? You see her as someone...someone old, instead of someone who's exceptionally kind, sweet, and loving, not to mention a person who has a lifetime of experiences to share with someone who's capable of appreciating her."

"That's not true!" I protested. "It's also completely unfair!"

"Then there's Winston," Nick continued. "A perfectly lovely fellow, if you ask me. I couldn't imagine anyone more gentlemanly. Yet you assume that because both he and Betty have a few years on you—okay, a few decades—that the only possible explanation for his interest in her has got to be something sinister."

"Nick, you're missing the whole—"

"Did it ever occur to you that Winston and Betty might simply *like* each other? That the two of them probably have a million things in common? They grew up at the same time, they lived through the same historic events, they probably enjoy listening to the same music...I bet there's a long list of other interests and experiences they share that would instantly bond them together."

I opened my mouth to protest. Almost immediately, I snapped it shut, figuring there was no point in trying to explain. Of *course* I recognized what a gem Betty was! Of *course* I wasn't surprised that a man who was her age would find it rewarding to be in her company!

But we weren't talking about just anybody. We were talking about Winston Farnsworth, who happened to have close ties to a dashing polo player who had recently been murdered. He also had a motive and, from what I'd heard, a bit of a past.

My concerns are completely legitimate, I told myself firmly.

Aren't they?

"Besides, we have much more relevant things to discuss," Nick insisted. He gestured toward the kitten lying on her back in my lap, swatting at the button on my shirt with her tiny paws. "Like this little girl's future."

That was an easy one. At least, in my opinion.

But there were others I needed to consider.

I glanced over at Cat, who was my first concern. I wondered how she would feel about adding another feline to the household. She'd wandered into the room as Nick and I discussed Betty's questionable love life, leaving her favorite spot in the kitchen to check out what all the commotion was about. She hovered nearby, watching the kitten. She seemed more curious than anything else—a good sign, I figured.

As for Max and Lou, they seemed to be taking the situation in stride, just as I would have expected. As my two sidekicks, regularly accompanying me on calls, they were both in the habit of encountering new animals all the time. They never seemed to feel threatened, and this situation was no exception. They were both too secure in the knowledge that the three of us were all part of the same pack, which created a bond that would never be broken.

"So what about it, Jess?" Nick urged. "Can you find room for one more in your menagerie?"

I nestled the darling little kitten against my cheek, marveling over how soft she was. I'd already picked out a name: Tinkerbell. "I think we can squeeze in someone this cute."

"In that case, how about *two* more?"

I frowned, confused. I half expected Nick to pull another kitten out of his pocket.

Instead, he said lightly, "You know, she's not the only one who's homeless."

It was then that I realized that Nick wasn't referring to a four-legged creature. He was referring to himself.

"Oh," I said, the single syllable coming out sounding more like a squeak that an actual word. "You mean you."

"The dogs already like me," he said, talking quickly. "Cat does, too. And Prometheus...well, ever since I taught him the pirate song, the two of us have been as thick as thieves, if you'll pardon the expression. Besides, I'm self-cleaning, like a cat. I'm capable of refilling my own water bowl. I've never met anybody who's allergic to me. I don't bite or shed. And did I mention that I'm completely housebroken?

"But I'm rambling, aren't I? I do that when I'm nervous. I guess a lot of people do. But it's because I really want us to live together, Jess. I love you, and I can't help thinking that being forced to move out of my apartment is a sign. Especially since we're both even busier than ever, with me back in school and all, and so living together is the perfect solution to the problem of finding time for each other as well as all the stuff we both have to do every day. So...what do you think?"

As he looked at me expectantly, I could feel a wave of terror rising up inside me. My hands got clammy, my skin felt warm, and I could feel a strange vibration near my hip.

It took me a few seconds to realize that the vibration wasn't physiological. It was my cell phone.

"Excuse me," I told Nick. "I'd better get this."

This was one of the few times in my life I was actually glad I'd been interrupted by a cell phone. Placing Tinkerbell on the cushion beside me, I pressed the green button. "Dr. Popper."

"It's me, Dr. Popper. Callie."

I hadn't recognized the high-pitched, frightened-sounding voice as hers.

"What's wrong, Callie?"

"You've got to come to Heatherfield," she insisted. "I

can't—" Her voice broke off, and she made a terrible choking sound.

"What is it?" I demanded. "What's going on?"

"Just *come*!" she insisted. "I'm here all alone...and whoever poisoned Eduardo has struck again!"

Chapter 15

C allie, quick," I instructed the terrified girl at the other end of the line. "Tell me your symptoms."

"It's not me," she replied in the same panicked voice. "It's Inez."

"Inez?" The idea that someone had targeted the MacKinnons' housekeeper was horrifying. "Callie, call nine-one-one!"

"She won't let me! She refuses to go to a hospital because she doesn't have any health insurance. She keeps saying she doesn't want to be any trouble. In fact, you're the only person she'd let me call. I'm here all alone, Dr. Popper. Please, you've got to come!"

I had already leaped off the couch and was dashing around the cottage madly, trying to locate my car keys.

"I'll be there as fast as I can," I told her. "Just stay calm!"

"Another emergency?" Nick asked as I hung up. His expression was grave.

"An emergency of the people variety," I replied. "Callie thinks Inez, the MacKinnons' housekeeper, has been poisoned! I hate to do this, but do you think you could hold down the fort while I—?"

"Of course. Just go, Jess." Scooping up the tiny kitten who was mewing in confusion, he added, "I'll take care of the dogs and everybody else."

"It's probably a good idea to keep Tinkerbell—that's what I'm calling her—away from the other animals. If you could put her in the bedroom—"

"We'll be fine," he assured me. "I promise."

"Thanks, Nick." I paused long enough to cast him a look of gratitude. Even in the heat of the moment, I realized that simply knowing that he was there to support me, as solid as a rock, went a long way in keeping me from going over the edge. "I don't think I could manage without you."

Flashing me a funny half-smile, he said, "That's what I keep trying to tell you."

I took the VW to Heatherfield, figuring it would get me there faster than my van. I struggled to follow the advice I'd given Callie and remain calm. Still, I had to make a point of reminding myself that clenching my jaw so hard that my teeth hurt wasn't going to help.

I had to admit that I was feeling a bit overwhelmed. First, Eduardo Garcia had been poisoned, a tragedy that had preoccupied me for the past two weeks. Then, that very morning, I had rushed to Heatherfield to treat a horse that had ingested poison.

Now, here I was only a few hours later, rushing to the aid of someone else at Heatherfield who looked like the victim of poisoning.

Of course, there was one major difference—one that

made my stomach tighten. In a way, I was responsible for this one.

The third anonymous note. It had warned that there would be another victim. Of course, at the time, I'd assumed it referred to *me*.

It had never occurred to me that my actions might be putting someone else in danger.

Even if I'd considered that possibility, I thought as I careened along a particularly treacherous curve on Turkey Hollow Road, I never would have imagined that poor Inez would have been chosen as the next victim.

And then suddenly, like a flash of lightning, the connection became ridiculously obvious.

Of *course*! I thought. Someone must have overheard Inez telling me about the argument between Diana Chase and Eduardo right before his murder! Or perhaps that person already knew that the MacKinnons' housekeeper had found out how angry Diana was...and figured that it was only a question of time before she broke her silence about the incriminating conversation that had occurred only days before he was poisoned.

She was only trying to be helpful, I thought mournfully, lurching to a stop and hurrying up the path connecting the MacKinnons' mansion with Inez's cottage. And look what happened.

As I hurried toward the tiny building nestled behind the MacKinnons' grand mansion, I saw that the front door was ajar. I paused in the doorway, softly calling, "Callie? Inez? It's me, Jessie Popper."

Then I saw Inez in the small living room, lying on her side on the sagging couch. Her head was nestled against a pillow and a blanket was draped over her. Callie sat perched on the edge of the chair next to her, her expression tense. She jumped up as soon as I came in.

"Thanks *so* much for coming, Dr. Popper," she said breathlessly. "Like I said on the phone, you seemed to be the only person Inez trusted enough to let me call. She doesn't look too good. I brought in the pillow and blanket from her bedroom. I figured at the very least, I should do everything I could to help her get more comfortable."

"That was very smart, Callie," I assured her. I only wished I felt as confident as I sounded. I was supposed to be in charge here. But as I surveyed the scene, I felt overwhelmed. Lying before me was a possible poisoning victim who refused to get medical treatment. And because I had no idea what she had ingested, it was impossible for me to know how to treat her myself.

I crouched down next to the couch, my face close to Inez's. "Inez, can you hear me? Are you able to talk?"

"Dr. Popper," she said weakly. "I theenk I will be fine. I just feel dizzy. Eet was probably nothing. Just something I ate, maybe."

"That's what we're afraid of," I told her. "Callie thinks you were poisoned."

"No!" she protested. "Ees not possible!"

"I'm afraid it's very possible. Sooner or later, we'll figure out what was used to poison Eduardo. Once that's done, I'm hoping it will become much easier to identify his killer." I hesitated. "Inez, I'm afraid that person might be trying to poison you with the same substance."

"I'm sure eet was nothing. A bad piece of fish, maybe. I'll be fine. I just—" Her voice broke off, as if she were no longer capable of speaking.

"Inez!" I cried, afraid I was losing her. If nothing else, I wanted her to remain conscious. "Tell me exactly what happened. What you ate, when you started feeling strange..."

"Eet was earlier tonight, right after I ate dinner here in my cottage." She spoke haltingly. "I—I started to feel dizzy. Then, the room started spinning around and I blacked out, just for a moment. I managed to get to the phone, and I called the house. Callie answered. She said she was all alone, but I asked if she would come."

"She looked really bad," Callie interjected.

"Bad, how?" I was still hoping that, somehow, I'd be able to figure out what Inez had ingested.

"She was just lying on the couch, moaning. The first thing I thought of was calling for help, but she wouldn't let me." Callie studied Inez. "Shouldn't we make her throw up or something? Isn't that what you're supposed to do when someone's poisoned?"

"It depends on what they ingested," I told her. "In some cases, vomiting can make it worse." I focused on Inez once again. "Inez, do you have any idea what you might have eaten? Was there anything unusual about what you had for dinner tonight? You mentioned that you had fish. Did it look strange or taste unusual?"

"I don't theenk so . . ." Her voice trailed off.

"It would have been so easy for somebody to sneak into her cottage and stick something bad in her food," Callie volunteered. "They could have just walked in and put whatever they wanted into something that was already in the refrigerator. This place is hardly ever locked. Besides, it's been warm and there's no air-conditioning, so Inez has been keeping the windows open. It would be really easy to get in without Inez or anyone else knowing."

"It's possible that it's just food poisoning or the flu," I said. But even I didn't believe it. Not in the face of all the horrifying events of the past few weeks. "Inez, it's really important that you get medical attention. Please, let me take you to the emergency room so you can see a doctor!"

"But you are a doctor!" she insisted.

"I'm an animal doctor," I reminded her. "I'm not qualified to treat people!"

"Please, eef I can just sleep..." All of a sudden, a look of alarm crossed her face. "I theenk I am going to be sick!" She threw off the blanket, jumped up, and dashed toward the bathroom.

"Dr. Popper?" Callie asked nervously. "Is she okay?"

"It might be the best thing," I assured her. "At least this will help get the poison out of her system."

Still, I went over to the bathroom, hesitating outside the closed door. From inside, I could hear violent retching sounds, followed by coughing. I waited until I heard the toilet flush before knocking softly.

"Inez? It's Dr. Popper. Can I come in?"

"Yes, of course," she replied in a weak voice.

I opened the door slowly and found her kneeling on the floor, in front of the toilet. Her face, half hidden behind a towel, was red. Her dark eyes burned with fear.

"Dr. Popper, please, do not call anyone," she begged. "I am feeling better already. I just ate something bad, but I theenk now I will be okay."

"Please reconsider," I pleaded. "We're talking about your health. We could even be talking about your life!"

"But ees so expensive at the hospital! Eef I can just rest—"

"All right, Inez." As frustrated as I was, I had to face the fact that I was never going to convince her that she should seek medical help. Besides, I was relieved to see that she really was starting to look better. The color was coming back into her face, and her eyes were beginning to lose their dull look.

"You and Callie, you can both go now," she continued. She stood up, holding onto the sink to steady herself. "I theenk I would like to sleep. I feel so much better now."

"I don't feel right, leaving you alone," I insisted.

"I am fine. Please, Dr. Popper. You are so kind to be

concerned. I will keep the telephone close by, but now I will rest. Tomorrow, all this will be just a bad memory."

I hoped she was right, especially since it was clear that she wouldn't have it any other way. I watched her shuffle into her bedroom, closing the door firmly behind her.

"Come on, Callie," I said reluctantly. "Let's go home."

"Is Inez going to be okay?" she asked, glancing at the closed bedroom door nervously.

"I think so." I hesitated. "I *hope* so."

"What about you, Dr. Popper? Are *you* okay?"

"I'm just very, very tired," I told her. I didn't bother to tell her I was also very worried.

I was about to get back into my car when I realized that I needed to use a bathroom first. While I'd used that as an excuse many times before as a way to snoop around someone's house, this time the need was sincere.

"Callie, before I hit the road, can I use your bathroom?"

"Of course, Dr. Popper. You know your way around, right? I'm going upstairs. Even though Shakespeare is the last thing I feel like facing right now, I've got a ton of homework." She cast me a grateful look. "Thanks for coming over. You really came through for us."

"You're welcome, Callie. I'm glad I could help." I was about to add that I was actually kind of pleased that she'd thought of calling me for help, and that she was welcome to do it again any time. But she'd already turned and headed up the stairs.

As I came out of the bathroom and walked toward the front door, I noticed that Callie had left one of her sketch pads out again. This one lay on a table in the living room, probably forgotten. Unable to resist, I picked it up and began leafing through.

Not surprisingly, Callie turned out to be just as adept at still-life drawing as she was at creating landscapes and portraits. *She really is talented,* I marveled, studying one rendering after another. The first three or four were groupings of common household objects. One featured a pencil mug and a stack of letters, another was of a teapot and several porcelain cups, a third pictured an ornate jewelry box with necklaces and strings of beads spilling out.

The next drawing was an unusual-looking flower, in a terra-cotta pot. It was a beautiful plant, with a slender stalk that curved gracefully, delicate leaves, and a large blossom that was shaped like a trumpet. I wasn't surprised to see that the drawing was as well executed as all the other pieces of artwork Callie had done.

I flipped over and saw another drawing of the same plant, this time from a different angle.

The next page was a rendering of a profusion of the same flowers. I recognized the area of the estate that Callie had captured on paper. It was the patio, where these plants flourished. I'd noticed them the night of Jillian's cocktail party.

I didn't know all that much about plants in general. They were interesting, but I'd always found animals so much more engaging. But as I stared at these particular drawings, something I'd learned about this one slowly came into focus.

And the limited knowledge I'd acquired had nothing to do with my formal training in biology. In fact, I remembered something I'd learned during my sophomore year of college.

In my Shakespeare class.

Datura. If the plant Callie had drawn was the one I thought it was, it had many different names: jimson-weed, locoweed, angel's trumpet, devil's trumpet, mad apple, green dragon.

Its mind-altering effects were well-known—which is why Shakespeare had found it so intriguing. It had proven very useful in *Romeo and Juliet,* when Juliet needed a way to appear dead. The Friar instructed Juliet to drink a potion containing *Datura* in order to induce a state of unconsciousness that would make her appear to be dead.

If my memory served me correctly, it was also extremely toxic.

Oh, my God, I thought, my mind racing. This highly poisonous plant was growing all over Heatherfield, just like the red maple leaves that poisoned Stryder. They had been right in front of me since Eduardo's murder, but not for a moment had I stopped to think about what a threat they were.

And I never would have if it hadn't been for the fact that Callie had singled it out. She'd chosen it as the subject for her artwork, again and again.

Which was an interesting fact, by itself.

It could just be coincidence, I told myself, trying not to jump to conclusions. She could have picked out this particular plant as a subject for her artwork simply because it was such an interesting specimen. And it *was* abundant here on the property.

So are a lot of other plant species, another voice inside my head pointed out.

Please, no, I thought. *It* can't *be Callie. I have to be misinterpreting this.*

I wasn't sure whether or not I was heading in a direction that made sense. But there was one thing I was sure of: It was time to talk to an expert.

My concern for Inez continued to weigh me down late the following morning as I drove my red VW into Brookside University Visitors' Parking Lot. It wasn't as if I didn't understand her fears about seeking help at an emergency room—and possibly being admitted to the hospital. The cost of medical care was astronomical. I suspected that her salary was barely enough to cover her usual costs, and she certainly didn't strike me as somebody who had a few dollars left over at the end of every week to stash into a savings account.

Still, I would have felt much better if she'd seen a doctor. The next best thing, I figured, was to find out if she really had been poisoned—and, if so, if it had been with the same substance that had been used to kill Eduardo.

I hadn't anticipated how strange it would feel to be back on a university campus. But as I strode across the wide green lawn of Brookside University's central quad, I found myself feeling oddly out of place.

It wasn't even the age difference between me and the students who walked together in twos and threes, although the fact that I spotted more pierced bellybuttons wandering through the quad than I could remember having seen in a long time didn't help. It was more the feeling that this college campus was a place that belonged to *them*, that this was their time to dedicate themselves to learning and exploring—at least, in terms of their intellectual life.

It also brought back all the pressure of college. I remembered the countless all-nighters I'd pulled, Suzanne and I fortifying ourselves with Diet Coke and take-out pizza that was about as tasty as the cardboard box it was delivered in. Sweating each grade, never forgetting for a minute that admission to veterinary school was so competitive that getting even one A-minus instead of an A could make the difference in deciding the future.

There's a sense of unreality that's part of the academic experience, I recalled, a loss of perspective about how the rest of the world functions. But at the same time, the stakes are so high at that point in life.

I mused about the fact that here I was, ten years after graduating from college, taking for granted so many things that at one time seemed like a dream. Yet I was lucky enough to be living it every day, pursuing the career I'd wanted since I was a little girl.

I wondered if Nick had been dealing with all this. Putting myself in his shoes, at least for the distance required to walk from the parking lot to the Life Sciences building, was certainly making me more sympathetic to what he was facing. I felt bad that I hadn't been more patient, and I vowed to be more understanding from now on.

At the moment, however, I had more pressing things on my mind.

"Room three-eighteen..." I muttered as I walked down the dim hallway on the third floor of the redbrick building that housed Brookside's biology department. When I'd telephoned and asked how I might get in touch with a botanist, the woman in Community Relations seemed to know immediately who the best person for me to speak with would be. I was glad I didn't have to go into too much detail about the kind of information I was seeking. Explaining why I wanted to know about a particular plant species' effectiveness as a poison wasn't exactly something that I expected would come tripping off my tongue.

Then I spotted it: Room 318. The door was closed, but through the glass insert I could see a lab similar to the ones from my college days. Beyond it stretched a sunny room with huge windows that appeared to serve as a greenhouse.

I knocked softly, nervous about disturbing the professor who did his research here.

A stocky man in his late fifties, dressed in a rumpled white lab coat, opened the door. His bushy salt-and-pepper hair contained more white than black, as did his full beard. Behind his wire-rimmed glasses, I could see serious, intelligent eyes.

"Dr. Newcomb?"

"Please, call me Harry. And you must be Dr. Popper."

"Jessie," I corrected him.

"Jessie, then. I got a call from Community Relations telling me you'd be stopping by."

"I hope this isn't a bad time," I said, glancing around uncertainly.

Smiling, he gestured behind him at the room filled with greenery. "Just as long as you don't do anything to keep my plants from growing, we'll do fine."

"I won't take up too much of your time," I assured him. "I wanted to show you some drawings and ask you what you thought."

I handed him Callie's sketchbook, which I'd opened to the first of her renderings of angel's trumpet.

"Very nicely done," he observed, studying her handiwork before flipping through the pages. "I see there are lots more. Whoever drew these is certainly talented."

"Yes, she is. But what I'm interested in is the subject of the drawings," I explained. "The plants themselves."

"I see. I suppose you already know that they're drawings of angel's trumpet, *Datura* stramonium?"

"That's what I thought."

"*Datura* is quite common in the United States, as well as Canada and the Caribbean," Dr. Newcomb continued. "It also grows in South America. Jimsonweed, green dragon, mad apple, locoweed...they're all members of a group of plants that's known as the belladonna family. You've heard of it, right?"

"Sure. I don't know much about it, though."

"If I remember my plant lore correctly, the name 'belladonna' comes from the women in Italy who used it because one of its effects was dilating their pupils, which they thought enhanced their looks." Dr. Newcomb chuckled. But he quickly grew serious. "These particular plants also happen to be popular with teenagers."

That was a new one. "What's their appeal?"

"In addition to causing feelings of confusion and disorientation, they can also have a hallucinogenic effect," he explained. "Kind of like LSD. But it's even easier to get hold of, so kids use it as a recreational drug. They smoke it, eat the seeds, or use it to make tea.

"But it's not as if modern kids discovered it. Homer wrote about it in *The Odyssey*, and Shakespeare used it in several of his plays. *Hamlet, Anthony and Cleopatra* . . . and let's not forget the famous climax of *Romeo and Juliet*."

"Yes, I remember learning about that in college," I told him. "The plant's ability to induce a deathlike state came in very handy when Shakespeare needed a heartbreaking ending for his play."

"This plant also happens to have played an important role in history. Any chance you remember Bacon's Rebellion, from the days you were a student of American history?"

I shook my head. "Sorry. If we covered it, I'm afraid it didn't stick."

"Bacon's Rebellion took place in Virginia in 1676. It's often considered the first step in what eventually became the Revolutionary War. However, there's an increasingly popular theory that it was largely the result of two gentlemen with particularly large egos. One was the governor of Virginia and the other was his rebellious young cousin, Nathaniel Bacon. The two of them were apparently doing battle for personal reasons that had nothing to do with politics. At any rate, Bacon, who had kind of a problem with authority, instigated a little skirmish. The British sent troops to suppress it. But when they got to the New World, they couldn't resist having a little fun with some *Datura* they found growing here. It ended up making them so silly that they were completely ineffective."

"So these plants can have a major effect on people, but they aren't lethal?"

"I didn't say that. In fact, they all contain toxins—two tropane alkaloids, hyoscyamine and scopolamine, also known as belladonna alkaloids. And believe me, they're heavy-duty chemicals."

By that point, my heart was pounding. "So people do die from ingesting it."

"Sure. It happens all the time, especially with the kids who are using it because of its hallucinogenic properties. Another common scenario is that someone who ingests it falls into a stupor and loses the ability to make sound judgments. That, combined with losing coordination, can cause them to die accidentally. You know, driving without their full faculties, stumbling over the side of a cliff—"

"Or falling off a horse." My mouth was so dry I could hardly say the words.

"That would certainly be consistent with the effects of the drug," Dr. Newcomb said, nodding. "But don't get me wrong; it can kill by itself. It causes anticholinergic toxidrome. There's a saying about the symptoms: 'blind as a bat, mad as a hatter, red as a beet, hot as a hare, dry as a bone...' In other words, the signs are warm, dry skin, dry mouth, tachycardia, seizures, sometimes delirium with hallucinations, and finally, coma. It could take hours or it could be immediate, depending on what part of the plant is ingested. The concentration of the toxins is much higher in the roots, compared to the leaves. As a result, the toxic effects from consuming the roots could occur right away, while someone who had eaten the leaves might not experience them for hours. The amount consumed would also make a difference. Anyone who ingested sufficient amounts would experience a spike in body temperature, paralysis, and—probably most important—a drastically increased heartbeat that could cause an arrhythmia and kill them."

He handed me back the drawing pad. "So what exactly do you want to know?"

"I think you've already told me what I wanted to find out," I told him.

"In that case," Dr. Newcomb said with a little shrug, "I'm glad I could be of help."

"Thank you for your time." I hesitated. "Actually, I found it surprisingly strange, being back on a college campus again."

"Yet it sounds like you're someone who keeps on learning," he observed.

"I suppose you're right," I said, turning to leave.

I didn't bother to tell him that at the moment, I felt as if everything I learned turned out to be bad news.

As I unlocked the door of my Volkswagen, I noticed it was another beautiful autumn afternoon. The sun was shining brightly, just a trace of briskness energized the air, and the leaves on the trees on the campus were tinged with red and gold. Yet the delightful afternoon did nothing to improve my dark mood. As hard as it was to face, my suspicion—that Callie had poisoned Eduardo, and that she'd used angel's trumpet to do it—now looked like a strong possibility.

Not only did she hate him, I thought grimly as I started the ignition, she had plenty of access to a plant that had the power to kill him. She'd made drawings of it, again and again. And the night poor Inez was poisoned, she was the only other person at Heatherfield. It all added up.

But she's a child! I reminded myself. *She's only*

fourteen years old! Surely she's not capable of something that horrendous!

My reluctance to believe that Callie could be a murderer was supported by the fact that I was still considering a long list of other possible suspects. And they were all much older, wiser, and craftier. *Please,* please, *let me be wrong about Callie,* I thought.

My newfound knowledge about *Datura* also increased my concern about Inez. I pulled out my cell phone and dialed Heatherfield, figuring I'd ask whoever answered how I could get in touch with her.

"Hello, MacKinnon residence," a familiar voice answered.

"Inez?" I asked, surprised.

"Dr. Popper!" she replied, dropping her formal tone. "I am so glad you called! I wanted to thank you for your help last night."

"That's why I'm calling," I told her. "Inez, I've gotten some more information about the poison that may have been used to kill Eduardo—and which you might have ingested yesterday. It's really important that you see a doctor—"

"I already have," she replied. "Thees morning, I told a friend of mine, a girl who works in a house nearby, what happened. Like you, she says I must go to the doctor. She knows a man who will not charge so much money. He says I am fine. Eet was maybe something I ate, some food that was bad, or maybe I had a touch of the flu."

"Did you tell him about what happened to Eduardo?" I asked her anxiously. "Inez, I think you have to consider the possibility—"

"I am fine, Dr. Popper," Inez insisted. "See? I am even back at work today. A leetle tired, maybe, and my stomach still does not feel so good, but I am—what ees the saying?—back on my feet again."

She thanked me again for my concern, then insisted that she had to get back to work.

At least she saw a doctor, I told myself as I hung up. And from the way she sounded, she seemed to be fine.

Yet the possibility that, like Eduardo, she had been a victim of poisoning continued to nag at me. While she seemed unwilling to consider that such a terrible thing had happened to her, I couldn't be as certain.

I was about to pull out of my parking space, still agonizing over whether Inez had gotten the medical care she really needed, when my cell phone rang. I put the car back into park and grabbed it off the front seat. Glancing at the familiar number on the screen told me Forrester was calling. My heart sank.

"Hey, Popper! Long time no hear from!" he greeted me. He hesitated for just a moment. "We're still friends, aren't we?"

"I've just been busy," I told him. Quickly, I added, "With veterinarian business. Seems like one emergency after another lately."

"I know the feeling. Sounds like being a vet is almost as bad as being a reporter. 'Crisis oriented'—isn't that what they call it? But I hope that doesn't mean you haven't had time to—you know, work on our little project."

"Actually..." I cleared my throat, stalling as I tried to come up with an excuse. "I'm sorry, Forrester, I'm getting beeped," I lied. "This could be a client. Can I call you back?"

"Sure, Popper. You know I'm always happy to hear from you." In a voice that, even in my distracted state, struck me as awfully flirty, he said, "Day *or* night."

As I hung up, I felt a little guilty for having held out on him. Yet I hadn't been able to bring myself to play Show and Tell. Something prevented me from telling him what I'd learned about Callie and angel's trumpet—and the conclusion that naturally arose.

Somehow, I just couldn't bring myself to say the words out loud, that such a young girl may have committed murder.

At least, not until I'd ruled out some of those other suspects—starting with the one in my very own backyard.

Chapter 16

"The wildest colts make the best horses."

—Plutarch

This time, I was actually glad to see Winston Farnsworth's cream-colored Rolls-Royce parked in front of Betty's house. As I pulled up outside my cottage, I tried to think of a way of luring him outside—while keeping Betty *inside*. Asking him to look at one of my tires, claiming that it appeared to be getting flat, struck me as a good possibility. Then, once I had him alone, I'd simply have to do some quick thinking about how to get him to come clean with whatever information he had about Eduardo Garcia's murder.

I rang Betty's bell, trying to ignore the knot in my stomach and hoping my acting abilities were good enough to convince her that there really was a problem with my tire. I was so befuddled over the prospect of lying to one of my closest friends that I actually jumped when Winston answered the door.

"Oh!" I cried. "I was expecting Betty." I could feel

my cheeks growing warm. After what had happened last night, I was relieved he didn't slam the door in my face and flee in terror.

In fact, he smiled warmly, making it clear there were no hard feelings. "Hello, Jessica. I'm afraid Betty isn't here. Apparently the ribbon on one of her ballet shoes tore off, and she's in Port Townsend, trying to find someone to repair it. But you're certainly welcome to come in and wait. Or simply to visit."

I strode inside. "Is Frederick with you?" I asked, as if visiting with a dachshund, rather than a mere human being, was a stronger reason to pay a call.

"He's at home," Winston said, "probably having the time of his life barking at squirrels." Chuckling, he added, "Goodness, you'd think that after all this time, dogs and squirrels would have called a truce."

"Right." At the moment, I wasn't feeling very friendly toward him. In fact, I kept glancing around, terrified that I'd see some sign of foul play. Just because Winston said Betty was out doing errands didn't mean he was telling the truth. After all, not trusting him was what had brought me here in the first place.

"Would you like a cup of tea?" Winston offered after leading me into the front parlor. "Not surprisingly, Betty is much better than I am at running a house. Not only does she have an entire collection of teacups, she actually has cookies and little cakes. I'm learning my way around her kitchen well enough to be able to—"

"Winston, I want you to be straight with me."

He looked startled. "Of course, Jessica. I've never had any intention of being anything but completely honest with you."

"Good. I hope that's true—especially since Betty is now part of your life." Narrowing my eyes, I said, "I'm giving you the benefit of the doubt here, Winston, in assuming that your interest in Betty is sincere."

"Of course it's sincere!" By this point, he looked very confused. "I know you're protective of Betty, Jessica, and that really is quite admirable. However, I'm afraid I'm not following where you're going with this."

I took a deep breath. Then, looking him in the eye, I said, "I want you to tell me what you know about Eduardo Garcia's murder."

"Oh, dear." Winston sank onto Betty's silk-covered Victorian sofa, his expression changing to one of distress. He stared at the thick Oriental carpet for what seemed like a very long time before finally raising his eyes to meet mine. "You've heard something about me, then."

"Yes," I told him, hoping I sounded convincing. "But because you and I both care about Betty, because the last thing either of us wants is for her to get hurt, I want to hear the truth from you."

"I certainly owe you that, don't I? For Betty's sake, if nothing else."

"For Betty's sake," I repeated. I lowered myself into a chair and folded my hands in my lap. Then I fixed my eyes on him expectantly.

"I suppose you're right, Jessica, that I can't remain silent anymore. Not with all that's gone on." Winston spoke in a somber tone, so softly that I had to struggle to hear. "I owe a great deal to Andrew. To Bill Johannsen and Harlan Chase, too. But things are getting out of hand. I can't simply stand by, watching it all unfold."

By that point, my heart was racing with alarming speed. I could see that Winston was also under a great deal of stress. His face was flushed, and he was having difficulty looking me in the eye. I was tempted to feel sorry for him. But I reminded myself that I needed to find out what he had to say before I decided whether or not he deserved my sympathy.

He took a deep breath. "I suppose it makes sense to start at the beginning. Isn't that usually the best way? About two years ago, the four of us—Andrew, Bill, Harlan, and I—came up with what we thought was an explosive idea for a major business venture. We decided to launch an extensive line of men's products that ran across all categories. A clothing line, personal-care products like aftershave and shampoo, lifestyle magazines, travel arrangements, car detailing, even home furnishings. It was something that had never been done before, certainly not on the scale we envisioned. And it was all going to revolve around Eduardo.

"He was going to be our spokesperson. Our symbol. In fact, he was the very inspiration for the idea. The four of us were sitting around the fire one evening drinking brandy and talking. Somehow, it came out that each one of us had made the same observation independently: Eduardo Garcia was what every man longs to be. He was so handsome, so charismatic, that he was attractive to both women and men. People were spellbound by him. But there was so much more to him. He was also athletic, disciplined, accomplished...and quite principled.

"As we spoke, we realized how remarkable it was that we had all come to the same conclusion. We also recognized, as experienced businessmen, that Eduardo's uniqueness was something the four of us were in an ideal position to take advantage of. That same evening, we came up with the idea of building an entire campaign around him. Our goal would be to convince men all over America and eventually all over the world that they could have what he had—that they could actually *become* him. All they had to do was buy our products."

"Like Ralph Lauren's 'Polo' line," I observed.

"Even bigger." Winston forced a smile. "And 'Polo' would have been an excellent name. Except, of course, that it had already been taken. But we hired an advertising agency that came up with something we thought was just as strong: Charisma.

"All four of us immediately threw ourselves into it. It was an exciting time. One idea led to another, momentum kept building...we were convinced we were onto something tremendous. By the beginning of August, just a few weeks ago, everything was in place. And that included financing. Each of us sank a huge amount of money into our new venture. There was no doubt in our minds that we'd all make it back, five and ten times over. Perhaps even much more than that. But we also brought in other investors. Some of them were our friends. Some of them were people who...well, who weren't so friendly." He hesitated. "And then something happened that none of us had anticipated."

I looked at him expectantly, holding my breath.

"Eduardo told us he was backing out."

I blinked, taking a moment to imagine the effect such an announcement would have had on four wealthy, powerful men who had just spent two years of their lives plus substantial sums of money on one man.

"But hadn't he signed a contract?" I asked. "Surely you and your investors are savvy enough to have made provisions for something like this."

"You're right. Even though we'd never dreamed that Eduardo would change his mind, we had done all the standard paperwork. In fact, we'd had the best lawyers in New York City draw up an airtight contract. But when Eduardo informed us that he'd lost interest in the project, he said he was planning to go back to Argentina. Back to the village he'd grown up in, in fact. He told us he'd decided that he no longer cared about money, that he'd tired of the glamorous life of a polo player. Instead, he yearned for the simple life."

I suddenly realized what Andrew MacKinnon had

been referring to when he'd remarked that losing Eduardo would have meant a loss to the game—and that it had nothing to do with Eduardo's unexpected death.

While that was suddenly clear, there was another question that still nagged at me. "Is it true that Eduardo owed money? I've heard rumors..."

"Yes, there were rumors," Winston agreed. "I don't know if there was anything to them. But it wouldn't surprise me if Eduardo had gotten himself into financial difficulties. He was young and impressionable. He hadn't been in this country long before he developed a taste for the finest things in life. Expensive sports cars, expensive wines, expensive women..."

He smiled sadly. "Not that I blame him. The man came from nothing. All of a sudden, the world was his oyster, if you'll excuse the cliché. Yet if he was in financial trouble, going through with this project would have been his way out of it. Which makes his decision to back out even more puzzling—and more distressing."

"But you said yourself you had a contract," I pointed out. "Surely you had legal recourse."

"First of all, waging a legal battle against someone living in South America—in a village that barely had electricity, no less—would have been a nightmare. Second of all, the litigation would have taken years. We already had orders that our customers expected us to fill by next spring. Bloomingdale's, Nordstrom, Neiman-Marcus, Abercrombie and Fitch...even Tiffany, which was extremely excited about our men's jewelry line. The one thing we didn't have was *time*."

"In that case, couldn't you have found someone else to create the image for the Charisma campaign? Pancho Escobar? Or even the other polo player on MacKinnon's team, Scott Mooney?"

Winston smiled like a patient parent who was about

to explain something rudimentary to a child. "You still have no idea, do you? Eduardo was magic. He had the looks of a movie star, the charm of Lady Diana, and a level of athletic ability that put him in the same class as Alex Rodriguez or Tiger Woods. He was aristocratic, but at the same time down-to-earth. Everyone had the utmost respect and admiration for him, yet it was easy to imagine having a beer with him while watching the game on television. The traits he possessed were truly a rare combination, something that's almost impossible to find. Eduardo Garcia was Michael Jordan, Brad Pitt, and John F. Kennedy, Jr., all rolled into one. And once we launched Charisma, he would have been an icon for his age."

Winston shook his head slowly. "Still, you're absolutely right. We could have found someone else, some good-looking model or even an established figure from the sports world. But the bottom line is that we'd sold the entire line based on images of Eduardo. For heaven's sake, we'd even brought him with us to meet the buyers from the top stores. It wouldn't have been easy, slipping in a substitute at the last minute. Possible, maybe. But not without losing a large part of our credibility, something that was extremely important for the entire project. You see, we were selling much more than pleasantly fragranced water in a bottle or button-down shirts or tours of Provence. We were selling Eduardo. Reneging on the promise we'd made would have affected us throughout the rest of our business careers."

Winston stared down at the floor, silent for a few seconds. "There was another level to all this, as well. A personal level. None of us could believe what Eduardo had done to us. He was our *friend*, for heaven's sake. We trusted him. By backing out, he hurt each and every one of us personally. It was extremely painful."

When he finally raised his eyes to meet mine, the look

in them was mournful. "You can see why I was reluctant to say anything about any of this."

"Actually, I *don't* see," I replied. "You clearly held Eduardo in high regard. If you have suspicions about who may have murdered him, why wouldn't you rush to tell the police?"

Winston's expression flagged even further. "Because the obvious conclusion is that one of the four of us murdered Eduardo Garcia."

I remained silent, even though my mind was racing. Winston simply stared at me, no doubt studying my face to gauge my reaction.

I'd barely formed the thought that Winston was a member of that guilty-looking foursome when he said, "It wasn't me. I know that's probably exactly what you're thinking, but you're wrong. Whether you believe me or not, I know that to be the truth. Which means I can only presume that it was either Andrew, Bill, or Harlan. By revealing what happened right before he was killed, I am basically incriminating one of my three closest friends. I understand that doing precisely that is my legal responsibility. But I owe these men so much! This entire situation has turned into quite a moral dilemma for me. I would do anything for any one of them. They're like brothers to me. But now, with other people in danger, I suppose I cannot remain silent any longer. Justice must prevail—even though it may well mean a terrible punishment for one of my dearest friends."

I had to agree. Based on what I'd just learned, it did seem likely that one of the four businessmen who had put their trust in Eduardo—not to mention their trust accounts—had killed him. Perhaps even Winston. While he seemed sincere, I would have been naïve to ignore the possibility that he'd only revealed this to me in order to throw suspicion away from himself should the authorities learn the truth—either on their own or from one of the other three men.

Winston was looking at me expectantly. "That's my story, Jessica. What do you suggest I do now?"

"I think you should go to the police," I told him gently. "Tell Lieutenant Falcone what you just told me."

He nodded. "I was afraid that was what you'd say. I know, in my heart, that you're right." He closed his eyes, as if he were steeling himself for something extremely difficult. "Damn it, I just hate being in this position."

"Perhaps you should bring one of the others with you," I suggested. "It might make it easier, having one of your friends there."

He gazed at me sadly. "The question is, which one?"

Given what I now knew about Winston Farnsworth, I felt I had no choice but to confront Betty.

Even though she returned home a few minutes later, another hour passed before the cream-colored Rolls-Royce disappeared from her driveway. Now that she was alone, I had no excuse for putting it off. As I trudged from my cottage to the Big House, I dreaded the next twenty minutes of my life as much as if I were on my way to a doctor's office for an unsavory medical procedure. I even thought about bringing the dogs along for moral support, but realized that relying on them to be a distraction would be cowardly.

"Hello, Jessica," Betty greeted me in an uncertain voice as she opened the front door. She was dressed in a long purple-and-turquoise dress, a batiked fabric covered with suns and stars and moons. The hem brushed the tops of her feet, which were bare except for several toe rings. Her smooth white hair was pushed back over her ears to reveal silver and gold earrings, two quarter-moons with tiny stars dangling from them. Looking me up and down, she added, "I hope you're unarmed."

"It was an honest mistake," I told her. "Can I come in?"

"If you mean am I alone, the answer is yes." She moved aside to let me enter.

The two of us stood in the foyer, awkward in each other's presence for the first time since the day I'd met her.

"Aren't you going to offer me tea?" I finally asked.

"Are you planning to stay?" she returned, raising her chin into the air defiantly.

"I suppose you think I should apologize," I began. "And I am sorry for acting in a way that someone could construe as ... outrageous."

"I'd say 'outrageous' is the perfect word," she agreed.

"But surely you realize that at the time, I thought I was protecting you!" In response to her look of bafflement, I added, "Betty, what do you think you're doing?"

She looked at me for a long time. And then a slow, dreamy smile crossed her face. "What I'm doing, Jessica, is having the time of my life."

"What about Charles?" I demanded. "I thought he was the love of your life!"

"He most certainly was," Betty replied archly. "But he's gone, Jessica. Has been for decades. And for heaven's sake, it's not as if Winston was the first man I've been involved with since Charles. You know that as well as I do."

"You just met him," I pointed out. "Friday night, in fact. Five nights ago."

"Is that all it is?" she mused. "It seems like we've known each other for years. Of course, we've hardly been out of each other's company since Saturday night.

That's when he took me dancing. Since then, we've been to the theater, to a horse race, and out to dinner at three of the most magnificent restaurants I've ever eaten at. Of course, we've had plenty of private time, too."

"But you hardly know anything about him!"

"I know what's in my heart," she replied firmly. "That's all I need to know."

At this point, I had no choice but to tell her what was really on my mind.

"There's something else," I said slowly, choosing my words with care. "Do you think we could sit down?"

Betty eyed me warily, then led me over to her living room couch. We sat side by side, but at an angle that enabled us to look each other in the eye.

Not that doing so was particularly easy. "I know you think Winston is a wonderful person," I began slowly, "but as your friend, I must tell you that I have my... suspicions."

"Suspicions?"

I nodded. "Do you remember that polo player who was murdered two weeks ago?"

"Of course. The Argentine fellow. Eduardo something, isn't it? It's terrible, absolutely terrible. But what does that have to do with Winston?"

"That's the problem," I replied evenly. "I'm not really sure."

Betty just stared at me, her blue eyes clouded. "Jessica! Surely you don't think Winston had anything to do with it!"

"To be perfectly honest, I don't know. He could have, Betty. There are things that Eduardo was involved in that could have—"

"Pshaw!" Betty insisted, reacting as if I'd just said the most ridiculous thing in the world. "I simply don't believe a word of it. It's impossible that Winston could have anything to do with *murder,* of all things! Why, he's one of the sweetest, kindest men I've ever known!"

I was silent for a few moments, trying to come up with the words that would convince her that she was treading on very dangerous ground. But before I could, she leaned forward and took both my hands in hers.

"Jessica," she said gently, "I know how your mind works. You can't help getting involved when you feel that some injustice has been done, and that's admirable. You're also extremely intelligent, with a wonderfully active imagination. But an imagination like yours can get out of hand, reading into things and interpreting them in the worst possible way.

"I appreciate your concern. I know you're only looking out for me, and that's very sweet. But I promise you: Winston had nothing to do with Eduardo's murder—or anything else that he'd need to be secretive about. Even though he and I have only been together for a very short time, I *know* him. I'm fine, Jessica. In fact, I'm more than fine—and it's all because of Winston."

"But there's more!" I insisted, frustrated over her refusal to heed my warning. "There are all kinds of rumors about him! That he's in financial trouble, that he's selling his estate, that he had to fire his housekeeper—"

"Oh, pshaw," Betty insisted, waving her hand in the air. "If I believed every rumor I'd ever heard in my life, if I'd ever given a hoot about anything anybody thought or said...well, I'd probably still be living back in Altoona. Maybe even still working at the Paper Plate Diner, although I probably would have been promoted to manager by now."

"Betty, I'm only telling you this for your own good."

Her expression softened. "I know you are, Jessica," she said, squeezing my hands. "I know you mean well, that your fears about Winston are rooted in your concern for me. But I'm a big girl, in case you haven't noticed. More than old enough to take care of myself."

"But what about Winston selling his estate?"

"He told me all about it."

My eyebrows leaped up to my hairline. "What did he say?"

"That he's too darned old and too darned lonely to be rattling around all alone in a huge house like that. He's looking for a smaller place. And that makes perfect sense, if you ask me."

"Did he say anything about selling his house because of economic reasons?"

"No, and I'm too much of a lady to ask him about his financial status. I'm not after his money, Jessica. I'm after his company."

"What about letting his housekeeper go?" I demanded.

"Dora had been talking about retiring for months. She'd been with him for twenty-three years!"

I opened my mouth to try another argument, but the expression on Betty's face told me that our discussion had come to an end.

"Just wish me the best, Jessica," Betty said earnestly. "I haven't been this happy for a long, long time. Be glad for me—and for goodness' sake, stop worrying so much! I really do have a good sense of who Winston is. I'm a fairly decent judge of character. For heaven's sake, I agreed to let you move in here when that overbearing real estate Misty or whatever her name is brought you by, didn't I?"

"That's true," I admitted.

"I have the same feeling about this man. He's special, Jessica. He's someone I could care about. And he's certainly no murderer."

I had to admit that Betty made a pretty good argument. I was close enough to her to know she was nobody's fool. Winston's willingness to come clean with me about Eduardo's last-minute change of plans and its shocking repercussions among the members of Winston's social set was pretty persuasive, too.

"Now, how about some tea?" Betty said, the familiar twinkle returning to her sapphire blue eyes.

"Tea sounds perfect," I told her, glad that our friendship was back on solid ground.

There was another reason for my great sense of relief: having at least one name I could cross off my list of suspects. The problem was, that still left me with a fairly long list—and Callie's name remained pretty high on it.

As I headed back to my cottage, I came up with one more reason it was unlikely that Winston had murdered Eduardo: motivation.

It wouldn't have made sense for him or any of the other businessmen who'd invested in Eduardo to have killed him, I thought. For all they knew, it might have been possible to change the polo player's mind at the eleventh hour. Or maybe he was bluffing. His announcement that he was returning to his village in Argentina could have been nothing more than a tactic to wangle more money out of the men who were counting on him. It seems to me that until the moment that Eduardo actually stepped onto an airplane bound for Buenos Aires, everything was negotiable.

Then again, I reminded myself, how often does murder have anything to do with logic? Winston—or Andrew or Bill or Harlan—could have tried to convince Eduardo to live up to his commitment, then become incensed when he wouldn't budge.

Yet poisoning someone was such a calculated act. It could hardly be considered a crime of passion, the result of flying into a rage.

The ringing of my cell phone put an end to my specu-
lation. Glancing at the number, I saw that someone from
Heatherfield was calling me.

What now? I thought, a wave of apprehension wash-
ing over me.

"Dr. Popper? Ees Inez," the familiar voice greeted me.

I was relieved—but only for a second. "Is everything
all right?" I asked.

"Everything ees fine. I am calling for—what do you
say, a personal reason. I would like to invite you to dinner this evening. Eet is my way of saying thank you for
helping me last night. I think I must have eaten something bad, but now I am fine. But you were so kind to
rush over when Callie called you last night. I know eet is
short notice, but I am hoping you will come."

Inez—the shy housekeeper who moved about the
shadows of Heatherfield, her presence rarely noticed
and hardly ever taken seriously. She had already turned
out to be a good source of information. After all, she
had overheard Diana arguing with Eduardo just before
he was murdered. It was possible that on some other occasion, she'd learned some other critical bit of information from walking into a room unexpectedly while
Callie and Eduardo were huddled together or serving
coffee while Andrew was meeting with his three business associates. Chatting with her over a casual dinner
could turn out to be the best way of finding another
piece of the puzzle—perhaps some tidbit that even she
didn't realize had significance. A discussion or an argument she'd overheard but didn't think anything of at the
time, a comment Callie or Andrew or Peyton had made
while talking on the phone, maybe even a note she'd
found on the floor, a few words scribbled on a scrap of
paper...

Of course, I recognized that returning to Heatherfield
carried a certain risk. Someone over there doesn't like

me, I reminded myself. Just showing my face amounts to asking for trouble.

For a fleeting moment, I pictured myself enjoying a quiet dinner with Inez, then jumping to my feet as a masked intruder leaped into the cottage through an open window....

Still, spending a couple of hours with the Mac-Kinnons' housekeeper could provide me with the information I needed to figure out who killed Eduardo Garcia.

"Inez, I'd love to," I told her. "What time?"

Chapter 17

"Horses do think. Not very deeply, perhaps, but enough to get you into a lot of trouble."
—Patricia Jacobson and Marcia Hayes,
"A Horse Around the House"

Once again, Heatherfield seemed strangely quiet. As I turned off Turkey Hollow Road, the sun was about to drop below the horizon, and the darkening sky was already settling over the estate like a blanket. The only sound was the chirping of birds and, in the distance, the whinny of one of Andrew MacKinnon's horses. I parked my VW on the driveway, then shut the car door behind me.

As I walked purposefully up the path toward Inez's cottage, I took my cell phone out of my purse and stuck it into my pocket. Nick was meeting with his study group tonight, and I wanted to be sure I'd hear it ring if he called. I'd used the chaos of the past few days as an excuse not to give him an answer about the future of our living arrangements—which pretty much amounted to the same thing as the future of our relationship. As a result, things between us were still a bit unsettled. Even if

I couldn't quite bring myself to offer to share my home with him, I wanted to be available if he tried to get in touch.

I found Inez standing in the doorway, watching for me. I gave her a little wave.

"It was so nice of you to invite me to dinner," I told her, stepping inside her small living room. Handing her the bouquet I'd brought, I added, "I thought these would cheer up the cottage. I know how much you like flowers."

"Thank you so much, Dr. Popper," she said, taking them from me. "You are very kind."

"Please, call me Jessie."

"Jessie, then." Her cheeks reddening, she lowered her eyes. "I will put these in water. But please, you must sit down."

As she disappeared into the kitchen, I lowered myself onto the sagging couch.

The coffee table in front of it had been set for dinner. Two mismatched plates were laid out side by side, along with two glasses of water and silverware. A loaf of warm bread was wrapped in a linen napkin that was slightly tattered at one end, and a huge serving of salad sat at each place.

"I thought it would be nicer to eat in the living room," Inez called in from the kitchen. She emerged a few seconds later, carrying the bouquet. It was now contained in what looked like a large mayonnaise jar.

"Goodness, you didn't have to go to so much trouble," I told Inez sincerely.

"Ees nothing," she said, setting the flowers on a rickety end table. "I am used to working hard. Cooking dinner for just two people is easy."

It wasn't until she sat down that I realized I hadn't fully hashed out my plan to pump Inez for more information. As I dug into my salad, I thought, *Okay, smarty.*

Now what? You can't exactly plunge right in and say, So, Inez, have you eavesdropped on any other conversations lately in which somebody mentioned wanting to murder Eduardo?

"Ees the salad all right?" Inez asked anxiously.

"Yes, it's fine," I told her. The truth was, I'd been so lost in thought that I'd barely noticed. Instead, I'd simply shoveled in forkful after forkful of the stuff, which was drenched in a thick, spicy dressing that masked the taste of everything else mixed into it. I did notice that she'd put a lot of effort into making it, which I found touching. In addition to the usual varieties of lettuce, she had cut up carrots, cucumbers, scallions, and half a dozen other vegetables.

"Would you like more? I have a big bowl in the refrigerator."

"No, thank you. This should be fine," I assured her.

"Good," she said with a little nod of her head. "I want to be certain you have enough."

"Inez," I began slowly, "do you remember that conversation between Eduardo and Diana Chase that you told me about a few days ago?"

"Of course." Before I had a chance to ask another question, she glanced over at my place setting and said, "I see you are done. Are you sure you don't want more? Please, let me bring out the bowl—"

"I'm fine," I assured her.

She hesitated. "Then I will bring these plates into the kitchen."

"I'll help you," I said, grabbing mine and standing up.

I followed her into the kitchen. As she busied herself with scraping and rinsing, I noticed that Inez had done some redecorating. She'd removed the large ornamental plants that she'd kept on the windowsill. Now, only the small pots of herbs remained. The window looked much bigger—probably the reason for the change, I figured.

As I stood idly, I ran my eyes over the photographs that covered the refrigerator. I'd noticed them the last time I'd been inside the cottage, but I hadn't taken the time to do more than glance at them. I've never found looking at photographs of strangers especially meaningful.

But this time, one photograph in particular caught my attention. There were two people in it, a boy and a girl about twelve years old standing with their arms loosely around each other's waists. But it was the girl's face that drew me in. Her expression was so blissful. She radiated happiness.

She also looked familiar. I leaned forward to peer at the picture more closely, wondering if the girl was Inez's younger sister. But I recognized the distinctive shape of her eyes. It had to be Inez, about ten years earlier.

When I glanced at the boy at her side, I blinked.

I could have been mistaken, but the boy in the photograph looked very much like a young version of Eduardo.

But how could that be? I puzzled. When Inez was that age, she was living in Puerto Rico and Eduardo was living far away in Argentina....

A cold, tingling feeling suddenly rushed over me. Was it possible that this photograph, and all the other photographs of Inez and her family, hadn't been taken in Puerto Rico, after all? That she hadn't been telling the truth when she claimed that was where she was from?

The wheels inside my head were turning. *There has to be a way to find out if Inez lied to me about her background,* I told myself.

And then I had an idea.

Struggling to sound matter-of-fact, I said, "You know, one of my best friends went to Puerto Rico on her honeymoon. She really loved it."

Inez glanced at me over her shoulder and beamed. "Ees so beautiful. I am not surprised."

"I remember her saying there was one area she particularly liked. La Perla, in San Juan?"

"Oh, yes. Ees very lovely. The beaches, the palm trees. Many tourists enjoy going there."

Inez's words echoed through my head. I replayed the image that had come into my mind when Suzanne had told me about her nightmare of a honeymoon in San Juan. Somehow, sitting in the one area of the city that tourists were warned against, trapped in a car surrounded by men who looked like drug dealers, didn't mesh with Inez's characterization of the place.

I struggled to make sense of what I was hearing—and what I was seeing. Why would she lie? I wondered. Why would Inez pretend to be from Puerto Rico when she really came from the same tiny Argentine village as Eduardo?

Even in my confusion, the answer was becoming alarmingly clear. *Because she isn't who she pretends to be.* Because she has a long history with Eduardo. Because she came to this country with him, so the two of them could be together.

Or maybe she followed him, uninvited.

Almost as if I were following directions that someone was feeding to me, I turned toward the windowsill above the kitchen sink and studied the neat row of potted plants. I thought back to the last time I'd been here, picturing the windowsill—*before* Inez had changed what was on it.

A distinctive-looking plant that could only have been angel's trumpet had been nestled among the herbs.

I tried to put together all the pieces of information tumbling through my brain. But for some reason, thinking straight was becoming increasingly difficult. I rubbed my forehead, realizing that my brain was beginning to feel foggy. I also felt light-headed.

"Inez, I'm going to sit down in the living room. I'm feeling a little dizzy." My voice sounded far away. It was almost as if someone in the next room was speaking, rather than me.

I sank onto the couch, shaking my head as if that was a way of banishing the muddled feeling. Inez stepped back into the room and leaned over me anxiously.

"Dr. Popper? Jessie? Are you okay? You are not looking so good."

"I'm fine," I assured her. "I'm probably just tired. Or maybe I'm coming down with something."

"I theenk you should lie down," Inez insisted. "Why don't you go into my bedroom?"

"Maybe I should just go home," I said.

"No! No, stay here. Eet would be bad for you to drive. Eet would be very dangerous, if you are dizzy."

"I could call Nick," I said, my voice seeming to echo around the room. "I could ask him to pick me up."

"No!" she cried. "No, you must not call anybody."

Something about the urgency in her tone helped me think clearly, at least for a few seconds.

Oh, my God, I thought. *She doesn't want me to leave, and she doesn't want me to call anyone. Is it possible...?*

I reached into my pocket, running one finger over the keys on my cell phone and dialing what I hoped was 911. *Please,* please, *let me hit the right numbers,* I begged silently.

I waited a few seconds, then said loudly, "I think I might have eaten something poisonous." When Inez remained silent, I said, "This might sound crazy, Inez, but did you put something in the salad you gave me?"

"Just stay here and rest, Dr. Popper," she replied. "Everything will be fine."

Despite the hazy feeling that had me in its grip, when I saw her walk over to the front door and lock it, I knew that my worst suspicions were true.

By that point, the room had begun to spin around. At the same time the walls seemed to be fading from view. I blinked hard, trying to fight off the weird sensation that I was drifting away. It didn't help.

"You poisoned me!" I cried. "Inez, it was you! *You* killed Eduardo Garcia!"

I wasn't even sure if she was still in the room. Then, in a low, angry voice I'd never heard before, she said, "You do not understand, Dr. Popper. Eduardo betrayed me."

"How did he betray you, Inez? Why did you kill him?"

"Eet was the only way," Inez said in the same hard voice. "You see, ever since we were children, Eduardo and me, we were together. We were so close—best friends. And then we became lovers. Everyone in our village knew that we would get married. I have always known, in my heart, that it was me that Eduardo really loved. We were meant to be together. But when he came to this country, he let himself be tricked. The money, the women...even Meester Mac, the way he treated Eduardo like he was a—a star. A celebrity.

"Eduardo had not been here long before he started to believe he was someone else. Someone so...*importante*. Too *importante* for me. But I know thees is wrong. Then he tells me he is going to make a big change in his life. He says he is waiting for the right time, and then he will tell me about it. But I do not have to know what eet is, because I already know that he will not want me to be part of it, that he will choose one of his other women. And if Eduardo will not stay with me, I will not let him stay with anybody."

"Tell me what happened right before he died," I said,

struggling with each word. "Exactly what happened? How did you do it, Inez?"

"Eet was the night before he fell from his horse, right before the party he was going to with all his fancy new friends," she replied in the same bitter tone. "I invited him for dinner, here at the cottage. No one saw him come. No one pays attention to what I do, because I am just the housekeeper. That night, I gave him salad with leaves from the locoweed. Eet grows everywhere here, just like in Argentina. But I grew my own plants, here in the cottage, so no one would ever see me cutting off the leaves."

"You did the same thing tonight, didn't you?" I accused, speaking as loudly as I could. "You put locoweed—angel's trumpet—in the salad you gave me."

"I had no choice, Dr. Popper. Surely you must understand that. You told me yourself the police were wrong to think he was poisoned at the party. At the *asado*, you said you were going to find out who he had been with the day before he died. I knew then that you were even smarter than the police and that it was only a matter of time before you figured out who killed Eduardo. That was why I started the fire. Only you didn't go inside the stable, the way I expected."

"But what about the other night, Inez?" I cried, my voice coming out in gasps. "I thought whoever murdered Eduardo had also poisoned you!"

"Eet was all an act. I knew that Callie would call you eef I told her to. Making you believe that I had been a victim of poisoning, just like Eduardo, seemed like the perfect way to keep you from thinking I had anything to do with his death. I picked a night when no one else but Callie was at home, because I knew eet would be easy to fool a leetle girl.

"And eet turned out to be just as easy to fool you." Inez laughed. "I found out I am not such a bad actress.

Even when I pretended I was throwing up in the bathroom, you believed me. But it was fake, all fake. I just act like I am sick!"

"So you killed Eduardo because you felt he had betrayed you, Inez," I said loudly, hoping the 911 operator could hear us both.

"Yes. And everything would have been fine, except for you. The way you were asking questions, talking to people...I knew you were a danger to me, Dr. Popper. Last night, after you left, I realized something *importante*: that even though I managed to make you think that I, too, had been poisoned, I was only fooling myself by thinking that in the end, you would not figure out that I had killed Eduardo. That maybe I even made a mistake by pretending that I, too, had been a victim because it made me more involved. You were trying so hard to find the murderer. I had no choice but to try again to stop you. Eet is the only way I can be safe."

Inez's voice sounded farther and farther away. Her words echoed through my head, making me feel as if I were falling deeper and deeper into a bottomless canyon.

"I don't understand. It took Eduardo more than twelve hours to die. But I—I..."

"Eduardo ate only the leaves, so it took a very long time for him to be poisoned. As long as no one knew he was here for dinner before the big party, no one could connect me to his death. But for you, I do not have so much time, so I added the root. In Santa Rosita, everyone say eet works so much faster."

Her words seemed to get softer and softer.

"Inez, please!" I cried, my voice sounding as far away as hers. "You've got to help me—"

I heard her shrill laughter.

My head was suddenly filled with a loud rumbling

sound, as if a train were running through it. And I kept blacking out, if only for a few seconds at a time.

I had to get outside.

Blindly, I staggered toward the kitchen, trying to find the back door. I walked with my arms outstretched to keep me from bumping into anything. Behind me, I could hear Inez, laughing and speaking in Spanish. Somewhere, in the back of my mind, it occurred to me that she might come after me and grab me. But I also knew that she'd already done her worst. Now, the only thing left for her to do was to let me die.

When I reached the back door, I clutched the knob, grateful that I'd found a way out. I stumbled outside, relieved to feel the fresh, cool air on my skin. But I realized after only a moment that even that wouldn't do me any good.

Then I remembered the phone—and my 911 call to Police Emergency. *Scream!* a voice inside my head urged. *Tell them to send an ambulance!*

I opened my mouth—at least, I thought that was what I was doing. But even though I tried, I couldn't manage to make any sound come out.

I stared straight ahead, trying to focus. I could see the bright yellow of the stable, and for some reason that struck me as a safe destination. I staggered toward it, blacking out every few seconds, finding it more and more difficult to concentrate or even to catch my breath.

The last thing I saw was the MacKinnons' barn cat, standing in my path and blinking at me in puzzlement. And then, nothing but darkness.

Chapter 18

"Anyone who is concerned about his dignity would be well advised to keep away from horses."
　　　　　　　　　　　　　—Prince Philip, Duke of Edinburgh

When I opened my eyes, I didn't recognize anything around me.

I blinked hard, trying to make sense of the pale green walls that surrounded me. I was lying in a narrow bed with an IV stuck in my arm, covered with a thin white sheet.

If I hadn't known better, I might have concluded that I was in a hospital.

"What happened?" I asked, even though I seemed to be alone. I was surprised by how difficult it was to get my mouth to work. "Where am I?"

"You're at North Country Hospital—and you're doing fine."

I stared at the grinning face that was suddenly looming over me. It took me a few seconds to remember who it belonged to.

"Forrester? What are you doing here?"

His cheeks turned pink. Running his fingers through his thick, disheveled hair, he said, "Making sure you're okay. I rushed over as soon as Falcone called me on my cell. You gave us a real scare, Popper."

"What time is it?" I asked Forrester. "What *day* is it?"

"It's still Wednesday night," he replied. "Good thing, too. If we'd waited much longer to get you to a hospital, you might not have made it."

"I feel like a hippopotamus stepped on my stomach," I groaned. "Right after somebody Roto-Rootered my throat."

"That's because they pumped your stomach." Sounding half teasing and half worried, he added, "You really should think about cutting back on the amount of angel's trumpet in your diet."

I suddenly felt as if a dark cloud had moved into the room. "It was Inez, wasn't it? She killed Eduardo and she tried to kill me! We have to call the police! We have to tell them what happened!"

"Don't worry, Popper," Forrester said with his usual breeziness. "Falcone nabbed her."

"But how did he know?"

"Your call to the police, of course. You did good, Popper. Dialing nine-one-one was nothing short of brilliant. Even Falcone admitted—begrudgingly, of course—that you'd done an incredible job. The cops have Inez's whole confession on tape. It couldn't have been better if they were right there in the room with you two. Right now, she's is in police custody, charged with murder one." Frowning, he added, "Attempted murder, too. Where you were concerned, she meant business."

"She left the anonymous notes and set the fire, too?" Forrester nodded.

"So Falcone got her—thanks to me." Even though every single molecule of my body felt as if I'd been zapped through time by a teletransporter, I managed to smile.

"By the way, he told me to give you a message. I don't really understand it, but he said you would. He said, 'Tell Dr. Popper I owe her—again.'"

"I'll keep that in mind. By the way," I added, "thanks for saving me."

He grinned. "Hey, I really wish I could take the credit. But I'm not the one who found you lying in the grass outside the stable and called the ambulance."

"Who did?"

"Our pal Johnny Ray. Guess he had a soft spot for you, after all. You're quite a charmer, Popper, winning over a crusty guy like him. It's a good thing, too. While the police knew you were in trouble from the nine-one-one call you made on your cell phone, they didn't know *where* you were."

"Dr. Popper?" I heard a female voice call softly.

Glancing across the room, I saw Luisa standing shyly in the doorway. She was the last person in the world I would have expected to visit me.

"Come in, Luisa," I told her. I glanced at Forrester, who looked equally surprised.

"The nurse said I could visit for a short time," she said. "Ees all right? I have something I would like to tell you, something I think ees maybe important."

I nodded, encouraging her to go on.

She looked over at Forrester uncertainly before she began. "Eduardo came to me the day before he died. It was late in the afternoon. Maybe five o'clock, five-thirty. Eduardo, he always makes me laugh. He tells me I am his mother here in America. That his real mother is at home in Argentina, so far away, but that God has sent him a second mother to look after him.

"Usually, Eduardo is so happy. Why not? He has everything here. The money, the horses, the women who treat him so special, even the men who have so much power, like Meester Mac. But that night, Eduardo is not laughing and having fun. In fact, he is very serious.

"He tells me he has made a very big, very important decision. He has decided to go home to Santa Rosita. He says the life he once thought was not good enough for him, living in his village with his *madre* and *padre* and raising a family of his own, is now the life he desires. He says he wants to go back and marry the one woman he has always loved, his sweetheart from the time he was a little boy."

"Inez," I said softly. "He was going home, and he planned to take her back with him."

"*Sí,*" she replied.

It took me a moment to comprehend what she was telling me. "When was he going to tell her?" I finally asked.

"He told me he had already tried," Luisa said. "Just a few days before, he had told Inez that he was about to make a big change in his life, one that would have an effect on her life, too. He could see that she had a very big... what is the word, reaction? That was when he decided to make his announcement special, to create a moment the two of them would remember for the rest of their lives. He wanted to make a big occasion.

"That was the reason he wanted to talk to me the day before he died—the night he had dinner with Inez at her cottage. He said he wanted to propose marriage to her in some very wonderful place. He asked me where I thought it should be. A restaurant, maybe, or a garden... I told him she loves flowers, and that maybe he should take her to a place with beautiful gardens. He thanked me and said he would do that, the very next day.

"But then... everything went wrong." She shook her head slowly. "I theenk Inez expected that he was going to tell her something very bad. Maybe that he was getting married to someone else. . . . She was so afraid she would lose him completely. And I believe she felt, in her heart, that she could not let anyone else have him. So the night before Eduardo was planning to propose marriage to Inez, the one thing she had been waiting for her entire life, ever since she was a leetle girl . . ." Luisa choked on her words, unable to go on.

"A day late and a dollar short," Forrester muttered. "Tough luck."

"What a tragedy." I closed my eyes, suddenly overwhelmed.

I opened them just as quickly. "Luisa, there's one more thing I have to know. What about Callie? What kind of relationship did she have with Eduardo?"

She sighed. "Poor Callie. I know she had a terrible— what is the word, crush? I used to tease Eduardo about it all the time. He would laugh and say that Callie was his little sister here in thees country the same way I was his mother. He even had a special name he called her: 'Nena,' which is—what is the word, slang?—for 'leetle girl.' But whenever he would tease her and tell her thees, she would get very angry. I could see she did not like Eduardo to treat her like a child, even though that was the only way he could see her."

"I'm sure she didn't like it at all," I commented, more to myself than to Luisa.

"Dr. Popper, I am so sorry for bothering you at a time like this," she said. "You must be very tired. I will leave you to rest."

"Thank you for coming," I told her. "And thank you for telling me about Eduardo."

As soon as she left, Forrester reached for his jacket. "Well, Popper, I should probably get going, too. I think you're supposed to be sleeping this off."

"Thanks for coming, Forrester," I said sincerely. "And for everything else."

"Listen, if you ever get tired of the veterinary biz, give me a call. I know some folks over at *Newsday* who'd be thrilled to have a top-notch reporter like you on staff." He hesitated, then leaned over and gave me a quick kiss on the cheek. "See you at the next murder, Popper. Until then, stay out of trouble, okay?"

As he strode out of the room, I heard him say, " 'Scuse me."

And then Nick was standing next to my bed, his face tense and drawn. "I came over as soon as I got a call," he said anxiously. "It was from some guy named Forrester, whoever that is. He assured me that the doctors say you're fine. How do you feel, Jess?"

"For someone who's had her Minimum Daily Requirement of hyoscyamine and scopolamine, I'd say I'm doing pretty well."

"I want to hear the whole story," Nick told me, reaching over and taking my hand.

"It's kind of what's known as a *long* story," I told him ruefully. "Right now, I'm not so sure I have the energy."

"Okay." He hesitated before adding, "We have a few other things to talk about, too. You know, you-and-me-type issues."

"I *know* I don't have the energy for those."

"You're right. This probably isn't the best time. I guess we can wait until you're out of the hospital."

"It's a deal."

"But in the meantime," Nick continued, "there's something I really need you to do."

"Anything."

He gave my hand a tight squeeze. "I want you to promise me that from now on, you'll keep as far away from murder as possible."

"But—"

"No buts, Jess. Maybe you're tough enough to handle nearly getting killed, but I'm not. Please?" Looking into his eyes, I saw an intensity I couldn't remember having seen before.

I blinked. "It's that important to you?"

"Of course it's that important!"

"In that case—" The annoying trill of my cell phone stopped me mid-sentence. Casting him an apologetic look, I grabbed it off the table next to me, where it sat along with my keys and other belongings. "Hello?"

"Jessie! I'm so glad I got you!" The desperation I heard in Suzanne's voice told me that she wasn't calling simply to complain about a glitch in her social life.

"Suzanne, what's wrong?"

"Jessie, you've got to help me! I—I don't know what to do! This whole thing is so crazy—"

"Slow down," I insisted. "What's happened?"

"Oh, Jessie, I've been accused of murder! Robert's fiancée was killed, and the police think *I* did it!"

"Jess?" Nick interrupted gently. "What's going on?"

I raised my eyes and just looked at him.

About the Author

CYNTHIA BAXTER is a native of Long Island, New York. She currently resides on the North Shore, where she is at work on the next *Reigning Cats & Dogs* mystery, which Bantam will publish in Summer 2006. Visit her on the web at www.cynthiabaxter.com.

Dear Reader,

In my next mystery, Jessica Popper's role as amateur sleuth takes on new urgency when one of her closest friends, veterinarian Suzanne Fox, finds herself the number one suspect in a murder.

Jessie's investigation leads her to Long Island's pastoral North Fork, once covered with potato fields but today home to more than two dozen vineyards and a booming wine industry. In writing the book, I tried to capture the area's beauty—as well as its colorful history, which includes notorious pirate Captain Kidd and his buried treasure.

As Jessie once again struggles to discover "whodunit," this time to save her friend, she encounters an intriguing collection of suspects, uncovers secrets and lies more numerous than the jewels in Captain Kidd's chest, and strives to decipher some surprising clues . . . purposely left behind by the victim herself.

I hope you enjoy this special preview!

Cynthia Baxter

Read on for an exclusive sneak peek at
the next
***Reigning Cats and Dogs* mystery**

by Cynthia Baxter

Coming in Summer 2006

A new *Reigning Cats and Dogs* mystery

On sale in summer 2006

"A kitten is more amusing than half the people one is obliged to live with."

—Lady Sydney Morgan

As I drove east to the island's wine region Saturday morning, retracing my steps of two days earlier, I was struck once again by how beautiful this part of Long Island is. In fact, I found it difficult to believe that I was in the same universe that contained the offices of Jerry Keeler, Attorney at Law.

There was one major difference between my last foray and this one, however: the traffic. Even though it was barely 11 a.m. on a weekend, a steady stream of cars was heading east along Route 35, a strange twist on the rush-hour concept. At first, I thought there must be road construction up ahead. Then I realized the reason for the congestion was that plenty of other people had discovered the East End wineries. While I was seeking information, however, they were heading to the North Fork in search of the perfect chardonnay—or at least a relaxing day spent tasting wine and enjoying the scenery.

I knew I'd reached Thorndike Vineyards when I spotted a huge white sign with a large gold "T" surrounded by a ring of dark green vines. I recognized it as the same logo that appeared on their label. I pulled into the parking lot, where sightseers were already vying for parking spaces. Of course, the two big tour buses that took up a good chunk of the pavement didn't help. I lucked into a spot when a couple who'd just loaded two cases of wine into the trunk of their BMW backed out hurriedly, probably rushing to the next winery on their list.

The day was surprisingly cool for late September. I was glad I'd worn my navy blue polyester fleece jacket. I was equally glad the Thorndike Vineyards Visitor Center was just a few steps away. It was a large, barnlike building that looked at least a hundred years old. At least on the outside. Stepping inside, I saw that the interior had been completely renovated, with high white walls and sleek wooden fixtures that gave it the look of a Manhattan boutique—one that just happened to have a bar running along one wall. Even though it wasn't yet noon, the room was lined with wine lovers who were taking advantage of the opportunity to taste.

All manner of wine-related paraphernalia was displayed on tables and shelves. Bottle stoppers topped with bunches of purple grapes or chubby sommeliers. Glittery gift bags designed to hold a single bottle of wine that would serve as a hostess gift. Fancy snack foods like paper-thin English crackers and obscure French cheeses that were the perfect accompaniment to a fine wine, along with ceramic plates hand-painted with vines to serve them on. Most people were just browsing, although a few were filling the straw baskets the shop supplied with the frenzy of last-minute Christmas shoppers.

Then there were the wines themselves. Two of the room's walls were lined with shelves displaying bottle after bottle of Thorndike wines. I saw chardonnays, pinot noirs, merlots, and a half dozen other varieties. Every label was emblazoned with the same logo I'd seen on my way in.

A large white sign proclaimed that Thorndike Vineyards had been named "Winery of the Year" at the previous year's "New York Wine Classic," and had won gold medals for its 1999 Merlot Grand Vintage and its 2002 Barrel Fermented Chardonnay. Pretty impressive, especially to someone like me who had always thought there were basically two varieties of wine: white and red.

"The eleven-thirty tour is about to get under way," a woman's voice announced, cutting through the din. "We still have one or two places available, if anyone is interested in touring the winery."

I thought you'd never ask, I thought, heading over to the small group gathered by the back door.

". . . Six, seven, eight," a pleasant-looking middle-aged woman whose blouse had the familiar "T" embroidered on it counted aloud. "I think that should do it. If you'll please follow me . . ."

Our tour guide—Marian, according to her name tag—led us through double doors at the back of the tasting room. We were suddenly in a warehouse-type area, except that it was very well ventilated, with walls that didn't quite reach all the way to the roof. Every inch was immaculate, from the huge shiny vats that lined one long wall to the smooth concrete floor.

"Thorndike Vineyards started twenty years ago with the first planting of vinifera," she began after shepherding us into a cluster. "These are the grapes that are planted in France and California. We began with only forty acres, then acquired more land in the years that followed. Today, we plant a total of ninety acres and produce nearly twenty thousand cases of wine annually.

"The key to making good wine is using sweet grape juice," she continued, "which means starting the process with ripe fruit and good sugar." She pointed to the wall of vats. "We begin the process by crushing the fruit in these vats. We use stainless steel because, unlike wooden vats, they don't impart any flavor to the wine. We only use wooden barrels at this stage if we specifically want to flavor the wine.

"Inside each vat, there's a membrane that inflates and deflates like a balloon, pressing the fruit against the outer wall and causing the juice that's released to drip down into a receiving container. From there, we pump the juice into a different set of stainless steel tanks that hold two to three thousand gallons. At that point, it's still fleshy because it's filled with protein particles. We let it sit for twenty-four hours to allow the solids to settle at the bottom."

Marian led us further into the drafty room. "Fermentation is the next stage," she continued. "The juice is transferred into wooden barrels made of French oak, where we inoculate it with a special strain of yeast. Basically, the yeast feeds on the sugar in the juice, and as the yeast digests the sugar, it creates carbon dioxide, which escapes into the air, and alcohol.

"The winemaker's task is creating just the right conditions so the natural process can occur. The ideal temperature for fermentation is fifty-five degrees Fahrenheit for white and eighty degrees for red. As the yeast feeds on the sugar in the juice, yeast cells begin to line the barrel. The result is a harmony between the fruit and the oak."

"How long does the wine fermentation

take?" a man in a New York Islanders T-shirt asked.

"From ten days to three weeks," the guide replied. "The sweetness or dryness of the wine depends on the sugar content of the grape and whether the winemaker arrests fermentation before all sugar is converted or just part." Pointing at the plastic tubes protruding from the top of each barrel, she added, "These tubes are called 'fermentation locks.' They let the fermentation gases escape. In the beginning, we stir every two days, but eventually we stir only once a week."

"What about all those crazy adjectives people use to describe wines?" another man asked. "Do those words mean anything or are they just showing off?"

A few members of the tour group chuckled. "The wooden barrels are made of French oak," the tour guide explained patiently. "The wood, which is made of starch, has its own distinctive flavor, which it imparts to the wine. For example, if someone describes a wine as having 'a hint of vanilla and butterscotch,' that comes from the barrel.

"By the end of May or early June, we return the wine to stainless steel tanks for blending. We use sterile filtration to get it into bottles, and then we cork it, cap it, and label it. The wine is placed onto pallets and moved to a temperature-controlled building, where it's stored at fifty-five to fifty-six degrees until it's sold. By the way, that room is also called the 'tax room,' because state or federal agents are free to inspect it. Wineries pay tax on every bottle of wine they produce, so it's important that we keep good records."

"How many grapes does it take to make a bottle of wine?" a teenaged girl asked.

"One ton of grapes yields seven hundred sixty bottles of wine," she replied. "If you do the math, that translates to roughly two and a half pounds of grapes per bottle."

"I thought you were supposed to serve red wine at room temperature," a woman interjected, "but I read somewhere that the French keep their rooms cooler than we do. What's the best temperature?"

With our guide distracted by questions, I figured it was a good time to do a little touring of my own. I edged my way toward the back of our group, then slipped behind a giant vat. I headed back into the main building, but this time found myself in a different section.

No tourists here. In fact, the hallway was blocked off by a sign perched atop one of those freestanding metal poles. It read, "Employees Only."

After glancing from side to side to make sure no one was watching, I ducked down the private corridor. When I reached the end, I found myself in a cavernous room that looked like a gigantic wine cellar. It served as a foyer, with four wooden doors leading off it. Offices, probably. The walls were made of red brick, the temperature was cool, and there was only one lighting fixture, perched high atop the back wall.

As soon as my eyes fully adjusted to the dim light, I saw that the lamp had been placed so that it illuminated a huge oil painting, over six feet high, in an ornate gilt frame. It faced the entryway, making it the focal point for anyone who entered.

The painting was a portrait of a tall, slender young woman with pale, luminescent skin and large blue-green eyes, their startling color emphasized even further by her thick, dark eyebrows. Gleaming straight black hair spilled down her back, the ends curving gently around her shoulders like a shawl. She stood erect, her chin held at a slightly defiant angle, as proud and as graceful as a gazelle.

She wore a long gown made of rich purple velvet and flowered gold brocade. The theatrical garment gave her the not-quite-of-this-world look of a woman in a pre-Raphaelite painting. The wreath of white and lavender flowers that encircled the crown of her head made her appear even more ephemeral, as if she were a goddess or an angel that some artist with an overdeveloped sense of drama had conjured up.

"Can I help you?"

I whirled around, surprised by the unexpected sound of a sharp voice. I hadn't realized that anyone else had come into the foyer, probably because I'd been so absorbed by the painting.

The man glowering at me looked as if he was in his late sixties, with a full head of thick silver hair. He was tall, with a dignified stance. He was also portly—a word that suited him well, not just because of his slightly rotund build, but also because he seemed as old-fashioned as the word. He was dressed in a dark blue plaid flannel shirt and a pair of those crisp, brand-new–looking jeans that older men tend to wear, the kind that emphasizes how flat their behinds are.

"This is a private area," he added, using the same cross tone.

"I was looking for the restroom," I lied, resorting to my favorite fallback excuse.

He cast a skeptical look at me. All right, so maybe it was hard to believe that a grown woman couldn't tell the difference between a sign that read "Employees Only" and one that featured male and female paper cutouts, the international symbol for people who have to pee.

"Okay, that's not exactly true," I admitted. "The truth is that I noticed this portrait as I was walking by, and I just had to get a better look."

"Ah. Well." That excuse seemed to placate him. He gazed up at the painting, the corners of his mouth drooping and his eyes dampening. "She was beautiful, wasn't she?"

"Who is she?" I asked, even though I was

pretty sure I already knew, thanks to the photos I'd seen splashed all over *Newsday*.

"Cassandra Thorndike. Gordon's daughter." As if he'd suddenly remembered that I was nothing more than an intruder, and therefore unlikely to know the people he had named, he added, "Gordon Thorndike founded Thorndike Vineyards."

"I see. Are you a member of the Thorndike family?"

"Me? No. I own Simcox Wineries, right next door." I guess he figured he'd already told me enough that it was time for an official introduction. "I'm Theodore Simcox," he said, extending his hand.

"I'm Jessica Popper," I replied as we shook hands.

"I'm a close friend of the Thorndike family." Raising his eyes to the portrait once again, he added, "Cassandra was like a daughter to me. You may have heard about the recent tragedy. She passed away earlier this week—"

We both jumped a little at the sound of footsteps traveling briskly across the terra-cotta–tiled floor. A short, plump woman in a gray wool skirt and a black sweater bustled into the foyer, closing the door of one of the offices behind her. Her hair matched her outfit, I noticed, black with gray accents. It was also just as severe, pulled back tightly into a low ponytail.

"Theodore, I really can't tell you how much I

appreciate you—" She stopped abruptly. "I'm sorry. I didn't realize you had a guest."

"I'm not a guest," I explained. "I just stepped in here to get a better look at this painting."

The woman drew her lips into a thin, straight line, as if she were trying to maintain her composure. Even so, her eyes filled with tears so quickly that I figured she'd been doing a good deal of precisely that over the past few days.

"You really shouldn't be in here," she said without much conviction.

"This is Mrs. Thorndike," Theodore Simcox said meaningfully.

"Oh! Mr. Simcox told me about your daughter. I'm so sorry."

She acknowledged my expression of sympathy with a nod.

In addition to being completely caught off guard by the realization that I'd just met Cassandra's mother, I also experienced a whole new level of understanding. Up until this point, I'd been so wrapped up in worrying about Suzanne that I'd barely thought about the people who had known and loved Cassandra Thorndike—and how much they were suffering. A young woman was dead. And that meant her parents would have to live with the terrible sadness of having lost their daughter for the rest of their lives. I felt a surge of determination to find out who had killed Cassandra Thorndike—not only for Suzanne's sake, but also for the people who had loved the poor young woman who had died.

Mrs. Thorndike turned her attention back to Theodore. "Thanks again for running the show for us for a few days, Theo."

"I'm glad there's at least something I can do, Joan," he replied earnestly.

"You've lifted a tremendous burden off my shoulders. I need to be at home. I just don't feel right, leaving Gordon on his own. He's devastated." Glancing back at me, she added, "Right now, all the wineries on the East End are gearing up for the busiest time of the year. Not only is autumn the time of the harvest; it's also the height of tourist season. From September through November, I think most of us feel that our business is orchestrating tastings and hayrides, instead of turning grapes into wine."

For a moment, a small smile lit up her face, and I could see a trace of liveliness I hadn't noticed before.

The smile faded quickly. "But right now, my husband and I simply can't cope with the day-to-day operation of the winery. In fact, the only reason I came in today is that one of our employees called to tell me one of the cats who help keep the mouse population down here at the winery, Coco, is ailing. I came to pick her up and take her to the vet."

"If you'd like, I could take a look at her." In response to her puzzled look, I added, "I'm a veterinarian with a mobile services unit. I guess you didn't notice my van on your way in, but it's right in your parking lot. I'd be happy to treat your cat."

"Oh, *would* you?" she asked gratefully. "It would make things so much easier. But could I trouble you to drive your van to my house? As I said, I feel I should be at home with Cassandra's father. He's having such a difficult time coping with his daughter's death, and every minute I'm away seems like too much."

I guess my expression reflected my confusion because she added, "I should probably explain that I'm actually Cassandra's stepmother. Her real mother passed away when she was a little girl. At any rate, would you mind coming over? I know it's a lot to ask."

"It's no trouble at all," I assured her.

"Terrific. I'll just grab Coco and meet you at the house."

She began giving me directions, then decided it would be simpler for me to follow her home.

Turning back to Theo, she said, "Feel free to close up early. I know you've got enough to take care of without doing double duty by running my vineyard as well as your own."

"Now, Joan, don't even think about it," he insisted. "You know that a lonely old bachelor like me doesn't have anything else to do on a Saturday. There's nothing on my schedule for the rest of the day except the roast beef special over at Clyde's."

She smiled gratefully. "Thanks, Theo. You're a real friend."

As I pulled out of the Thorndike Vineyards parking lot, I could scarcely believe my good fortune. I'd been wondering how I'd ever manage to get inside the world that Cassandra Thorndike had occupied, and here the perfect opportunity had just fallen into my lap.

Right, I thought. Nothing but pure luck. That—and a little scheming, a bit of acting, and the good fortune to own a clinic-on-wheels that gave me the perfect excuse to visit people's homes.

The Bantam Dell
BREAKING & ENTERING
Consumer Sweepstakes Official Rules

NO PURCHASE NECESSARY. Open to legal residents of the U.S. and Canada (excluding Puerto Rico and Quebec), who are 18 years of age or older as of May 31, 2005. Sweepstakes ends September 1, 2005.

TO ENTER:
Mail-in Entry:
Hand-print your complete name and address, including zip code, and phone number (optional) on an Official Entry Form or 3" x 5" piece of paper. Mail entry in a hand-addressed (#10) envelope to: *Breaking & Entering Sweepstakes*, c/o Bantam Marketing, Mail Drop 24-3, 1745 Broadway, NY, NY, 10019. Entries must be postmarked by September 1, 2005 and received by September 15, 2005. **You may enter as often as you wish via mail but limit one entry per outer mailing envelope.**

Online Entry:
Enter online beginning at 12:00 Midnight, U.S. Eastern Time (ET), Tuesday, May 31, 2005 through 11:59 PM, U.S. Eastern Time (ET), September 1, 2005, at www.breaking-and-entering.com; follow the BREAKING & ENTERING sweepstakes directions and provide your complete name, address and email address. Limit one entry per person and/or email address per day. Sponsor is not responsible for lost/late/misdirected entries or computer malfunctions.

WINNER SELECTION:
One Hundred (100) Grand Prize Winners will be selected in a random drawing from all eligible entries, conducted on or about September 23, 2005, by Bantam Dell Marketing personnel, whose decisions are final. Odds of winning depend on the number of eligible entries received.

PRIZES:
One Hundred (100) Grand Prizes—A set of six (6) "B&E" paperback copies signed by the author, and one custom-created "B&E" coffee mug. (Approximate Retail Value: $47.00 U.S.)

WHO CAN PARTICIPATE:
Open to legal residents of U.S. and Canada who are 18 years of age or older as of May 31, 2005. Employees of Random House, Inc., Bantam Dell Publishing Group, their parent, subsidiaries, affiliates, agencies, and immediate families and persons living in the same household of such employees are not eligible. Void in Puerto Rico and Quebec, and where prohibited.

GENERAL CONDITIONS:
Taxes will be the responsibility of the Winners. Potential Winners from Canada will be required to answer a time-limited arithmetic skill-testing question in order to qualify as a Winner. Potential Winners may be required to execute an Affidavit/Publicity/Liability Release within 14 days of attempted notification or prize will be forfeited and an alternate Winner selected. No transfer/cash substitution of prize permitted. Sponsor reserves the right to post, remove and/or modify this sweepstakes on the Internet at any time. Sponsor reserves the right to disqualify entries from anyone tampering with the Internet entry process. If, for any reason, the sweepstakes or any drawing is not capable of running as planned by reason of damage by computer virus, worms, bugs, tampering, unauthorized intervention, technical limitations or failures, or any other causes which, in the sole opinion of the Sponsor, could compromise, undermine or otherwise affect the Official Rules, administration, security, fairness or proper conduct of the sweepstakes, the Sponsor reserves the right and absolute discretion to modify these Official Rules and/or to cancel, terminate, modify or suspend the sweepstakes. In the event of termination or cancellation, the Winners will be selected from all eligible entries received before termination. Sponsor assumes no responsibility for any error, omission, interruption, deletion, defect, delay in operation or transmission, communications line failure, theft, destruction, or unauthorized access to the site. Sponsor not responsible for injury or damage to any computer, other equipment, or person relating to or resulting from participation in the sweepstakes, or from downloading materials or accessing the site. Sweepstakes subject to applicable laws and regulations in U.S. and Canada. Participants release the Sponsor, its agencies, and assigns from any liability and/or loss resulting from participation in sweepstakes or acceptance or use of any prize. By their entry, participants agree to these rules. By acceptance of prize, Winners agree to rules and Sponsor's use of name/likeness for commercial purposes without notification/compensation, except where prohibited by law.

TO OBTAIN THE NAMES OF THE WINNERS:
For the names of the Winners, available after October 1, 2005, send a self-addressed, stamped envelope to be received by October 1, 2005 to: "BREAKING & ENTERING" Winners, Bantam Marketing, Mail drop 24-3, 1745 Broadway, NY, NY 10019.

Promotion Sponsor is Bantam Dell Publishing Group, a division of Random House, Inc., 1745 Broadway, New York, NY 10019